The Wordsworth Dickens Dictionary

Some other books by Rodney Dale

For Wordsworth Editions:
The Wordsworth Dictionary of Culinary and Menu Terms (2000)
The Wordsworth Dictionary of Abbreviations and Acronyms
   (with Steve Puttick) (1997; 2nd edition 1999)
The Wordsworth Book of Urban Legend (2005)

For the British Library:
Cats in Books (1998)
The *Discoveries and Inventions* series (1992-94)

For Fern House:
About Time a work of fiction (1995)
Halcyon Days – recollections of post-war vintage motoring (1999)

For Hodder Educational:
Teach Yourself Jazz (2004)

Miscellany:
Louis Wain, the Man who drew Cats (1968; 1991)
Catland (1977)
From Ram Yard to Milton Hilton (1979; 1982)
The World of Jazz (1980)
The Sinclair Story (1985)
The Manna Machine (1978)
The Book of When? (2004)
The Book of Where? (2004)
The Book of Who? (2004)
The Book of What? (2004)

The Wordsworth
DICKENS
DICTIONARY

Compiled and Edited by
RODNEY DALE

Wordsworth Reference

Readers who are interested in other titles from
Wordsworth Editions are invited to visit our website at
www.wordsworth-editions.com

For our latest list and a full mail-order service contact
Bibliophile Books, 5 Thomas Road, London E14 7BN

Tel: +44 0207 515 9222   Fax: +44 0207 538 4115
e-mail: orders@bibliophilebooks.com

First published 2005 by Wordsworth Editions Limited
8B East Street, Ware, Hertfordshire SG12 9HJ

ISBN 1 84022 307 3

Typeset by Antony Gray
Printed and bound in Great Britain by
Mackays of Chatham, Chatham, Kent

TO
ANGHARAD, MADELEINE,
LOUIS, SAMUEL AND TRISTAN
With love from G'Pa

My grateful thanks, as always, to
CHARLOTTE EDWARDS
whose diligent application
made this work possible

Little Charles Dickens at the blacking warehouse – Fred Barnard

Contents

Note: Part of the introduction to each section of the Dictionary appears below to facilitate comparison.

INTRODUCTION

A collection of short pieces; Dickens's first attempts at authorship. They were originally contributed to *The Monthly Magazine* (*The Old Monthly*, as it was called to distinguish it from Colburn's *New Monthly*), *The Morning Chronicle*, and *Bell's Life in London*. In 1836 they were brought together and republished, with illustrations by George Cruikshank, in two series, of which the former was contained in two volumes and the latter in one. The very first of those 'Sketches', 'Mrs Joseph Porter', appeared in *The Monthly Magazine* for January 1834. The first in which Dickens assumed the pseudonym of 'Boz' was the second part or chapter of 'The Boarding House', which came out in the same magazine in August 1834.

2   POSTHUMOUS PAPERS OF THE PICKWICK CLUB   36

This work was issued in monthly shilling numbers, with green covers - a form of publication which Dickens adopted in all his subsequent monthly serials. The first number appeared in March 1836, with four illustrations by Robert Seymour. However, Seymour died suddenly before the publication of the second number (for which, however, he had furnished three plates), so Robert W Buss was chosen to succeed him, and two plates 'drawn and etched' by this gentleman appeared in No 3. But they were so inferior, both in conception and execution, that he was dismissed, and Hablot Knight Browne was selected as the illustrator of the work, furnishing two plates for No 4. In No 5 he used for the first time the pseudonym 'Phiz', which he retained thereafter. In the second edition of the work, the publishers cancelled the two plates by Buss which appeared in No 3, and substituted two others by Phiz.

The greater part of this tale was originally published during the years 1837 and 1838 in *Bentley's Magazine*, of which Dickens was at that time the editor. It was begun in the second number (February, 1837), and was illustrated by George Cruikshank. On its completion, it was issued in three volumes by Mr Bentley.

These reports appeared in *Bentley's Miscellany* in 1837 and 1838, while Dickens was the editor of that periodical. They were designed to satirise the proceedings of the British Association for the Advancement of Science, which had then been recently established. (For a happy consonance, note the Pugwash Conferences (named after the first held at Pugwash, Nova Scotia in 1957) to promote International co-operation on the social responsibility of science.)

This story was begun a few months after the completion of the *Pickwick Papers* (September 1837); *Oliver Twist*, which followed that work, having been begun in February 1837, and carried on simultaneously with it for several months. *Nicholas Nickleby* was issued in monthly shilling numbers, and was illustrated by Phiz. On its completion in 1839, it was brought out in volume form, with a prefixed portrait of Dickens, engraved by Finden from a painting by Maclise. It was dedicated to W G Macready (1793–1873), the actor and theatre manager.

This collection was published in 1840.

7   MASTER HUMPHREY'S CLOCK

Dickens started a miscellany under this title in April 1840, which was to be issued in weekly numbers, at three pence each, and which was to consist of short, detached papers, with occasional continuous stories. The work extended to eighty-eight numbers, covering a period of nearly two years. It was brought out in the form of an imperial octavo, was excellently printed on good paper, and was illustrated with engravings (instead of etchings on steel) by George Cattermole, Phiz, George Cruikshank, and Daniel Maclise – the latter artists, however, furnishing but one sketch each. On the completion of the eighty-eight numbers, the work was issued in three volumes – of which the first appeared in 1840, and the last two in 1841.

8   THE OLD CURIOSITY SHOP

This story originally appeared in the serial miscellany *Master Humphrey's Clock*, the first chapter in the fourth number. When first published, it bore the subtitle 'Personal Adventures of Master Humphrey'.

9   BARNABY RUDGE

This first appeared in 1841, in *Master Humphrey's Clock*; and in 1849 it was published apart from the machinery of that serial miscellany.

10   A CHRISTMAS CAROL

This work was printed and published for the author by Messrs Bradbury and Evans, in December 1843, in one volume, 12mo, with four coloured etchings on steel by John Leech.

11 THE LIFE AND ADVENTURES OF MARTIN CHUZZLEWIT 140

This novel was begun after Dickens's return from his first visit to America in 1841–42, and was issued in twenty monthly shilling parts, the first part making its appearance in January, 1843. The work was completed and published in one volume in 1844. It was illustrated with twenty etchings on steel by Phiz.

12 THE CHIMES 163

This, the second of the Christmas books, was brought out in 1844 by Bradbury and Evans. It was illustrated with a frontispiece and title on steel by Daniel Maclise, and with woodcuts from drawings by John Leech, Richard Doyle, and Clarkson Stanfield. The tale is divided into 'Quarters'.

13 THE CRICKET ON THE HEARTH 167

Published in 1845, inscribed to Lord Jeffrey, and illustrated with a frontispiece and title page by Maclise, and woodcuts from drawings by Doyle, Leech, Clarkson Stanfield, and Landseer. The tale is divided into 'Chirps'.

14 THE BATTLE OF LIFE 171

Published in 1846, with a frontispiece and title page engraved on wood from drawings by Maclise, and with woodcuts inserted in the text, from designs by Doyle, Leech, and Stanfield.

15 DOMBEY AND SON 174

On 1 October 1846, Messrs Bradbury and Evans issued the first number of a new serial novel under the title of 'Dealings with the Firm of Dombey and Son, Wholesale, Retail, and for Exportation'. Each part was illustrated with two engravings on steel by Phiz. The publication of the work extended over twenty months; and on its completion, in 1848, it was brought out in a single octavo volume.

16 THE HAUNTED MAN & THE GHOST'S BARGAIN 195

Published in 1848, and illustrated with a frontispiece and title-page engraved on wood from drawings by John Tenniel, and with woodcuts in the text from sketches by Stanfield, Leech, and Stone.

17 THE PERSONAL HISTORY OF DAVID COPPERFIELD THE YOUNGER 201

This work was originally brought out under the title: 'The Personal History, Adventures, Experiences, and Observations of David Copperfield the Younger, of Blunderstone Rookery (which he never meant to be published on any account)'. It was issued in twenty monthly parts, with two illustrations by Phiz in each part. The first number appeared 1 May 1849, and the preface was dated October 1850.

18 BLEAK HOUSE 225

In the preface to *David Copperfield*, Dickens promised to renew his acquaintance with the public by putting forth again 'two green leaves once a month'. This he did by bringing out, in 1852, in the familiar serial form, the first number of a new novel, called *Bleak House*. It was published by Bradbury and Evans, was illustrated by Phiz, and ran through the usual twenty numbers.

19 HARD TIMES 247

This tale was originally published in *Household Words*; the first chapter making its appearance in No 210 (April 1851), and the last in No 229 (12 August 1854). In the same year it was brought out, independently, in one octavo volume of 352 pages.

20 THE SEVEN POOR TRAVELLERS 257

Published in *Household Words*, 1854.

21 THE HOLLY-TREE 259

Published in *Household Words*, December 1855.

22 LITTLE DORRIT 261

The first number of this tale was issued on the first day of December 1856, and the twentieth and last number made its appearance in June 1857. It was illustrated by Phiz.

23 A TALE OF TWO CITIES 279

The first portion of this story was published in the first number of *All the Year Round*, 30 April 1859. It was concluded in No 31, 26 November 1859. It was also issued in eight monthly parts, with two

Phiz illustrations in each. On its completion, it was published as an independent volume by Chapman and Hall.

24 HUNTED DOWN 291

This tale was written specially for *The New York Ledger*, in which paper it appeared in the numbers for 20 & 27 August and 3 September 1859 (Vol 15, No 24–26), illustrated with seven woodcuts. It was republished in 1860 in *All the Year Round*, 4 & 11 August (First series, Nos 67 and 68).

25 UNCOMMERCIAL TRAVELLER 293

In December 1860, 17 papers on a variety of topics, which had previously appeared at intervals in *All the Year Round*, were published in a collective form by Chapman and Hall under the above title. A cheap edition in 1865 added a further 11 pieces, and an 1871 edition, with illustrations, carried 36 pieces. Finally, the Gadshill edition of 1890 at last presented all the 37 pieces.

26 GREAT EXPECTATIONS 300

This tale originally appeared in *All the Year Round*, starting on 1 December 1860. On its completion in 1861, it was published by Chapman and Hall in three volumes, with illustrations by Marcus Stone.

27 SOMEBODY'S LUGGAGE 314

Published in *All the Year Round*, in December 1862

28 MRS LIRRIPER'S LODGINGS 316

Published in *All The Year Round* in December 1863

29 MRS LIRRIPER'S LEGACY 318

Published in *All The Year Round* in December 1864

30 OUR MUTUAL FRIEND 321

Like most of its predecessors, this novel made its first appearance in twenty monthly parts. The first part was issued 1 May 1864, and the last in November 1865. The illustrations were on wood from drawings by Marcus Stone. On its completion, the work was published in two octavo volumes by Chapman and Hall.

31 DOCTOR MARIGOLD   339

Originally published as part of the collection of tales entitled 'Doctor Marigold's Prescriptions', which formed the Christmas number of *All the Year Round* for 1865.

32 BARBOX BROTHERS   341

This story is one of a number of tales included in 'Mugby Junction', the extra Christmas number of *All the Year Round* for 1866.

33 THE BOY AT MUGBY   344

This tale as originally published, formed the third portion of 'Mugby Junction', the extra Christmas number of *All the Year Round* for 1866.

34 TWO GHOST STORIES   345

34.1 THE TRIAL FOR MURDER

The first of the two stories reprinted under the above title was originally published as the sixth of 'Doctor Marigold's Prescriptions', the extra Christmas number of *All the Year Round* for 1865.

34.2 THE SIGNALMAN

The second Ghost Story is an account of an incident occurring on one of the branch lines leading from Mugby Junction. It forms the fourth division of the extra Christmas number bearing that name, which was published in 1866, in connection with *All the Year Round*.

35 HOLIDAY ROMANCE   347

This story in four parts was written expressly for *Our Young Folks* (a juvenile magazine published in America), and appeared during the months of January, March, April, and May 1868. It was also brought out in England, in *All the Year Round*, in January, February, and March of the same year.

36 GEORGE SILVERMAN'S EXPLANATION   351

This tale was written expressly for *The Atlantic Monthly*, and was published in that magazine in the months of January, February and March 1868. It was republished, the same year, in *All the Year Round*.

37 NEW UNCOMMERCIAL SAMPLES   354

Published in *All The Year Round* in 1869

38 THE MYSTERY OF EDWIN DROOD   356

This first number of this work was issued by Messrs Chapman and
Hall on 1 April 1870, with two illustrations on wood from drawings
by S L Fildes. The story was to be completed in twelve monthly
parts, but Dickens died soon after the third part was published. He
left three more parts for publication, so half the story did appear in
print.

39 REPRINTED PIECES   363

Under this name, thirty-one sketches, all of them originally published
in *Household Words*, between the years 1850 and 1856, were first
brought together in 1858, and published in the twelfth volume of
the 'Library Edition' of Dickens's works, issued jointly by Messrs
Chapman and Hall, and Messrs Bradbury and Evans.

1

Sketches by Boz

This collection of short pieces comprises Dickens's first attempts at authorship. They were originally contributed to *The Monthly Magazine* (*The Old Monthly*, as it was called to distinguish it from Colburn's *New Monthly*), *The Morning Chronicle*, and *Bell's Life in London*. In 1836 they were brought together and republished, with illustrations by George Cruikshank, in two series, of which the former was contained in two volumes and the latter in one. The very first of those 'Sketches', 'Mrs Joseph Porter', appeared in *The Monthly Magazine* for January 1834. The first in which Dickens assumed the pseudonym of 'Boz' was the second part or chapter of 'The Boarding House', which came out in the same magazine in August 1834. According to Dickens: ' "Boz" was the nickname of a pet child, a younger brother [Augustus Dickens], whom I had dubbed Moses in honour of the Vicar of Wakefield; which, being shortened, became Boz. "Boz" was a very familiar household word to me long before I was an author; and so I came to adopt it.'

Of 'The Sketches' Dickens later wrote (in the Preface to the 1850 edition) that they are often 'extremely crude and ill-considered, bearing obvious marks of haste and inexperience, particularly in that section of the volume which is comprised under the general head of Tales'.

CHARACTERS

1 Our Parish

THE BEADLE

SIMMONS – Parish beadle.

THE FOUR SISTERS

DAWSON, Mr – A surgeon, &c, in attendance on Mrs Robinson at the time of her confinement.

ROBINSON, Mr – A gentleman in a public office, who marries the youngest Miss Willis, though he has to court her three sisters also, as they are all completely identified one with another.

WILLISES, The four Miss – Four sisters in 'our parish', who seem to have no separate existence, and who drive the neighbourhood distracted by keeping profoundly secret the name of the fortunate one who is to marry Mr Robinson.

ELECTION FOR BEADLE

BUNG, Mr – A man of thirty-five years of age, with five small children; a candidate for the office of beadle, which he obtains by a large majority (see below).

PURDAY, Captain – A bluff and unceremonious old naval officer on half-pay (first introduced, though not mentioned by name, in the sketch entitled 'The Curate'). He is a determined opponent of the constituted authorities, whoever they may chance to be, and zealously supports Bung for beadle.

SPRUGGINS, Mr Thomas – Defeated candidate for beadle; a little thin man, fifty years old, with a pale face expressive of care and fatigue – owing, perhaps, to the fact of his having ten small children (two of them twins) and a wife.

SPRUGGINS, Mrs – His wife. She solicits votes for her husband, and increases the general prepossession which at first prevails in his favour by her personal appearance, which indicates the probability of an imminent addition to his already large family.

THE BROKER'S MAN

BUNG, Mr – A broker's assistant, afterwards the parish beadle (see above). One of those careless, good-for-nothing, happy fellows who float cork-like on the surface for the world to play at hockey with.

FIXEM – A broker, who assumes the alias of Smith; Bung's master.

JOHN – A servant.

THE LADIES' SOCIETIES

BROWNS, The three Miss – Members of various visitation committees and charitable societies, and admirers of the curate, who is a young man and unmarried.

The broker's man – George Cruikshank

PARKER, Mrs Johnson – The mother of seven extremely fine girls – all unmarried – and the founder of a Ladies' Bible and Prayer-Book Distribution Society, from which the Miss Browns are excluded.

OUR NEXT-DOOR NEIGHBOUR

WILLIAM – A young man who overtasks himself to earn a support for himself and his widowed mother, and at last dies in her arms.

2 *Scenes*

THE STREETS – NIGHT

MACKLIN, Mrs – An inhabitant of No 4 in one of the little streets in the suburbs of London.

PEPLOW, Mrs – A neighbour of Mrs Macklin.

PEPLOW, Master – Her son.

SMUGGINS, Mr – A little round-faced man, in the comic line, with a mixed air of self-denial and mental consciousness of his own powers.

WALKER, Mrs – An inhabitant of No 5 in the same street as Mrs Macklin.

SEVEN DIALS

MARY – A woman who has taken 'three-outs' enough of gin and bitters to make her quarrelsome.

SARAH – A vixen who falls out with Mary, and settles the difficulty by a resort to blows.

DOCTORS' COMMONS

BUMPLE, Michael – Promoter, or complainant, against Mr Sludberry, in a brawling case.

SLUDBERRY, Thomas – A little red-faced, sly-looking, ginger-beer seller, defendant in the case of 'Bumple against Sludberry'; sentenced to excommunication for a fortnight and payment of costs.

LONDON RECREATIONS

BILL, Uncle – One of a party of Sunday pleasurers at a tea-garden; considered a great wit by his friends.

SALLY – His niece, joked by Uncle Bill about her marriage, and her first baby, because a certain young man is 'keeping company' with her.

THE RIVER

DANDO – A boatman.

ASTLEY'S

WOOLFORD, Miss – A circus-rider.

PRIVATE THEATRES

LARKINS, Jem – An amateur actor in the genteel comedy line, known to the public as Mr Horatio St Julian.

LOGGINS, Mr – A player who takes the part of Macbeth, and is announced on the bills as Mr Beverley.

VAUXHALL GARDENS BY DAY

GREEN, Mr – An aeronaut.

GREEN, Mr, Junior – His son and assistant.

THE LAST CAB-DRIVER AND THE FIRST OMNIBUS-CAD

BARKER, Mr William – commonly called 'Bill Boorker *or* Aggera-watin' Bill'. An omnibus-cad, with a remarkable talent for enticing the youthful and unwary, and shoving the old and helpless into the wrong bus.

A PARLIAMENTARY SKETCH

CAPTAIN, The – A spare, squeaking old man, always damning his own eyes or 'somebody else's' and a complete walking-reservoir of spirits and water.

JAYE – The Hebe of 'Bellamy's' or the refreshment-room of the Houses of Parliament. She has a thorough contempt for the great majority of her visitors, and a great love of admiration.

NICHOLAS – The butler of 'Bellamy's', who has held the same place, dressed exactly in the same manner, and said precisely the same things, ever since the oldest of its present visitors can remember.

TOM, Honest – A metropolitan member of the House of Commons.

THE FIRST OF MAY

SLUFFEN, Mr – of Adam-and-Eve Court. A speaker at the anniversary dinner given to the chimney-sweeps on Mayday at White Conduit House.

THE PAWNBROKER'S SHOP

HENRY, Mr – A pawnbroker, whose shop is near Drury Lane.

JINKINS – A customer, dirty, intoxicated, and quarrelsome.

MACKIN, Mrs – Another customer, slipshod and abusive.

TATHAM, Mrs – An old woman who tries to borrow eighteen pence or a shilling on a child's frock and 'a beautiful silk 'ankecher'.

3 *Characters*

THOUGHTS ABOUT PEOPLE

SMITH, Mr – A poor clerk, a mere passive creature of habit and endurance.

A CHRISTMAS DINNER

GEORGE, Aunt – The hostess at whose house the Christmas family-party assembles.

GEORGE, Uncle – Her husband.

JANE, Aunt – Another member of the family.

MARGARET, Aunt – Married to a poor man, and treated coldly by her relations in consequence.

ROBERT, Uncle – Husband to Aunt Jane.

THE NEW YEAR

DOBBLE, Mr – A clerk in a public office, who gives a quadrille party on New Year's Eve.

DOBBLE, Mr Jun – His son.

DOBBLE Miss Julia – His eldest daughter.

DOBBLE, Mrs – His wife.

TUPPLE, Mr – A junior clerk in the same office with Mr Dobble; a young man with a tendency to cold and corns, but 'a charming person', and 'a perfect ladies' man'.

MISS EVANS AND THE EAGLE

EVANS, Miss Jemima – (called 'J'mima Ivins' by her acquaintances). A shoe-binder and straw bonnet maker, affianced to Mr Samuel Wilkins.

EVANS, Miss Tilly – One of her sisters.

EVANS, Mrs – Her mother.

WILKINS, Mr Samuel – A journeyman carpenter of small dimensions, 'keeping company' with Miss Jemima Evans.

THE PARLOUR ORATOR

ELLIS, Mr – A sharp-nosed man, with a very slow and soft voice, who considers Mr Rogers 'such improving company'.

ROGERS, Mr – A stoutish man of about forty, with a red face and a confident oracular air, which marks him as a leading politician, general authority, and universal anecdote-relater. Proof is what he requires – proof, not assertions – in regard to anything and everything whatsoever.

TOMMY – A little chubby-faced greengrocer, of great good sense, who opposes Mr Rogers, and is denounced by him, in consequence, as 'a willing slave'.

THE HOSPITAL PATIENT

JACK – A young fellow who treats his paramour so brutally as to cause her death, and yet is so loved by her, even to the last, that she cannot be persuaded to swear his life away, but dies praying God to bless him.

THE MISPLACED ATTACHMENT OF MR JOHN DOUNCE

DOUNCE, Mr John – A fat, red-faced, white-headed old boy, a retired glove and braces maker, and a widower. He falls in love with a bewitching barmaid, who trifles with his affections, and at last tells him plainly that she 'wouldn't have him at no price'; whereupon he offers himself successively to a schoolmistress, a landlady, a feminine tobacconist, a housekeeper, and his own cook, by the last of whom he is accepted, married – and thoroughly henpecked.

HARRIS, Mr – A law stationer and a jolly old fellow; a friend of Mr Dounce.

JENNINGS, Mr – A robe maker; also a friend of Mr Dounce, and a sad dog in his time.

JONES, Mr – Another friend, a barrister's clerk, and a rum fellow – capital company – full of anecdote.

THE MISTAKEN MILLINER

MARTIN, Miss Amelia – A milliner and dressmaker who has an ambition to 'come out' as a public singer, and tries it, but fails miserably.

RODOLPH, Mr and Mrs Jennings – Her friends and counsellors.

THE DANCING ACADEMY

BILLSMETHI, Signor – A popular dancing-master.

BILLSMETHI, Master – His son.

BILLSMETHI, Miss – His daughter, a young lady with her hair curled in a crop all over her head, and her shoes tied in sandals all over her ankles. She sets her cap for Mr Cooper and, not succeeding in securing him for a husband, brings a suit for breach of promise, but finally compromises the matter for twenty pounds, four shillings, and sixpence.

COOPER, Mr Augustus – A young gentleman of Fetter Lane, in the oil and colour business, just of age, with a little money, a little business, and a little mother.

MAKING A NIGHT OF IT

POTTER, Mr Thomas – A clerk in the City, with a limited income, and an unbounded friendship for Mr Smithers.

SMITHERS, Mr Robert – Also a clerk in the City, knit by the closest ties of intimacy and friendship to Mr Potter. On the receipt of their quarter's salary, these two 'thick-and-thin pals', as they style themselves, spend an evening together, and proceeding by degrees from simple hilarity to drunkenness, commit various breaches of the peace; are locked up in the station-house for the night; brought before the police court in the morning, and each fined five shillings for being drunk, and thirty-four pounds for seventeen assaults at forty shillings a head.

THE PRISONERS' VAN

BELLA – A young girl, not fourteen, forced by a sordid and rapacious mother to a life of vice and crime, which she loathes, but cannot escape from.

EMILY – Her sister, hardened in depravity by two additional years' experience of the debauchery of London street-life, and priding herself on being 'game'.

4 Tales

THE BOARDING HOUSE

AGNES – Mrs Bloss's maid.

BLOSS, Mrs – The wealthy widow of a cork-cutter, whose cook she had been. Having nothing to do, she imagines she must be ill but eats amazingly, and has the appearance of being remarkably well. She makes the acquaintance of Mr Gobler, and marries him.

CALTON, Mr – A superannuated beau, exceedingly vain, inordinately selfish, and the very pink of politeness. He makes himself agreeable to Mrs Maplesone, and agrees to marry her but, failing to do so, she sues him for breach of promise, and recovers a thousand pounds.

EVENSON, Mr John – A stern, morose, and discontented man, a thorough radical, and a universal fault-finder.

GOBLER, Mr – A lazy, selfish hypochondriac, whose digestion is so much impaired, and whose interior so deranged, that his stomach is not of the least use to him.

HICKS, Mr Septimus – A tallish, white-faced, spectacled young man who has the reputation of being very talented. He falls in love with Miss Matilda Maplesone, whom he marries, but afterwards deserts.

JAMES – A servant to Mrs Tibbs.

MAPLESONE, Mrs – An enterprising widow of fifty; shrewd, scheming, and good-looking, with no objection to marrying again if it would benefit her dear girls.

MAPLESONE Miss Julia – Her younger daughter; married to Mr Simpson.

MAPLESONE, Miss Matilda – Her elder daughter; married to Mr Septimus Hicks.

O'BLEARY, Mr Frederick – A patriotic Irishman, recently imported in a perfectly wild state; in search of employment, and ready to do or be anything that might turn up.

ROBINSON – A female servant to Mrs Tibbs.

SIMPSON, Mr – One of the 'walking gentlemen' of society; an empty-headed young man, always dressed according to the caricatures published in the monthly fashions.

TIBBS, Mr – A short man, with very short legs, but a face peculiarly long, by way of indemnification. He is to his wife what the o is in 90 – of some importance with her, but nothing without her.

TIBBS, Mrs – His wife, mistress of the boarding-house; the most tidy, fidgety, thrifty little person that ever inhaled the smoke of London.

TOMKINS, Mr Alfred – Clerk in a wine-house; a connoisseur in paintings, and with a wonderful eye for the picturesque.

WISBOTTLE, Mr – A clerk in the Woods and Forests Office, and a high Tory; addicted to whistling, and having a great idea of his singing powers.

WOSKY, Doctor – Mr Bloss's medical attendant, who has amassed a fortune by invariably humouring the worst fancies of his female patients.

MR MINNS AND HIS COUSIN

BROGSON, Mr – An elderly gentleman visiting at Mr Budden's.

BUDDEN, Mr Octavius – A retired corn-chandler, residing at Amelia Cottage, Poplar Walk, Stamford Hill. He is a cousin to Mr Minns.

BUDDEN, Mrs Amelia – His wife.

BUDDEN, Master Alexander Augustus – Their son, a precocious child, and the pride of his parents.

JONES, Mr – A little man with red whiskers, a visitor at Mr Budden's, and a 'devilish sharp fellow', who talks equally well on any subject.

MINNS, Mr Augustus – A clerk in Somerset House, and a precise, tidy, retiring old bachelor, who is always getting into trouble when he leaves his own snug and well-ordered apartments, and who is thoroughly disgusted with a visit which he is compelled to make to his cousin, Mr Octavius Budden.

SENTIMENT

BUTLER, Mr Theodosius – A very wonderful genius, author of a pamphlet entitled 'Considerations on the Policy of Removing the Duty on Beeswax'. This he presents to Cornelius Brook Dingwall, Esq, MP, under the assumed name of Edward M'Neville Walter, and thus gains admission to his house, and an opportunity of winning the heart of his supersentimental daughter.

CRUMPTON, Miss Amelia – A very tall, thin, skinny, upright, yellow, and precise maiden lady, with the strictest possible idea of propriety.

CRUMPTON, Miss Maria – The exact counterpart of her sister, in conjunction with whom she carries on Minerva House, a finishing-school for young ladies.

DADSON, Mr – Writing-master at the Miss Crumptons' school.

DADSON, Mrs – His wife.

DINGWALL, Cornelius Brook, Esq, MP – A very haughty, solemn, and portentous man, having a great opinion of his own abilities, and wonderfully proud of being a Member of Parliament.

DINGWALL, Mrs Brook – His wife.

DINGWALL, Frederick – Son of Mr and Mrs Brook Dingwall; one of those public nuisances – a spoiled child.

DINGWALL, Miss Lavinia Brook – Their daughter, the most romantic of all romantic young ladies; in love with Edward M'Neville Walter (otherwise Mr Theodosius Butler), a young man much her inferior in life. She is therefore sent to the Miss Crumptons' educational establishment, to eradicate the sentimental attachment from her young mind, on the supposition that she can have no opportunity of meeting him there. She does meet him, however, and runs away, with and marries him in haste, only to repent at leisure.

HILTON, Mr – Master of the ceremonies at a ball at Minerva House.

JAMES – Servant to Mr Brook Dingwall.

LOBSKINI, Signor – A singing-master, with a splendid tenor voice.

PARSONS, Miss Letitia – A brilliant musical performer.

SMITHERS Miss Emily – The belle of Minerva House.

WILSON, Miss Caroline – Her bosom-friend, and the ugliest girl in Hammersmith – or out of it.

THE TUGGSES AT RAMSGATE

AMELIA, Jane and Mary Anne – Young ladies who take part in games of chance in a concert-room at Ramsgate.

SLAUGHTER, Lieutenant – A friend of Captain Waters.

TIPPIN, Mr – A comic singer at Ramsgate.

TIPPIN, Mrs – His wife; a concert-singer from the London theatres.

TIPPIN, Master – Their son.

TIPPIN, Miss – Their daughter; a performer on the guitar.

TUGGS, Mr Joseph – A little pursy London grocer, with shiny hair, twinkling eyes, and short legs. By the unexpected decision of a long-pending lawsuit, he comes into possession of twenty thousand pounds, whereupon he incontinently puts on airs, closes his shop, and starts with his family for Ramsgate, that being a fashionable watering-place.

TUGGS, Mrs – His wife; in charge of the cheesemongery department.

TUGGS, Miss Charlotte – Their only daughter. When her father becomes rich, she calls herself Charlotta.

TUGGS, Mr Simon – Their only son; a young gentleman with that elongation in his thoughtful face, and that tendency to weakness in his interesting legs, which tell so forcibly of a great mind and romantic disposition. At first, he is a bookkeeper in his father's shop but, when the fortune falls to the family, he styles himself Cymon, attempts to play the gentleman, and roundly abuses his father for not appearing aristocratic. Going to Ramsgate, he is neatly taken in and swindled by Captain Waters and his wife, whom he meets there, and greatly admires – especially the wife. He escapes with the loss of his veneration for appearances, and of fifteen hundred pounds in money.

WATERS, Captain Walter – A pretended military man, and a sharper.

WATERS, Mrs Belinda – His wife; a young lady with long black ringlets, large black eyes, brief petticoats, and unexceptionable ankles.

HORATIO SPARKINS

BARTON, Mr Jacob – Brother of Mrs Malderton; a large grocer, who never scrupled to avow that he wasn't above his business. 'He made his money by it, and he didn't care who know'd it'.

FLAMWELL, Mr – A little spoffish toad-eater, with green spectacles, always pretending to know everybody, but in reality knowing nobody; a friend of Mr Malderton.

Horatio Sparkins – George Cruikshank

JOHN – A man in Mr Malderton's service, half-groom, half-gardener but, on great occasions, touched up and brushed to look like a second footman.

MALDERTON, Mr – (of Oak Lodge, Camberwell). A man who has become rich in consequence of a few successful speculations, and who is hospitable from ostentation, illiberal from ignorance, and prejudiced from conceit. The whole scope of his ideas is limited to Lloyds, the Exchange, the India House, and the Bank.

MALDERTON, Mrs – His wife; a little fat woman, with a great aversion to anything low.

MALDERTON Miss Marianne – Their younger daughter; a sentimental damsel.

MALDERTON, Miss Teresa – Their older daughter; a young lady of eight-and-twenty, who has flirted for ten years in vain, but is still on the look-out for a husband.

MALDERTON, Mr Frederick – Their eldest son; the very *beau idéal* of a smart waiter, and the family authority on all points of taste, dress, and fashionable arrangement.

MALDERTON, Mr Thomas – Their younger son snubbed by his father on all occasions, with a view to prevent his becoming 'sharp' – a very unnecessary precaution.

SPARKINS, Mr Horatio – A young man whose dashing manners and gentlemanlike appearance so dazzle the Maldertons that they think he must be a man of large fortune and aristocratic family. They even go so far as to suspect that he may be a nobleman, and are greatly mortified at last to discover that he is a mere clerk in a linen-draper's shop, and owns to the plebeian name of Smith.

THE STEAM EXCURSION

BRIGGS, Mrs – A widow lady; a rival of Mrs Taunton.

BRIGGS, Miss – One of her three daughters.

BRIGGS, Miss Julia – Another daughter.

BRIGGS, Miss Kate – Another daughter.

BRIGGS, Mr Alexander – Her younger son, articled to his brother. He is remarkable for obstinacy.

BRIGGS, Mr Samuel – Her elder son; an attorney, and a mere machine; a sort of self-acting, legal walking-stick.

EDKINS, Mr – (of the Inner Temple). A pale young gentleman in a green stock and green spectacles, who makes a speech on every occasion on which one can possibly be made.

FLEETWOOD, Mr – One of the excursion party.

FLEETWOOD, Mrs – His wife, who accompanies him.

FLEETWOOD, Master – Their son; an unfortunate innocent of about four years of age.

HARDY, Mr – A stout, middle-aged gentleman with a red face, a somewhat husky voice, and a tremendous laugh. He is a practical joker, is immensely popular with married ladies, and a general favourite with young men.

HELVES, Captain – A military gentleman with a bass voice and an incipient red moustache; a friend of the Tauntons.

NOAKES, Mr Percy – A law student, smart, spoffish, and eight-and-twenty. With a few friends he attempts to get up an excursion party to which no one shall be invited who has not received the unanimous vote of a committee of arrangements. But the obstinate Mr Alexander Briggs being a member of this committee, and blackballing everybody who is proposed by Mr Noakes or his friends, the original plan is abandoned; and every gentleman is allowed to bring whom he pleases. The party start on a Wednesday morning for the Nore, and reach it after a pleasant trip; but on the return a violent squall comes up; the pitching and tossing of the boat bring on a general seasickness; and, when they get back to the wharf at two o'clock the next morning, everyone is thoroughly dispirited and worn out.

STUBBS, Mrs – A dirty old laundress with an inflamed countenance.

TAUNTON, Mrs – A good-looking widow of fifty, with the form of a giantess and the mind of a child. The sole end of her existence is the pursuit of pleasure, and some means of killing time. She is a particular friend of Mr Percy Noakes, and a mortal enemy of the Briggses.

TAUNTON, Miss Emily – Her daughter; a frivolous young lady.

TAUNTON, Miss Sophia – Another daughter, as light-minded as her sister.

THE GREAT WINGLEBURY DUEL

BROWN, Miss Emily – A young lady beloved by both Mr Trott and Mr Hunter, but finally married to the latter.

HUNTER, Mr Horace – Rival of Mr Trott for the hand of Miss Emily Brown.

MANNERS, Miss Julia – A buxom and wealthy woman of forty, formerly engaged to be married to a Mr Cornberry, who died leaving her a large property unencumbered with the addition of himself. Being in want of a young husband, she falls in love with a certain wild and prodigal nobleman, Lord Peter, who falls in love with her handsome fortune of three thousand pounds a year; but in the end she marries plain Mr Trott.

OVERTON, Joseph, Esq – Solicitor, and mayor of Great Winglebury.

PETER, Lord – A dissipated sprig of nobility, attached to Miss Manners (or her money); killed by being thrown from his horse in a steeple-chase.

THOMAS – A waiter at the Winglebury Arms.

TROTT, Mr Alexander – A cowardly young tailor (or umbrella maker). He desires to marry Miss Emily Brown, but is deterred by the hostile attitude of Mr Horace Hunter, who challenges him to mortal combat for daring to think of such a thing. He accepts the challenge in a bloodthirsty note, but immediately sends another, and an anonymous one, to the mayor of Great Winglebury, urging that Mr Trott be arrested forth with. By a ludicrous blunder, he is mistaken for Lord Peter, who is expected at the Winglebury Arms for the purpose of meeting Miss Julia Manners, his intended, and who is to be seized and carried off as an insane person, in order that his relatives may not discover him. Thus it happens that Trott is taken away in a carriage with Miss Manners, and mutual explanations having been made, that he marries her instead of the adorable Miss Emily Brown.

WILLIAMSON, Mrs – Landlady of the Winglebury Arms.

MRS JOSEPH PORTER

BALDERSTONE, Mr Thomas – *called* 'UNCLE TOM'. A rich brother of Mrs Gattleton, always in a good temper, and always talking and joking.

BROWN, Mr – A performer on the violoncello at the private theatricals.

CAPE, Mr – A violinist.

EVANS, Mr – A tall, thin, pale young gentleman, with lovely whiskers, and a remarkable talent for writing verses in albums, and for playing the flute. He is the *Roderigo* of the private theatricals.

GATTLETON, Mr – A retired stockbroker, living at Rose Villa, Clapham Rise. He is infected, as are the other members of his family, with a mania for private theatricals, acting himself as prompter.

GATTLETON, Mrs – His wife; a kind-hearted, good-tempered, vulgar soul, with a natural antipathy to other people's unmarried daughters, a fear of ridicule, and a great dislike for Mrs Joseph Porter.

GATTLETON, Miss – One of their three daughters.

GATTLETON, Miss Caroline – Another daughter; the *Fenella* of the private theatricals.

GATTLETON, Miss Lucina – Another daughter, who plays the part of *Desdemona*.

GATTLETON, Mr Sempronius – Their son, at once stage-manager and *Othello*.

HARLEIGH, Mr – A singer, who takes the part of *Masaniello*.

JENKINS, Miss – A piano-player.

PORTER, Mrs Joseph – A sarcastic scandalmonger, who delights in making other people uncomfortable. At the private theatricals of the Gattletons, she indulges her propensity to mischief-making by setting on Mr Jacob Barton (who prides himself on his accurate knowledge of Shakespeare) to interrupt the performers, in the very midst of the play, by correcting their numerous mistakes.

PORTER, Miss Emily – Her daughter.

WILSON, Mr – The *Iago* of the private theatricals.

A PASSAGE IN THE LIFE OF MR WATKINS TOTTLE

IKEY – The factotum of Mr Solomon Jacobs's sponging-house.

JACOBS, Mr Solomon – A bailiff, living in Cursitor Street.

JEM – A sallow-faced, red-haired, sulky boy in charge of the door of Mr Jacobs's private lock-up.

JOHN – Servant to Mrs Parsons.

LILLERTON, Miss – A prim spinster of uncertain age, with a complexion as clear as that of a wax doll, and a face as expressive.

MARTHA – Servant to Mrs Parsons.

PARSONS, Mr Gabriel – An elderly and rich sugar-baker, who mistakes rudeness for honesty, and abrupt bluntness for an open and candid manner.

PARSONS, Mrs Fanny – His wife.

TIMSON, The Reverend Charles – A friend of Mr Parsons. He marries Miss Lillerton.

TOTTLE, Mr Watkins – A plump, clean, rosy bachelor of fifty; a compound of strong uxorious inclinations and an unparalleled degree of anti-connubial timidity. Having been arrested for debt, and confined in a sponging-house, his friend Parsons engages to pay the debt, and take him out, if he will agree to marry Miss Lillerton, who has five hundred pounds a year in her own right. On being released, he offers himself to that lady, but after such an awkward and ambiguous fashion, that she quite mistakes his meaning, and answers him in a way that makes him think himself accepted. On being sent by her with a note – respecting their marriage, as he supposes – to the Reverend Mr Timson, it transpires that she has been engaged to that gentleman for several weeks. The upshot of the whole affair is that Mr Parsons renounces the friendship and acquaintance of Mr Tottle, who takes refuge from 'the slings and arrows of outrageous fortune' by walking into the Regent's Canal.

WALKER, Mr – An imprisoned debtor, inmate of Mr Solomon Jacobs's private lock-up.

WILLIS, Mr – Another inmate of the same establishment.

THE BLOOMSBURY CHRISTENING

DANTON, Mr – A young man with a considerable stock of impudence, and a very small share of ideas, who passes for a wit. He is a friend of Mr Kitterbell's, and a great favourite generally, especially with young ladies.

DUMPS, Mr Nicodemus – *called* 'Long Dumps'. An old bachelor, never happy but when he is miserable, and always miserable when he has the best reason to be happy, and whose only real comfort is to made everybody about him wretched. He is uncle to Mr Charles Kitterbell and, having been invited to stand as godfather to that gentleman's infant son, reluctantly does so, but takes his revenge by suggesting the most dismal possibilities of sickness and accident as altogether likely to happen to the child, and by making a speech at the supper after the christening so lugubrious and full of gloomy forebodings as to throw Mrs Kitterbell into violent hysterics, thus breaking up the party, and enabling him to walk home with a cheerful heart.

KITTERBELL, Mr Charles – A small, sharp, spare man, with an extra-ordinarily large head and a cast in his eye; very credulous and matter-of-fact.

KITTERBELL, Mrs Jemima – His wife; a tall, thin young lady with very light hair, a particularly white face, a slight cough, and a languid smile.

KITTERBELL, Master Frederick Charles William – Their first baby.

THE DRUNKARD'S DEATH

TOM – One of the officers who arrest young Warden.

WARDEN – A confirmed and irreclaimable drunkard. Remorse, fear, and shame; the loss of friends, happiness, and station; the death of his wife from grief and care; the murder of one of his sons, whom he had driven from home in a drunken fit; his own betrayal of another son into the hangman's hands from a like cause; his final desertion by his daughter, who has stayed by him and supported him for years; the utmost extremity of poverty, disease, and houseless want; – do not avail to conquer his fierce rage for drink, which drives him remorselessly until at last he seeks release in death by drowning himself in the Thames.

WARDEN, Mary – His daughter.

WARDEN, William – His son. He avenges his brother's death by killing the gamekeeper who shot him; flees from justice to his father's solitary attic room in the obscurest portion of the Whitefriars; is discovered by the officers in the consequence of his father's getting intoxicated and betraying his hiding-place; and is seized, handcuffed, carried off, and made to suffer the penalty of his crime.

2

Posthumous Papers of the Pickwick Club

This work was issued in monthly shilling numbers, with green covers – a form of publication which Mr Dickens adopted in all his subsequent monthly serials. The first number appeared in March 1836, with four illustrations by Robert Seymour. However, Seymour died suddenly before the publication of the second number (for which, however, he had furnished three plates), so Robert W Buss was chosen to succeed him, and two plates 'drawn and etched' by this gentleman appeared in No 3. But they were so inferior, both in conception and execution, that he was dismissed, and Hablot Knight Browne was selected as the illustrator of the work, furnishing two plates for No 4. In No 5 he used for the first time the pseudonym 'Phiz', which he retained thereafter. In the second edition of the work, the publishers cancelled the two plates by Buss which appeared in No 3, and substituted two others by Mr Browne.

Dickens gave the following account of the origin of the work:

> The idea propounded to me was that the monthly something should be a vehicle for certain plates to be executed by Mr Seymour; and there was a notion, either on the part of that admirable humorous artist, or of my visitor – Mr Chapman of the publishing house of Chapman and Hall – (I forget which), that a 'Nimrod Club', the members of which were to go out shooting, fishing and so forth, and getting themselves into difficulties through their want of dexterity, would be the best means of introducing these. I objected, on consideration, that, although born and partly bred in the country, I was no great sportsman, except in regard of all kinds of locomotion; that the idea was not novel, and had been already much used; that it would be infinitely better for the plates to arise naturally out of the text; and that I should like to take my own way, with a freer range of English scenes and people, and was afraid I should ultimately do so in any case, whatever course I might prescribe to myself at starting. My views being deferred to, I thought of Mr Pickwick, and wrote

the first number; from the proof-sheets of which Mr Seymour made his drawing of the club, and that happy portrait of its founder by which he is always recognised, and which may be said to have made him a reality. I connected Mr Pickwick with a club because of the original suggestion; and I put in Mr Winkle expressly for the use of Mr Seymour.

The conception of Mr Pickwick as an elderly little gentleman, somewhat pursy, with a bland face, bald head, circular spectacles, fawn-coloured tights, and black gaiters, is said to have originated in a description by Mr Chapman of a like odd-looking character whom he had met at Richmond. The ludicrous name of 'Pickwick' is not a fabrication of the novelist, as many suppose, but is also 'founded on fact'. It was actually borne by the proprietor of a line of stages running between London and Bath.

CHARACTERS

ALLEN, Arabella – Sister of Benjamin Allen; afterwards the wife of Mr Winkle. {28, 30, 39, 48, 53, 54, 56, 57}

ALLEN, Benjamin – A medical student, and the devoted friend of Mr Bob Sawyer, to whom he purposes marrying his sister Arabella. Mr Allen does not succeed in his project, however, as Mr Winkle, with the assistance of Mr Pickwick, carries the girl off, and marries her without the consent of either her brother or Mr Bob Sawyer. {30, 32, 38, 48, 50, 51, 52, 54, 57} *See* **SAWYER**, *Bob*.

AYRESLEIGH, Mr – A prisoner for debt, whom Mr Pickwick meets in the 'coffee-room' at Coleman Street. {40}

BAGMAN, The One-eyed – A stout, jovial, middle-aged man with a 'lonely eye', whom Mr Pickwick meets, first at The Peacock Inn, Eatanswill, and afterwards at The Bush, in Bristol. He is the narrator of 'The Bagman's Story', and of 'The Story of the Bagman's Uncle'. {14, 48, 49} *See* **SMART**, *Tom*.

BAMBER, Jack – A little, high-shouldered, keen-eyed old man, whom Mr Pickwick casually meets at The Magpie and Stump. He relates 'The Old Man's Tale about a Queer Client'. {20}

BANTAM, Angelo Cyrus, Esq, MC – A charming young man of not much more than fifty, whom Mr Pickwick meets at Bath; friend of Captain Dowler, and master of ceremonies at the ball which Mr Pickwick attends. {35}

BARDELL, Mrs Martha – Mr Pickwick's landlady in Goswell Street. Becoming impressed with the idea that Mr Pickwick has offered to marry her, she is highly indignant when she finds herself mistaken. In fact, she insists that she is not mistaken, and forthwith brings an action against him for breach of promise. {12, 26, 34, 46}

BARDELL, Master Tommy – The hopeful son of Mrs Bardell. {12, 26, 46}

BETSEY – Servant-girl at Mrs Raddle's. {32}

BLADUD, Prince – Mythical founder of Bath; hero of the 'True Legend' discovered by Mr Pickwick. {36}

BLOTTON, Mr – (of Aldgate). A member of the Pickwick Club. Having been accused by Mr Pickwick, at a meeting of the club, of acting in 'a vile and calumnious manner', he retorts by calling Mr Pickwick 'a humbug'; but it finally being made to appear that they both used the words not in a common, but in a parliamentary or merely technical or constructive sense, and that each personally entertains the highest regard and esteem for the other, the difficulty is readily settled, and the gentlemen express themselves mutually satisfied with the explanations which have been made. {1}

BOLDWIG, Captain – A fierce little man, very consequential and imperious; owner of the premises on which Mr Pickwick and his friends trespass while shooting. Mr Pickwick, having fallen asleep under the influence of too much cold punch, is left there by the rest of his party, and is discovered by the captain, who indignantly orders him to be taken to the pound in a wheelbarrow. {19}

BOLO, Miss – A fashionable lady at Bath. {35}

BUDGER, Mrs – A little old widow, with plenty of money; Mr Tupman's partner in a quadrille at the charity ball at The Bull Inn, Rochester, which he attends in company with Mr Jingle. {2}

BULDER, Colonel – Head of the garrison at Rochester, and one of the company at the same ball. {2, 4}

BULDER, Mrs Colonel – His wife. {2}

BULDER, Miss – Their daughter. {2}

BUZFUZ, Serjeant – Mrs Bardell's counsel remarkable for his brutal and bullying insolence to the witnesses on Mr Pickwick's side. {34}

CHANCERY PRISONER, The – An old man whose acquaintance Mr Pickwick makes in the Fleet. He has been confined there for twenty years, but gets his release at last from the hands of his Maker, and accepts it with a smile of quiet satisfaction. {42, 44}

The sagacious dog – Robert Seymour

CLERGYMAN, The – One of the guests at Mr Wardle's. He sings the song of 'The Ivy Green', and relates the story of 'The Convict's Return'. {6, 11, 28}

CLUBBER, Sir Thomas – A fashionable gentleman at Rochester, Commissioner at the head of the dockyard there. {22}

CLUBBER, Lady – His wife. {2}

CLUBBER, The Misses – His daughters. {2}

CLUPPINS, Mrs Betsey – A bosom-friend of Mrs Bardell's. {26, 24, 46}

CRADDOCK, Mrs – Mr Pickwick's landlady at Bath. {36, 37}

CROOKEY – An attendant at the sponging-house in Coleman Street. {40}

CRUSHTON, The Honourable Mr – A gentleman whom Mr Pickwick meets at Bath; a friend of Captain Dowler's. {35}

DISMAL JEMMY – *See* **HUTLEY**, Jem.

DODSON and FOGG – Attorneys for Mrs Bardell. {20, 24, 53}

DOWLER, Captain – A blustering coward, formerly in the army, whom Mr Pickwick meets at the travellers' room at The White Horse Cellar. {25, 36, 38}

DOWLER, Mrs – Wife of Capt Dowler. {35, 36}

DUBBLEY – One of the special officers of the Mayor's Court at Ipswich; a dirty-faced man, over six feet high, and stout in proportion. {24}

DUMKINS, Mr – A member of the All-Muggleton Cricket Club. {7}

EDMUNDS, John – Hero of the story of 'The Convict's Return'; a sullen, wilful young man, condemned to death for crime but, by commutation of his sentence, transported for fourteen years. A repentant and altered man, he returns to his old home, only to find his mother buried, and to see his father die suddenly from the effects of passion and terror – the same hardhearted and ferocious brute that he had always known him. {6}

EDMUNDS, Mr – His father; a morose, dissolute, and savage-hearted man. {6}

EDMUNDS, Mrs – His mother; a gentle, ill-used, and heart-broken woman. {6}

EMMA – A servant-girl at Mr Wardle's. {28}

FITZ-MARSHALL, Charles – *See* **JINGLE**, Alfred.

FIZKIN, Horatio, Esq – (of Fizkin Lodge, near Eatanswill). A candidate for Parliament, defeated by the Honourable Samuel Slumkey. {13}

FLASHER, Wilkins – A stockbroker. {55}

FOGG, Mr – *See* **DODSON** *and* **FOGG**.

GOODWIN – Servant to Mrs Pott. {18}

GROFFIN, Thomas – One of the jury in the case of Bardell *v.* Pickwick. He desires to be excused from attendance on the ground that he is a chemist, and has no assistant. {34}

GRUB, Gabriel – Hero of Mr Wardle's 'Story of the Goblins who stole a Sexton'; a cross-grained, surly, solitary fellow, who is made good-natured and contented by his remarkable experiences on Christmas Eve. {29}

GRUMMER, Daniel – A constable in attendance upon the Mayor's Court at Ipswich. {24, 25}

GRUNDY, Mr – A friend of Mr Lowten's, and a frequenter of The Magpie and Stump Inn. {20}

GUNTER, Mr – A friend of Mr Bob Sawyer's. {32}

GWYNN, Miss – Writing and ciphering governess at Westgate House Establishment for Young Ladies, at Bury St. Edmunds. {38}

HARRIS – A greengrocer. {38}

HENRY – A character in 'The Parish Clerk'; cousin to Maria Lobbs, whom he finally marries. {17}

HEYLING, George – Hero of 'The Old Man's Tale about a Queer Client'. He is a prisoner for debt in the Marshalsea. During his confinement, his little boy is taken sick and dies; and his wife, who thereupon shares her husband's lot, soon follows, sinking uncomplainingly under the combined effects of bodily and mental illness. Released from prison by the sudden death of his father, a very wealthy man who had disowned him, and had meant to disinherit him, he devotes himself unremittingly to avenge the death of his wife and child upon his wife's father, who had cast him into prison, and had repulsed daughter and grandchild from his door when they sued at his feet for mercy. In this scheme of vengeance he is successful, suffering the old man's boy to drown before his eyes, though he might easily have saved him, and afterwards pursuing the father until he reduces him to utter destitution. He intends to consign him to the hopeless imprisonment which he himself so long endured – but, on announcing his purpose, his victim falls lifeless, and Heyling disappears, leaving no clue to his subsequent history. {21}

HEYLING, Mary – His wife. {19}

HOPKINS, Jack – A medical student, whom Mr Pickwick meets at Mr Bob Sawyer's party. {32}

HUMM, Anthony – Chairman of the Brick Lane Branch of the United Grand Junction Ebenezer Temperance Association. {33}

HUNT – Gardener to Captain Boldwig. {19}

HUNTER, Mrs Leo – A literary lady whom Mr Pickwick meets at Eatanswill. {15}

HUNTER, Mr Leo – Mrs Leo Hunter's husband. {15}

HUTLEY, Jem – called 'Dismal Jemmy'. An itinerant actor, who 'does the heavy business'; brother to Job Trotter, and friend of Mr Alfred Jingle, who introduces him to Mr Pickwick. He relates to them 'The Stroller's Tale', in which he himself figures. {3, 5}

ISAAC – A friend of Mr Jackson's. {46}

JACKSON, Mr – A clerk in the office of Dodson and Fogg. {20, 31, 46}

JEMMY, Dismal – *See* **HUTLEY**, *Jem*.

JINGLE, Alfred – An impudent strolling actor, who palms himself off on Mr Pickwick and his travelling-companions of the club as a gentleman of consequence, sponges good dinners and borrows money from them, and finally gets into the Fleet Prison where, some time afterwards, Mr Pickwick finds him in great destitution and distress, and benevolently pays his debts and releases him, on satisfactory evidence of penitence, and on promise of reformation, which is faithfully kept. Mr Jingle is a very loquacious person, talking incessantly; rarely speaking a connected sentence, however, but stringing together mere disjointed phrases, generally without verbs. He first meets Mr Pickwick and his party at the coach-stand in Saint Martin's-le-Grand. {2, 3, 7–10, 15, 25, 42, 45, 47, 53}

JINKINS, Mr – A character in 'The Bagman's Story'; a rascally adventurer with a wife and six babes – all of them small ones – who tries to marry a buxom widow, the landlady of a roadside inn, but is prevented by Tom Smart, who marries her himself. {14}

JINKS, Mr – A pale, sharp-nosed, half-fed, shabbily-clad clerk of the Mayor's Court at Ipswich. {24, 25}

JOE, The Fat Boy – Servant to Mr Wardle; a youth of astonishing obesity and voracity, who has a way of going to sleep on the slightest provocation, and in all sorts of places and attitudes. {4–9, 28, 54, 56}

The warden's room – Robert William Buss

JOHN – A low pantomime actor, and an habitual drunkard, whose death is described in 'The Stroller's Tale'; related to Mr Pickwick and his friends by Mr Rutley. {3}

KATE – A character in the story of 'The Parish Clerk'; cousin to Maria Lobbs. {17}

LOBBS, Maria – A character in Mr Pickwick's story of 'The Parish Clerk'; a pretty girl, beloved by Nathaniel Pipkin, and also by her cousin Henry, whom she marries. {17}

LOBBS, Old – Father to Maria Lobbs; a rich saddler, and a terrible old fellow when his pride is injured, or his blood is up. {17}

LOWTEN, Mr – A puffy-faced young man, clerk to Mr Perker. {20, 21, 31, 34, 40, 47, 53, 54}

LUCAS, Solomon – A seller of fancy dresses. {15}

LUFFEY, Mr – Vice-president of the Dingley Dell Cricket Club. {7}

MAGNUS, Peter – A red-haired man, with an inquisitive nose and blue spectacles, who is a fellow-traveller with Mr Pickwick from London to Ipswich. {22, 24}

MALLARD, Mr – Clerk to Mr Serjeant Snubbin. {31, 34}

MARTIN, Mr – A prisoner confined in the Fleet Prison. {42}

MARTIN – A coachman. {48}

MARTIN – A gamekeeper. {19}

MARTIN, Jack – Hero of 'The Story of the Bagman's Uncle'. {49}

MARY – A servant-girl at Mr Nupkins's; afterwards married to Sam Weller. {25, 39, 47, 53, 54, 56}

MATINTER, The two Misses – Ladies attending the ball at Bath. {35}

MILLER, Mr – A guest at Mr Wardle's. {6, 28}

MIVINS, Mr – *called* 'The Zephyr'. A fellow-prisoner with Mr Pickwick in the Fleet. {41, 42}

MUDGE, Mr Jonas – Secretary of the Brick Lane Branch of the United Grand Junction Ebenezer Temperance Association. {33}

MUTHANED, Lord – A fashionable gentleman whom Mr Pickwick meets at a ball in Bath; a friend of Captain and Mrs Dowler. {35}

MUZZLE, Mr – An undersized footman, with a long body and short legs, in the service of George Nupkins, Esq. {24, 25}

NAMBY, Mr – A sheriff's officer who arrests Mr Pickwick. {11}

NEDDY – A prisoner for debt, confined in the Fleet; a phlegmatic and taciturn man. {42, 43}

NODDY, Mr – A friend of Mr Bob Sawyer. {32}

NUPKINS, George, Esq – Mayor of Ipswich, before whom Mr Pickwick and his friend Mr Tupman are brought. {24, 25}

NUPKINS, Mrs – Wife of George Nupkins, Esq. {25}

NUPKINS, Miss Henrietta – Their daughter. {25}

PAYNE, Doctor – Surgeon of the Forty-third regiment, and a friend of Doctor Slammer. {2, 3}

PEEL, Mr Solomon – An attorney at the Insolvent Court in Portugal Street; a fat, flabby, pale man, with a narrow forehead, wide face, large head, short neck, and wry nose. {43, 55}

PERKER, Mr – Election-agent for the Honourable Samuel Slumkey; afterwards Mr Pickwick's attorney – a little, high-dried man, with a dark, squeezed-up face, small, restless black eyes, and the air of one in the habit of propounding regular posers. {10, 13, 31, 34, 35, 47, 53, 54}

PHUNKY, Mr – Junior counsel with Serjeant Snubbin in the case of Bardell *v.* Pickwick; regarded as 'an infant barrister', as he has not been at the Bar quite eight years. {31, 34}

PICKWICK, Samuel – Founder of the Pickwick Club. Mr Pickwick starts out upon his travels with the other members of the Corresponding Society of the Pickwick Club and meets with many laughable and interesting adventures. {1–28, 30–32, 34–37, 39–48, 50–56}

PIPKIN, Nathaniel – The 'Parish Clerk' in Mr Pickwick's tale of that name. He is a harmless, good-natured little being, of a very nervous temperament, and with a cast in his eye and a halt in his gait. He falls in love with the beautiful Maria Lobbs, but sees her married to another. {17}

PODDER, Mr – A member of the All-Muggleton Cricket Club. {7}

POTT, Mr – Editor of *The Eatanswill Gazette.* {13, 15, 18}

POTT, Mrs – Wife of the editor of *The Eatanswill Gazette.* {13, 15, 18, 51}

PRICE, Mr – A coarse, vulgar young man, with a sallow face and a harsh voice; a prisoner for debt whom Mr Pickwick encounters in the 'coffee-room' of the sponging-house in Coleman Street. {40}

PRUFFLE – A servant to a scientific gentleman at Bath. {39}

RADDLE, Mr – Husband to Mrs Raddle. {32, 46}

RADDLE, Mrs Mary Ann – Mr Bob Sawyer's landlady; sister to Mrs Cluppins, and a thorough shrew. {32, 46}

ROGERS, Mrs – A lodger at Mrs Bardell's. {46}

ROKER, Mr Tom – A turnkey at the Fleet Prison. {40–45}

SAM – A cab-driver. {2}

SANDERS, Mrs Susannah – A bosom-friend of Mrs Bardell's. {25, 34}

SAWYER, Bob – A medical student whom Mr Pickwick meets at Mr Wardle's. He afterwards sets up (Sawyer, late Nockemorf) as a medical practitioner in Bristol, where Mr Winkle meets him. He has a very nice place; but 'half the drawers have got nothing in 'em, and the other half don't open. Indeed, hardly anything real in the shop but the leeches; and *they* are second-hand'. {30, 32, 38, 48, 50–52}

SHEPHERD, The – See **STIGGINS**, The Reverend Mr

SIMMERY, Frank, Esq – A smart young stockbroker. {55}

SIMPSON, Mr – A prisoner in Fleet. {43}

SKIMPIN, Mr – Junior counsel with Serjeant Buzfuz for Mrs Bardell, in her suit against Mr Pickwick. {34}

SLAMMER, Doctor – Surgeon of the Ninety-seventh Regiment, present at a charity ball at The Bull Inn, Rochester. {2, 3}

SLUMKEY, The Honourable Samuel – Candidate for Parliament from the borough of Eatanswill. He is successful in the contest, beating his opponent, Horatio Fizkin, Esq. {13}

SLURK, Mr – Editor of *The Eatanswill Independent*. {51}

SMANGLE – A fellow-prisoner with Mr Pickwick in the Fleet. {41, 42, 44}

SMART, Tom – Hero of 'The Bagman's Story'. {14}

SMAUKER, John – Footman in the service of Angelo Cyrus Bantam, Esq. {35, 37}

SMIGGERS, Joseph – Perpetual Vice-President of the Pickwick Club. {1}

SMITHERS, Miss – A young lady-boarder at Westgate House, Bury St Edmunds. {16}

SMITHIE, Mr – A gentleman present at the charity ball at The Bull Inn, Rochester. {2}

SMITHIE, Mrs – His wife. {2}

SMITHIE, The Misses – His daughters. {2}

SMORLTORK, Count – A famous foreigner whom Mr Pickwick meets at Mrs Leo Hunter's fancy-dress breakfast. {15}

SMOUCH, Mr – A sheriffs assistant, who takes Mr Pickwick to the Fleet Prison. {40}

SNIPE, The Honourable Wilmot – Ensign of the Ninety-seventh; one of the company at the ball in Rochester attended by Mr Tupman. {2}

SNODGRASS, Augustus – A poetic member of the Corresponding Society of the Pickwick Club. {1–6, 8, 11–15, 18, 24–26, 28, 30–32, 34–36, 44, 47, 54, 57}

SNUBBIN, Serjeant – Senior counsel for Mr Pickwick in his suit with Mrs Bardell. {31, 34}

SNUPHANUPH, Lady – A fashionable lady whom Mr Pickwick meets in the Rooms at Bath. {35, 36}

STAPLE, Mr – A little cricket-player who makes a big speech at the dinner which succeeds the match-game at Dingley Dell. {7}

STARELEIGH, Mr Justice – The judge who presides, in the absence of the chief justice, at the trial of Bardell *v.* Pickwick. {34}

STIGGINS, The Reverend Mr – called 'The Shepherd'. An intemperate, canting, and hypocritical parson, who ministers to a fanatical flock, composed largely of women, at Emanuel Chapel. {27, 33, 45, 52}

STRUGGLES, Mr – A cricketer of Dingley Dell. {7}

TADGER, Brother – A member of the Brick Lane Branch of the United Grand Junction Ebenezer Temperance Association. {33}

TAPPLETON, Lieutenant – Doctor Slammer's second. {2, 3}

TOMKINS, Miss – Principal of Westgate House, a boarding-school for young ladies at Bury St. Edmunds. {16}

TOMLINSON, Mrs – Postmistress at Rochester, and one of the company at the charity ball at The Bull Inn there. {2}

TOMMY – A waterman. {2}

TROTTER, Job – The confidential servant of Mr Alfred Jingle, and the only man who proves too sharp for Sam Weller. {16, 20, 23, 25, 42, 45–47, 53, 57}

TRUNDLE, Mr – A young man who marries Isabella Wardle. He is repeatedly brought upon the scene as an actor, but not once as an interlocutor. {4, 6, 8, 16, 17, 19, 28, 57}

TUCKLE – A footman at Bath. {37}

TUPMAN, Tracy – One of the Corresponding Society of the Pickwick Club; of so susceptible a disposition, that he falls in love with every pretty girl he meets. {1–9, 11–15, 18, 19, 24–26, 28, 30, 32, 34, 35, 44, 47, 57}

UPWITCH, Richard – A greengrocer; one of the jurymen in the case of Bardell *v*. Pickwick. {34}

WARDLE, Mr – (of Manor Farm, Dingley Dell). A friend of Mr Pickwick and his companions; a stout, hearty, honest old gentleman, who is most happy when he is making others so. {4, 6–11, 16–19, 28, 30, 54, 56}

WARDLE, Miss Emily – One of his daughters. {4, 6–11, 28, 30, 54, 57}

WARDLE, Miss Isabella – Another daughter. {4, 6–8, 28, 57}

WARDLE, Miss Rachael – His sister; a spinster of doubtful age, with a peculiar dignity in her air, majesty in her eye, and touch-me-not-ishness in her walk. The too susceptible Mr Tupman falls in love with her, only to be circumvented by the adroit Mr Jingle, who steals her heart away from him, and elopes with her, but is pursued, overtaken, and induced to relinquish his prize in consideration of a cheque for a hundred and twenty pounds. {4, 6–9}

WARDLE, Mrs – Mother of Mr Wardle and Miss Rachael, very old and very deaf. {6–9, 28, 57}

WATTY, Mr – A bankrupt client of Mr Perker, whom he keeps pestering about his affairs, although they have not been in Chancery four years. {31}

WELLER, Samuel – Mr Pickwick's valet; a compound of wit, simplicity, quaint humour, and fidelity, who may be regarded as an embodiment of London low life in its most agreeable and entertaining form. {10, 12, 13, 15, 16, 18–20, 22–28, 30–35, 36–48, 50–52, 55–57}

WELLER, Tony – Father to Samuel Weller; one of the old plethoric, mottled-faced, great-coated, many-waistcoated stage-coachmen that flourished in England before the advent of railways. Being a widower, and therefore feeling rather lonely at times, he is inveigled by a buxom widow, who keeps a public-house, into marrying again. {10, 12, 13, 27, 33, 34, 43, 45, 52, 55, 56}

WELLER, Mrs Susan – Wife of Mr Tony Weller, formerly Mrs Clarke. {27, 45}

WHIFFERS – A footman at Bath. {37}

WICKS, Mr – Clerk in office of Dodson and Fogg. {20}

WILKINS – Gardener to Captain Boldwig. {19}

WINKLE, Mr, Senior – Father of Nathaniel Winkle; an old wharfinger at Birmingham, and a thorough man of business, having the most methodical habits, and never committing himself hastily in any

First appearnnce of Mr Samuel Weller –
Hablot K Browne *alias* Phiz

affair. He is greatly displeased at his son's marriage to Miss Arabella Allen, but finally forgives him, and admits that the lady is 'a very charming little daughter-in-law, after all'. {50, 56}

WINKLE, Nathaniel – A member of the Corresponding Society of the Pickwick Club, and a cockney pretender to sporting skill. {1–5, 7, 9, 11–13, 15, 18, 19, 24–26, 28, 30–32, 34–36, 38, 39, 44, 47, 54, 56, 57}

WITHERFIELD, Miss— A middle-aged lady, affianced to Mr Magnus. {22, 24}

WUGSBY, Mrs Colonel – A fashionable lady whom Mr Pickwick meets at Bath. {35, 36}

ZEPHYR, The – *See* **MIVINS, Mr.**.

PRINCIPAL INCIDENTS

{1} Meeting of the Pickwick Club; Mr Blotton calls Mr Pickwick a 'humbug' in a 'Pickwickian sense'. {2} The Pickwickians get into trouble with a cabman at the Golden Cross Inn; they meet Mr Alfred Jingle; the journey to Rochester; after supper at The Bull Inn, Mr Tupman and Mr Jingle attend the ball, Mr Jingle wearing Mr Winkle's coat; Mr Jingle excites the jealousy of Dr Slammer, who challenges Mr Winkle in consequence; the duel, which is interrupted by Dr Slammer discovering that Mr Winkle is 'not the man'. {3} Dismal Jemmy relates 'The Stroller's Tale'; Dr Slammer recognises Mr Jingle. {4} The military review at Rochester; meeting with Mr Wardle and his party. {5} The drive to Dingley Dell; Mr Winkle, dismounting, is unable to remount; and, Mr Pickwick going to his assistance, his horse runs away, leaving the Pickwickians to walk the rest of the way. {6} The party at Mr Wardle's; the clergyman recites 'The Ivy Green' and relates 'The Convict's Return'. {7} Mr Winkle attempts to shoot the rooks, and wounds Mr Tupman; the cricket-match at Muggleton, and the dinner that followed. {8} Mr Tupman proposes to Miss Rachael, and is discovered by the fat boy; Joe relating the discovery to old Mrs Wardle, is overheard by Mr Jingle, who determines to supersede Mr Tupman in the spinster's affections. {9} Finding his arts successful, he elopes with her; Mr Wardle and Mr Pickwick follow, and are just on the point of overtaking the fugitives, when their carriage breaks down. {10} Sam Weller's first appearance as 'boots' at The White Hart Inn; his account of his father's marriage; Mr Wardle questions Sam, and finds that Jingle and Miss Rachael are at the White Hart; Mr Jingle is bought off, and the lady returns with her brother. {11} The disappearance of Mr Tupman, and the journey of Pickwick, Snodgrass, and Winkle in search of him; Mr Pickwick discovers the stone with the famous inscription; the madman's manuscript; the discussion occasioned among the learned societies by Mr Pickwick's discovery. {12} Mr Pickwick, informing Mrs Bardell of his determination to employ a valet, finds himself in an awkward situation, in which he is discovered by his friends; Mr Pickwick engages Sam Weller as his valet. {13} Some account of Eatanswill, and the rival factions of the Buffs and Blues; Mr Perker explains how election is managed, and introduces the Pickwickians to Mr Pott, editor of *The Gazette*, who invites Mr Pickwick and Mr Winkle to his house; Sam Weller relates to his master some tricks of the election; speeches of the rival candidates, and success of the Hon Samuel Slumkey. {14} 'The Bagman's Story'. {15} Mr Leo Hunter waits upon Mr Pickwick, and invites him and his friends to a *fête champêtre*, to be given by Mrs Leo Hunter; dispute and reconciliation of Mr Pickwick and Mr Tupman; the fancy ball at Mrs Hunter's, and reappearance of Alfred Jingle as Mr Charles Fitz-Marshall; recognising Mr Pickwick, he suddenly departs, and is followed by Mr Pickwick and Sam to The Angel at Bury St Edmunds. {16} Sam gives Mr Pickwick some account of his bringing up; Sam discovers Mr Job Trotter, who reveals the plans of Mr Charles Fitz-Marshall for eloping with a young lady from the boarding-school; Mr Pickwick's adventure in the boarding-school; he is relieved from his unpleasant situation by the appearance of Mr Wardle and Mr Trundle. {17} Mr Pickwick reads to Mr Wardle the 'Story of the Parish Clerk'. {18} Mr Putt, having his jealousy of Mr Winkle excited by an article in *The Independent*, denounces that gentleman, whereupon a scene ensues, ending in the departure of Mr Winkle; Messrs Winkle, Snodgrass, and Tupman join Mr Pickwick at The Angel, at Bury St. Edmunds; Mr Pickwick receives a letter from Messrs Dodson and Fogg, informing him of Mrs Bardell's action for breach of promise. {19} Account of the shooting-party and the extraordinary skill of Messrs Tupman and Winkle; Sam Weller explains the mysteries of 'weal pie'; Mr Pickwick, having imbibed punch very freely, falls asleep in a wheelbarrow, and is left alone while the party continue their sport; he is discovered by Captain Boldwig, who orders him to be wheeled off to the pound, from which he is rescued by Mr Wardle and Sam Weller. {20} Mr Pickwick and

Sam visit the office of Dodson and Fogg, after which they call at a tavern, where Sam unexpectedly encounters his father; from him they learn that Jingle and Job Trotter are at Ipswich, and Mr Pickwick decides to seek them there at once; Mr Pickwick finds Mr Lowten at the head of a convivial party at The Magpie and Stump, and is invited to join them. {21} Jack Bamber relates some stories about Gray's Inn and also 'A Tale of a Queer Client'. {22} Mr Pickwick, going to Ipswich, meets Mr Peter Magnus going to the same place, and learns from that gentleman his object in visiting that city; Mr Pickwick, retiring for the night, leaves his watch upon the table and, returning to seek it, loses his way, and gets into the wrong room, which proves to be the chamber of a middle-aged lady. {23} Sam Weller unexpectedly encounters Mr Job Trotter, and begins his return-match. {24} Mr Magnus introduces Mr Pickwick to his betrothed, and is astonished at their behaviour; Miss Witherfield waits upon George Nupkins Esq, and enters a complaint against Mr Pickwick, in consequence of which that gentleman and Mr Tupman are arrested and, in attempting a rescue, Sam Weller and the other Pickwickians share the same fate. {25} The trial before George Nupkins Esq, which is brought to an unexpected termination by Mr Pickwick exposing Mr Alfred Jingle and his designs; Mr Weller also exposes Job Trotter; the first passage of Mr Weller's first love. {26} Sam visits Mrs Bardell, and assists in a conversation which throws some light on the action of Bardell *v.* Pickwick. {27} Sam goes to Dorking, and makes the acquaintance of his mother-in-law and the Revd Mr Stiggins, and also has an interview with Mr Weller senior. {28} The Pickwickians and Sam Weller go to Dingley Dell, and attend the wedding of Mr Trundle and Miss Isabella Wardle; Mr Pickwick speaks at the wedding breakfast, and dances with old Mrs Wardle in the evening; Mr Wardle sings a 'Christmas Carol'. {29} Mr Wardle relates 'The Story of the Goblins who stole a Sexton'. {30} The Pickwickians make the acquaintance of Mr Ben Allen and Mr Bob Sawyer; Mr Winkle exhibits his skill in the accomplishment of skating; Mr Pickwick's fall through the ice, and rescue; breaking up of the party. {31} Mr Jackson, of the house of Dodson and Fogg, subpœnas the friends and servants of Mr Pickwick; Mr Pickwick and Sam go to Mr Perker's, Sam relating on the way the mysterious disappearance of a respectable tradesman; Mr Perker informs Mr Pickwick that he has retained Serjeant Snubbin as his advocate, and is amazed at Mr Pickwick's determination to see that eminent

Sam Weller at the White Hart – Cecil Aldin

personage; Mr Pickwick's interview with Serjeant Snubbin, in which they are joined by Mr Phunky. {32} Mr Bob Sawyer, proposing to give a bachelor party, has some trouble with his landlady; the party, getting noisy, is ordered out by Mrs Raddle. {33} Mr Sam Weller, going to meet his father at The Blue Boar, has his attention attracted by a valentine in a shop window and, purchasing paper and pens, he indites a valentine to Mary, which Mr Weller senior, criticises and approves; Mr Weller and Sam attend the meeting of the Brick Lane Branch of the United Grand Junction Ebenezer Total Abstinence Association; Mr Stiggins also attends in a state which astonishes the members, and causes the dispersion of the meeting. {34} Commencement of the memorable trial, Bardell *v.* Pickwick; dramatic effect of Mrs Bardell's appearance; address of Serjeant Buzfuz, followed by the examination of the witnesses, and the important testimony of Sam Weller; verdict for the plaintiff. {35} The Pickwickians, going to Bath, make the acquaintance of Captain Dowler, also of Angelo Cyrus Bantam Esq MC; Sam goes on an errand to Queen Square, and meets a resplendent footman; the ball-night in the assembly-room at Bath, where Mr Pickwick does himself no credit at cards. {36} Mr Pickwick takes lodgings for himself and friends in the Royal Crescent; he finds the 'True Legend of Prince Bladud'; Mr Dowler, sitting up for his wife, who has gone to a party, falls asleep; on her return in a sedan-chair, Mr Winkle is the first person aroused, and he proceeds, in dressing-gown and slippers, to open the door, when it is blown to behind him, and he rushes into the sedan-chair; exciting Chase of Mr Winkle by Mr Dowler. {37} Sam Weller receives an invitation to a 'friendly swarry' by the Bath footmen, which he attends under the patronage of Mr John Smauker; Mr Pickwick relates to Sam the story of Mr Winkle's flight, and commissions him to find and bring him back. {38} Mr Winkle, having fled to Bristol, unexpectedly finds himself in the presence of Mr Bob Sawyer and Mr Ben Allen; Mr Allen explains to Mr Winkle his intentions in regard to his sister Arabella; Mr Winkle, returning to his hotel, is greatly astonished to find Mr Dowler; mutual explanation and reconciliation. {39} Sam Weller appears, and undertakes to find Miss Arabella Allen; his unexpected meeting with the pretty housemaid, through whom he finds and has an interview with Miss Allen; Mr Pickwick arranges and assists at a meeting between Mr Winkle and Miss Arabella, and casts new light on the studies of a scientific gentleman. {40} Mr Pickwick is arrested;

Mr Perker visits him, but is unable to induce him to pay the damages adjudged, and Mr Pickwick is carried to the Fleet. {41} Sam relates the story of the Chancery prisoner; Mr Pickwick makes the acquaintance of Messrs Mivins and Smangle. {42} Mr Smangle's attempt to get possession of Mr Pickwick's linen is frustrated by Sam Weller; Mr Pickwick is 'chummed' upon No 27 in the third, and takes possession of his quarters, but finding his presence disagreeable to his chums, and learning that he *can* live elsewhere, he hires a room in the coffee-house flight; he visits the poor side of the prison, and encounters Mr Alfred Jingle and Mr Job Trotter; Mr Pickwick dismisses Sam. {43} Sam arranges with his father a little plan, by which he gets himself arrested and sent to the Fleet as a prisoner, in which character he astonishes Mr Pickwick. {44} Sam relates to his master the story of the man 'as killed hisself on principle'; he makes the acquaintance of his chum, the cobbler; Mr Pickwick is visited by Messrs. Tupman, Snodgrass, and Winkle; death of the Chancery prisoner. {45} Sam Weller is visited by his father, his mother-in-law, and the shepherd; he is overwhelmed with astonishment at encountering Mr Job Trotter; Mr Trotter introduces Mr Pickwick and Sam to a 'whistling-shop'. {46} Mrs Bardell is visited by some friends, with whom and her lodger she goes to The Spaniard Tea Gardens; their tea-party is interrupted by Mr Jackson, of Dodson and Fogg, by whom Mrs Bardell is carried to the Fleet, in execution for costs in the case of Bardell *v.* Pickwick. {47} Mr Perker, having received notice of this from Sam, visits Mr Pickwick; Mr and Mrs Winkle appear, to confess their marriage; Mr Snodgrass and Mr Tupman also arrive; and Mr Pickwick finally yields to their united appeals, and consents to release himself from prison. {48} Mr Bob Sawyer and Mr Ben Allen, discussing the prospects, business and matrimonial, of the former, are visited by an aunt of the latter, also by Mr Pickwick and Sam; Mr Pickwick's explanation reconciles all parties to the marriage of Miss Allen with Mr Winkle; Mr Pickwick again meets the one-eyed bagman. {49} He relates 'The Story of his Uncle'. {50} Mr Pickwick having arranged with Mr Ben Allen to accompany him to Birmingham, to explain matters to the elder Mr Winkle, is surprised at Mr Sawyer's determination to go with them; humorous conduct of that gentleman on the journey; the three visit Mr Winkle, senior; unfavourable result of the interview. {51} The party, returning to London, stops at The Saracen's Head, Towcester, where they find Mr Pott; arrival of Mr Slark, and desperate encounter of the rival editors. {52} Sam receives news of the death of his mother-in-law, and goes to Dorking to see his father; Mr Stiggins pays a visit of sympathy to the widower, by whom he is kicked out of doors, and ducked in the horse-trough. {53} Mr Pickwick calls to consult Mr Perker on Mr Winkle's affairs, and meets Mr Jingle and Job Trotter, who finally take their leave of him and of the reader; Mr Pickwick gives Messrs Dodson and Fogg his opinion of their character. {54} The fat boy announces the arrival of his master; Mr Wardle astonishes Mr Pickwick with the story of the attachment of Mr Snodgrass and Miss Emily Wardle; Mr Snodgrass, visiting Miss Emily, is discovered by the fat boy, who is bribed to keep the secret; Mr Wardle and his party returning earlier than expected, Mr Snodgrass conceals himself in an inner room, from which he is unable to escape; unaccountable behaviour of Joe, which is explained by the appearance of Mr Snodgrass, and his story. {55} Mr Weller, advised by Sam, has his late wife's will probated, and sells his share in the funds, through the aid of Wilkins Flasher, Esq. {56} Mr Weller, senior, consigns his property into the hands of Mr Pickwick; Mr Pickwick advises Sam, with his father's consent, to marry, but Sam stoutly refuses to leave his master; Mr Winkle, senior, calls on his daughter-in-law, and becomes reconciled to his son's marriage. {57} Mr Pickwick announces the dissolution of the club; marriage of Snodgrass and Emily Wardle, and subsequent history of the principal characters.

3

The Adventures of Oliver Twist

The greater part of this tale was originally published during the years 1837 and 1838 in *Bentley's Magazine*, of which Dickens was at that time the editor. It was begun in the second number (February, 1837), and was illustrated by George Cruikshank. On its completion, it was issued in three volumes by Mr Bentley.

In *Oliver Twist* Dickens assailed the abuses of the poor-law and workhouse system. Of his more general object in writing the work, he has himself given the following account:

I have yet to learn that a lesson of the purest good may not be drawn from the vilest evil. I have always believed this to be a recognised and established truth, laid down by the greatest men the world has ever seen, constantly acted upon by the greatest and wisest natures, and confirmed by the reason and experience of every thinking mind. I saw no reason, when I wrote this book, why the dregs of life, so long as their speech did not offend the ear, should not serve the purpose of a moral, at least as well as its froth and cream. Nor did I doubt that there lay festering in Saint Giles's as good materials towards the truth as any to be found in Saint James's.

In this spirit, when I wished to show in little Oliver the principle of good surviving through every adverse circumstance, and triumphing at last; and when I considered among what companions I could try him best, having regard to that kind of men into whose hands he would most naturally fall – bethought myself of those who figure in these chapters. When I came to discuss the subject more maturely with myself, I saw many strong reasons for pursuing the course to which I was inclined. I had read of thieves by scores – seductive fellows (amiable for the most part), faultless in dress, plump in pocket, choice in horse-flesh, bold in bearing, fortunate in gallantry, great at a song, a bottle, pack of cards, or dice-box, and fit companions for the bravest; but I had never met (except in

Hogarth) with the miserable reality. It appeared to me that to draw a knot of such associates in crime as really do exist; to paint them in all their deformity, in all their wretchedness, in all the squalid poverty of their lives; to show them as they really are, for ever skulking uneasily through the dirtiest paths of life, with the great, black, ghastly gallows closing up their prospect, turn them where they may – it appeared to me that to do this would be attempting to do something which was greatly needed, and which would be a service to society. And therefore I did it as best as I could.

CHARACTERS

ANNY – A pauper. {24, 51}

Artful Dodger, The – *See* **Dawkins**, *John*

Barney – A villainous young Jew, with a chronic catarrh, employed at The Three Cripples Inn, Little Saffron Hill. {15, 22, 42, 45}

Bates, Charley – A thief; one of Fagin's apprentices. {9, 10, 12, 13, 16, 18, 25}

Bayton – One of the poor of the parish. {5}

Becky – Barmaid at The Red Lion Inn. {21}

Bedwin, Mrs – Mr Brownlow's housekeeper. {7, 14, 17, 41, 51}

Bet or Betsy – A thief in Fagin's service, and a companion of Nancy. {9, 13, 16, 18}

Bill – A grave-digger. {5}

Blathers *and* **Duff** – Bow Street officers. {31}

Bolter, Morris – See **Claypole**, Noah.

Brittles – A servant at Mrs Maylie's. {28, 30, 31, 53}

Brownlow, Mr – A benevolent old gentleman, who takes Oliver into his house and treats him kindly. {10–12, 16, 41, 46, 49, 51–53}

Bull's-eye – Bill Sikes's dog. {13, 15, 16, 19, 39, 48, 50}

Bumble, Mr – A beadle puffed up with the insolence of office. He visits the branch workhouse where Oliver Twist is 'farmed', and is received with great attention by Mrs Mann, the matron. Mrs Corney being matron of the workhouse, and the death of Mr Stout, the master of the establishment, being daily expected, Mr Bumble, who stands next in order of succession, thinks it might be a good opportunity for 'a joining of hearts and house-keepings'. With this idea in his mind, he pays the lady a visit, and, while she is out of the room for a few moments, counts the spoons, weighs the sugar-tongs, closely inspects the silver milk-pot, takes a mental inventory of the furniture, and makes himself acquainted with the contents of a chest of drawers. Upon her return, after some billing and cooing, she says 'the one little, little, little word' he begs to hear, and bashfully consents to become Mrs Bumble as soon as ever he pleases. But the course of Mr Bumble's love does not run smooth after marriage; for his wife turns out to be a thorough shrew. When the first tiff occurs Mrs Bumble bursts into tears, but they do not serve to soften the heart of Mr Bumble; for he smilingly bids her keep on. 'It opens the lungs', he tells her, 'washes the countenance, exercises the eyes. and softens the temper: so cry away'. When, however, she changes her tactics, boldly flies at him, and gives him a sound and well-merited drubbing, he yields incontinently and indulges in sad and solitary reflections. 'I sold myself' he says, 'for six tea-spoons, a pair of sugar-tongs, and a milk-pot, with a small quantity of second-hand furniter, and twenty pound in money. I went very reasonable, cheap – dirt cheap'. This precious pair are afterwards guilty – first, of selling certain articles which were left in the workhouse by the mother of Oliver Twist, and which are necessary to his identification; and, secondly, of witnessing what they suppose to be the destruction of these articles. Brought before Mr Brownlow, they are confronted with proofs and witnesses of their rascality ; but Bumble excuses himself by saying, 'It was all Mrs Bumble. She *would* do it'. Notwithstanding this disclaimer of any personal responsibility in the matter, Mr Bumble loses his situation, and retires with his wife to private life. {1, 3–5, 7, 17, 18, 37, 38, 49}

Charlotte – Servant to Mrs Sowerberry; afterwards goes to London with Noah Claypole. {4–6, 27, 42, 53}

Chitling, Tom – An 'apprentice' of Fagin's; a 'half-witted dupe', who makes a rather unsuccessful thief. {18, 25, 39, 50}

Claypole, Noah – A chuckle-headed charity-boy, apprenticed to Mr Sowerberry the undertaker. He afterwards goes to London, and becomes a thief. {5, 6, 27, 42, 43, 45–47, 53}

Corney, Mrs – Matron of a workhouse; afterwards married to Mr Bumble. {23, 24, 27, 37, 38, 51}

Crackit, Toby – A housebreaker. {23, 25, 28, 39, 50}

Dawkins, John – *called* 'The **Artful Dodger**'. A young pickpocket in the service of Fagin the Jew. When Oliver Twist runs away from his master, and sets out for London, he meets the Artful Dodger on the road, who gives him something to eat, and afterwards takes him to Fagin's den. Although the Dodger is an adept in thieving and knavery, he is detected at last in attempting to pick a gentleman's pocket, and is sentenced to transportation for life. While in court, he maintains his accustomed coolness, impudently chaffs the police-officers, asking the jailer to communicate 'the names of them two files as was on the bench', and generally does full justice to his bringing-up, and establishes for himself a glorious reputation. When brought into court, he requests to know what he is 'placed in that 'ere disgraceful sitivation for'. The evidence against him is direct and conclusive, but the Dodger continues unabashed and, when the magistrate asks him if he has anything to say, he affects not to hear the question. {8–10, 12, 13, 16, 18, 19–25, 39, 43}

Dick, Little – Companion of Oliver Twist at a branch workhouse where infant paupers are tended with parochial care. {8, 17}

Dodger, The Artful – *See* **Dawkins**, *John*.

Duff – A Bow Street officer. *See* **Blathers** *and* **Duff**.

Fagin – A crafty old Jew, a receiver of stolen goods, with a number of confederates of both sexes. He also employs several boys (styled 'apprentices') to carry on a systematic trade of pilfering. After a long career of villainy, he is sentenced to death for complicity in a murder. Having been taken to prison, he is placed in one of the 'condemned cells', and left there alone. {8, 9, 12, 13, 15, 16, 19, 20, 25, 26, 34, 39, 42–45, 47, 52}

Fang, Mr – A violent and overbearing police-magistrate. Oliver Twist, charged with stealing a handkerchief from Mr Brownlow as he stands quietly reading at a bookstall, is brought before Mr Fang for trial; Mr Brownlow appearing as witness. The keeper of the bookstall, however, who saw the affair, and knows that Oliver is not guilty, just at this moment hastily enters the room, demands to be heard, and testifies that it was not Oliver, but his companion (the 'Artful Dodger'), who picked Mr Brownlow's pocket; and that Oliver, apparently much terrified and astonished by the proceeding, ran off, was pursued, knocked down, arrested, and taken away by a police-officer. This evidence, though unwillingly received by the magistrate, acquits the boy, who is compassionately taken by Mr Brownlow to his own house, where he is laid up with fever, and is carefully nursed till he recovers. {11}

Fleming, Agnes – Mother of Oliver Twist. {1, 53}

Fleming, Rose – *See* **Maylie**, *Rose*.

Gamfield – A chimney-sweep. {3}

Giles, Mr – Mrs Maylie's butler and steward. {28–31, 34, 35, 53}

Grimwig, Mr – An irascible but warm-hearted friend of Mr Brownlow's. {14, 17, 41, 51, 53}

Kags – A returned transport. {50}

Leeford, Edward – *See* **Monks**

Limbkins – Chairman of the Workhouse Board. {2, 3}

Lively, Mr – A salesman in Field Lane, and a dealer in stolen goods. {26}

Losberne, Mr – *called* '**The Doctor**'. A friend of the Maylie family; a surgeon, fat rather from good-humour than from good living, and an eccentric bachelor, but kind and large-hearted withal. {29–36, 41, 49, 51, 53}

Mann, Mrs – Matron of the branch workhouse where Oliver Twist is 'farmed'. {1, 17}

Martha – A pauper. {23, 24, 51}

Maylie, Harry – Son of Mrs Maylie; afterwards married to Rose. {34, 36, 51, 53}

Maylie, Mrs – A lady who befriends Oliver Twist. {29–31, 33, 34, 41, 51, 53}

Maylie, Rose – Her adopted daughter; an orphan, whose true name is Rose Fleming, and who turns out to be Oliver Twist's aunt. {28, 29, 30–33, 35, 36, 40, 41, 46, 51, 53}

Monks – A half-brother of Oliver Twist. His real name is Edward Leeford. His father, while living apart from his wife, from whom he has long been separated, sees and loves Agnes Fleming, daughter of a retired naval officer. The result of their intimacy is a child (Oliver), who is born while Mr Leeford is in Rome, where he is suddenly taken ill and dies. His wife and her son join him as soon as they hear of his illness, that they may look after his large property, which they take possession of immediately upon his death, destroying a will, which leaves the great bulk of it to Agnes Fleming and her unborn child. Believing that this child will yet appear to claim his rights, young Leeford, under the assumed name of Monks, endeavours to find him out and, after a long search, discovers that he was born in a workhouse, but has left there. He pursues the boy,

Mr Fagin and his pupil recovering Nancy – George Cruikshank

and finds him at last in London, in the den of Fagin the Jew, whom he makes his accomplice and confidant, giving him a large reward for keeping the boy ensnared. The proofs of Monks villainy are discovered by Mrs Brownlow, and he is compelled to give up one-half (three thousand pounds) of the wreck of the property remaining in his hands, after which he leaves the country, and ultimately dies in prison. {26, 33, 34, 37–39, 49, 51, 53}

Nancy – A thief in Fagin's service; and mistress to Sikes, to whom, brutal as she is, she is always faithful and devoted. {9, 13, 15, 16, 19, 20, 26, 39, 40, 44–47}

Sally, Old – An inmate of the workhouse, who robs Agnes Fleming (Oliver's mother) when on her deathbed. {24}

Sikes, Bill – A brutal thief and housebreaker, with no gleam of light in all the blackness of his character. He first appears on the scene during a squabble between Fagin and the Artful Dodger, in which Fagin throws a pot of beer at Charley Bates. The pot misses its mark, and the contents are sprinkled over the face of Sikes, who just then opens the door. Later in the story, after murdering Rose Mayalie, Sikes flees into the country but, after wandering for miles and miles in momentary fear of capture, he finally resolves to return to London, thinking he can 'lay by' for a while, and then escape to France. He seeks refuge in an old den in Jacob's Island – the filthiest, strangest, and most extraordinary of the many localities that are hidden in the great city – but his old companions shrink from him, and one cries aloud for help to the officers and others below, who have tracked the ruffian to his retreat. The crowd swarm about the building and endeavour, with thick and heavy strokes, to break down the strong doors and window-shutters. Sikes escapes to the roof and attempts, by means of a rope, to drop into a ditch at the back of the house. {8, 15, 16, 19–22, 28, 39, 44, 47, 48, 50}

Sowerberry, Mr – A parochial undertaker, to whom Oliver Twist is apprenticed. {4, 5, 7}

Sowerberry, Mrs – His wife, 'a short, thin, squeezed-up woman, with a vixenish countenance' and disposition. {4–7}

Twist, Oliver – A poor, nameless orphan boy, born in the workhouse of a small town, whither his young mother, an outcast and a stranger, had come to lie down and die. He is 'brought up by hand' and 'farmed out' at a branch establishment, where twenty or thirty other juvenile offenders against the poor-laws are starved, beaten, and abused by an elderly woman named Mrs Mann. On his ninth birthday, Mr Bumble, the beadle, visits the branch, and removes Oliver to the workhouse to be taught a useful trade. After serving a short apprenticeship to Mr Sowerberry, parish undertaker, and being cruelly abused, Oliver runs off and makes his way, under the guidance of Mr John Dawkins (*alias* The Artful Dodger) to London, where he is decoyed into the den of Fagin, an old Jew, and a receiver of stolen goods, who employs a number of young persons of both sexes to carry on a systematic trade of theft. From this haunt of vice, where he is cautiously and gradually instructed in the art of larceny, he is temporarily rescued (*see FANG*), but is recaptured, and watched more closely than before to prevent his escape. His assistance, however, being very necessary to the execution of a contemplated burglary, he is forced to accompany two confederates of Fagin (Sikes and flash Toby Crackit) on their house-breaking expedition. But the plan fails, as the family are alarmed; and the robbers flee, taking with them Oliver, who has been shot, and severely wounded. Being closely pursued, they drop the boy into a ditch and dart off at full speed. On recovering his senses, Oliver wanders about till he comes to the very house he had entered. On being admitted, he is kindly cared for by the lady of the house, Mrs Maylie, and her niece Rose who, on hearing his story, save him from arrest, and educate him and love him. The detection and punishment of Fagin and his accomplices, and the identification of Oliver through the zealous efforts of his new friends (among whom he finds an aunt in Rose Maylie), bring the tale to a happy conclusion. {1–12, 14–16, 18, 20–22, 28–36, 41, 51–53}

PRINCIPAL INCIDENTS

{1} Oliver Twist is born; his mother dies. {2} He is farmed' with Mrs. Mann; Mr Bumble visits Mrs. Mann, explains how Oliver received his name, and takes him to the workhouse; Oliver is brought before the 'Board' and assigned to picking oakum; appointed by lot among the starved boys, he asks for 'more', and is duly punished for his temerity. {3} Mr Gamfield's negotiations for Oliver. {4} Mr Sowerberry converses with Mr Bumble on parish undertaking and juries; takes Oliver, who {5} becomes acquainted with Noah Claypole; on account of his 'interesting expression of melancholy', Oliver is promoted to be a 'mute', and attends his first funeral. {6} He

Fagin in the condemned cell – J Mahoney

knocks down Noah Claypole; the excitement caused by this exhibition of spirit. {7} His punishment; he runs away. {8} Experiences divers hardships and ill treatment; meets Jack Dawkins, the 'Artful Dodger'; goes with him to London. {9} Hears Fagin's soliloquy over a box of stolen watches and jewellery. The 'Artful Dodger' and Charley Bates report their success in pocket picking at an execution. {10} Oliver goes out to operate with them; is arrested. {11} His trial. {12} His illness at Mr Brownlow's; Mr Brownlow visits him, and in surprised by his familiar look; reception of the Dodger and Charley Bates by Fagin, after Oliver's arrest. {13} Bill Sikes, with his dog, enters Fagin's room; their altercation; Nancy goes to the police officer to learn where Oliver is. {14} Mr Brownlow's kindness to Oliver; his conversation with him; with Mr Grimwig; Oliver is sent with a parcel to a bookseller. {15} He is caught by Nancy. {16} Impression produced on Fagin's thieves by his return and good clothes; Oliver's grief at having Mr Brownlow's money and the parcel of books taken from him; he attempts to run away; Nancy protects him when retaken; her rage against Sikes and Fagin. {17} Mr Bumble visits the 'parochial' nursery; Dick astounds him by desiring that someone may write a note expressing his love for Oliver, and his wish to die; Mr Bumble sees Mr Brownlow's advertisement for Oliver, and calls on him; tells a very unfavourable story of Oliver's parentage and character. {18} The 'Dodger' advises Oliver to become a 'prig', to make friends with Fagin, and to steal, because, if he didn't, somebody else would; Oliver becomes acquainted with Tom Chitling, just out of the House of Correction. {19} Sikes and Fagin plan a burglary in which Oliver must assist. {20} Fagin tells Oliver he must go with Sikes, and gives him a book of murders to read till sent for; Nancy takes him to Sikes, who gives him his instructions. {21} Their journey. {22} Preparations for the burglary by Sikes and Toby Crackit; Oliver's grief and terror at learning their plan, and that he must aid in executing it; he enters the house of Mrs Maylie, is shot, and carried off by Sikes and Crackit. {23} Mrs Corney makes a cup of tea, and has some reflections over it; Mr Bumble calls, and discusses the obstinacy of paupers, and the great 'porochial' safeguard – to give them exactly what they don't want; takes a cup of tea with Mrs Corney, and becomes tender. {24} An old pauper-woman on her deathbed gives hints of a revelation concerning Oliver's mother. {25} A game of whist at Fagin's; Toby Crackit reports to Fagin the ill success of the burglary. {26} Fagin seeks intelligence of Sikes among the traders in stolen goods; at The Three Cripples; at Sikes's own room; almost betrays his own guilt to Nancy; has a conference with Monks. {27} Hints of great things that might be said concerning beadles; Mr Bumble, having weighed and counted Mrs Corney's silver plate while she was at Old Sally's deathbed, on her return concludes his courtship; on his way home interrupts Noah Claypole eating oysters. {28} Abandonment of Oliver by Sikes and Crackit after the burglary; conversation between Giles and Brittles while pursuing them; Oliver recovers consciousness, and wanders to the house he had entered the previous night: Giles's report to the other servants of the incidents of the burglary; in the midst of his narrative Oliver knocks and, after considerable hesitation, is admitted. {29} Rose Maylie; the doctor comes to dress Oliver's wound. {30} Mrs Maylie and Rose look at Oliver sleeping and Rose pleads for mercy toward him; he tells his story; the doctor challenges Giles and Brittles to identify Oliver as the boy who had broken into Mrs Maylie's house. {31} Blathers and Dull examine the premises, and report their opinion of the burglary; after taking some spirits they become loquacious, and tell how Conkey Chickweed robbed himself; they look at Oliver, and contemn Giles and Brittles for their contradictory testimony. {32} Oliver expresses his gratitude to Rose; the doctor takes him to see Mr Brownlow, and at Chertsey Bridge rushes into the house Oliver points out as the one from which Sikes and Crackit had gone to commit the burglary; Oliver's disappointment at finding that Mr Brownlow had gone to the West Indies; his duties and delights in the country house to which Mrs Maylie moved in the spring. {33} Rose is taken sick; Oliver goes to the market town with a letter for the doctor; encounters Monks; Rose comes out of the crisis of her fever to live. {34} Oliver, overjoyed, walks out, and meets Giles with Harry Maylie; Harry tells his mother his love for Rose; Giles's gallantry on the night of the burglary rewarded; Oliver sleeps, and dreams that Fagin and Monks are watching him; wakes, and finds it real. {35} The fruitless search for them; Harry tells Rose his love; she explains why she must not become his wife. {36} The doctor and Harry Maylie leave Mrs Maylie's. {37} Mr Bumble as master of the workhouse; discussion of prerogative between him and Mrs (Corney) Bumble; settled decisively in her favour; Mr Bumble, going into a public-house to regain his composure, meets Monks, who makes numerous inquiries concerning Oliver's mother and the woman who nursed her. {38} Mr and Mrs Bumble go to Monks's hiding-place; Mrs Bumble, after demanding and receiving twenty pounds, relates what Old Sally told her about Oliver's mother; hands Monks a locket containing two locks of hair and a gold wedding-ring, which he drops through a trap-door into the river, and then dismisses Mr and Mrs Bumble. {39} Sikes recovers from a fever; Fagin and his boys bring refreshments; Nancy goes with Fagin for some money for Sikes; she overhears a conversation between Fagin and Monks; gives an opiate to Sikes; goes to find Miss Maylie. {40} She repeats what she heard Monks tell Fagin about Oliver; Rose pleads with her to abandon her wretched course of life. {41} Oliver accidentally discovers Mr Brownlow; Rose goes to his house with Oliver; Mr Grimwig's excitement at hearing her account of Oliver; joyful surprise of Mr Brownlow and Mrs Bedwin at seeing Oliver; discussion of the best mode of clearing up the mystery of his parentage, and securing Monks. {42} Noah Claypole and Charlotte, having robbed Mr Sowerberry, go to London; they stop at The Three Cripples; Fagin overhears their conversation; shows that he knows of their theft, and proposes that they join his gang; Noah enters heartily into his plan, and agrees to undertake stealing money from children sent on errands. {43} Fagin explains how Noah cannot take care of himself without having special regard to Fagin's interests; the 'Artful Dodger' is arrested; Fagin expatiates to his other boys on the unusual glory of attaining to the dignity of transportation for life at the 'Dodger's' tender age; Noah (now Morris Bolter) goes to the police-office to learn the 'Dodger's fate; his examination and committal. {44} Nancy tries to keep her appointment with Rose, on Sunday night, but is prevented by Sikes; Fagin observes her efforts, and resolves to learn her secret, and so strengthen his influence over her. {45} He sends Noah to follow her the next Sunday night. {46} Noah dogs her steps to London Bridge, where Mr Brownlow and Rose Maylie meet her; she tells them why she tailed to meet them before; describes Monks; is urged to forsake her vile companions, but declares she cannot. {47} Fagin tells Sikes of her disclosures; Sikes, in a frenzy of rage, goes to his room, tells Nancy she was watched and overheard at London Bridge, and kills her. {48} His flight; at an inn a pedlar offers to take a blood-stain out of his hat; he hears the murder talked of at the mail-coach; tries to sleep, but the murdered girl's eyes and figure haunt him; helps at a fire; goes back to London. {49} Mr Brownlow causes Monks to be seized; tells him the story of his father, mother, and

Oliver; convinces him that his villainy, and the proofs of it, are well known; makes him promise a complete statement of facts in regard to Oliver, and full restitution of money of which he had defrauded him. {50} Jacob's island, where Fagin's gang took refuge after his arrest; Chitling's account of Fagin's capture; Sikes's dog, which he had vainly tried to drown, reaches the island; Sikes himself comes, fearfully haggard; Charley Bates so horrified as to attack him; his hiding-place is discovered, and a fierce crowd try to capture him; his frantic efforts to escape; accidentally hangs himself; and his dog – springing at him – falls, and dashes out his brains. {51} Oliver's sensations as he goes to his native town; he is shocked at the sight of Monks; aided by Mr Brownlow, Monks relates to Oliver's father, and describes the will and letter he left; the destruction of the will by Monks's mother; his promise to hunt down Oliver; his bribing to ensnare Oliver, and his own exposure; Mr and Mrs Bumble are summoned; Mrs Bumble denies all knowledge of Monks and the locket, but two old pauper-women, who overheard Old Sally's confession, refresh her memory; Mr Bumble's opinion of the law, which supposes that the wife acts under her husband's direction; Rose's parentage made known; Harry, having reduced his circumstances to match hers, and become a clergyman, wins her hand. {52} Fagin on trial; his sentence; his last days and nights; Mr Brownlow and Oliver visit him; he tells Oliver where he put the papers given him by Monks. {53} Last look at the principal surviving characters.

4

Full Report of the First (and Second) Meeting of the Mudfog Association for the Advancement of Everything

These reports appeared in *Bentley's Miscellany* in 1837 and 1838, while Dickens was the editor of that periodical. They were designed to satirise the proceedings of the British Association for the Advancement of Science, which had then been recently established. The first meeting is 'holden in the town of Mudfog'; some of the sections sitting at The Original Pig, and others at The Pig and Tinder-box: the second meeting is at Oldcastle; and the various sections obtain accommodation at the two rival inns – The Black Boy and Stomachache, and The Bootjack and Countenance.

CHARACTERS

BELL, Mr Knight – (MRCS) A member of the association, who exhibits a wax preparation of the interior of a man who, in early life, had swallowed a door-key. At a *post mortem* examination, it is found that an exact model of the key is distinctly impressed on the coating of the stomach. This coating a dissipated medical student steals, and hastens with it to a locksmith of doubtful character, who makes a new key from the novel pattern. With this key the student enters the house of the deceased gentleman, and commits a burglary to a large amount, for which crime he is tried and executed. The deceased gentleman had always been much accustomed to punch, and it is supposed that the original key must have been destroyed by the acid. After the unlucky accident, he was troubled with nightmare, under the influence of which he always imagined himself a wine-cellar door.

BLANK, Mr – A member who exhibits a model of a fashionable annual, composed of copperplates, gold leaf, and silk boards, and worked entirely by milk and water.

BLUBB, Mr – A member who lectures learnedly upon a cranium which proves to be a carved coconut-shell.

BLUNDERUM, Mr – Contributor of a paper, 'On the Last Moments of the Learned Pig'.

BROWN, Mr – (of Edenburg) A member.

BUFFER, Doctor – Another member.

CARTER, Mr – President of Section D (Mechanical Science), at the first meeting of the association.

COPPERNOSE, Mr – Author of a proposition of great magnitude and interest, submitted, at the first meeting of the association, to Section B (Display of Models and Mechanical Science), illustrated by a vast number of models, and explained in a treatise entitled 'Practical Suggestions on the Necessity of Providing some Harmless and Wholesome Relaxation for the young Noblemen of England'.

CRINKLES, Mr – Inventor and exhibitor of a beautiful pocket-picking machine.

DOZE, Professor – Vice-president of Section A (Zoology and Botany), at the first meeting of the association.

DRAWLEY, Mr – Vice-president of Section A at the second meeting.

DULL, Mr – Vice-president of Supplementary Section E (Umbugology and Ditchwateristics).

DUMMY, Mr – Another vice-president of the same section.

FEE, *Doctor W R* – A member of the association.

FLUMMERY, Mr – Another member.

GRIME, Professor – Another member.

GRUB, Mr – President of Supplementary Section E (Umbugology and Ditchwateristics).

GRUMMIDGE, Doctor – A physician who gives an account of his curing a case of monomania by the heroic method of treatment

JOBBA, Mr – Exhibitor of a forcing-machine on a novel plan, for bringing joint-stock railway shares prematurely to a premium.

JOLTERED, Sir William – President of Section A (Zoology and Botany), at the second meeting of the association.

KETCH, Professor John – A member who is called upon to exhibit the skull of the late Mr Greenacre, which he produces with the remark 'that he'd pound it as that 'ere 'spectable section [the section of Umbugology and Ditchwateristics] had never seed a more gamerer cove nor he vos'. The 'professor' finds, however, that he has made a slight mistake, and has displayed a carved coconut instead of the skull that he intended to show.

KUTANKUMAGEN, Doctor – (of Moscow). A physician, who succeeds in curing an alarmingly healthy man by a persevering use of powerful medicine, low diet, and bleeding, which method of treatment so far restores him as to enable him to walk about with the slight assistance of a crutch and a boy.

KWAKLEY, Mr – A member who submits the result of some ingenious statistical inquiries relative to the difference between the value of the qualification of several members of parliament, as published to the world, and its real nature and amount.

LEAVER, Mr – Vice-president of Section B (Display of Models and Mechanical Science) at the Oldcastle meeting.

LEDBRAIN, Mr X – Vice-president of Section C (Statistics) at the Mudfog meeting. He reads a very ingenious paper showing that the total number of legs belonging to one great town in Yorkshire is, in round numbers, forty thousand; while the total number of chair and stool legs is only thirty thousand. Allowing the very favourable average of three legs to a seat, he deduces the conclusion that ten thousand individuals (or one-half the whole population) are either destitute of any seats at all, or pass the whole of their leisure time in sitting upon boxes.

LONG EARS, The Honourable and Reverend Mr – A member of the association.

MALLET, Mr – President of Section B (Display of Models and Mechanical Science) at the second meeting.

MISTY, Mr X – A member.

MISTY, Mr X X – Author of a communication on the disappearance of dancing-bears from the streets of London, with observations on the exhibition of monkeys as connected with barrel-organs.

MORTAIR, Mr – Vice-president of Section C (Anatomy and Medicine) at the Oldcastle meeting.

MUDDLEBRAINS, Mr – Vice-president of Section A (Zoology and Botany), at the Oldcastle meeting.

MUFF, Professor – A member of the association, remarkable for the urbanity of his manners and the ease with which he adapts himself to the forms and ceremonies of ordinary life. At the first meeting, at Mudfog, he tries some private experiments, in connection with

Professor Nogo, with prussic acid, upon a dog. The animal proves to have been stolen from an unmarried lady in the town, who is rendered nearly distracted by the loss of her pet (named Augustus, in affectionate remembrance of a former lover), and avenges his death by a violent attack on the two scientific gentlemen, in which the expressive features of Professor Muff are much scratched and lacerated, while Professor Nogo, besides sustaining several severe bites, loses some handfuls of hair. Professor Muff subsequently relates to the association an extraordinary and convincing proof of the wonderful efficacy of the system of infinitesimal doses. He had diffused three drops of rum through a bucketful of water, and given the whole to a patient who was a hard drinker. Before the man had drunk a quart, he was in a state of beastly intoxication; and five other men were made dead drunk with the remainder.

MULL, Professor – A member of the association, who criticises some of the ideas advanced by Mr X X Misty in his paper on dancing-bears and barrel-organ monkeys.

NEESHAWTS, Doctor – A medical member.

NOAKES, Mr – Vice-president of Section D (Statistics) at the meeting held at Oldcastle.

NOGO, Professor – Exhibitor of a model of a wonderful safety fire-escape.

PESSELL, Mr – Vice-president of Section C (Anatomy and Medicine), at the meeting at Oldcastle.

PIPKIN, Mr – (MRCS). Author of a paper which seeks to prove the complete belief of Sir William Courtenay (otherwise Thom), recently shot at Canterbury, in homeopathy; and which argues that he might have been restored to life if an infinitesimal dose of lead and gunpowder had been administered to him immediately after he fell.

PROSEE, Mr – A member.

PUMPKINSKULL, Professor – An influential member of the council of the association.

PURBLIND, Mr – A member of the association.

QUEERSPECK, Professor – Exhibitor of a model of a portable railway, neatly mounted in a green case, for the waistcoat pocket. By attaching this instrument to his boots, any bank or public-office clerk could transport himself from his place of residence to his place of business at the easy rate of sixty-five miles an hour. The professor explains that City gentlemen would run in trains, being handcuffed together to prevent confusion or unpleasantness.

RUMMUN, Professor – A member.

SCROO, Mr – Vice-president of Section B (Display of Models and Mechanical Science) at the second meeting of the association.

SLUG, Mr – A celebrated statistician. 'His complexion is a dark purple, and he, has a habit of sighing constantly'. He presents to Section C the result of some investigations he has made regarding the state of infant education and nursery literatures among, the middle classes of London. He also states some curious calculations respecting the dogs'-meat barrows of London, which have led him to the conclusion that, if all skewers delivered daily with the meat could be collected and warehoused they would, in ten years' time, afford a mass of timber more than sufficient for the construction of a first-rate vessel of war, to be called *The Royal Skewer*, and to become, under that name, the terror of all the enemies of Great Britain.

SMITH, Mr – (of London). A member of the association.

SNIVEY, Sir Hookham – A member who combats the opinion of Mr Blubb.

SNORE, Professor – President of Section A (Zoology and Botany) at the meeting of Mudfog.

SNUFFLETOFFLE, Mr O J A – member present at the second meeting of the association.

SOEMUP, Doctor – President of Section C (Anatomy and Medicine) at the second meeting.

SOWSTER – Beadle of Oldcastle; a fat man with an immense double-chin and a very red nose, which he attributes to a habit of early rising.

STYLES, Mr – Vice-president of Section D (Statistics), at the second meeting of the association.

TICKLE, Mr – Exhibitor of a newly-invented kind of spectacles, which enable the wearer to discern in very bright colours objects at a great distance (as the horrors of the West India plantations), and render him wholly blind to those immediately before him (as the abuses connected with the Manchester cotton-mills).

TIMBERED, Mr – Vice-president of Section C (Statistics) at the meeting held at Mudfog.

TOORELL, Doctor – President of Section B (Anatomy and Medicine) at the same meeting.

TRUCK, Mr – One of the vice-presidents of Section D (Mechanical Science) at the same meeting.

WAGHORN, Mr – Another of the vice-presidents of the same section, at the same meeting.

WHEEZY, Professor – One of the vice presidents of Section A (Zoology and Botany) at the same meeting.

WIGSBY, Mr – Exhibitor of a cauliflower somewhat larger than a chaise umbrella, raised by the simple application of highly-carbonated soda-water as manure. He explains that, by scooping out the head (which would afford a new and delicious species of nourishment for the poor) a parachute could at once be obtained; the stalk, of course, being kept downwards.

WOODENSCONCE, Mr – President of Section C (Statistics) at the meeting held at Mudfog.

5

The Life and Adventures of Nicholas Nickleby

This story was begun a few months after the completion of the *Pickwick Papers* (September 1837); *Oliver Twist*, which followed that work, having been begun in February 1837, and carried on simultaneously with it for several months. *Nicholas Nickleby* was issued in monthly shilling numbers, and was illustrated by 'Phiz' (Hablot K Browne). On its completion in 1839, it was brought out in volume form, with a prefixed portrait of Dickens, engraved by Finden from a painting by Maclise. It was dedicated to W G Macready (1793–1873), the actor and theatre manager.

The main object of the work was to expose 'the monstrous neglect of education in England, and the disregard of it by the State, as a means of forming good or bad citizens, and miserable or happy men' by showing up, as a notable example, the cheap Yorkshire schools which were in existence at that time. The author's purpose was answered. In the Preface to a later edition of *Nicholas Nickleby*, he was able to speak of the race of Yorkshire schoolmasters 'in the past tense' and to say: 'Though it has not yet disappeared, it is dwindling daily'.

CHARACTERS

ADAMS, Captain – One of the seconds in the duel between Sir Mulberry Hawk and Lord Frederick Verisopht. {1}

AFRICAN KNIFE-SWALLOWER, The – A member of Mr Crummles's theatrical company. {48}

ALICE – See **YORK, The Five Sisters of**

ALPHONSE – Mrs Wititterly's page; so diminutive 'that his body would not hold, in ordinary array, the number of small buttons which are indispensable to a page's costume; and they were consequently obliged to be stuck on four abreast'. {21, 28, 32}

BELLING, Master – One of Mr Squeers's pupils at Dotheboys Hall. {4}

BELVAWNEY, Miss – A lady in Mr Vincent Crummles' theatrical company. {23–25, 29}

BLOCKSON, Mrs – A charwoman employed by Miss Knag. {18}

BOBSTER, Mr – A ferocious old fellow into whose house Nicholas Nickleby is introduced one evening by Newman Noggs, whom he has commissioned to find out where Madeline Bray lives, and who makes the ludicrous mistake of discovering the wrong person. {40}

BOBSTER, Miss – His daughter; mistaken by Newman Noggs for Miss Madeline Bray, and persuaded by him to see Nicholas, and to hear him speak for himself. {11}

BOLDER – A pupil at Mr Squeers's school. {8}

BONNEY Mr – A friend of Ralph Nickleby's, and the prime organiser of the 'United Metropolitan Improved Hot Muffin and Crumpet Baking and Punctual Delivery Company'. {2}

BORUM, Mr – A gentleman at whose house Nicholas Nickleby and Miss Snevellicci call (accompanied by Miss Ninetta Crummles, the 'Infant Phenomenon') to induce him to put his name to Miss Snevellicci's 'bespeak'. {24}

BORUM, Mrs – His wife; mother of six interesting children. {24}

BORUM, Augustus – Their son; a young gentleman who pinches the Infant Phenomenon behind to ascertain whether she is real. {24}

BORUM, Charlotte – One of their daughters, who filches the Infant Phenomenon's parasol, and carries it off. {24}

BORUM, Emma – Another daughter. {24}

BRAVASSA, Miss – One of the members of Mr Crummles's theatrical company. {23–25, 29}

BRAY, Madeline – Daughter of a gentleman who married a very particular friend of the Cheeryble Brothers. Her mother dies while she is a mere child and her selfish and profligate father is later reduced, between sickness and poverty, to the verge of death. Although she braves privation, degradation, and affliction for the sake of supporting him, he is on the point of forcing her to marry a rich old miser named Gride, when death suddenly carries off the unnatural parent, and Madeline is removed to Mrs Nickleby's house. She afterwards marries Nicholas. {16, 40, 46, 47, 51, 52, 54–56, 63, 65}

BRAY, Mr Walter – Father to Madeline, a broken-down, irritable, and selfish debauchee. {46, 47, 52–54}

BROOKER – A felon and an outcast; a former clerk to Nickleby. Being ill-treated by his master, and hating him, he takes advantage of favouring circumstances to think his only son has died and been buried, during his temporary absence from home – though, in reality, the boy has been left at a Yorkshire school, with the design of one day making the secret a means of getting money from the father. But the plan fails and Mr Nickleby, in the hot pursuit of bad ends, persecutes and hunts down his own child to death. {44, 60, 65}

BROWDIE, John – A stout, kind-hearted Yorkshireman. He is betrothed to Miss Matilda Price, whom he afterwards marries. At his first meeting with Nicholas Nickleby he becomes furiously jealous of him. Finding however that Nicholas has no intention of making trouble between him and his intended, he conceives a more favourable opinion of the young gentleman, and they become good friends. {4, 8, 39, 42, 43, 45, 64}

BULPH, Mr – A pilot, who keeps a lodging-house at which Mr Crummles lives. {23}

CHEERYBLE BROTHERS, The (Charles and Edwin) – Twin brothers, partners in business, and the benefactors and employers of Nicholas Nickleby. Dickens says of them in his Preface that they are 'drawn from life', and that 'their liberal charity, their singleness of heart, their noble nature, and their unbounded benevolence, are no creations of the author's brain, but are prompting every day (and oftenest by stealth) some munificent and generous deed in that town of which they are the pride and honour'. Dickens, however, never saw these gentlemen, or interchanged any communication with them during his life. Having been encouraged to tell his story to one of the brothers, whom he has accidentally met in the street, Nicholas is hurried into an omnibus and taken straight to the warehouse, where he is introduced to the other brother and, after some inquiries and private conference, is taken into their employment. {35, 37, 40, 43, 46, 49, 55, 59, 60, 61, 63, 65}

CHEERYBLE, Frank – Nephew of the Cheeryble Brothers. He finally marries Kate Nickleby. {43, 49, 55, 57, 59, 61, 63, 65}

CHOWSER, Colonel – One of the guests at a dinner-party given by Ralph Nickleby. {19, 50}

COBBEY – A pupil at Squeers's school. {8}

CROWL, Mr – A fellow-lodger of Newman Noggs. {14, 15, 32}

CRUMMLES, Mr Vincent – The manager of an itinerant theatrical company. Meeting Nicholas Nickleby and Smike at an inn not far from Portsmouth, he advises them to adopt the stage for a profession, and offers to bring them out. 'There's genteel comedy,' he tells Nicholas, 'in your walk and manner, juvenile tragedy in your eye, and touch-and-go farce in your laugh.' The result is that Nicholas, after a little deliberation, declares it a bargain, and he and Smike become a part of Mr Crummles's company. Mr Crummles treats them very kindly, and when he finally separates from them – on the occasion of his departure with his family for America – he puts out his hand, with 'not a jot of his theatrical manner' remaining, and says with great warmth: 'We were a very happy little company. You and I never had a word. I shall be very glad tomorrow morning to think that I saw you again; but now I almost wish you hadn't come.' {23– 25, 29, 30, 48)

CRUMMLES, Mrs – Wife of Mr Vincent Crummles. {23–25, 29, 30, 48)

CRUMMLES, Master – One of their sons, and a member of the theatrical company. {22, 23, 30, 48}

CRUMMLES, Master Percy – Another son. {22, 23, 30, 48}

CRUMMLES, Miss Ninetta – Their daughter, known and advertised as the 'Infant Phenomenon'. {23–25, 29, 48}

CURDLE, Mr – A Portsmouth gentleman, whom Miss Snevelicci calls upon to request that he would put his name to her 'bespeak', he being a great critic, and having quite the London taste in matters relating to literature and the drama. He is the author of a pamphlet of sixty-four pages, post octavo, on the character of the nurse's deceased husband in *Romeo and Juliet*. {24}

CURDLE, Mrs – His wife. {24}

CUTLER, Mr and Mrs – Friends of the Kenwigses. {14}

DAVID – Butler to the Cheeryble Brothers. {37, 63}

DIGBY – Smike's theatrical name; *See* **Smike**

FOLAIR, Mr – A dancer and pantomimic actor belonging to Mr Crummles's company. {23–25, 29, 30}

GAZINGI, Miss – An actress in the theatrical company of Mr Vincent Crummles. {23}

GENTLEMAN, The, In Small-Clothes – *See* **Nickleby, Mrs**

GEORGE – A friend of the Kenwigses. He is a young man who had known Mr Kenwigs when he was a bachelor, and is much esteemed by the ladies as bearing the reputation of a rake. {14}

GRAYMARSH – A pupil at Squeers's school. {8}

GREEN, Miss – A friend of the Kenwigses. {14}

GREGSBURY, Mr – A Member of Parliament to whom Nicholas Nickleby applies for a situation as private secretary. The requirements, however, are so many, and so difficult to meet, that the situation is declined. {16}

GRIDE, Arthur – An old miser. {47, 51, 53, 54, 56, 59, 65}

GROGZWIG, Baron of – *See* **KOËLDWETHOUT**, *Baron Von*

GRUDDEN, Mrs – An actress attached to Mr Crummles's theatrical company, and an assistant to Mrs Crummles in her domestic affairs. {23, 24, 29, 30, 49}

HANNAH – Servant to Miss La Creevy. {3}

HAWK, Sir Mulberry – A fashionable gambler, *roué*, and knave, remarkable for his tact in ruining young gentlemen of fortune. He insults Kate Nickleby, and is punished by her brother. He afterwards fights a duel with his pupil and dupe, Lord Frederick Verisopht, in which the latter is killed. {19, 26–28, 32, 38, 50, 65}

INFANT PHENOMENON – See **CRUMMLES**, Miss Ninetta

JOHNSON, Mr – The stage name given by Mr Crummles to Nicholas Nickleby

KENWIGS, Mr – A turner in ivory, and a lodger in the same house with Newman Noggs; 'looked upon as a person of some consideration on the premises, inasmuch as he occupied the whole of the first floor, comprising a suite of two rooms'. {14–16, 36, 53}

KENWIGS, Mrs – His wife; quite a lady in her manners, and of a very genteel family, having an uncle [Mr Lillyvick] who collected a water-rate; besides which distinction, the two eldest of her little girls went twice a week to a dancing-school in the neighbourhood, and had flaxen hair tied with blue ribbons hanging in luxuriant pigtails down their backs, and wore little white trousers with frills round the ankles, for all of which reasons – and many more, equally valid but too numerous to mention – she was considered a very desirable person to know'. {14–16, 37, 52}

KENWIGS, Morleena – Her eldest daughter, 'regarding whose uncommon christian-name it may be stated, that it was invented and composed by Mrs Kenwigs previous to her first lying-in, for the special distinction of her eldest child, in case it should prove a daughter'. {14–16, 36, 52}

KNAG, Miss – Forewoman in Madame Mantalini's millinery establishment, and her successor in the business. {17, 18, 20, 21, 49}

KNAG, Mr Mortimer – Her brother; a young man whom unrequited affection has made miserable. {18}

KOLËDWETHOUT, Baron Von – Hero of one of the tales told at a roadside inn when Nicholas Nickleby and Squeers, with other passengers, were detained there by an accident to the stage-coach in which they were travelling. The baron is described as dwelling 'once upon a time' with numerous retainers, in an old castle at Grogzwig in Germany. He is a young, jolly, roistering blade, and a perfect Nimrod of a hunter. Becoming tired of his monotonous bachelor-life, he marries a daughter of the Baron von Swillenhausen, by whom he is soon well snubbed and effectually subdued. As the baroness makes it a point that the family pedigree shall receive an addition yearly, and as the Grogzwig coffers are not as inexhaustible as her relatives suppose them to be, Koëldwethout at last loses heart, and resolves to make away with himself. But, before doing so, he smokes one last pipe, and tosses off one last measure of wine, the effect of which is to conjure up an apparition – the 'Genius of Suicide and Despair' – with which he has a conference that ends in his deciding to put a good face on the whole matter, and try the world a little longer. This he does; and dies, many years after, a happy man, if not a rich one. {6}

KOËLDWETHOUT, Baroness Von – His wife. {6}

LA CREEVY, Miss – A good-hearted elderly miniature-painter, who becomes a fast friend of the Nicklebys, and finally marries Tim Linkinwater, the old clerk of the Cheeryble Brothers. {3, 5, 10, 20, 31, 33, 35, 38, 49, 61, 63, 65}

LANE, Miss – Governess in Mr Borum's family. {24}

LEDROOK, Miss – A member of Mr Crummles's dramatic company. {23, 25, 30}

LENVILLE, Thomas – A tragic actor in Mr Crummles's theatre. {23, 24, 29}

LENVILLE, Mrs – His wife; a member of the same profession. {23, 29}

LILLYVICK, Mr – A collector of water-rates; uncle to Mrs Kenwigs, at one of whose anniversary wedding-parties he meets Miss Henrietta Petowker, an actress, and is smitten with her charms. He finally follows her to Portsmouth – where she has engaged to appear in Mr Crummles's theatre – and marries her, much to the disgust of the Kenwigses, who have considered themselves his heirs. But Miss Petowker soon proves to be false, and elopes, leaving the collector disconsolate. He returns to London, where he meets Newman Noggs, and is prevailed upon to go to the house of his relative, where a ludicrously affecting scene ensues. A boy has been born to the Kenwigses during his absence. Mr Lillyvick informs them that he never shall expect them to receive his wife, as she has deserted him. {14–16, 25, 30, 36, 48}

LINKINWATER, Miss – Sister to Tim Linkinwater. {37, 63}

LINKINWATER, Tim – Chief clerk of the Cheeryble Brothers. {35, 37, 40, 43, 49, 55, 59–61, 63, 65}

LUMBEY, Mr – A doctor who attends on Mrs Kenwigs in her last confinement. {35}

MANTALINI, Madame – A fashionable milliner and dressmaker. {10, 17, 18, 21, 34, 44}

MANTALINI, Mr Alfred – Her husband. When Madame refuses to supply his demands, he at first resorts to flattery and honeyed words; then declares that, being a burden, he will put an end to his existence, which generally has the effect of softening her heart, and bringing her to terms. She is at last, however, driven into bankruptcy by his reckless extravagance and, the suicide dodge having been tried once too often, insists on a separation, and declares her firm determination to have nothing more to do with such a man. The elegant and dashing fop's butterfly life is soon ended, and he goes 'to the demnition bow-wows'. He gets into prison, and is taken out by a vixenish washerwoman, who is at first captivated by his handsome person and graceful manners but, becoming disenchanted, keeps him constantly turning a mangle in the cellar in which she lives, 'like a demd old horse in a demnition mill' – making his life, as he says, 'one demd horrid grind'. {10, 17, 22, 34, 44, 64}

MOBBS – A pupil at Squeers's school. {8}

NICKLEBY, Mr Godfrey – Father of Ralph and the elder Nicholas, to the former of whom he left three thousand pounds in cash, and to the latter 'One thousand and the farm, which was as small a landed estate as one would desire to see'. {1}

NICKLEBY, Nicholas the elder – Son of Mr Godfrey Nickleby, brother of Ralph, and father of Nicholas and Kate. By his wife's advice he took to speculating with what little capital he had and, losing it all, lost heart too, took to his bed, and died. {1} *See* **Nickleby, Ralph**.

NICKLEBY, Nicholas – the younger. The character from whom the story takes its name; a young man who finds himself, at the age of nineteen, reduced to poverty by the unfortunate speculations and death of his father but possessed, notwithstanding, of a good education, and with abounding energy, honesty, and industry. His mother being determined to make an appeal for assistance to her deceased husband's brother, Mr Ralph Nickleby, he accompanies her, with his sister, to London. On their first interview their relative receives them very roughly, and takes a dislike to his nephew, amounting to positive hatred; but he procures him a situation as assistant tutor at Dotheboys Hall – a school kept by Mr Wackford Squeers, in Yorkshire. Nicholas proceeds thither to assume his new duties but such is the meanness, rapacity, and brutality of Mr Squeers, that he soon forcibly interferes on behalf of the 'pupils', gives the master a sound drubbing, and then turns his back upon the place, taking with him a poor, half-starved, and shamefully-abused lad named Smike. He returns to London only to find that the story of his adventure, highly magnified and distorted, has preceded him. Learning that his sister will lose a situation she has obtained if he remains at home, he quits London again and goes to Portsmouth, where he joins a theatrical company, and becomes an actor. He is, however, suddenly summoned back to London to protect his sister from the insults and persecutions of two aristocratic *roués*, one of whom he chastises severely under circumstances of great provocation. He then takes his mother and sister under his own protection, and soon after makes the acquaintance of two benevolent merchants – the Cheeryble Brothers – gains their respect and confidence; is, after a while, admitted into the firm; and finally marries a friend and *protégée* of his benefactors. {3–9, 12, 13, 15, 16, 20, 22–25, 29, 32, 33, 35, 37, 40, 42, 43, 45, 46, 48, 49, 51–55, 58, 61, 63–65}

NICKLEBY, Ralph – A miser and usurer; uncle to the younger, and brother to the elder Nicholas Nickleby. On the death of his father, he is placed in a mercantile house in London; applies himself passionately to his old pursuit of money-getting; soon has a spacious house of his own in Golden Square; and enjoys the reputation of being immensely rich. When his brother's widow presents herself in London with her two children, seeking his assistance, he gives her to understand that he is not to be looked to 'as the support of a great hearty woman and a grown boy and girl'. He makes them work, therefore, for their bread and, taking an intense dislike to his nephew, tries in every way to humble and ruin him; but his machinations are all defeated, his illegal operations detected, his evil deeds discovered; and he finally hangs himself in a fit of mingled frenzy, hatred, and despair. {1–4, 10, 19, 20, 28, 31, 33, 35, 44, 45, 47, 51, 54, 56, 59, 60, 62}

NICKLEBY, Kate – Sister of Nicholas; she marries Frank Cheeryble. {3, 5, 10, 11, 17–21, 27, 28, 33, 35, 38, 41, 43, 45, 51, 55, 61, 63–65}

NICKLEBY, Mrs – Widow of the elder, and mother of the younger Nicholas Nickleby; a well-meaning woman, but weak withal; very fond and proud of her children; very loquacious; very desirous of being considered genteel; and remarkable for the inaccuracy of her memory, the irrelevancy of her remarks, and the general discursiveness and inconsequence of her conversation. When she leaves her quarters in London, and goes with Nicholas to live at Bow, her attention is attracted by the singular deportment of an elderly gentleman who lives in the next house. He is so plainly struck with Mrs Nickleby's appearance, and becomes so very demonstrative that, although she feels flattered by his homage, she determines, nevertheless, to acquaint her son with the facts. Mrs Nickleby is finally convinced that her admirer is insane, which nobody else is slow to perceive; but she will not admit it until the old gentleman has transferred his admiration to Miss La Creevy; though she persists in thinking that her rejection of his addresses is the unhappy cause of his madness. {3, 5, 10, 11, 18–20, 21, 26–28, 33, 35, 38, 41, 43, 45, 55, 61, 63, 65}

NOGGS, Newman – Mr Ralph Nickleby's clerk and drudge. This man was once a gentleman but, being of an open and unsuspicious nature, he falls into the hands of Ralph Nickleby and other knaves, who ruin him. Reduced to poverty, he enters Nickleby's service as clerk and drudge, both because he is proud and there are no other drudges there to see his degradation, and because he is resolved to find Nickleby out, and hunt him down. He befriends and assists Nicholas, aids in unravelling his master's wicked plots, and at last has the satisfaction of telling him what he has done, 'face to face, man to man, and like a man'. {2–6, 11, 14–16, 22, 28, 31, 33, 34, 40, 44, 47, 51, 52, 57, 59, 63, 65)

PETOWKER, Miss Henrietta – An actress who marries Mr Lillyvick, and then elopes with a 'half-pay captain'. {14, 15, 25, 30, 36, 48}

PHOEBE, *or* **PHIB** – Miss Squeers's maid. {12}

Newman Noggs leaves the ladies in the empty house –
Hablot K Brown *alias* Phiz

PLUCK, Mr – A creature of Sir Mulberry Hawk's. {19, 27, 28, 38, 50}

PRICE, Matilda – A friend of Miss Fanny Squeers, engaged to John Browdie, whom she afterwards marries. {9, 12, 39, 42, 43, 45, 64}

PUGSTYLES, Mr – One of Mr Gregsbury's constituents, and the spokesman of a deputation which waits on that gentleman to request him to resign his seat in parliament. {16}

PUPKER, Sir Matthew – A member of parliament, and chairman of a meeting called to organise 'The United Metropolitan Improved Hot Muffin and Crumpet Baking and Punctual Delivery Company'. {2}

PYKE, Mr – Toad-eater in ordinary to Sir Mulberry Hawk. {19, 27, 28, 38, 50}

SCALEY, Mr – A sheriff's officer. {21}

SIMMONDS, Miss – A workwoman of Madame Mantalini. {17}

SLIDERSKEW, Peg – Arthur Gride's housekeeper; a short, thin, weazen, blear-eyed old woman, palsy-stricken, hideously ugly, and very deaf. {51, 53, 54, 57, 65}

SMIKE – An inmate of Squeers's house. Left with Mr Squeers at an early age, and no one appearing, after the first year, to claim him, or to pay for his board and tuition, he is made use of as a drudge for the whole family. Starved and beaten, he becomes broken-spirited and nearly half-witted. When Nicholas Nickleby arrives at Dotheboys Hall as Squeers's assistant, his heart is filled with pity for the poor lad, and he treats him with great gentleness and kindness; when Squeers undertakes to flog the boy within an inch of his life for attempting to run away, Nicholas interferes, compels the ruffian to desist, and gives him as severe a beating as Smike himself was to have had. The two then leave the school and the village together and, after various wanderings, fall in with Mr Crummles, who is much struck with Smike's haggard countenance, and secures him for his theatrical company as 'an actor for the starved business', bringing him out as the apothecary in *Romeo and Juliet*, under the stage-name of Digby. Smike is subsequently captured by Squeers, who meets him in London, and takes him to Snawley's house; but he is helped to escape by John Browdie, and succeeds in finding his way back to Nicholas, who refuses to give him up. Introduced to Mrs Nickleby and Kate and Miss La Creevy, and surrounded by all the comforts and pleasures of a home, Smike gradually becomes accustomed to the new life upon which he has

Affectionate behaviour of Messrs Pyke and Pluck –
Hablot K Browne *alias* Phiz

entered, and recovers much of his natural intelligence; but it is not long before he begins to droop and, though he rallies once or twice, grows weaker and weaker till he dies. It is afterwards ascertained that he was the son of Ralph Nickleby. {7, 8, 12, 13, 15, 20, 22, 23, 25, 29, 30, 32, 35, 37–40, 45, 49, 55, 58}

SNAWLEY, Mr – A sanctimonious, hypocritical rascal, who places his two little step sons in the care of Squeers at Dotheboys Hall, with the tacit understanding that they are to have no vacations, and are to 'rough it a little'. Acting as the tool of Ralph Nickleby, he afterwards claims Smike, his son, for the purpose of separating him from Nicholas and restoring him to the custody of Squeers; but his villainy is discovered and, to secure his own safety, he divulges the whole scheme, naming Ralph Nickleby as his employer, and implicating Squeers as a confederate. {3, 38, 45, 59}

SNAWLEY, Mrs – His wife. {38, 59}

SNEVELLICCI, Miss – A member of Mr Crummles's dramatic company. {23–25, 29, 30, 48}

SNEVELLICCI, Mr – Her father; an actor belonging, to the same company. {30}

SNEVEILLICCI, Mrs – Her mother. {30}

SNEWKES, Mr – A friend of the Kenwigses. {14}

SNOBB, The Honourable Mr – A guest at the dinner party given by Ralph Nickleby. {14}

SQUEERS, Wackford – A brutal, rapacious, and ignorant Yorkshire schoolmaster. To this person Nicholas Nickleby engages himself as a scholastic assistant on the faith of an advertisement in the London papers. {4–9, 13, 34, 38, 39, 42, 45, 56, 57, 59, 60, 65}

SQUEERS, Mrs – Wife of Mr Wackford Squeers. {7, 8, 9, 13, 64}

SQUEERS, Miss Fanny – Daughter of Mr and Mrs Wackford Squeers; a young lady in her three-and-twentieth year, resembling her mother in the harshness of her voice and the shrewishness of her disposition, and her father in the remarkable expression of her right eye, something akin to having none at all. {9, 12, 13, 15, 39, 41, 44}

SQUEERS, Master Wackford Junior – Son of Mr and Mrs Wackford Squeers. {8, 9, 13, 29, 34, 38, 42, 64}

SWILLENHAUSEN, Baron Von – Neighbour and father-in-law to the Baron of Grogzwig. {6}

SWILLENHAUSEN, Baroness Von – His wife. {6}

TIMBERRY, Mr Snittle – An actor belonging to Mr Crummles's theatre. {21}

TIX, Mr Tom – A broker who makes an inventory of the stock in Madame Mantalini's millinery establishment on the occasion of her sudden failure. {48}

TOM – Clerk at the General Agency Office. {16, 43}

TOMKINS – One of Squeers's pupils. {13}

TRIMMERS, Mr – A friend of the Cheeryble Brothers. {35}

VERISOPHT, Lord Frederick – A silly young noble man, the tool of Sir Mulberry Hawk. He becomes enamoured of Kate Nickleby, and has an angry altercation concerning her with Sir Mulberry. The quarrel leads to a duel, in which Lord Frederick is killed. {19, 26–28, 38, 50}

WESTWOOD, Mr —One of the seconds in the duel between Sir Mulberry Hawk and Lord Verisopht. {50}

WILLIAM – A waiter at the Saracen's Head Inn. {5}

WITITTERLY, Mrs Julia – A lady of the middle class, who apes the airs and style of the aristocracy, and with whom Kate Nickleby lives for a while as companion. {21, 27, 28}

WITITTERLY, Mr Henry – Husband to Mrs Wititterly. Being informed that Kate has applied for a situation as companion to his wife, he discusses the matter for some time with Mrs Wititterly in whispers. {21, 27, 28, 33}

YORK, The Five Sisters of – The title of a story told by a grey-haired gentleman at a roadside inn between Grantham and Newark, for the amusement of his fellow-passengers, when their stage-coach breaks down. The five sisters are represented as living in York in the early part of the sixteenth century, in an old house belonging to the black monks of St Benedict. While engaged in embroidering a complicated and intricate pattern, they are visited by one of the monks, who urges them to take the veil but, under the influence of the youngest sister (named Alice), they refuse to do so, believing that peace and virtue can be found beyond as well as within a convent's walls. Years pass by, bringing change and separation and sorrow; but at last the four elder sisters meet again in the old home; and again the same black monk urges them by all the sad memories of the past to seek consolation and peace within the sheltering arms of the Church. Remembering how the young heart of their lost sister had sickened at the thought of cloistered walls, they again refuse. As a work of piety, however, as well as a memorial of affection, they cause to be executed in five compartments of stained glass, fitted into a large window in York Minster (which is still shown there under the name of the Five Sisters), a faithful copy of their old embroidery-work, through which the sun may shine brightly on a flat stone in the nave, which bears the name of Alice. {6}

PRINCIPAL INCIDENTS

{1} Sketch of the history of the Nickleby family previous to the time of our story, and death of Mr Nickleby, father of its hero. {2} Description of Mr Ralph Nickleby, and of his business; formation of the Crumpet Company. {3} Ralph Nickleby receives the news of his brother's death, and the arrival of the widow and her children in London; he finds them in lodgings at Miss La Creevy's, and proceeds to provide for them by promising to secure Nicholas a situation as assistant in the academy of Mr Wackford Squeers in Yorkshire. {4} Interview between Mr Squeers and Mr Snawley; Ralph and his nephew call upon Mr Squeers, and Nicholas secures the situation; Nicholas informs Newman Noggs of his uncle's intentions in regard to him. {5} Nicholas bids adieu to Miss La Creevy, and leaves the house without disturbing his mother and sister; how Mr Squeers and his boys breakfasted; Ralph, Mrs Nickleby, and Kate come to see Nicholas off, also Newman Noggs, who secretly gives him a letter. {6} On the journey to Yorkshire the coach is overturned; while waiting for another, one gentleman entertains his fellow-passengers with the story of the Five Sisters of York; and another one relates the story of the Baron of Grogzwig; they leave the stage at Greta Bridge, and Mr Squeers 'stretches his legs', as he has frequently done on the journey. {7} They reach Dotheboys Hall, with which Nicholas is not favourably impressed; he is introduced to Mrs Squeers; notices the sad appearance of Smike, and gets an idea of the internal economy of Squeers's establishment; he reads Newman Noggs's letter. {8} Mrs Squeers improves the boys' appetites by dosing them with brimstone and treacle; Mr Squeers shows his practical mode of teaching, makes a report to the school of his journey to London, and adds a liberal discipline with the cane; Nicholas shows his sympathy for Smike. {9} Mrs Squeers expresses her opinion of Nicholas; Miss Fanny Squeers makes an errand into the schoolroom, in her father's absence, for the purpose of inspecting Nicholas; his appearance being satisfactory, she at once falls in love with him, and hastens to inform her bosom friend, Miss Price, of her attachment and its return; Miss Squeers makes a little party for the purpose of introducing Nicholas to her friends; he excites the jealousy of Mr John Browdie, and Miss Price does the same service for Fanny Squeers. {10} La Creevy paints Kate Nickleby's portrait; discussing the character of Ralph Nickleby, they are interrupted by the appearance of that gentleman; Ralph informs Kate and her mother of the situation he has obtained for her in the establishment of Madame Mantalini; Kate has an interview with Mr and Madame Mantalini. {11} Newman Noggs moves Mrs Nickleby and Kate into the house of which Ralph Nickleby has given them possession. {12} Miss Price informs Miss Squeers that her wedding day is fixed; Nicholas in his solitary walk is met by Miss Squeers and her friend, and a scene follows in which he declares his sentiments for the schoolmaster's daughter; Nicholas has a conversation with Smike. {13} Smike runs away, is pursued in one direction by Squeers, and in another by Mrs Squeers, who overtakes him and brings him back; Mr Squeers is about to flog Smike, when he is stopped by Nicholas, who beats the brute severely, and leaves the house; meeting John Browdie, that worthy individual is greatly delighted to hear of Nicholas's exploit, and assists him on his way; Nicholas is joined by Smike. {14} Newman Noggs attends the party of the Kenwigses on their wedding day, and is called away by the arrival of Nicholas and Smike. {15} Newman reads to Nicholas a copy of Fanny Squeers's letter to Ralph Nickleby; Nicholas rescues the infant Kenwigs from a dangerous position, and makes a favourable impression on the company. {16} Nicholas, visiting a register office in search of employment, is struck with the appearance of a young lady whom he meets there; being referred to Mr Gregsbury, MP, he visits that gentleman just as he is waited upon by a deputation of his constituents; he finds the situation not adapted to his wants, and he accepts, as Mr Johnson, the position of private tutor to the Kenwigs' children; enters upon the duties of that position under the inspection of Mr Lillyvick. {17} Kate Nickleby commences her labours at Madame Mantalini's, and is introduced to Miss Knag. {18} Miss Knag conceives a warm affection for Kate, and makes the acquaintance of Mrs Nickleby; Kate and her mother go home with Miss Knag to her brother's, and learn something of the history of that gentleman; Kate, being preferred by some ladies to Miss Knag, loses the forewoman's good opinion. {19} Ralph Nickleby invites Kate to dine with him; she is astonished to find his house richly furnished; Ralph introduces her to his guests, Lord Frederick Verisopht and Sir Mulberry Hawk; Kate bears their insulting manner as long as she can, and then hurries from the room; Sir Mulberry finds her alone and, pursuing his attentions, is interrupted by Ralph Nickleby; Ralph and Sir Mulberry understand each other. {20} Miss La Creevy has an interview with Miss Knag; Miss La Creevy is astonished at the return of Nicholas, and undertakes to prepare his mother and Kate for his coming; Ralph visits the widow to inform her of her son's misdemeanours, and is confronted by Nicholas himself, who repels his charges; for the sake of his mother and Kate, he leaves them to the care of his uncle, and departs. {21} Madame Mantalini's establishment falls into the hands of the sheriff; Mr Mantalini threatens suicide; and Kate finds herself without a situation; Mrs Nickleby urges Kate to answer an advertisement for a companion, and she applies for and secures a situation in that capacity in the family of Mrs Wititterly. {22} Nicholas and Smike leave London for Portsmouth in search of fortune; Nicholas attempts to revive Smike's recollections of his childhood; they fall in with Mr Vincent Crummles, witness the rehearsal of a stage-combat by the Masters Crummles, and Nicholas embraces the offer of Mr Crummles, and joins the theatrical profession. {23} They proceed to Portsmouth, Mr Crummles giving an account of his wonderful pony by the way, and Nicholas is introduced to the company; Mr Crummles announces a new play, of which Nicholas is to be the author, and shows him how to make use of the French original; Nicholas dines with Mr and Mrs Crummles, and then finds lodgings for himself and Smike. {24} Mr Folair and Mr Lenville give Nicholas some hints of value in his task of composition; Nicholas accompanies Miss Snevellicci in her calls on the occasion of her 'bespeak'; Nicholas appears in his new piece, and meets with decided success. {25} Mr Crummles's company is joined by Miss Henrietta Petowker from London, and Mr Lillyvick follows her; Mr Lillyvick makes known to Nicholas his intentions in regard to Miss Petowker; Mr Lillyvick and Miss Petowker are married, and have their wedding-breakfast; Nicholas instructs Smike in the part of the Apothecary. {26} Lord Frederick Verisopht and Sir Mulberry Hawk determine to find Kate Nickleby, and Lord Frederick learns her address from Ralph; they encounter Mrs Nickleby, and show her particular attention, which sets that good lady castle-building. {27} Messrs Pyke and Pluck call upon Mrs Nickleby as the friends of Sir Mulberry Hawk, and invite her to make one of their party at the play; at the play she finds herself in the next box to Kate, who is in company with the Wititterlys; Sir Mulberry makes a division of the party, so as to secure Kate's society to himself, and becomes more insulting in his attentions. {28} Sir Mulberry and Lord Frederick, backed by Pyke and Pluck, follow up their advantage, and call at the Wititterlys; Kate, harassed beyond endurance, seeks her uncle, and claims his protection, but he declines to interfere. {29} Mr Lenville, jealous of Nicholas's increasing popularity, threatens him with punishment; attempting to execute his threat in the presence of the company, he finds himself disappointed; Nicholas receives warning from Newman Noggs that his presence in London may be necessary for Kate's protection. {30} Mr Crummles arranges three 'last appearances' for Mr Johnson; Nicholas, at Miss Snevellicci's earnest invitation, accompanies that young lady home, when he becomes the hero of the dinner-feast, and Miss Snevellicci gives way to her feelings; the appearance of a London manager in the audience creates an unusual excitement behind the curtain; Nicholas receives another letter from Newman, and hurries his departure for London. {31} Ralph Nickleby detects Newman watching him; Newman consults with Miss La Creevy in regard to Kate and the return of Nicholas. {32} Nicholas returns to London and, not finding Newman or Miss La Creevy, strolls into an hotel where he overhears Sir Mulberry and his party insolently jesting about Kate, and demands satisfaction; receiving only insult in reply, he assaults Sir Mulberry as he is entering his carriage to leave, the horse takes fright, and Sir Mulberry receives serious injury. {33} Newman relates to Nicholas the position of affairs in regard to Kate, and Nicholas loses no time in removing her from Mrs Wititterly's; he also removes his mother and Kate back to the lodgings at Miss La Creevy's, and returns the key of Ralph Nickleby's house to the owner. {34} Madame and Mr Mantalini transact a little business with Ralph Nickleby; Mr Mantalini informs Ralph of the altercation between Nicholas and Sir Mulberry Hawk; Mr Squeers surprises Ralph by calling upon him; they plan to retaliate upon Nicholas through his affection for Smike. {35} Smike is introduced to Mrs Nickleby and Kate; Nicholas tries the register office again for employment, and meets Mr Charles Cheeryble, who takes him to his warehouse, where he meets Mr Ned

Cheeryble and Tim Linkinwater; he enters the employ of Cheeryble Brothers, and removes his mother and Kate to a cottage which his employers let him at Bow. {36} The Kenwigses, rejoicing over an addition to their family, have their joy turned to grief by the news Nicholas brings of the marriage of Mr Lillyvick. {37} Nicholas's labours meet the entire approval of Tim Linkinwater; Cheeryble Brothers give Tim Linkinwater a dinner on his birthday; Mrs Nickleby informs Nicholas of the strange proceedings of their next-door neighbour. {38} Miss La Creevy notices a sorrowful change in Smike; Ralph Nickleby waits upon Sir Mulberry Hawk, and they discuss his injury from the attack of Nicholas; Lord Frederick refuses to be a party to any assault upon Nicholas; Smike is arrested in the street by Mr Squeers, and carried to Snawley's house. {39} John Browdie and his wife, with Miss Squeers, arrive in London, and stop at The Saracen's Head; Mr Squeers reports to them the capture of Smike; accepting the schoolmaster's invitation to tea at Mr Snawley's, John Browdie feigns illness, and helps Smike to escape. {40} Smike finds his way to Newman Noggs, and is restored to Nicholas; Nicholas encounters a young lady in the room of Mr Charles Cheeryble, whom he recognises as the one he met at the register office, and falls in love with her at once; Nicholas employs Newman to follow her servant, and find out who she is; Newman faithfully performs his trust, and appoints a meeting, on keeping which Nicholas finds that his mediator has made a mistake in the lady. {41} Mrs Nickleby and Kate, conversing in the garden, are interrupted by the gentleman next door, who proceeds to declare his passion for Mrs Nickleby, when he is arrested by his keeper. {42} Nicholas takes supper with Mr and Mrs John Browdie at The Saracen's Head, and hears from John the particulars of Smike's escape from Squeers; sudden appearance of Miss Squeers, with her father and brother; her indignation, and her departure with her relatives. {43} Nicholas first meets Mr Frank Cheeryble; Charles Cheeryble and his nephew take tea with the Nicklebys. {44} Ralph Nickleby learns that Sir Mulberry Hawk has left the country; Ralph is accosted by a beggar who claims an old acquaintance with him; he refuses to help him, and threatens him with arrest; Ralph witnesses a falling-out between Mr and Madame Mantalini; returning home, Ralph finds Squeers and Snawley, and goes away with them; Newman Noggs, following, encounters a stranger, in whom he becomes greatly interested. {45} Mr and Mrs John Browdie spend a merry evening at the Nicklebys'; their pleasure is interrupted by the entrance of Ralph Nickleby and Squeers, who claim Smike in the name of his father, who they produce in the person of Snawley; Nicholas refuses to give up Smike; and Squeers gets some rough treatment from John Browdie. {46} Nicholas, relating the circumstances to Mr Charles Cheeryble, finds that Ralph has been before him; Mr Charles relates to Nicholas the history of the young lady whom he has met, and employs him as his confidential messenger in communicating with her, and Nicholas makes his first call upon Miss Bray. {47} Newman Noggs, concealing himself in a closet in his room, becomes witness to an interview between Ralph Nickleby and Arthur Gride, in which the latter details his plans for securing Madeline Bray as his bride, and compounds with Ralph for his assistance; they visit Bray, and urge Gride's suit for his daughter's hand. {48} Nicholas encounters Mr Vincent Crummles, and attends a farewell supper given to that gentleman and his family before they depart for America; Nicholas discusses the morality of a certain class of playwrights, and takes his final leave of the Crummleses. {49} Mrs Nickleby appropriates to herself the attentions of Mr Frank Cheeryble; Frank and Tim Linkinwater drop in at the Nicklebys'; they are astonished at the entrance, down the chimney, of the Gentleman in Small-Clothes; an abrupt change in his manner towards Mrs Nickleby convinces her of his insanity, of which she thinks herself the cause; Nicholas becomes alarmed at Smike's melancholy. {50} Sir Mulberry Hawk threatens revenge on Nicholas, and Lord Frederick remonstrates; a quarrel between them in a gambling-booth at Hampton Races leads to a duel, in which Lord Frederick is killed. {51} Arthur Gride selects his wedding-garments; Newman Noggs bears a letter from his master to Gride, and takes an opportunity to acquaint himself with its contents; Ralph questions Newman about Brooker, but without satisfactory result; Newman informs Nicholas of the plot between Ralph and Gride, by which the latter is to marry Madeline Bray; in the absence of the Cheeryble Brothers, Nicholas determines to take upon himself the responsibility of remonstrating with Miss Bray. {52} Mr Lillyvick returns to the Kenwigses, and relates the story of his wife's elopement. {53} Pursuing his purpose, Nicholas counsels Miss Bray to prevent the approaching marriage; finding she will sacrifice herself for her father's sake, he goes to Gride, and tries threats upon him, but without effect. {54} Arthur Gride and Ralph Nickleby go to

Mr Bray's for the marriage; while waiting for the appearance of Bray and Madeline, they are surprised by the entrance of Nicholas and Kate; sudden death of Mr Bray; Nicholas accuses Ralph and Gride of their evil designs, threatens them with discovery and punishment, and carries Madeline from the house. {55} Mrs Nickleby surprises Nicholas by informing him of her discovery that Frank Cheeryble has fallen in love with Kate; Smike becomes very ill, and Nicholas takes him to Devonshire. {56} Ralph Nickleby and Gride return to the latter's house, and find it closed; forcing an entrance they find that Peg Sliderskew has robbed Gride of his papers, and absconded; Ralph Nickleby sends for Squeers, informs him of the theft of the papers, and engages him to recover them. {57} Squeers, having found Mrs Sliderskew and secured her confidence, proceeds to examine the stolen papers; Frank Cheeryble and Newman Noggs steal in upon them, and prevent the destruction of a will in which Madeline is interested. {58} Smike has his fears excited by the apparition of the man who first carried him to Dotheboys Hall; Smike confesses to Nicholas his love for Kate and dies. {59} Ralph is surprised by the absence of Newman Noggs, and also by the appearance of Mr Charles Cheeryble, to whom he refuses to listen, Ralph goes in search of Squeers, but does not find him, and then to Gride's, who refuses him entrance; he then goes to Cheeryble Brothers, where Newman Noggs confronts him, and tells him how he has watched his actions and overheard his plots; they also relate to Ralph the discoveries they have made in regard to the imposture of Snawley, the occupation of Squeers, his arrest, and the implication of Ralph in these villainies; he spurns their counsel and defies them to do their worst. {60} Ralph visits Squeers at the police-office, learns that the will in favour of Madeline Bray has been lost to him, and that Squeers no longer will aid his schemes; Tim Linkinwater carries the announcement of a fresh discovery to Ralph, and conveys him again to Cheeryble Brothers' counting-room, where they tell him of Smike's death and confront him with Brooker, who proves to him that Smike was his (Ralph's) own son. {61} Nicholas confesses to Kate his love for Madeline, and she informs him that she has declined the hand of Frank Cheeryble; Nicholas also makes known the state of his feelings to Mr Charles Cheeryble; Mr Cheeryble informs Nicholas of the occurrences of the preceding day, and that his uncle has fixed an appointment for a meeting with him. {62} Ralph Nickleby, on leaving the Cheeryble Brothers, goes home filled with remorse; on

keeping his appointment, they find him dead, hanged by his own act.
{63} The Cheeryble Brothers invite the Nicklebys and Miss La
Creevy to a dinner, where they are surprised to find Frank Cheeryble
and Madeline Bray; Brother Charles explains the position of
Madeline's affairs, and approves of her choice of Nicholas, and also
the union of Frank with Kate; Tim Linkinwater and Miss La Creevy
agree to unite their fortunes; Newman Noggs appears in a new
character. {64} Nicholas and Kate discover Mr Mantalini in reduced
circumstances; Nicholas visits John Browdie in Yorkshire; breaking
up of Dotheboys Hall. {65} Conclusion, in which the subsequent
history of the characters is briefly told.

The internal economy of Dotheboys Hall – Hablot K Browne *alias* Phiz

6

Sketches of Young Couples

Published in 1840

THE YOUNG COUPLE

ADAMS, Jane – A housemaid.

ANNE – A housemaid at 'No 6'; friend to Jane Adams.

FIELDING, Miss Emma – A young lady about to be married to a Mr Harvey, who is 'an angel of a gentleman'.

HARVEY, Mr – A young gentleman engaged to Miss Fielding.

JOHN, Mr – A servant in the house of Miss Fielding's father.

THE LOVING COUPLE

LEAVER, Augustus and Augusta – Two married persons, so tender, so affectionate, so given to the interchange of soft endearments, as to be well-nigh intolerable to everybody else.

STARLING, Mrs – A widow-lady enraptured with the affectionate behaviour of Mr and Mrs Leaver, whom she considers a perfect model of wedded felicity.

THE CONTRADICTORY COUPLE

CHARLOTTE and EDWARD – A married pair who seem to find a positive pleasure in contradiction, and agree in nothing else.

CHARLOTTE, Miss – Their daughter.

JAMES, Master – Their son.

THE COUPLE WHO DOTE UPON THEIR CHILDREN

SAUNDERS, Mr – A bachelor-friend of the Whifflers.

WHIFFLER, Mr and Mrs – A married pair, whose thoughts at all times and in all places are bound up in their children, and have no sphere beyond. They relate clever things their offspring say or do, and weary every company with their prolixity and absurdity.

THE COOL COUPLE

CHARLES and LOUISA – A husband and wife, well-bred, easy, and careless, who rarely quarrel, but are unsympathising, and indifferent to each other's comfort and happiness.

THE PLAUSIBLE COUPLE

WIDGER, Mr Bobtail and Mrs Lavinia – People of the world, who adapt themselves to all its ways, all its twistings and turnings; who know when to close their eyes, and when their ears; when to crawl upon their hands and knees; when to stoop; and when to stand upright.

THE NICE LITTLE COUPLE

CHIRRUP, Mr – A warm-hearted little fellow, with the smartness, and something of the brisk, quick manner, of a small bird.

CHIRRUP, Mrs – His wife; a sprightly little woman, with an amazing quantity of goodness and usefulness – a condensation, indeed, of all the domestic virtues.

THE EGOTISTICAL COUPLE

SILVERSTONE, Mr – A clerical gentleman, who magnifies his wife on every possible occasion by launching out into glowing praises of her conduct in the production of eight young children, and the subsequent rearing and fostering of the same.

SILVERSONE, Mrs – His wife; always engaged in praising her husband's worth and excellence.

THE COUPLE WHO CODDLE THEMSELVES

CHOPPER, Mrs – Mother to Mrs Merrywinkle.

MERRYWINKLE, Mr and Mrs – A married pair, who have fallen into excessive habits of self-indulgence, and forget their natural sympathy and close connection with everybody and everything in the world around them; thus depriving themselves of the best and truest enjoyment.

THE OLD COUPLE

ADAMS, Jane – An aged servant, who has been a nurse and story-teller to two generations.

CROFTS – A barber.

7

Master Humphrey's Clock

Dickens started a miscellany under this title in April 1840, which was to be issued in weekly numbers, at three pence each, and which was to consist of short, detached papers, with occasional continuous stories. These were introduced and connected together by means of a fiction, describing an old gentleman named Master Humphrey, and a kind of club, which meets once a week at his house, in a quaint old room in which there is a tall old-fashioned clock, from the case of which the members of the club draw forth piles of dusty papers which they themselves have written, and placed there to be read at their meetings. The work extended to eighty-eight numbers, covering a period of nearly two years. It was brought out in the form of an imperial octavo, was excellently printed on good paper, and was illustrated with engravings (instead of etchings on steel) by George Cattermole, 'Phiz' (H K Browne), George Cruikshank, and Daniel Maclise – the latter artists, however, furnishing but one sketch each.

The public did not take kindly to the machinery of Master Humphrey and his friends and, to revive their flagging interest, Mr Pickwick and the two Wellers were again brought upon the scene, as was also a third Weller – a young Tony – who is Sam's son, and a counterpart in miniature of his grandfather. This device was successful, and the work won a way steadily to general favour. But Dickens considered that the connecting fiction of Master Humphrey interfered too much with the continuity of the principal stories, and gave the whole work too desultory a character. He therefore eventually cancelled the introductory, intercalary, and concluding chapters in which this fiction was contained, though on the completion of the eighty-eight numbers of which the work consisted, it was issued in three volumes – of which the first appeared in 1840, and the last two in 1841.

CHARACTERS

ALICE, Mistress – Heroine of the tale told by Magog, the Guildhall giant, to his companion, Gog; the beautiful and only daughter of a wealthy London bowyer of the sixteenth century. She elopes with a young cavalier, by whom she is conveyed abroad, where shame and remorse overtake her. Her father, dying, leaves all his property and trade to a trusted 'prentice named Hugh Graham, charging him with his latest breath to revenge his child upon the author of her misery, if ever he has the opportunity. Twenty years afterwards, Alice suddenly returns and Master Graham (who was formerly an aspirant for her hand, and who still loves her) gives her lodging in his house – once hers – taking up his own abode in a dwelling near by. Soon after, he encounters the man who wrought her ruin. The two exchange a few high, hot words, and then close in deadly contest. After a brief struggle, the noble falls, pierced through the heart with his own sword by the citizen. A riot ensues, and at last Graham is shot dead on his own doorstep. On carrying him upstairs, an unknown woman is discovered lying lifeless beneath the window.

BELINDA – A distracted damsel, who writes a letter to Master Humphrey about her faithless lover.

BENTON, Miss – Master Humphrey's housekeeper. Mr Weller, senior, in a moment of weakness, falls in love with her, but she prefers Mr Slithers the barber; and the old gentleman, recovering his 'native hue of resolution', conjures his son Samuel to put him in a strait waistcoat until the fit is passed, in the event of his ever becoming amorous again.

DEAF GENTLEMAN, The – An intimate friend of Master Humphrey's, and a cheerful, placid, happy old man. It is his humour to conceal his name, or he has a reason and purpose for doing so. Master Humphrey and the other members of the club respect his secret, therefore; he is known among them only as the Deaf Gentleman.

GOG – One of the Guildhall giants.

GRAHAM, Hugh – A bowyer's 'prentice, in love with his master's daughter.

JINKINSON – The subject of an anecdote related by Sam Weller.

MAGOG – One of the Guildhall giants.

MARKS, Will – The hero of a tale which Mr Pickwick submits to Master Humphrey and his friends as a 'qualification' for admission to their club. Will is a wild, roving young fellow, living at Windsor in the time of James I. He volunteers to keep watch by night at a gibbet near Kingston, for the purpose of identifying some witches who have been holding hideous nocturnal revels there; but he finds, instead of witches, two gentlewomen weeping, and wailing for an executed husband and brother. He suffers himself to be conducted to Putney, where he is introduced to a masked cavalier who induces him to take the body of the dead man by night for burial to St Dunstan's Church in London. This task, though a difficult and dangerous one, he performs and on his return home, finding the whole neighbourhood worked up to a high pitch of mystery and horror over his disappearance, he adds to the excitement by telling them a most extraordinary story of his adventures, describing the witches' dance to the minutest motion of their legs, and performing it in character on the table, with the assistance of a broomstick.

MASTER HUMPHREY – A kind-hearted, deformed old gentleman, living in an ancient house in a venerable suburb of London. He is the founder of a sort of club, which meets in his room one night in every week, at the hour of ten. In this room are six chairs, four of which are filled by Master Humphrey and his friends – Jack Pedburn, Mr Owen Miles, and the 'Deaf Gentleman'. The two empty seats are reserved until they can fill them with two men to their mind; Mr Pickwick eventually becomes the occupant of one of them, while Mr Jack Bamber is proposed as a candidate for the other. In a snug corner stands a quaint old clock in a huge oaken case, curiously and richly carved; and in the bottom of this case the members of the club, from time to time, deposit manuscript tales of their own composition, which are taken out and read at their weekly meetings. Among these are the two well-known stories called *The Old Curiosity Shop* (the secondary title of which, as at first published, was 'Personal Adventures of Master Humphrey' and *Barnaby Rudge*.

MILES, Mr Owen – A wealthy retired merchant of sterling character; a great friend and admirer of Jack Redburn.

PICWICK, Mr Samuel – The hero of *The Pickwick Papers*. Reading Master Humphrey's account of himself, his clock, and his club, he is seized with a strong desire to become a candidate for one of the two vacant chairs in the club, and accordingly furnishes a witch-story of the time of James I, as his qualification, which procures him the honour.

The deaf gentleman then fills and lights his pipe, and we once more take our seats round the table before mentioned, Master Humphrey acting as president – if we can be said to have any president, where all are on the same social footing – and our friend Jack as secretary.

Hablot K Brown *alias* Phiz

PODGERS, John – A character in Mr Pickwick's tale; a stout, drowsy, fat-witted old fellow, held by his neighbours to be a man of strong sound sense; uncle to Will Marks.

REDBURN, Jack – One of Master Humphrey's friends, and his factotum. Mr Miles is his inseparable companion, and regards him with great admiration, believing not only that 'no man ever lived who could do so many things as Jack, but that no man ever lived who could do anything so well'.

SLITHERS, Mr – Mr Pickwick's barber; a very bustling, active little man, with a red nose and a round bright face. He falls in love with Miss Benton, Master Humphrey's house keeper, and finally marries her.

TODDYHIGH, Joe – An old playmate of the Lord Mayor elect of London. The two had been poor boys together at Hull; and when they separated, and went out into the world in different directions to seek their fortunes, they agreed always to remain fast friends. But time works many changes; and so it happens that the Lord Mayor elect receives his old companion very coldly when he suddenly appears in his counting-room, and claims acquaintance, at a late hour on the very night before the grand inauguration. Ashamed and distrustful of his old friend, he gets rid of him as quickly as possible – giving him, however, a ticket to the grand dinner on the morrow. Joe takes it without a word, and instantly departs. The next day he goes to Guildhall, but, knowing nobody there, lounges about, and at last comes into an empty little music-gallery, which commands the whole hall. Sitting down, he soon falls asleep; and when he wakes, as the clock strikes three, he is astonished to find the guests departed, and to see the statues of the great giants Gog and Magog (the guardian genii of the city) endowed with life and motion, and to hear them speak in grave and solemn voices, agreeing to while away the dreary nights with legends of old London and with other tales; Magog making a beginning by relating the first of the 'Giant Chronicles'.

WELLER, Samuel – Mr Pickwick's body-servant; 'the same true, faithful fellow' that he used to be in the days of the Pickwick Club, retaining all his native humour too, and all his old easy confidence, address, and knowledge of the world.

WELLER, Tony – the elder. The old plethoric coachman of *The Pickwick Papers*; father to Sam Weller. When Mr Pickwick, attended by Sam, visits Master Humphrey on club-nights, old Mr Weller accompanies them as part of Mr Pickwick's bodyguard. While the members of Master Humphrey's Clock are holding their meeting in the study upstairs, Miss Benton the housekeeper, and her friend, Mr Slithers the barber, entertain the two Wellers in the kitchen. The old 'whip' presides with great dignity, and observes the strictest rules of parliamentary law; thus, when Sam, in the course of some remarks, refers to a class of gentlemen as 'barbers', and Mr Slithers rises, and suggests that 'hair-dressers' would be more 'soothing' to his feelings, Mr Weller rules that 'hair-dressers' is the only designation proper to be used in the debate, and that all others are out of order. Having taken a decided fancy to Miss Benton, but being afraid that she is a 'widder', Mr

Weller gets Sam to inquire as to the fact. He is told that she is a spinster. Mr Weller insists upon the two words being synonymous, but is finally assured that Miss Benton is not a widow, which gives him great satisfaction.

WELLER, Tony, the younger – A son of Sam Weller; named after his grandfather. He is a very small boy, about two feet six from the ground, having a very round face strongly resembling Mr Weller's, and a stout little body of exactly his build, firmly set upon a couple of very sturdy legs. When Mr Weller is first introduced to Master Humphrey, he immediately goes off, as he always does, into praises of his namesake.

It is again midnight. My fire burns cheerfully; the room is filled with my old friend's sober voice; and I am left to muse upon the story we have just now finished.

8

The Old Curiosity Shop

This story originally appeared in the serial miscellany called *Master Humphrey's Clock*, the first chapter in the fourth number. It is supposed to be narrated by Master Humphrey (who figures as the Single Gentleman, the brother of Little Nell's grandfather) and, as at first published, it bore the subtitle 'Personal Adventures of Master Humphrey'.

The author says of this tale: 'The many friends it won me, and the many hearts it turned to me when they were full of private sorrow, invest it with an interest in my mind which is not a public one, and the rightful place of which appears to be "a more removed ground". I will merely observe, therefore, that in writing the book I had it always in my fancy to surround the lonely figure of the child [Little Nell] with grotesque and wild, but not impossible companions, and to gather about her innocent face and pure intentions associates as strange and uncongenial as the grim objects that are about her bed when her history is first foreshadowed'.

CHARACTERS

BACHELOR, The – A kind old gentleman at a village where Little Nell and her grandfather stay in the course of their wanderings {3, 54, 55, 61, 68, 69, 83}

BARBARA – A housemaid at Mrs Garland's; afterwards the wife of Kit Nubbles {22, 38–40, 58, 69, 73}

BARBARA'S MOTHER – {39, 40, 61, 68, 69, 73}

BRASS, Sally – Sister and partner of Sampson Brass {33–38, 51, 56, 58–60, 63–67, 73}

BRASS, Sampson – A villainous attorney of Bevis Marks, with a cringing manner and a very harsh voice; Quilp's legal adviser. He is a tall, meagre man, with a nose like a wen, a protruding forehead, retreating, eyes, and hair of a deep red {11–13, 33, 35, 37, 38, 49, 51, 56–60, 62–64, 66, 67, 83}

CHEGGS, Mr – A market-gardener; a rival of Mr Swiveller's for the hand of Sophy Wackles, whom he finally marries {8}

CHIGGS, Miss – His sister {8}

CHUCKSTER, Mr – Clerk in the office of Witherden the notary, a member of the Lodge of Glorious Apollos, and a mortal enemy of Kit Nubbles {14, 20, 38, 40, 46, 60, 65, 69, 73}

CLERGYMAN, The – A very kind pastor at the village where Nell and her grandfather stay for a time {52, 73}

CODLIN, Tom – One of the Punch-and-Judy showmen with whom Little Nell and her grandfather travel for a few days {16–19, 27, 73}

DAVID, Old – Assistant to the old sexton in the village where Little Nell dies {54}

EDWARDS, Miss – A pupil at Miss Monflathers's educational establishment {31, 32}

EVANS, Richard – One of Mr Marton's pupils {52}

GARLAND, Mr – A little, fat, placid-faced, and very kind-hearted old gentleman, with whom Kit Nubbles lives after he leaves Little Nell {14, 20, 22, 38–40, 60, 67–70, 72}

GARLAND, Mrs – His wife; a little old lady, plump and placid, like himself {14, 20, 22, 38–40, 67–69, 73}

GARLAND, Mr Abel – Their son, articled to Mr Witherden the notary, whose partner he afterwards becomes {14, 20, 38–41, 60, 65, 67–69, 73}

GEORGE – Driver of Mrs Jarley's caravan; afterwards her husband {26, 28, 47}

GEORGE, Mrs – A neighbour and friend of Mrs Quilp's {4}

GRANDFATHER, Little Nell's – Proprietor of the Old Curiosity Shop. Possessed by an overmastering desire to provide for his granddaughter, he is drawn to the gaming-table, and tries his luck again and again, until at last he becomes – for her sake – a confirmed gambler. Losing heavily and constantly, but confident that fortune will finally favour him, he borrows money from Quilp, a rich dwarf, pledging his little stock as security for the debt. His resources, however, are soon all exhausted, his shop and its contents taken in execution, and he himself is thrown upon the world, a beggar, shattered in intellect, and tottering on the verge of the grave. Little Nell leads him away from London; and they wander together through the country. But the passion for play only slumbers in him, and is ready to awake with the first opportunity that offers. But in the seclusion of a quiet village where they at last find a home, such temptation no longer comes; and his hopes and fears, and all his thoughts, are turned to the gentle object of his love, who soon begins to sink under the effects of her past trials and sufferings. When by dint of such inquiries as the utmost vigilance and sagacity could set on foot he at last discovers the place of the wanderer's retreat, it is only to find Little Nell dead, and her grandfather a mere wreck. Even Kit Nubbles, his old servant, who accompanies the younger brother, has no power to move him. They then take the old man out while Little Nell is removed to the churchyard; but, upon his return, he repairs straight to her chamber {1–3, 4, 6, 7, 15–19, 24–32, 42–46, 52, 54, 55, 71, 72}

GRINDER, Mr – A showman {17}

GROVES, James – Landlord of The Valiant Soldier Inn {29, 73}

HARRIS, Mr – *alias* **Short Trotters**, but commonly called either '**Short**' or '**Trotters**'. One of the showmen with whom Little Nell and her grandfather travel for a few days {16–19, 27, 73}

HARRY – A schoolboy; Mr Marton's favourite pupil {24, 25}

JARLEY, Mrs – Proprietor of 'Jarley's Wax Works'. Little Nell is engaged by this lady to point out the figures to visitors {26–29, 31, 32, 47, 73}

JERRY – Proprietor of a troop of dancing-dogs {17, 19, 37}

JINIWIN, Mrs – The mother of Mrs Quilp, with whom she lives, and with whose husband she wages perpetual war, though she stands in no slight dread of him {4–6, 23, 49, 50, 73} *See* **Quilp**, *Daniel.*

JOWL, Joe – A gambler, who tempts Little Nell's grandfather to rob Mrs Jarley {29, 42, 73}

LIST, Isaac – A gambler and knave {29, 30, 42, 73}

MARCHIONESS, The – A name given to the small servant at Sampson Brass's, by Dick Swiveller, who eventually marries her {34–36, 51, 57, 58, 64–66, 73}

MARTON, Mr – An old schoolmaster who befriends Little Nell and her grandfather {24–26, 45, 46, 52–54, 72, 73}

MONFLATHERS, Miss – Principal of a select boarding school for young ladies {31}

NELL, Little – *See* **Trent**, *Little Nell*

NUBBLES, Christopher or Kit – A shock-headed, shambling, awkward

'Aquiline!' cried Quilp, thrusting in his head – Charles Green

lad, with an uncommonly wide mouth, very red cheeks, a turned-up nose, and a peculiarly comical expression of face. He is very much attached to Little Nell, whose grandfather employs him as an errand-boy. After a while, however, the old man takes it into his head that Kit has told of his gambling habits, and that this is the reason why he cannot succeed in borrowing any more money. He therefore forbids his ever coming into his presence again. After the disappearance of his old master, Kit gets employment in the family of a kind old gentleman named Garland. At length he falls into trouble, being falsely accused of larceny and is arrested, and thrown into prison; but his innocence is soon established, and he is set at liberty. He afterwards marries Barbara, Mrs Garland's servant {1, 3, 6, 10, 11, 13, 14, 20–22, 38–41, 48, 56–61, 63, 64, 68–72}

NUBBLES, Jacob – Brother to Kit {10, 13, 21, 22, 39, 41, 51, 69, 72}

NUBBLES, Mrs – Mother to Kit Nubbles; a poor but industrious widow, very pious, and very constant in her attendance at a dissenting chapel called Little Bethel. When the Single Gentleman at last gains tidings of Little Nell and her grandfather, he desires Mrs Nubbles, as being an acquaintance of Nell's, and a kind and motherly person, to accompany him for the purpose of bringing the wanderers back. There being urgent need of haste in the matter, Kit is despatched for his mother. He does not find her at home, however, and feeling sure that she must, therefore, be at chapel, he takes his way to Little Bethel {10, 13, 21, 22, 39, 41, 47, 48, 61, 63, 69, 72}

OWEN, John – A schoolboy; one of Mr Marton's pupils {52}

QUILP, Daniel – A hideous creature, full of ferocity and cunning. Quilp having absented himself from home for some time, and not having been heard from, it is finally supposed that he is dead; and Mr Sampson Brass, the attorney, is called in to write a descriptive advertisement in hopes of finding the body. Quilp returns, however, just at this moment, and resolves to steal upon his wife unawares. Quilp comes to his end by falling into the Thames, and being drowned on a dark night, in an attempt to escape from some officers who are on the point of arresting him for various crimes. His property falls to his wife, who bears her bereavement with exemplary resignation, and marries again, choosing the exact opposite of the dear departed {3–6, 9, 11–13, 23, 27, 30, 41, 48–51, 60, 62, 64, 67, 73}

QUILP, Mrs Betsey – His wife; 'a pretty little mild-spoken, blue-eyed woman, who having allied herself in wedlock to the dwarf, in one of those strange infatuation of which examples are by no means scarce, performed a sound practical penance for her folly every day of her life' {4–6, 13, 21, 23, 49, 50, 67, 73}

SCOTT, Tom – Quilp's boy. Although she is habitually beaten and abused by Quilp, Tom retains a strange sort of affection and admiration for his master. His favourite amusement is to stand on his head; he also adopts this attitude when he wishes to show his defiance of Mr Quilp's instructions, or to revenge himself upon him. Being cast upon the world by his master's death, he determines to go through it upon his head and hands, and accordingly becomes a professional 'tumbler', adopting the name of an Italian image-lad of his acquaintance, and meeting with extraordinary success {4–6, 11, 13, 27, 49–51, 67, 73}

SEXTON, The Old – An old man at the village where Little Nell and her grandfather find a home. {53–55, 70, 72}

SHORT – *See* **Harris, Mr**

SIMMONS, Mrs Henrietta – A neighbour of Mrs Quilp. {4}

SINGLE GENTLEMAN, The – Brother to Little Nell's grandfather. He proves to be Master Humphrey, the narrator of the story {34–38, 40, 41, 47, 48, 55, 56, 66, 69–73}

SLUM, Mr – A writer of poetical advertisements. {28}

SPHYNX, *Sophronia* – *See* **Marchioness, The**.

SWEET WILLIAM – A silent man, who earns his living by showing tricks upon cards, and who has rather deranged the natural expression of his countenance by putting small leaden lozenges into his eyes and bringing them out at his mouth. {19}

SWIVELLER, Dick – Friend to Fred Trent, and clerk to Sampson Brass. He is first introduced on the occasion of a visit which young Trent makes to his grandfather for the purpose of demanding to see his sister. Mr Swiveller and Fred enter into a sort of conspiracy to marry the former to Little Nell, and thus get possession of the enormous wealth which it is supposed the old man is hoarding up for her. After the disappearance of Little Nell and her grandfather, Dick makes a friend of Quilp, who obtains for him a situation as clerk in the office of Sampson Brass. Here he makes the acquaintance of the Marchioness. After the arrest of Kit Nubbles, in consequence of the false testimony of Sampson Brass, Dick, who has sided with the poor boy, is discharged. He takes his little bundle under his arm, intending to go to Kit's mother, and comfort and assist her. In the end, Kit is released and returned to his friends. Dick comes into an annuity of one hundred and fifty pounds a year, and, being very grateful to the Marchioness yet, his first thought is of her. 'Please God', he says, 'we'll make a scholar of the poor Marchioness yet! And she shall walk in silk attire, and siller have to spare, or may I never rise from this bed again!' {2, 3, 7, 8, 13, 21, 23, 34–38, 48, 50, 56–66, 73}

TRENT, Frederick – Brother to Little Nell. {2, 3, 7, 8, 23, 50, 73}

TRENT, Little Nell – A small and delicate child of angelic purity of character and sweetness of disposition, who lives alone with her grandfather, an old man possessed by a mania for gambling; his object being to make her rich and happy. The account of their wanderings, after the old man loses the last of his property, and is turned into the streets a beggar and an imbecile, forms the thread of the story. Nell and her grandfather fall into the company of many strange people during their wanderings, among whom are Messrs Codlin and Short, a couple of itinerant showmen, who take it into their heads that the old man has stolen the child, and is endeavouring to elude pursuit, and that there will surely be a reward offered for their apprehension; whereupon they resolve to keep them in their company until the right time comes for surrendering them. Little Nell divines the object of these men; and, fearing that her grandfather, in case they should be handed over to the authorities, may be confined in some asylum, she escapes from the showmen, and shortly afterwards falls in with Mrs Jarley, the proprietress of 'Jarley's Wax Work', who engages her to point out the figures to visitors. While walking one evening, near the town where Mrs Jarley is exhibiting her works, Nell and her grandfather are overtaken by a severe storm, and are forced to seek shelter for the night at a roadside inn called The Valiant Soldier. Behind a screen some men are playing at cards and, with the sight of this, all the slumbering passion of the old man is aroused. The old man plays until their little purse is exhausted, and nothing is left with which to pay for their entertainment. In this strait, Nell, after much hesitation, and fearful that her grandfather will observe her, takes from her dress a small gold piece which she has kept concealed there, in anticipation of some great emergency, and pays the reckoning, hiding the change which she receives, before rejoining her grandfather. Shortly afterwards she retires for the night. Shocked beyond measure by the sight, the child returns to her room; but during the night, she steals again to her grandfather's side and finds him asleep. By tears and entreaties, Nell succeeds in leading her grandfather away from the old temptation, which has again beset him, and forms fresh hopes of saving him; but these are soon dissipated. Herself, unseen, she discovers him in company with the same gamblers, and witnesses their cunning endeavours to induce him to rob Mrs Jarley in order to obtain the means of winning back all he had lost – and perhaps of securing still greater gains. They suffer much privation after this,

The giants meet the dwarfs – Hablot K̄ Browne *alias* Phiz

and the old man complains piteously of hunger and fatigue; but the child trudges on, with less and less of hope and strength, indeed, but with an undiminished resolution to lead her sacred charge somewhere – anywhere, indeed – away from guilt and shame. At last they encounter Mr Marton, a poor but kind-hearted schoolmaster, whom they had met once before. He is travelling on foot to a distant village, where he has been appointed clerk and teacher; on learning from Little Nell the full story of her trials and sufferings and wanderings, he asks her and her grandfather to accompany him, promising to use his best endeavours to find them some humble occupation by which they can subsist. Little Nell gladly embraces his offer; and they journey on together. Arrived at the village, their kind friend exerts himself successfully in their behalf, procures them a pleasant home and a light employment in connection with the parish church, which brings them money enough to live on. But the quiet and happy life they begin to lead is destined to be of short duration. Long exposure and suffering have been too much for the child's delicate organisation, and her health fails. Slowly, but surely, the end draws on, and at last she dies. {1–6, 9–12, 15–19, 24–32, 42–46, 52–55, 71, 72}

TROTTERS – *See* **Harris, Mr**

VUFFIN – A showman; proprietor of a giant, and of a little lady without legs or arms. {19}

WACKLES, Miss Jane – Youngest daughter of Mrs Wackles, and instructor in the art of needlework, marking, and samplery, in the 'Ladies' Seminary' presided over by her mother. {8}

WACKLES, Miss Melissa – Teacher of English grammar, composition, geography, and the use of the dumb-bells, in her mother's seminary for young ladies. She is the eldest daughter, and verges on the autumnal, having seen thirty-five summers, or thereabouts. {8}

WACKLES, Miss Sophy – A fresh, good-humoured, buxom girl of twenty; Mrs Wackles's second daughter, and teacher of writing, arithmetic, dancing, and general fascination in the 'Ladies' Seminary'. Mr Swiveller at one time supposes himself to be in love with Miss Sophy. {8}

WACKLES, Mrs – Proprietor of a very small day-school for young ladies at Chelsea; an excellent but rather venomous old lady of threescore, who takes special charge of the corporal punishment, fasting, and other tortures and terrors of the establishment. {8}

WEST, Dame – The grandmother of a favourite pupil of Mr Marton's the schoolmaster. {25}

WHISKER – A pony belonging to Mr Garland, obstinate, independent, and freakish, but 'a very good fellow if you know how to manage him'. {14, 20, 22, 38, 40, 41, 51, 63, 65, 66, 73}

WILLIAM, Sweet – *See* **SWEET WILLIAM**.

WITHERDEN, Mr – A notary; short, chubby, fresh-coloured, brisk and pompous. {14, 20, 38, 40, 41, 61, 63, 65, 66, 73}

PRINCIPAL INCIDENTS

{1} Little Nell enquires the way of Master Humphrey; he goes home with her to the Old Curiosity Shop, and meets her grandfather; return of Kit from his errand; Master Humphrey is surprised to hear that the old man is going out, leaving Little Nell alone. {2} Returning, drawn by curiosity, a few days after, Master Humphrey interrupts an angry controversy between the old man and his grandson; Fred Trent calls in his friend Mr Swiveller, who gives some pacific advice; Little Nell returns. {3} She is followed by Quilp; the old man keeps his secret closely. Mrs Quilp and her mother, discussing with some neighbours the character of Mr Quilp, are interrupted by the entrance of that gentleman; Quilp's kind treatment of his wife. {5} Mr Quilp goes to his wharf, where he quarrels with his boy; Nell comes to him there with a letter. {6} Quilp takes Nell to his home on Tower Hill, where he forces Mrs Quilp to endeavour to find out from the child her grandfather's secret, while he listens behind the door. {7} Fred Trent, supposing his grandfather to be very rich, conspires with Dick Swiveller to get possession of his property by the marriage of Little Nell to the latter gentleman, involving the probable disappointment of the matrimonial expectations of Miss Sophy Wackles. {8} Mr Swiveller dines his friend at the expense of the cook-shop keeper; Miss Sophy Wackles plays off Mr Cleggs against Mr Swiveller, and loses Mr Swiveller. {9} Nelly pleads with her grandfather to give up their way of living, and become beggars and be happy; Quilp enters, unperceived, and hears their conversation; Quilp informs the old man that he has discovered the secret of his gambling, and the old man denies that he ever played for his own sake, but always for Nelly's good; Quilp throws the old man's suspicions upon Kit. {10} Kit, after watching the house until midnight, goes home, and is soon followed by Nelly, who informs him of the illness of her grandfather, and that he blames Kit himself as the cause. {11} Quilp, accompanied by Sampson Brass, takes possession of the old man's property; Kit has a secret interview with Little Nell. {12} The old man recovers, and is warned by Quilp to leave the house; he and Nell leave secretly, not knowing where they shall go. {13} Mr Quilp, opening the door to his wife, falls into the hands of Mr Richard Swiveller; Mr Swiveller's astonishment at what has happened; Kit fights with Quilp's boy for the possession of Nelly's bird, and wins. {14} Kit minds the horse of Mr and Mrs Garland, while their son, Mr Abel, is being articled to Mr Witherden, and gets overpaid for the job. {15} Nelly and her grandfather escape from London, and are befriended by a cottager's family. {16} They encounter Messrs Codlin and Short, itinerant showmen, in the churchyard. {17} Little Nell's interview with the aged widow of a young husband; Codlin and Short invite Nell and her grandfather to go with them to the races; they encounter the stilt-walkers. {18} Arrived at The Jolly Sandboys, they are joined by other showmen, and have supper. {19} Codlin makes warm professions of friendship, and both he and Short keep close watch over the fugitives; Nelly and her grandfather escape from their companions. {20} Kit goes to work out the odd sixpence paid him by Mr Garland. {21} He is engaged by Mr Garland for six pounds a year; Quilp and Mr Swiveller pursue their inquiries for the fugitives at the house of Mrs Nubbles; the dwarf draws from Mr Swiveller the details of the scheme he has formed with Fred Trent, and promises his assistance. {22} Kit becomes an inmate of Abel Cottage. {23} Mr Richard Swiveller bemoans his orphan state; Quilp and Fred Trent, for different reasons, unite in the scheme for entrapping Nelly into a marriage with Dick Swiveller. {24} Escaped from the showmen, Nell and her grandfather find their way to a quiet village, where they are kindly received by the schoolmaster. {25} Nell spends the morning in the schoolroom; the schoolmaster takes Nell to the sickroom of his favourite pupil, little Harry; Harry's death. {26} After leaving the schoolmaster, Nelly and the old man encounter Mrs Jarley taking tea outside her caravan; she gives them some supper, and carries them on their way. {27} Mrs Jarley explains her business to the child and, finding they are begging their living, offers her employment, which she gladly accepts; the child is terrified at the sight of Quilp, but luckily escapes being seen by him. {28} Mr Slum receives an order from Mrs Jarley; Nell learns the histories of Mrs Jarley's wax figures.

A black and dreadful place – George Cattermole

{29} Nell and her grandfather, wandering through the fields, are caught in a storm, and take refuge in The Valiant Soldier; the old man becomes excited at the sight of gambling, secures the child's purse, plays, and loses. {30} The old man robs Nell of the little she has left. {31} She tells him of the robbery, in the hope that he will confess it; he bids her keep silent about it; Miss Monflathers receives Nell with dignity; she lectures Miss Edwards for her impropriety in doing Nell a kindness, and refuses her patronage to Mrs Jarley's exhibition. {32} The old man gambles away all Nelly's earnings; Mrs Jarley's schemes for making her exhibition more popular. {33} Sally Brass reproves her brother for taking a clerk; he justifies it as the request of his best client, Mr Quilp; Quilp introduces Mr Swiveller, who is installed as Sampson Brass's clerk. {34} Dick defines his position, and tells how he came in it; he lets the lodgings to the Single Gentleman. {35} The new ledger remains singularly silent for a long time; Sampson Brass refreshes Mr Swiveller's memory in regard to the statement made by the Single Gentleman, who is at length aroused, and expresses his desires to Mr Richard Swiveller. {36} Mr Swiveller finds favour in the eyes of Sally Brass; he witnesses the feeding of the small servant. {37} The Single Gentleman shows an extraordinary interest in Punch and Judy shows; he entertains Messrs Codlin and Short, and makes particular inquiries in regard to Little Nell and her grandfather. {38} Kit's progress in his new place; he meets the strange gentleman at Mr Witherden's, who questions him closely about the old man and the child, and enjoins silence thereupon; Dick Swiveller finds Kit can keep a secret. {39} How Kit and his mother, and Barbara and her mother, enjoyed their half holiday. {40} Kit receives with some surprise the intelligence that the strange gentleman desires to take him into his service, and declines to leave Mr Garland; the Single Gentleman informs Kit that Nell and the old man have been found; Kit declines his proposal to take him with him to bring them back, on account of the old man's feeling towards him, but recommends his mother instead. {41} Kit finds his mother at Little Bethel Chapel, where he is astonished to see Quilp also; the Single Gentleman and Mrs Nubbles start on their journey. {42} Little Nell overhears the gamblers tempting her grandfather to rob Mrs Jarley, until he consents; she sets this knowledge before him as a terrible dream she has had, and bids him fly with her from a place where such dreams come. {43} The fugitives are befriended and carried on their way by some rough boatmen. {44} Lost in the busy

Quilp's Wharf – Frank Reynolds

streets of a manufacturing town, they are taken by a poor workman to a foundry, where they remain through the night, in the warmth of the furnaces. {45} They wander on in search of the open country, Nell growing very weak from hunger and fatigue; she is about to beg of a traveller on the road, when she recognises in him their old friend the schoolmaster, and falls senseless at his feet. {46} The schoolmaster carries her to a neighbouring inn, where she is restored; he informs them of his change of fortune, and they accompany him to his new home. {47} The Single Gentleman and Mrs Nubbles reach Mrs Jarley's, to find that lady just married to George, and to learn that the child and her grandfather disappeared a week before, and all attempts to find them have failed. {48} Quilp's appearance at the inn to which the Single Gentleman goes, and how he came to be there. {49} Quilp returns home, and interrupts the arrangements Mr Sampson Brass and Mrs Jiniwin are making for the recovery of his body, supposing him to be drowned. {50} Quilp establishes himself as a jolly bachelor in the counting-house on his wharf; he pays a visit to Mr Swiveller, whom he finds disconsolate at the marriage of Sophy Wackles to his rival, Cheggs; the dwarf learns from Dick that his friend Fred Trent and the Single Gentleman have met, with no good result; Mrs Quilp importunes her husband to return home, but he drives her away. {51} Quilp has an interview with Miss Brass's small servant; Quilp informs Sampson and Sally Brass that he wants Kit put out of the way, and they agree to do it. {52} The schoolmaster arranges that Nell and her grandfather shall have the care of the church, and they take possession of their new home; their kind reception by the clergyman and the bachelor; the bachelor introduces the schoolmaster to his new pupils. {53} Nell's talk with the old sexton. {54, 55} The sexton's impatience with old David; Nelly's health fails, and her friends grow anxious about her. {56} Mr Swiveller goes into mourning on the occasion of the marriage of Miss Sophy Wackles; Mr Chuckster complains to Mr Swiveller that his merits are not appreciated; Sampson Brass calls Kit into his office, and begins to put his plot against him into execution. {57} Progress of the plot; Dick Swiveller discovers the small servant eavesdropping; he teaches her to play cribbage, and bestows upon her the title of Marchioness. {58} He learns from her how she is kept by Miss Sally; Mr Swiveller relieves his melancholy by a little flute-playing; Miss Sally reports to Dick that some small thefts have occurred in the office; she suspects Kit, whom her brother stoutly defends. {59} Consummation of the plot,

and arrest of Kit for larceny. {60} Kit begs to be taken to Mr
Witherden's office; on the way they encounter Quilp, who bestows
his blessing on the party; astonishment of the Garlands and Mr
Witherden at the charge against Kit. {61} Kit in prison is visited by
his mother and Barbara's mother; Mr Swiveller shows his sympathy
in a mug of beer. {62} Sampson Brass visits Quilp in his den; pleasant
behaviour of the facetious dwarf; he demands the discharge of Mr
Swiveller. {63} Trial and conviction of Kit; Mr Swiveller gets his
discharge. {64} Mr Swiveller awakes from a delirious sickness to find
himself in the care of the Marchioness; she informs him how she
came there, and gives him the particulars of his sickness; the
Marchioness also relates to Dick the details of the plot against Kit,
which she overheard through the keyhole; she goes in search of Mr
Abel Garland. {65} She finds him, and brings him to Dick's lodgings,
where she repeats the story to him. {66} The Garlands and their
friends take Mr Swiveller and the Marchioness under their
protection; they attempt to draw a confession from Sally Brass, but
the conference is interrupted by Sampson, who confesses the whole
conspiracy; Dick Swiveller inherits a fortune, which is smaller than it
might have been. {67} Mrs Quilp carries to her husband a letter from
Sally Brass, informing him of the discovery of their schemes, and
warning him of his danger; he drives his wife away and, groping in
the darkness to escape the officers, who are already on his track, he
falls into the river, and is drowned. {68} Kit is released, and welcomed
home by his friends; Mr Garland notifies him to prepare for a
journey to meet Nell and her grandfather. {69} Kit has an
understanding with Barbara; the Single Gentleman, Mr Garland,
and Kit start on their journey; the Single Gentleman relates his story
to Mr Garland. {70} They arrive at the village after midnight; the old
sexton is disturbed; Kit discovers the old man brooding over the fire.
{71} The old man knows neither Kit nor his brother; Nelly is dead.
{72} Her burial is kept a secret from her grandfather; the old man is
found dead on the child's grave. {73} Sampson Brass, after serving out
his sentence, joins his sister in the wretched neighbourhood of St
Giles's; Mrs Quilp marries again and lives happily; Mr Abel Garland
becomes the head of a family; Mr Swiveller bestows upon the small
servant the name of Sophronia Sphynx, educates, and finally marries
her; sad end of Frederick Trent; the Single Gentleman rewards all
who befriended his brother; the family history of Kit and Barbara.

9

Barnaby Rudge

A Tale of the Riots of the 'Eighties

BARNABY RUDGE is an historical novel, based upon the Lord George Gordon, or London Protestant, riots of 1780. It first appeared in 1841, in *Master Humphrey's Clock*; and in 1849 it was published apart from the machinery of that serial miscellany.

CHARACTERS

AKERMAN, Mr – Head jailer at Newgate. {64, 77}

BLACK LION, The – Landlord of a London inn of the same name; so called because he had instructed the artist who painted his sign to convey into the features of the lordly brute whose effigy it bore, as near a counterpart of his own face as his skill could compass and devise. He is such a swigger of beer, that most of his faculties have been utterly drowned and washed away – except the one great faculty of sleep, which he retains in surprising perfection. {31}

CHESTER, Mr – *afterwards* **Sir John**. An elegant and punctiliously polite, but thoroughly heartless and unprincipled, gentleman. Mr Chester attempts, but unsuccessfully, to break off the match between his son Edward and Miss Emma Haredale, both because the girl is poor, and because he is bent on an alliance which will add to his own wealth and importance. {10–12, 14, 15, 23, 24, 26–30, 32, 40, 43, 53, 75, 81}

CHESTER, Edward – His son; in love with and finally married to Miss Emma Haredale. {1, 2, 5, 6, 14, 15, 19, 29, 32, 67, 71, 72, 79, 82}

COBB, Tom – General chandler and post-office keeper; a crony of old Willet's, and a frequent visitor at The Maypole Inn. {1, 30, 33, 54}

CONWAY, General – A member of parliament, and an opponent of Lord George Gordon. {49}

DAISY, Solomon – Parish clerk and bell-ringer of Chigwell; a little man, with little round, black, shining eyes like beads, and studded all down his rusty black coat, and his long flapped waistcoat, with queer little buttons, like nothing except his eyes, but so like them that he seems all eyes from head to foot. {1–3, 11, 30, 33, 54, 56}

DENNIS, Ned – Ringleader of the Gordon rioters. Having formerly been a hangman, and therefore entertaining a profound respect for the law, he desires that everything should be done in a constitutional way. Yet, as an adept in the art of 'working people off', he thinks it the better and neater method to hang everybody who stands in the way of the rioters; and he is frequently disgusted by the refusal of his fellow-insurgents to adopt his suggestions. When the riot is at last suppressed, and Dennis is arrested and condemned to death, he suddenly discovers that the satisfaction which he has experienced for so many years in executing the capital sentence upon his follow-mortals was, in all probability, not shared by the subjects of his skill; and he shrinks in the most abject fear from his fate. {36–40, 44, 49, 50, 52–54, 59, 60, 63–65, 69–71, 74–77}

GASHFORD, Mr – Lord George Gordon's secretary; a tall, bony, high-shouldered, and angular man. {35–38, 43, 44, 48–50, 52, 53, 71, 82}

GILBERT, Mark – One of the ''Prentice Knights, or United Bull-Dogs', a secret society formed by the apprentices of London for the purpose of resisting the tyranny of their masters. {8–39}

GORDON, Colonel – Member of parliament, and an opponent of his kinsman Lord George Gordon. {49}

GORDON, Lord George – Third son of Cosmo George, third duke of Gordon; born 19 Sept 1750; noted as the chief instigator of the Protestant or 'No Popery' riots, which took place in London in 1780, and were a result of the passage of a bill by parliament relieving Roman Catholics from certain disabilities and penalties. In these riots (which lasted for several days) many Roman Catholic churches were destroyed, as were also Newgate Prison, the residence of Lord Chief Justice Mansfield, and numerous other private dwellings. Lord George was arrested on a charge of high treason, and was committed to the Tower; but, the offence not having been proved, he was acquitted. He died 1 Nov 1793. {35–37, 43, 48–50, 57, 73, 82}

GREEN, Tom – A soldier. {58}

GRIP – A raven; the constant companion of Barnaby Rudge; a very knowing bird, supposed to be a hundred and twenty years old, or thereabouts. {5, 6, 10, 17, 25, 41–47, 57, 58, 68, 73, 75–77, 79, 82}

GRUEBY, John – Servant to Lord George Gordon; a square-built, strong-made, bull-necked fellow, of the true English breed, self-possessed, hard-headed, and imperturbable. {35, 37, 38, 57, 66, 82}

HAREDALE, Mr Geoffrey – A country gentleman, burly in person, stern in disposition, rough and abrupt in manner, but thoroughly honest and unselfish. He resides at a mansion called The Warren, on the borders of Epping Forest, and not far from The Maypole Inn. Being a rigid Roman Catholic, he is made a special object of vengeance by the Lord Gordon mob. He kills Sir John Chester in a duel, and thereupon quits England for ever, ending his days in the seclusion of a religious establishment abroad. {1, 10–12, 14, 20, 25–27, 29, 34, 42, 43, 56, 61, 66, 67, 71, 76, 79, 81, 82}

HAREDALE, Miss Emma – His niece; daughter of Mr Reuben Haredale, who is mysteriously murdered. She is finally married to Edward Chester. {1, 4, 12–15, 20, 25, 27–29, 32, 59, 70, 71, 79, 81}

HUGH – A wild, athletic, gypsy-like young fellow, with something fierce and sullen in his features. He is at first a hostler at The Maypole Inn, and afterwards a leader in the Gordon riots. He turns out to be a natural son of Sir John Chester, who, when urged to save him from the gallows, treats the appeal with the utmost sang froid, and permits him to be executed, without making the least effort in his behalf. {10–12, 20, 22, 23, 28, 29, 34, 35, 37–40, 44, 48–50, 52–54, 59, 60, 63–65, 67–69, 74, 76–78}

LANGDALE, Mr – A vintner and distiller; a portly, purple-faced, and choleric old gentleman. {8, 61, 66, 67, 81}

MIGGS, Miss – The single domestic servant of Mr Varden. When the Gordon riots break she forsakes her old master and mistress to follow and watch over Mr Sim Tappertit. After the dispersion of the rioters, Miss Miggs returns to Mr Varden's house, quite as a matter of course, expecting to be reinstated in her old situation. But Mrs Varden, who is at first amazed at her audacity, orders her to leave the house instanter; whereupon the young lady relieves her mind. Cast upon a thankless, undeserving world, and baffled in all her schemes, matrimonial and otherwise, Miss Miggs turns sharper and sourer than ever. It happens, however, that just at this time, a female turnkey is wanted for the county Bridewell, and a day and hour is appointed for the inspection of candidates. Miss Miggs attends, and is instantly chosen from a hundred and twenty-four competitors, and installed in office, which she holds till her decease more than thirty years afterwards. {7, 9, 13, 18, 19, 22, 27, 31, 36, 39, 41, 51, 63, 70, 71, 80, 82}

PARKES, Phil – A ranger who frequents The Maypole Inn; a tall man, very taciturn, and a profound smoker. {1, 11, 30, 33, 54}

PEAK – Sir John Chester's valet. {23, 24, 32, 75, 82}

RUDGE, Barnaby – A fantastic youth, half crazed, half idiotic. Wandering listlessly about at the time of the Gordon riots, he is overtaken by the mob, and eagerly joins them in their work of destruction. His strength and agility make him a valuable auxiliary and he continues fighting, until he is at last overpowered, arrested, and condemned to death. 'Aha, Hugh!' says he to his companion on the eve of their execution, 'we shall know what makes the stars shine *now*'. A pardon is finally procured for him by Mr Varden. {3–6, 10–12, 17, 25, 26, 45–50, 52, 53, 57, 58, 60, 62, 65, 68, 59, 73, 75–77, 79, 82}

RUDGE, Mrs – Mother of Barnaby. {4–6, 16, 17, 25, 26, 42, 45–50, 57, 62, 69, 73, 76, 79, 82}

RUDGE, Mr – Father of Barnaby, and a former steward of Reuben Haredale's. One morning in the year 1733, Mr Haredale is found murdered, and the steward is missing. Afterwards a body is discovered, which is supposed to be that of Rudge; but it is so disfigured as not to be recognisable. After the lapse of many years, it is proved that Rudge was the real murderer, and that the body, which was taken to be his, was really that of another of his victims. He is finally captured and executed. {1–3, 5, 6, 16–18, 33, 45, 46, 55, 56, 61, 62, 65, 68, 69, 73, 76}

STAGG – A blind man; proprietor of a drinking-cellar and skittle-ground. {8, 18, 45, 46, 62, 69}

TAPPERTIT, Simon – Apprentice to Mr Gabriel Varden, and a sworn enemy to Joe Willet, who has rivalled him in the affections of his master's daughter Dolly. Mr Tappertit is captain of the ''Prentice Knights' (afterwards called the 'United Bull-Dogs'), whose objects were vengeance on their tyrant masters (of whose grievous and insupportable oppression no 'prentice could entertain a moment's doubt) and the restoration of their ancient rights and holidays. He takes a leading part in the Lord George Gordon riots, but finally receives a gunshot wound in his body, and has his precious legs crushed into shapeless ugliness. After being removed from a hospital to a prison, and thence to his place of trial, he is discharged, by proclamation, on two wooden legs. By the advice and aid of his old master, to whom he applies for assistance, he is established in business as a shoe-black, and quickly secures a great run of custom; so that he thinks himself justified in taking to wife the widow of an eminent bone and rag collector. {4, 7–9, 18, 19, 22, 24, 27, 31, 34, 39, 48–52, 59, 60, 62, 70, 71, 82}

VARDEN, Dolly – A bright, fresh, coquettish girl, the very personification of good humour and blooming beauty. She is finally married to Joe Willet. {4, 13, 19–22, 27, 31, 59, 70, 71}

VARDEN, Gabriel – A frank, hearty, honest old locksmith, at charity with all mankind; father to Dolly Varden. {2–7, 13, 14, 19, 21, 22, 26, 27, 41, 42, 51, 63, 64, 71, 72, 74–76, 79, 80, 82}

VARDEN, Mrs Martha – His wife. {4, 7, 8, 19, 21, 22, 27, 36, 41, 42, 51, 71, 72, 80, 82}

WILLET, John – Landlord of The Maypole Inn at Chigwell; a burly, large-headed man, with a fat face, which betokened profound obstinacy and slowness of apprehension, combined with a very strong reliance upon his own merits. {1–3, 10–14, 19, 20, 24, 29, 30, 33, 35, 54–56, 72, 78, 82}

WILLET, Joe – Son of John Willet; a broad-shouldered, strapping young fellow, whom it pleases his father still to consider a little boy, and to treat accordingly. After being bullied, badgered, worried, fretted, and browbeaten, until he can endure it no longer, Joe runs away and joins the army. At the time of the London riots, however, he turns up, and renders good service to his friends, notwithstanding the loss of an arm at the siege of Savannah. The father is only too glad to welcome him back; never speaks of him to a stranger afterwards without saying proudly: 'My son's arm was took off at the defence of the – Salwanners – in America, where the war is'. Joe finally marries Dolly Varden, whom he has long loved. {1–3, 8, 14, 19, 21, 22, 30, 31, 41, 58, 67, 71, 72, 78, 80, 82}

PRINCIPAL INCIDENTS

{1} John Willet, landlord of The Maypole, and his guests, discuss the weather; a suspicious-looking stranger asks questions about The Warren, and is answered by Joe Willet; one of the guests sets out to walk to London through the storm; Joe Willet is lectured for his

Barnaby in Newgate – Hablot K Browne *alias* Phiz

forwardness by his father and his friends; Solomon Daisy relates the story, of the murder of Mr Reuben Haredale twenty-two years before. {2} The suspicious-looking stranger sets out for London, and rides furiously through the darkness; he encounters Gabriel Varden on the road; Gabriel goes back to The Maypole. {3} Joe Willet rebels against his father's authority, and threatens to run away; Gabriel advises him to think better of it; going on to London, Gabriel is attracted by loud outcries, and finds Barnaby Rudge standing over a bloody and apparently lifeless body. {4} Mr Varden's home described; Mr Simon Tappertit is introduced; Mr Varden gives his daughter an account of his last night's adventure on the road, and also his difficulty in finding Miss Emma Haredale; Dolly's confusion on hearing of Joe Willet; the jealousy of Mr Tappertit is aroused. {5} Varden goes to Mrs Rudge's to inquire about Mr Edward Chester, the young man whom he rescued; he is astonished to find her receiving a call from the ruffian he encountered on the road. {6} She declines to make any explanation, but begs him to keep silent; Gabriel sees Mr Edward Chester, who gives him an account of his adventure; and Varden recognises in his assailant the same man he himself met; Barnaby and his raven. {7} Gabriel's reception by Mrs Varden and Miggs on his return home. {8} Sim Tappertit secretly leaves the house, and goes to the rendezvous of the ' 'Prentice Knights', where he is received by Stagg; the ''Prentice Knights' admit a new member; confidence between the captain and the novice. {9} Miss Miggs witnesses Sim's exit from the house, and receives him on his return. {10} Mr John Chester visits The Maypole, and sends a note to Mr Haredale, requesting him to meet him there; Barnaby returns with Mr Haredale's answer. {11} Speculations of Mr Willet's customers in regard to the meeting of Mr Chester and Mr Haredale; interview between these gentlemen, in which they discuss the attachment of Mr Edward Chester and Miss Emma Haredale, and agree, though on different grounds, to oppose it. {12} Surprise of John Willet at finding Mr Chester uninjured. {13} Joe Willet sets out for London to pay his father's rent; he goes to The Warren for any message Miss Emma may have for Edward Chester; Joe goes to the Vardens', where the bouquet he had prepared for Dolly meets an inglorious fate; Dolly goes to a party, and Joe goes home disappointed. {14} On the road home Joe is joined by Mr Edward Chester; Edward calls on Miss Haredale, and is dismissed from the house by her uncle; finding his father at The Maypole, Edward avoids meeting him, and returns to town. {15} Interview between Mr John Chester and his son, wherein he explains the poverty of their resources and the necessity for his son's forming a wealthy marriage. {16} Condition of London streets at the time of the story; appearance among the outcasts of the ruffian who assaulted Mr Chester; he follows Mrs Rudge to her home, and gains admittance. {17} Terror of the widow lest he should be seen by her idiot son ; Barnaby tells his mother of his search for the robber, who, concealed in a closet, overhears their conversation; the ruffian threatens her with a sure and slow revenge, if she betrays him, and leaves her. {18} After wandering through the streets nearly all night, he sees the departure of Sim Tappertit from the rendezvous of the 'Prentices, and obtains shelter with Stagg. {19} Edward Chester calls at Mr Varden's to request Dolly to be the bearer of a letter to Miss Haredale; Mr Varden proposes to take his wife and daughter to The Maypole, and how Mrs Varden receives the proposal; they arrive at The Maypole; Dolly goes to The Warren, carrying Mr Edward's letter. {20}

Old John asleep in his cosy bar – George Cattermole

Leaving Miss Haredale, on her return with the answer she is met by Mr Haredale, who questions her in regard to her errand, and proposes to her to become Miss Haredale's companion; returning to The Maypole, Dolly is assaulted by Hugh, and rescued by Joe Willet. {21} She discovers the loss of her bracelet and of Miss Haredale's letter; Hugh questions her about the man who assaulted her, secretly warning her not to betray him; the Vardens returning home, Joe accompanies them on the way, and they are soon joined by Hugh. {22} Hugh rides back with Joe; Miggs repeats Dolly's adventure to Mr Tappertit, who denounces Joe. {23} Hugh waits upon Mr John Chester, and gives him Miss Haredale's letter to his son, telling him how he obtained it; how Mr Chester received it; and how he cautioned Hugh about robbing on the highway. {24} Mr Tappertit calls upon Mr Chester, and complains of the treatment he has received from his son; recommends him to see Mrs Varden, and prevent Dolly's being a go-between for the lovers; and warns him against the character of Joe. {25} Mrs Rudge and Barnaby go to Chigwell; she has an interview with Mr Haredale, and rejects the assistance she has received from him since her husband's supposed murder, for reasons which she declines to give. {26} Mr Haredale informs Varden of the singular conduct of Mrs Rudge, and Mr Varden gives him an account of his adventure with the ruffian, and of Mrs Rudge's conduct towards him; they go to Mrs Rudge's house together, and find Mr John Chester there alone, who informs them of the disappearance of the widow and her son, but cannot tell where they have gone. {27} Mr Chester leaves them, and calls upon Mrs Varden; he makes insinuations against the character of his son, and requests Mrs Varden's influence in breaking off the engagement between Edward and Miss Haredale. {28} Mr Chester finds Hugh asleep on the stairway; Hugh gives him a letter from Dolly Varden to Miss Haredale, which Mr Chester receives with less pleasure than Hugh expects. {29} Mr Chester goes to Chigwell again, and stops at The Maypole; Hugh shows his activity; Joe Willet upon his 'patrols;' Mr Chester encounters Miss Haredale, and endeavours to poison her mind against Edward; they are interrupted by Mr Haredale. {30} Joe rebels against his father's authority, punishes Tom Cobb for interfering, and escapes from the house. {31} He meets a recruiting-sergeant; Joe seeks an interview with Dolly Varden, who seems indifferent to him, and he enlists. {32} Mr Chester and his son have an interview, in which Edward gives his father offence, and is dismissed from his roof with his curse. {33} After an interval of five years, John Willet and his friends are sitting again in the public room of The Maypole, a severe storm raging without; sudden entrance of Solomon Daisy in great fright; he relates what he has just heard and seen at the church. {34} Mr Willet resolves to communicate to Mr Haredale what Daisy has witnessed, and summons Hugh to accompany him to The Warren; Mr Willet's story has a marked effect on Mr Haredale. {35} Returning home, Mr Willet encounters Lord George Gordon and his attendants, who go to The Maypole to spend the night; interview between Lord George Gordon and his secretary; John Grueby expresses his disgust at his lord's proceedings. {36} Lord George and his secretary in council consider the accessions to their cause in men and means; Gashford sowing seed. {37} Lord George Gordon's cause and its progress; Lord George and his attendants journey to London; interview between Gashford and Dennis, in which Dennis shows his desire for active work in the No-Popery cause. {38} Hugh presents himself, bringing one of the handbills dropped by Gashford, and is enrolled m the Great Protestant Association; Hugh and Dennis take a look at the Houses of Parliament, and then repair to The Boot. {39} Mr Tappertit bestows his patronage upon Hugh, and reminds him of former times; Dennis gives his companion some particulars of his trade, without exposing himself. {40} Hugh makes a call at Sir John Chester's; how Sir John obtained his title; Hugh informs Sir John that he has joined the Protestant Association, and made the acquaintance of Dennis; Sir John's underhand plotting. {41} Mr Varden defends himself for joining the Volunteers; Dolly questions her father about Mr Haredale's absence from home; Dolly's agitation at her father's mention of Joe Willet. {42} Mr Haredale meets the locksmith, and informs him that he intends to pass the night in watching at Mrs Rudge's old home; and Mr Varden leaves him there. {43} How Mr Haredale kept his watch; Mr Haredale encounters Sir John Chester and Gashford in Westminster Hall; Lord George Gordon joins them, and Sir John introduces Mr Haredale as a Papist; Mr Haredale, assaulted by the crowd, retaliates upon Gashford, and is rescued from the revenge of the mob by John Grueby. {44} Gashford joins Dennis and Hugh, and incites them to punish Haredale. {45} Mrs Rudge and Barnaby, in the quiet village home they had secured, are saluted by a blind wayfarer; he proves to be Stagg, and the agent of the ruffian from whom the widow had fled, in whose name he demands twenty pounds. {46} Stagg excites in Barnaby a desire to see the world; the widow gives Stagg her little hoard, and early in the morning leaves her home with Barnaby, to lose themselves in the crowds of London. {47} Harsh treatment of the widow and her son by a 'fine old country gentleman'. {48} The travellers arrive at Westminster Bridge just as the crowd of Lord Gordon's adherents are passing over to the city; Barnaby is enticed to join them by Lord George himself; he is recognised by Hugh, and drawn into the ranks. {49} The crowd of Lord George Gordon's followers meet at the House of Commons; they are confronted by General Conway and Colonel Gordon; the mob are opposed by the military, and Barnaby strikes down a soldier with his flagstaff. {50} Gashford finds Dennis and Hugh at The Boot, and suggests to them greater acts of violence. {51} Mr Tappertit returns home, boasting of the part he has taken in the disturbance of the day, gives Mrs Varden a 'protection' from Lord George Gordon, and escapes from Mr Varden, who attempts to detain him; Gabriel destroys his wife's collection-box and the 'protection'. {52} Hugh and Sim Tappertit plan an expedition against Mr Haredale's house; the rioters despoil churches and dwellings, and make bonfires of the plunder. {53} Gashford informs Hugh of the reward offered for the ringleaders of the mob; the rioters set out on their expedition to Chigwell. {54} Mr Willet gives the 'evidence of his senses' against the reports of the London riots; his cronies start for London to see for themselves; the mob visit The Maypole, despoil the house, bind old John to his chair, and hasten on to The Warren. {55} After the departure of the mob, a man comes to the inn, and is questioning Willet, when he is startled by the ringing of the bell at The Warren; the mob destroy Mr Haredale's house, and disperse. {56} The Maypole cronies, on the way to London, meet Mr Haredale on horseback, who takes Daisy up behind him, and hurries on to Chigwell; they find Mr Willet bound as the mob left him; he informs Mr Haredale of the call he has received from 'a dead man'; Mr Haredale hastens on to the ruins of his house, follows a shadowy form up the tower-stairs, and grapples with Rudge, the murderer of his brother. {57} Barnaby, on guard at The Boot, is visited by Lord Gordon and his servant; Grueby excites the anger of Lord George by calling Barnaby mad; a company of soldiers surround The Boot, and Barnaby is taken prisoner. {58} Barnaby notices a one-armed man among his guard; Barnaby is committed to Newgate. {59} Sim Tappertit, Dennis, and Hugh, having dispersed the rioters, convey Emma Haredale and Dolly Varden in a carriage to London, where they confine them in a miserable cottage, and warn them against any disturbance. {60} Returning to The Boot, Hugh and his companions find it in possession of the soldiers, and repair to the Fleet Market; a one-armed man brings the news of the arrest of Barnaby. {61} Mr Haredale hastens to London with his prisoner, and applies to the lord mayor for his committal; meeting with no success, he obtains a warrant from Sir John Fielding, and sees the murderer confined in Newgate. {62} Stagg visits Rudge in prison, who relates to him the particulars of his crime; Stagg forms a plan for releasing him; the father and son meet in the prison. {63} The rioters, carrying out their designs on Newgate, repair to Gabriel Varden's; he refuses to comply with their demand that he shall pick the prison look; Sim Tappertit orders Miggs to be released, and sends her to join Emma and Dolly. {64} Varden refuses the demands of the mob in front of Newgate, and is rescued from their fury by the one-armed man and another, and conveyed away through the crowd; the rioters burn down the jail-door, and gain entrance to the interior. {65} Rudge and Barnaby are released by the mob; Dennis visits the criminals condemned to be hanged; Hugh releases these criminals against the remonstrances of Dennis. {66} Mr Haredale seeks his niece without avail; fearing the release of the murderer, he goes to Newgate, but is met by Mr Langdale, who conveys him, in an exhausted condition, to his home; progress of the riot. {67} The rioters, led by Hugh, attack the house of Mr Langdale; Langdale and Mr Haredale, escaping by a secret passage, are met by Edward Chester and Joe Willet, who, disguised as rioters, have found this means of rescuing them; Joe Willet proves to be the one-armed man. {68} Barnaby and his father escape to Clerkenwell, and find shelter in a poor shed; Barnaby rejoins the rioters on Holborn Hill just as Hugh is struck down by Edward Chester, rescues Hugh, and carries him to the place where Rudge is concealed. {69} Barnaby goes in search of Stagg, with whom he returns; Dennis joins them, and, at a signal from his a body of soldiers advance, and arrest all but Stagg, who is shot in attempting to escape. {70} Dennis goes to the house where Emma and Dolly are imprisoned; Miggs informs him that Miss Haredale is to be removed the next night; and he imparts his scheme for disposing of Dolly. {71} Gashford attempts to induce Emma to trust in him, and go with him, when Mr Haredale and his friends enter, rescue the captives, and all repair to The Black Lion. {72} Mr Willet makes up his mind that Joe's arm has 'been took off'; interview between Dolly and Joe. {73} Dispersion of the rioters; interview between Barnaby and his mother in his dungeon; Mrs Rudge makes a vain attempt to move her husband to repentance. {74} Dennis's terror of Hugh on being confined in the same cell with him; Hugh tells Dennis of his mother's fate. {75} Gabriel Varden calls upon Sir John Chester, informs him that he believes Hugh to be his son, and begs Sir John to see him, and attempt to rouse in him a sense of his guilt; Sir John's callousness. {76} The execution of Rudge; agony of Dennis at his approaching fate. {77} Hugh and Dennis are led out to execution, and Hugh pleads for Barnaby. {78} Dolly seeks out Joe Willet, and declares her affection for him. {79} Mr Haredale and Edward Chester meet at Mr Varden's house; Mr Haredale now approves of Edward's attachment to his niece, and blesses their union; Gabriel is brought home in triumph by the crowd, accompanied by Barnaby, for whom he has obtained a pardon. {80} Happiness of the locksmith and his family; Miggs receives her discharge from Mrs Varden; Mr Haredale visits the ruins of The Warren, where he encounters Sir John Chester, with whom he has an altercation, ending in a duel, in which Sir John is killed. {81} Subsequent career of the principal characters.

The landlord of the Maypole
– Charles Pears

10

A Christmas Carol

In Prose; Being a Ghost-Story of Christmas

This work was 'printed and published for the author by Messrs Bradbury and Evans, in December 1843, in one volume, 12mo, with four coloured etchings on steel by John Leech'. In the Preface to the edition of the Christmas books published in 1850, Mr Dickens said of this, as well as of the others: 'My purpose was, in a whimsical kind of masque, which the good humour of the season justified, to awaken some loving and forbearing thoughts, never out of season in a Christian land'.

CHARACTERS

BELLE – A comely matron, whom the Ghost of Christmas Past shows to Scrooge, and in whom he recognises an old sweetheart. {# 2}

CAROLINE – Wife of one of Scrooge's debtors, shown to him in a dream by the Ghost of Christmas Yet To Come. {# 4}

CRATCHIT, Bob – Clerk to Scrooge. He works in a dismal little cell – a sort of tank leading out of Scrooge's counting room. {# 1, 3, 4, 5}

CRATCHIT, Mrs – His wife. {# 3, 4}

CRATCHIT, Belinda – Their second daughter. {# 3, 4}

CRATCHIT, Martha – Their eldest daughter. {# 3, 4}

CRATCHIT, Master Peter – One of their sons. {# 3, 4}

CRATCHIT, Tim – *called* 'Tiny Tim'. Their youngest son, a cripple. {# 3}

DILBER, Mrs – A laundress whom the Ghost of Christmas Yet To Come shows to Scrooge. {# 4}

FAN – A little girl, Scrooge's sister (afterwards the mother of Fred, his nephew) whom the Ghost of Christmas Past shows to Scrooge in a dream. {# 2}

FEZZIWIG, Mr – A kind-hearted, jolly old merchant, to whom Scrooge was a 'prentice, when a young man, and whom the Ghost of Christmas Past brings before him in a vision when he has become an old man and a miser. {# 2}

FEZZIWIG, Mrs – His wife, 'worthy to be his partner in every sense of the term'. At the ball which her husband gave to his workpeople on Christmas Eve, and which the Ghost of Christmas Past shows to old Scrooge, 'in came Mrs Fezziwig, one vast, substantial smile'. {# 2}

FEZZIWIG, The Three Misses – Their daughters, beaming and loveable, with six young followers, whose hearts they break. {# 2}

FRED – Scrooge's nephew. {# 1, 3, 5}

GHOST OF CHRISTMAS PAST – A phantom that shows Scrooge 'shadows of things that have been' in his past life. {# 2}

GHOST OF CHRISTMAS PRESENT – A jolly spirit, glorious to see, of a kind, generous, hearty nature, who invisibly conducts old Scrooge through various scenes on Christmas Eve. {# 3}

GHOST OF CHRISTMAS YET TO COME – An apparition which shows Scrooge 'shadows of things that have not happened', but which may happen in the time before him. {# 4}

JOE – A marine-store dealer, and a receiver of stolen goods, shown to old Scrooge by the Ghost of Christmas Yet To Come. {# 4}

MARLEY, The Ghost of Jacob – A spectre that visits Scrooge on Christmas Eve; Marley was in life Scrooge's partner in business. {# 1}

SCROOGE, Ebenezer – The hero of the *Carol*; surviving partner of the firm of Scrooge and Marley. One Christmas Eve, after having declined in a very surly manner to accept an invitation to dinner the next day from his nephew Fred, and having reluctantly given his clerk Bob Cratchit permission to be absent the whole day, Scrooge goes home to his lodgings where, brooding over a low fire, he is visited by the ghost of old Marley, who has been dead seven years. Being much in need of repose, whether from the emotion he had undergone, or the fatigues of the day, or his glimpse of the invisible world, or the lateness of the hour, or from all combined, Scrooge goes straight to bed, without undressing and falls asleep upon the instant. When he wakes, it is nearly one o'clock. The hour soon strikes ; and, as the notes die away, the curtain of the bed are drawn aside, and a child stands before him. It is the Ghost of Christmas Past. The spirit bids him follow, and takes him to scenes long past. His childhood comes back to him. His sister Fan is before him. His old master Fezziwig reappears and Dick Wilkins, the companion of his boyish days. It is Christmas time, and he and

Marley's Ghost – John Leech

Dick and many are made happy by their master's liberality. The scene changes, and Scrooge sees himself in the prime of life. 'His face had not the harsh and rigid lines of later years, but it had begun to wear the signs of avarice'; and a young girl stands beside him, and tells him that another idol, a golden one, has displaced her, and that she releases him. 'May you be happy in the life you have chosen!' she says sorrowfully, and disappears. 'Spirit!' says Scrooge, 'show me no more; conduct me home.' But the ghost points again, and the wretched man sees a happy home – husband and wife, and many children; and the matron is she whom he might have called his own. The spirit vanishes and Scrooge, exhausted and drowsy, throws himself upon the bed, and sinks into a heavy sleep. He awakes as the bell is upon the stroke of one; and the Ghost of Christmas Present is before him. It shows him the Cratchit family at table, with their Christmas goose and all the trimmings. At last all is finished and cleared; Bob then proposes the health of Mr Scrooge and, although his wife does not relish the toast, yet, at the solicitation of her husband, she consents to drink it for her husband's sake and the day's. Again the scene changes, and Scrooge finds himself in the bright gleaming house of his nephew, where a merry company are enjoying themselves, and are laughing at his surly refusal to join their Christmas festivities. The third and last Spirit comes at the same hour, and introduces itself as the ghost of Christmas Yet To Come. It shows Scrooge a room in which a dead man is lying. The Spirit points to the head, covered by the thin sheet, but Scrooge has no power to pull it aside and view the features. As they leave the room, however, he beseeches the Spirit to tell him what man it is who lies there so friendless and uncared for. The ghost does not answer, but conveys him to a churchyard, neglected, overgrown with weeds, 'choked up with too much burying, fat with repleted appetite. A worthy place!' The Spirit stands among the graves, and points to one, and Scrooge beholds upon the stone of the neglected grave his own name – 'Ebenezer Scrooge'. Scrooge asks if there is no hope; if these sights are the shadows of what *must* or what *may* come to him? The kind hand trembles; and Scrooge sees room for hope. And he does make amends most amply. The lesson of his dream is not forgotten. He instantly sends to the Cratchits a prize turkey, twice the size of Tiny Tim, and gives half-a-crown to the boy who goes and buys it for him. He surprises his nephew by dining with him, and the next day raises Bob Cratchit's salary. In short, 'he became as good a friend, as good a master, and as good a man, as the good old city knew, or any other good old city, town, or borough in the good old world.'

TINY TIM – *See* **Cratchit, Tim**.

TOPPER, Mr – One of the guests at Fred's Christmas dinner-party; a bachelor, who thinks himself a wretched outcast because he has no wife, and consequently keeps his eye upon one of Scrooge's niece's sisters. {# 3}

WILKINS, Dick – A fellow-'prentice of Scrooge's. {# 2}

Scrooge and Bob Cratchit – John Leech

11

The Life and Adventures of Martin Chuzzlewit

This novel was begun after Dickens's return from his first visit to America in 1841–42, and was issued in twenty monthly shilling parts, the first part making its appearance in January, 1843. The work was completed and published in one volume in 1844. It was illustrated with twenty etchings on steel by 'Phiz', and was dedicated to Miss (later Baroness) Burdett-Coutts.

'My main object in this story', says the author in his preface, 'was to exhibit in a variety of aspects the commonest of all the vices; to show how selfishness propagates itself, and to what a grim giant it may grow from small beginnings'.

Of the American portion of the book Dickens says that it 'is in no other respect a caricature than as it is an exhibition, for the most part, of the ludicrous side of the American character – of that side which is, from its very nature, the most obtrusive, and the most likely to be seen by such travellers as young Martin and Mark Tapely. As I have never, in writing fiction, had any disposition to soften what is ridiculous or wrong at home, I hope (and believe) that the good-humoured people of the United States are not generally disposed to quarrel with me for carrying the same usage abroad'. Our author's American readers did, however, quarrel with him very generally and very seriously, as they had previously done for his strictures on their social usages and political institutions in his 'American Notes'. But, as Emerson says (in his essay on 'Behaviour', in *The Conduct of Life*) 'the lesson was not quite lost: it held bad manners up, so that the churls could see the deformity'. On his second visit to the United States, Dickens frankly and gracefully, and 'as an act of plain justice and honour', bore testimony (in his farewell speech at New York, April 18, 1868) to the astonishing progress which had taken place in the country during the quarter of a century that had elapsed since his first visit. It is 'a duty', he said, 'with which I henceforth charge myself, not only here, but on every suitable occasion whatsoever and wheresoever, to express my high and grateful sense of my second reception in America, and to bear my honest testimony to the national generosity and magnanimity; also to declare how astounded I have been by the changes that I have seen around me on every side – changes moral, changes physical, changes in the amount of land subdued and peopled, changes in the rise of vast new cities, changes in the growth of older cities almost out of recognition, changes in the graces and amenities of life, changes in the press, without whose advancement no advancement can be made anywhere. Nor am I, believe me, so arrogant as to suppose, that, in five-and-twenty years, there have been no changes in me, and that I had nothing to learn, and no extreme impressions to correct when I was here first'. We should remember also that absence makes the heart grow fonder, and familiarity breeds acceptance.

CHARACTERS

BAILEY, Junior – The 'boots' at Mrs Todger's Commercial Boarding House; 'a small boy with a large red head, and no nose to speak of. He afterwards becomes 'tiger' to Tigg Montague, and finally engages with Mr Sweedlepipe in the barber business. {8, 10, 11, 27–29, 38, 41, 42, 49, 52}

BEVAN, Mr – A sensible, warm-hearted Massachusetts man, whom Martin Chuzzlewit meets at his boarding house in New York, and who afterwards advances him money to enable him to return to England. {16, 17, 21, 33, 34, 43}

BIB, Julius Washington Merryweather – An American gentleman in the lumber line; one of a committee that waits upon the Honourable Elijah Pogram. {34}

BRICK, Jefferson – The war correspondent of *The New York Rowdy Journal.* {16} He is introduced by Colonel Diver, the editor of the newspaper, to Martin Chuzzlewit, who had at first supposed him to be the colonel's son.

BRICK, Mrs Jefferson – His wife, and the mother of the 'two young Bricks'. She is taken by Martin Chuzzlewit for a 'little girl'; but he is put right by Colonel Diver, who informs him that she is a 'matron'. {16, 17}

BUFFUM, Mr Oscar – A member of a committee that 'Waits upon the Honourable Elijah Pogram for the purpose of requesting the honour of his company "at a little le-Vee" in the ladies' ordinary at the National Hotel'. {34}

BULLAMY – A porter in the service of the Anglo-Bengalee Disinterested Loan and Life Insurance Company. {27, 51}

CHOKE, General Cyrus – An American militia general, whose acquaintance Martin Chuzzlewit makes in a railway car. He is a member of the Eden Land Corporation, belongs to the Watertoast Association of United Sympathisers and, taken all in all, is 'one of the most remarkable men in the country' {21}

CHOLLOP, Major Hannibal – A man who calls upon Martin Chuzzlewit at Eden. {33, 34}

CHUFFEY, Mr – Clerk to Anthony Chuzzlewit; a little, blear-eyed, weazen-faced old man, looking as if he had been put away and forgotten half a century before, and had just been found in a lumber closet. He hardly understands anyone except his master, but always understands him, and wakes up quite wonderfully when Mr Chuzzlewit speaks to him. {11, 18, 19, 25, 26, 46, 48, 49, 51, 54}

CHUZZLEWIT, Anthony – Father of Jonas, and brother of Martin Chuzzlewit the elder; an old man with a face wonderfully sharpened by the wariness and cunning of his life. {4, 8, 12, 18, 19}

CHUZZLEWIT, George – A bachelor, who claims to be young, but has been younger. He is inclined to corpulency, overfeeds himself, and has such an obvious disposition to pimples, that the bright spots on his cravat, and the rich pattern on his waistcoat, and even his glittering trinkets, seem to have broken out upon him, and not to have come into existence comfortably. {4, 54}

CHUZZLEWIT, Jonas – Son of Anthony, and nephew of old Martin Chuzzlewit; a sly, cunning, ignorant young man, who is in pecuniary matters a miser, and in instinct and disposition a brute. His rule for bargains is 'Do other men; for they would do you'. 'That's the true business precept', he says. 'All others are counterfeit'. Tired of the prolonged life of his father, and eager to come into possession of his property, he attempts to poison him, and believes that he has succeeded, as the old man dies shortly afterwards. The truth is, however, that his attempt has been discovered by his intended victim and an old clerk named Chuffey, who privately remove the poison. But the thought of his son's ingratitude and unnatural wickedness breaks old Anthony's heart, and in a few days he dies, having first made Chuffey promise not to reveal the dreadful secret. Jonas now marries Mercy, the younger daughter of Mr Pecksniff, and treats her very cruelly. Believing that he has murdered his father, and that the secret has in some way become known to Montague Tigg, a swindling director of the Anglo-Bengalee Disinterested Loan and Lifes' Insurance Company, Jonas is forced, as a condition of his secrecy, not only to come into the company himself, but to pay large sums to Tigg as hush-money. At last, goaded to desperation, he follows Tigg into the country, where he waylays and murders him. The deed, though very cunningly devised and executed, is soon traced to him, and he is arrested, but poisons himself on his way to prison. {4, 8, 11, 18–20, 24, 26–28, 38, 44, 46–48, 51}

CHUZZLEWIT, Martin, Senior – A very rich and eccentric old gentleman; brother of Anthony, and grandfather of young Martin. He is nearly driven mad by the fawning servility and hollow professions of his covetous relatives, and even quarrels with and disinherits his grandson, the only one among them all for whom he has ever cared. He receives a visit from his cousin, Mr Pecksniff, under whose assumption of honest independence he instantly detects the selfishness, deceit, and low design of his true character. Notwithstanding this, the old man, for purposes of his own, goes to reside with Mr Pecksniff, and pretends to be entirely governed by his wishes. When young Martin returns from America, rendered humble and penitent by his hard experience, he sees Pecksniff drive him from the door, and yet does not interpose a word. But the time soon comes when having thoroughly tested both, and proved his grandson true and Pecksniff false, Chuzzlewit Senior makes ample amends to the former, and awards the latter his just deserts. {3, 4, 10, 24, 30, 31, 43, 50–54}

CHUZZLEWIT, Martin, The Younger – The hero of the story. He has been brought up by a rich grandfather, who has intended making him his heir. But the young man presumes to fall in love with a young lady (Mary Graham) of whom the old man does not approve and he is, therefore, disinherited, and thrown upon his own resources. He goes to study with Mr Pecksniff, with a vague intention of becoming a civil engineer. His grandfather, upon ascertaining this fact, intimates to Mr Pecksniff (who is his cousin), that he would find it to be for his own advantage if he should turn young Martin out of the house. This Mr Pecksniff immediately proceeds to do, and Martin again finds himself without money, or the means of obtaining it. He determines to go to America, and accordingly makes his way to London, where he meets Mark Tapley, who has saved a little from his wages at The Blue Dragon, and who wishes to accompany him. They take steerage passage on the packet-ship *Screw*, with sanguine expectations of amassing sudden wealth in the New World. Soon after their arrival at New York, Martin is led into investing the little money remaining to himself and Mark in a lot of fifty acres in the thriving city of Eden, in a distant part of the country, and they set out for it immediately. They find the city – which on paper had looked so fair, with its parks and fountains, its banks, factories, churches, and public buildings of all kinds – a dreary and malarious marsh, with a dozen log-cabins comprising the whole settlement. Worse than all, Martin is seized with fever and ague, and barely escapes with his life and, before he is fairly convalescent, Mark is also stricken down. When they are at last able to move about a little, they turn their faces toward England, and after some time arrive home. Martin seeks an interview with his grandfather, but finds that Mr Pecksniff's influence over him is paramount, and that not even a frank and manly avowal of error, coupled with a request for forgiveness, avails to revive the old love, or to save him from the indignity of being ordered out of the house. Miss Graham, however, has remained faithful to him, and with this one comfort he again turns his face towards London to make his way in the great world as best he can. In the sequel he finds, much to his surprise, that his grandfather, distracted by suspicions, doubts, and fears, has only been probing Pecksniff, and accumulating proofs of his duplicity, and that, all through their separation, he himself has remained the old man's favourite. {5–7, 12–17, 21, 22, 33–35, 43, 48–50, 52–54}

CICERO – A Negro truckman in New York, formerly a slave. {17}

CODGER, Miss – A Western literary celebrity. {35}

CRIMPLE, David – A pawnbroker, afterwards secretary of the Anglo-Bengalee Disinterested Loan and Life Insurance Company. His name was originally Crimp, but as this was susceptible of an awkward construction, and might be misrepresented, he altered it to Crimple. {13, 27, 28, 49, 51}

DIVER, Colonel – Editor of *The New York Rowdy Journal*; a sallow man, with sunken cheeks, black hair, small twinkling eyes, and an expression compounded of vulgar cunning and conceit. {15}

DUNKLE, Doctor Ginery – One of a committee of citizens that waits upon the Honourable Elijah Pogram to request the honour of his company at a little le-Vee at the National Hotel. Although he has the appearance of a mere boy with a very shrill voice, he passes for 'a gentleman of great poetical elements'. {34}

FIPS, Mr – A lawyer who, as the agent of an unknown person (old Martin Chuzzlewit), employs Tom Pinch as librarian. {39, 40, 53}

FLADDOCK, General – A corpulent American militia officer, starched and punctilious, to whom Martin Chuzzlewit is introduced at the Norris's in New York, as having come over from England in the same vessel as himself. The general does not recognise him, and Martin is obliged to explain that, for the sake of economy, he had been obliged to take passage in the steerage – a confession which at once stamps him as a fellow of no respectability, who has gained an entrance into good society under false pretences, and whose acquaintance must forthwith be disavowed. {15, 17}

GAMP, Sairey – A professional nurse. Mrs Gamp is represented as constantly quoting or referring to a certain Mrs Harris – a purely imaginary person – as an authority for her own fancies and fabrications. {19, 25, 26, 29, 40, 46, 49, 51, 52}

GANDER, Mr – A boarder at Mrs Todgers's. {9}

GRAHAM, Mary – Companion of old Martin Chuzzlewit, and betrothed to young Martin, whom she finally marries. {3, 5, 6, 24, 30, 31, 33, 43, 52, 53}

GROPER, Colonel – One of a committee who wait upon the Honourable Elijah Pogram to request his attendance at a little le-Vee at the National Hotel, given to him by the citizens. {34}

HOMINY, Mrs – A literary celebrity introduced to Martin Chuzzlewit. She is 'one of our chicest spirits, and belongs toe one of our most aristocratic families'. {22, 23, 34}

IZZARD, Mr – One of the deputation of citizens who beg the attendance of the Honourable Elijah Pogram at a little le-Vee at the National Hotel. {34}

JACK – Driver of a stage-coach plying between London and Salisbury. {36}

JANE – Mr Pecksniff's female servant. {31}

JINKINS, Mr – The oldest boarder at Mrs Todgers's; a gentleman of a fashionable turn, who frequents the parks on Sundays, and knows a great many carriages by sight. {9–11, 54}

JOBLING, Doctor John – Medical officer of the Anglo-Bengalee Disinterested Loan and Life Insurance Company. {27, 28, 38, 41}

JODD, Mr – A member of the committee of citizens that waits upon the Honourable Elijah Pogram to solicit the favour of his company at a little le-Vee at the National Hotel. {34}

KEDGICK, Captain – Landlord of the National Hotel, at which Martin Chuzzlewit stays on his way to Eden, and also on his return to New York. {22, 34}

KETTLE, La fayette – An inquisitive, bombastic American, whom Martin Chuzzlewit meets while travelling; secretary of the Watertoast Association of United Sympathisers. {21, 22}

LEWSOME, Mr – A young man bred a surgeon, and employed by a general practitioner in London as an assistant. Being indebted to Jonas Chuzzlewit, he sells him the drugs with which old Anthony Chuzzlewit is poisoned, though he has reason to suspect the use which will be made of them. After the death of the old man, he makes a voluntary confession of his agency in the matter, being impelled to do so by the torture of his mind and the dread of death caused by a severe sickness. {25, 29, 48, 51}

LUPIN, Mrs – Landlady of The Blue Dragon Inn at Salisbury; afterwards the wife of Mark Tapley. {3, 4, 7, 31, 36, 37, 43, 44, 52}

MODDLE, Mr Augustus – 'The youngest gentleman' at Mrs Todgers's Commercial Boarding House. He falls desperately in love with Miss Mercy Pecksniff and, becoming very low-spirited after her marriage to Jonas Chuzzlewit, is entrapped into an engagement with her sister Charity, but loses his courage and breaks his word at the last moment, sending the injured fair one a letter to inform her that he is on his way to Van Diemen's Land, and that it will be useless for her to send in pursuit, as he is determined never to be taken alive. {9–11, 32, 37, 46, 54}

MONTAGUE, Tigg – *See* **Tigg, Montague**.

MOULD, Mr – An undertaker; a little bald elderly man, with a face in which an attempt at melancholy was at odds with a smirk of satisfaction. {19, 25, 29, 38}

MOULD, Mrs – His wife. {25, 29}

MOULD, The Two Misses – Their daughters: fair, round, and chubby damsels, with their peachy cheeks distended as though they ought of right to be performing on celestial trumpets. {25}

MULLIT, Professor – A very short gentleman, with a red nose, whom

Martin Chuzzlewit meets at Mrs Pawkins's boarding-house in New York. He is a professor 'of education', a man of 'fine moral elements', and author of some powerful pamphlets, written under the signature of Suturb, or Brutus reversed. {16}

NADGETT, Mr – Tom Pinch's landlord, employed by Montague Tigg as a detective. {27, 28, 38, 40, 41, 47, 51}

NORRIS, Mr – A New York gentleman; wealthy, aristocratic and fashionable; a sentimental abolitionist, and 'a very good fellow in his way', but inclined 'to set up on false pretences', and ridiculously afraid of being disgraced by moneyless acquaintances. {17}

NORRIS, Mrs – His wife; much older and more faded than she ought to have looked. {17}

NORRIS, The Two Misses – Their daughters; one eighteen, the other twenty, both very slender, and very pretty. {17}

PAWKINS, Major – A New York politician; a bold speculator (or swindler), an orator and a man of the people, and a general loafer. {16}

PAWKINS, Mrs – His wife; keeper of a boarding house. {16}

PECKSNIFF, Seth – A resident of Salisbury; ostensibly an architect and land surveyor, though he had never designed or built anything, and his surveying was limited to the extensive prospect from the windows of his house. Mr Pecksniff is a cousin of old Martin Chuzzlewit, and when the old man is lying ill at The Dragon, a general council and conference of his relatives is held at Mr Pecksniff's house in order to devise means of inducing him to listen to the promptings of nature in the disposal of his large property. The meeting is far from being harmonious, and Mr Pecksniff is compelled to listen to some very plain truths, Mr Anthony Chuzzlewit telling him bluntly not to be a hypocrite. Meeting Mr Chuzzlewit in a stage-coach some time afterwards, Mr Pecksniff takes occasion to remark, incidentally, but cuttingly: 'I may be a hypocrite, but I am not a brute'. During the journey, Pecksniff imbibes copious refreshment from a brandy bottle, and is thereafter moved to give utterance to various moral precepts and weighty sentiments. Mr Pecksniff receives young Martin Chuzzlewit into his family as a student, and manifests a very strong interest in him; but, on a hint from the elder Mr Chuzzlewit, he humiliatingly turns him out of his house, and renounces him for ever. This he does because Martin's grandfather has expressed his desire for a better understanding between himself and Mr Pecksniff than has hitherto existed, and has declared his intention to attach him to himself by ties of interest and expectation. Systematic self-server that he is, in order to secure the old man's great wealth, Mr Pecksniff sedulously studies his likings and dislikings, falls in with all his prejudices, lies, fawns, and worms himself (as he thinks) into his favour, through concessions and crooked deeds innumerable, through meanness and vile endurance, and through all manner of dirty ways; but in the end he finds that, after all, his labour has been for nought, that his duplicity has been fathomed to the bottom, and a servile character thoroughly unmasked. Yet he remains the same canting hypocrite even in shame and discovery, and in the drunkenness and beggary in which he ends his days. {2-6, 8-12, 18-20, 24, 30, 31, 35, 43, 44, 47, 52, 54}

PECKSNIFF, Mercy – called '**Merry**'. His younger daughter; a giddy, vain, and heartless girl, and a hypocrite like her father. Mr Jonas Chuzzlewit, a thoroughly sordid and despicable villain, after making love to her sister, abruptly proposes to herself. She accepts and marries him – partly to spite her sister, and partly because he has money. She soon finds out that he is a brute as well as a rascal and she suffers much from his cruelty. {2, 4-6, 8, 10, 11, 20, 22, 24, 26, 28, 36, 40, 46, 47, 51, 54}

PINCH, Ruth – Governess in a wealthy brass and copper founder's family at Camberwell; sister to Tom Pinch; afterwards the wife of John Westlock. {9, 36, 37, 39, 40, 46, 48, 50, 52-54}

PINCH, Tom – An ungainly, awkward-looking man, extremely short-sighted, and prematurely bald. He is an assistant to Mr Pecksniff, for whom he has an unbounded respect, and in whose pretensions he has a wonderful faith; his nature being such that he is timid and distrustful of himself, and trustful of all other men – even the least deserving. Tom's faith in his master remains unshaken for a long time; but his eyes are opened at last, and he sees him to be a consummate hypocrite and villain. Pecksniff, knowing himself to have been found out, discharges Tom, who goes to London to try his fortune and is befriended by old Martin Chuzzlewit, secretly at first, but afterwards openly. {2, 5-7, 9, 12, 14, 20, 24, 30, 31, 36-40, 45, 46, 48, 50, 52-54}

PIP, Mr – A theatrical character, and a 'capital man to know'; a friend of Montague Tigg. {38}

Meekness of Mr Pecksniff and his charming daughters –
Hablot K Browne *alias* Phiz

PIPER, Professor – One of a deputation chosen to wait upon the Honourable Elijah Pogram, to request the honour of his company at a little le-Vee, at the National Hotel. {34}

POGRAM, The Honourable Elijah – A member of Congress, and 'one of the master minds of our country', whose acquaintance Martin Chuzzlewit makes on his return from Eden to New York. He is especially noted as the author of the 'Pogram Defiance', 'which rose so much contest and preju-dice in Europe'. Mr Pogram is waited on at the National Hotel by a committee of the citizens, and tendered a public reception, or 'levee', the same evening. {34}

PRIG, Betsey – A nurse; a bosom-friend of Mrs Gamp. These two ladies often 'nuss together, turn and turn about, one off, one on'. They are both engaged by John Westlock to take care of an acquaintance of his who lies dangerously ill at a public-house in London. The patient at last recovers sufficiently to admit of his being removed to the country, and Mrs Gamp and Mrs Prig superintend the arrangements for the journey. The arrangements are finally completed and, as Mrs Gamp is to accompany the invalid, she bids farewell to Mrs Prig. The two friends have a falling out at last, however. Mrs Prig has been invited to take tea with Mrs Gamp, on which occasion the latter informs her of another prospective job of nursing in partnership. {25, 29, 49}

SCADDER, Zephaniah – Agent of the Eden Land Corporation. He dupes Martin Chuzzlewit into buying for the ridiculously small sum of a hundred and fifty dollars, a little lot of fifty acres in the city from which the company takes its name, and which looks wonderfully thriving on paper, but proves to consist of a few log-houses in the midst of a hideous and pestilential morass.

SIMMONS, William – Driver of a van who carries Martin Chuzzlewit from near Salisbury to Hounslow after his dismissal by Mr Pecksniff. {13}

SLYME, Chevy – A very poor and shiftless relative of old Martin Chuzzlewit, and anxious to come into a share of his property. He is a friend of Montague Tigg. {4, 7, 51}

SMIF, Putnam – A young and ardent clerk in a dry-goods store, who 'aspirates' for fame, and applies to Martin Chuzzlewit for assistance. {22}

SOPHIA – A pupil of Ruth Pinch's, called by Mrs Todgers 'a syrup' (meaning a seraph or a sylph); a premature little woman of thirteen years old, who had already arrived at such a pitch of whalebone and education, that she had nothing girlish about her. {9, 36}

SPOTTLETOE, Mr – A relative of old Martin Chuzzlewit, with testamentary designs upon his property. He is so bald, and has such big whiskers, that he seems 'to have stopped his hair, by the sudden application of some powerful remedy, in the very act of falling off his head, and to have fastened it irrevocably on his face'. {4, 54}

SPOTTLETOE, Mrs – His wife; a woman 'much too slim for her years, and of a poetical constitution'. {4, 54}

SWEEDLEPIPE, Paul – *called* 'Poll'. A bird-fancier, who is an easy shaver and a fashionable hairdresser also; Mrs Gamp's landlord. {19, 26, 29, 49, 52}

TACKER – Foreman and chief mourner of Mr Mould the undertaker. {19, 25}

TAMAROO – An old woman in the service of Mrs Todgers; successor to Bailey. {32, 54}

TAPLEY, Mark – Hostler at The Blue Dragon Inn, kept by Mrs Lupin; a young fellow of some five or six and twenty, with a whimsical face and very merry pair of blue eyes, and usually dressed in a remarkably free and fly-away fashion. He believes that there never 'was a man as could come out so strong under circumstances that would make other men miserable' as himself, if he could 'only get a chance' – but that he finds difficult. He takes the situation at The Dragon in consequence of having made up his mind that it is the dullest little out-of-the-way corner in England, and that there would be some credit in being jolly in such a place. But he leaves it because there is no dullness there whatever; skittles, cricket, quoits, ninepins, comic songs, choruses, company round the chimney-corner every winter evening, making the little inn as merry as merry can be. Going to London, he meets Martin Chuzzlewit and, finding him moneyless, and resolved to go to America, he begs permission to accompany him as his manservant. After some opposition, Martin consents, and they take passage in the steerage of the packet ship *Screw*. Arrived at New York, Martin invests all his own means, and Mark's, in the purchase of a fifty-acre lot in the distant 'city' of Eden, which is represented to them as a flourishing town, with banks, churches, markets, wharfs, and the like. It is Martin's intention to establish himself here as an architect and he takes Mark into partnership, in consideration of his having furnished much the larger share of their joint stock. On reaching the place, however, after a long and fatiguing journey of many days, they find it to be a hideous swamp, exhaling deadly miasmata, and containing only a few scattered log-cabins. Martin is terribly disheartened on discovering the outrageous swindle that has been practised upon him, and soon sinks under an attack of the fever that prevails throughout the settlement. Martin no sooner recovers than Mark is prostrated. For many weary days and nights he lies burnt up with fever but, as long as he can speak, he assures Martin that he is still 'jolly', and when, at last, he is too far gone to speak, he feebly writes 'jolly' on a slate. After a long and lingering illness, he slowly recovers and, when able to get about once more, they both set their faces towards Old England, where they arrive in due time. Mark turns his steps towards The Blue Dragon, and finds his old friend Mrs Lupin alone in the bar. Wrapped up as he is in a greatcoat, she does not know him at first, but soon utters a glad cry of recognition, and he catches her in his arms. This love-passage ends in the marriage of Mark to the fair widow, and the conversion of The Blue Dragon into The Jolly Tapley. 'A sign of my own invention', said Mark; 'wery new, conwivial, and expressive'. {5, 7, 8–15, 17, 21–23, 33–35, 43, 48, 51–53}

TIGG, Montague – *alias* **TIGG MONTAGUE**. A needy sharper, and a friend of Chevy Slyme. At a later period, having come into the possession of a few pounds, he unites with David Crimple, a pawnbroker who has saved a few pounds (*see* **Crimple**, *David*), and reversing his name, and making it Tigg, Montague, Esquire, organises a swindling concern called the Anglo-Bengalee Disinterested Loan and Life Insurance Company, and, peculating on a grander scale than formerly, becomes a grander man altogether. Obtaining private information of Jonas Chuzzlewit's attempt to poison his father, Tigg makes use of his knowledge of the fact to compel him not only to invest largely in the stock of the Anglo-Bengalee out of his own wealth, but to persuade his father-in-law, Mr Pecksniff, to do so likewise. Jonas finding his secret known, and himself baffled, hunted, and beset, watches his opportunity, and murders Tigg; but his crime is discovered, and he is arrested, and put into a coach to be carried to prison, but poisons himself on the way. {4, 7, 12, 13, 22, 28, 38, 40–42, 44, 47}

TODGERS, Mrs M — Keeper of a commercial boarding-house in

London; a bony and hard-featured lady, with a row of curls in front of her head, shaped like little barrels of beer. Though not a handsome woman, Mrs Todgers is a very kind-hearted one, and when Mrs Jonas Chuzzlewit (Mercy Pecksniff), heartbroken and destitute, applies to her for sympathy and assistance, she extends both ready hand and heart. {8–11, 32, 37, 46, 54}

TOPPIT, Miss – A literary lady whom Mrs Hominy introduces to the Honourable Elijah Pogram. {34}

WESTLOCK, John – A young man who has been a pupil of Pecksniff, but has a difference with him, and leaves him. He is a warm friend of Tom Pinch, whose sister Ruth he finally marries. {2, 12, 25, 29, 36, 37, 39, 40, 45, 48, 49, 51–53}

WOLF, Mr – A friend and confederate of Montague Tigg; introduced to Jonas Chuzzlewit as a literary character connected with a remarkably clever weekly paper. {28}

PRINCIPAL INCIDENTS

{1} Concerning the pedigree of the Chuzzlewit family. {2} Mr Pecksniff, about to enter his house, is unceremoniously overturned down the steps by the wind slamming the door in his face; his daughters discover him, and bear him into the house; Mr Pecksniff's business, and his method of obtaining pupils, described; Pecksniff moralises, and announces to his daughters the engagement of a new pupil; Tom Pinch tries to intercede for John Westlock, but Mr Pecksniff will listen to no advances from Tom, or from John himself, who leaves in disgust; John tries to open Tom's eyes to the true character of Pecksniff, but without effect; John Westlock's departure for London. {3} Martin Chuzzlewit, sensor, and Mary Graham, arrive at The Blue Dragon; Martin is very ill, and the landlady sends for Mr Pecksniff; Mrs Lupin mistakes the relation existing between Mr Chuzzlewit and Mary; Mr Chuzzlewit destroys a paper he had with great difficulty written in bed; Mr Pecksniff arrives at The Blue Dragon, and is greatly scandalised by the landlady's story of her lodgers; his surprise at finding in the invalid his cousin Mr Chuzzlewit; Martin acquaints Mr Pecksniff with the facts of his wealth, and his distrust of all who court his favour. {4} Mr Pecksniff comes in violent contact with Mr Montague Tigg at the door of Mr Chuzzlewit's chamber; Mr Tigg eulogises his friend, Mr Chevy Blyme, and informs Mr Pecksniff of the arrival of Mr Chuzzlewit's relations; a meeting of these relatives is held at Mr Pecksniff's house; the meeting proves anything but harmonious, each person accusing every other of designs on the property of Mr Chuzzlewit, and Pecksniff is called some very hard names by his friends; the meeting breaks up on the announcement that Mr Chuzzlewit has gone no one knows where. {5} Tom Pinch drives to Salisbury to meet the new pupil, taking up Mark Tapley on the way; Mark informs Tom of his intention to leave The Dragon, and seek a new situation where he can get some credit for being jolly; meeting of Tom Pinch and the new pupil, and their first impressions of each other; Tom relates to young Martin the circumstances of his playing the organ in the church, and of the frequent appearance there of a beautiful young lady; Mr Pecksniff and his daughters affect surprise at the early arrival of Martin; Mr Pecksniff shows his house to Martin and, after supper (on a scale that surprises Tom Pinch) shows him to his bedroom, and takes an opportunity to give him a hint of Tom's position. {6} Mr Pecksniff announces his intention of going to London, and taking his daughters with him, and gives Martin some suggestions as to his employment during his absence; Tom and Martin, left alone together, become confidential, and Tom learns of Martin's attachment to Mary Graham, and consequent misunderstanding with his grandfather; he also finds that his beautiful visitor in the church was Mary. {7} Tom and Martin are surprised by the appearance of Mr Montague Tigg, who explains that he and Chevy Slyme are detained at The Dragon in default of payment of their bills, and Martin and Tom assume the obligation; Mr Slyme shows his independent nature; Mr Tigg improves a favourable opportunity, and begs the loan of a half-sovereign from Tom Pinch; Mark Tapley takes leave of The Blue Dragon. {8} Mr Pecksniff and his daughters, journeying to London by the stage-coach, are joined by Anthony Chuzzlewit and his son Jonas, and Mr Jonas becomes attentive to the young ladies; Mr Pecksniff arrives with his daughters at Mrs Todgers's Commercial Boarding-house, and that lady makes arrangements for their accommodation; situation of Todgers's described. {9} Mr Pecksniff returns a favourable answer to Mr Jinkins's round-robin; Pecksniff and his daughters call on Tom Pinch's sister; they patronise Miss Pinch, and offend the gentleman of the house; Bailey gives sundry dark hints in regard to the bill of fare for the approaching feast; the gentlemen boarders are presented to the young ladies; the successful dinner, graced by the presence of the young ladies, where Mr Jinkins is triumphant, and Mr Moddle becomes despondent and jealous; Mr Pecksniff, under the influence of wine, becomes a little particular in his attentions to Mrs Todgers; Mr Pecksniff is put to bed under difficulties. {10} Old Martin Chuzzlewit calls on Mr Pecksniff, apologises for his former rudeness, and asks an introduction to that gentleman's daughters; Mr Chuzzlewit instructs Pecksniff to dismiss young Martin from his employ, and asks him and the young ladies to befriend Mary who, he is careful to tell them, has no expectations from him; Mr Chuzzlewit warns Pecksniff that the world will accuse him of mercenary motives in carrying out this and takes his leave; Mrs Todgers's youngest boarder is incensed against Mr Jinkins; Mr Pecksniff reproves Mrs Todgers for dissimulation. {11} Mr Jonas Chuzzlewit invites the young ladies to view the sights of London; after a look at all the free spectacles, Jonas takes them to his home; they are introduced to old Chuffey; Chuffey's dependence upon Mr Anthony Chuzzlewit; Miss Charity makes the tea, and receives particular attention from Jonas; Jonas entertains the sisters through the evening, and then accompanies them home; the young gentlemen of Mrs Todgers's serenade the young ladies on the eve of their departure from London; Mr Bailey receives a gratuity and makes himself useful; Mr Anthony Chuzzlewit and Jonas call to take leave, and the Pecksniffs start for home. {12} Young Martin patronises Tom Pinch, and tells him what he shall do for him when he himself is successful; John Westlock invites Tom and Martin to dine with him at Salisbury; they walk to Salisbury to keep the appointment; John and Martin discuss the amiability of Tom Pinch and the hypocrisy of Pecksniff; Tom defends Pecksniff against John's prejudices; John returns Tom the money he had lent Tigg, and cautions him against trusting that gentleman any further; John Westlock, watching Tom and Martin as they set out for home, is impressed with a sense of Martin's selfish misappreciation of Tom's character; Martin and Tom turn out to meet Mr Pecksniff and his daughters on their return, and Martin is astonished to receive no recognition from them; Martin demands an explanation, and is dismissed by Pecksniff; he determines to go to America; Tom Pinch gives him his last half-sovereign. {13} Martin meets a friendly carter who helps him on his way, and gives him an account of his friend who went to the United States; Martin encounters Mr Montague Tigg at a pawnbroker's, and makes ineffectual attempts to find employment in London; he receives a twenty-pound note from an unknown hand; Mark Tapley introduces himself to Martin, and asks to be taken into his service, and allowed to go to America with him; Martin relates his history to Mark; Mark installs himself in Martin's service, and secures a meeting between his master and Mary. {14} Martin and Mary meet in the Park; he informs her of his intention to go to America, and consigns her to the care of Tom Pinch; Mark escorts Mary home after her farewell to Martin, and she sends by him her diamond ring to her lover. {15} Mr Mark Tapley, on board the ship *Screw*, bound for America, has an opportunity to be 'jolly', and makes himself useful to his poor fellow-passengers; Martin avoids the cabin-passengers; the travellers land in New York. {16} They encounter Colonel Diver, who eulogises his country; colloquy between the captain of the *Screw* and Colonel Diver; Martin accompanies the colonel to the office of *The Rowdy Journal*, and is introduced to Mr Jefferson Brick; Mr Brick gives a toast; they all go to the boarding-house of Mrs Pawkins, where Martin is astonished at the voracity of the boarders, and makes the acquaintance of some of 'the most remarkable men of the country'; Mr Bevan accosts Martin, and explains some of the characteristics of the colonel. {17} Mr Bevan surprises Martin by his criticisms of America; they find Mark Tapley at the office of *The Rowdy Journal*, in company with a former slave, whose story he repeats to them; Mr Bevan introduces Martin to the family of Mr Norris; Martin is much pleased with them, until the entrance of General Fladdock, who was a cabin-passenger in the *Screw*. Martin is now obliged to acknowledge that he himself came in the steerage from poverty, and finds a sudden coldness on the part of his hosts; Mrs Jefferson Brick describes her attendance on certain lectures; Mark Tapley revives Martin's spirits by administering a sherry-cobbler. {18} Jonas Chuzzlewit, surreptitiously examining his father's will, is startled by the appearance of Mr Pecksniff; Anthony informs Pecksniff that Jonas will be his heir, and advises him to bind him to one of his daughters while he is in the mood; sudden death of Anthony Chuzzlewit. {19} Mr Pecksniff goes in quest of Mrs Gamp; Mr Mould, the undertaker, commends the affectionate regrets of Mr Jonas, who has ordered no limitation of expense in the funeral arrangements; Chuffey's grief at the death of his old master; sensitiveness of Jonas under his affliction; how old Anthony was buried, and no expense spared; Jonas is alarmed lest Chuffey should 'talk some precious nonsense'. {20} Jonas questions Mr Pecksniff in regard to the dowry he will give his daughter in case she should secure such a husband as himself; how Jonas treated Pecksniff, and how Pecksniff paid the bill; Pecksniff, recalling the memory of old Anthony, is warned by Jonas never to revive the subject; Mr Pecksniff takes Jonas home with him, and they surprise Cherry in the performance of her household duties; Jonas proposes to Mercy in the presence of her sister, much to the disappointment of the older sister's hopes; Tom Pinch announces the approach of old Martin Chuzzlewit and Mary Graham. {21} Young Martin and Mark Tapley, on the way to Eden, discuss the attractions of that locality; Mr La Fayette Kettle and General Choke give Martin some information, new to him, in regard to his own country; the general advises the travellers in regard to settling in Eden; Martin takes Mark into partnership; they consult the agent of the Eden Land Corporation witness the flourishing condition (upon paper) of that city, and purchase an eligible site; they attend a great meeting of the Watertoast Sympathisers, and witness the end of that association. {22} Martin is lionised by the citizens, and invited to deliver a lecture; on declining he is forced to hold a 'le-Vee'; Mrs Hominy is introduced; Captain Kedgick gives Mark the secret of Martin's popularity. {23} The travellers proceed on their journey to Eden, leaving Mrs Hominy at New Thermopylæ; arrived at Eden, they find it to consist of a few log-houses in a swamp, and Martin, giving way, is taken ill with fever and ague. {24} Pecksniff receives Old Martin and Mary with assumed surprise; he prepares Mr Chuzzlewit's mind for a meeting with Jonas, whom he eulogises as a model and dutiful son; Tom Pinch lights Mr Chuzzlewit and Mary home to The Blue Dragon; returning, he encounters Jonas, who assaults him, and gets the worst of it; Jonas ascribes his injury to accident, but Charity suspects Tom to be the cause of it, and thanks him for it; old Martin tries to arouse Mercy to a sense of her future unhappiness if she marries Jonas; Jonas asks Mercy to fix the day. {25}. Mrs Gamp calls upon the Moulds, and discourses on the changes of life; she obtains Mr Mould's permission to night-watch a gentleman in connection with taking care of Mr Chuffey, who has been left in her charge in the absence of Jonas; John Westlock calls at The Ball to inquire about Mrs Gamp's new patient; Betsey Prig introduces Mrs Gamp to her new patient, whose mind is wandering. {26} Mr Bailey calls upon Poll Sweedlepipe, and hears of the marriage of Jonas; going with Poll to Jonas's house to fetch Mrs Gamp, she is surprised to learn that Jonas has married 'the merry one'; the bride's welcome home. {27} Mr Montague Tigg appears as Tigg Montague, Esq, chairman of the Anglo-Bengalee Disinterested Loan and Life Insurance Company of which David Crimple is secretary; meeting of the board of the Anglo-Bengalee; Dr Jobling introduces Jonas Chuzzlewit, who has an interview with Tigg, in which the latter makes himself known to Jonas, and invites him to join the company; Montague instructs Nadgett to bring him all the information he can obtain in regard to Jonas Chuzzlewit. {28} Jonas dines with Mr Tigg and a few friends at that gentleman's house; he is carried home drunk by Mr Bailey; Jonas curses his wife, and strikes her. {29} Mr Bailey has an easy shave at the hands of Poll Sweedlepipe; Mrs Gamp's opinion of Mr Lewsome's sickness; Mrs Gamp and Betsey Prig prepare their patient for a journey; Lewsome tells John Westlock he has a secret weighing on his mind. {30} Mr Pecksniff reproves his eldest daughter for her jealousy of her sister and, at her request, contents to place her at Mrs Todgers's in the city; Pecksniff informs Martin of Charity's proposed departure, and invites him to come and stay with him for the sake of Mary; Mr Pecksniff meets Mary and forces her to listen to an offer of marriage, which she spurns, and he threatens to use his influence with Mr Chuzzlewit against his grandson unless she submits; Cherry informs Tom Pinch of her intended departure. {31} Pecksniff witnesses in the church an interview between Tom Pinch and Mary, in which she opens Tom's eyes to the true character of his employer; Pecksniff complains to Mr Chuzzlewit that he has been cruelly deceived by Thomas Pinch; he accuses Tom, in the presence of Chuzzlewit, of addressing proposals of love to Mary in the church; Tom makes no reply, but returns to Pecksniff his double eyeglass which he had found in the church, and leaves the house; Tom declines Mrs Lupin's invitation to stay at The Dragon, and goes to Salisbury. {32} Miss Pecksniff arrives at Mrs Todgers's, and receives a pathetic account of the state of Mr Augustus Moddle; Charity becomes attentive to Mr Moddle, and draws him on to a proposal of marriage which, of course, she accepts. {33} Mr Mark Tapley finds that his fellow-passengers on the *Screw* are his next-door neighbours in Eden; Mr Hannibal Chollop calls upon the new settlers; Mark's free speaking does not please him, and he warns him to restrain it; Martin recovers, after many weeks, and Mark is then taken ill: by these experiences Martin learns the lesson of self-sacrifice and, upon Mark's recovery, consults him in regard to returning home; Martin writes to Mr Bevan for assistance, on receipt of which they start homeward. {34} Martin is introduced to the Honourable Elijah Pogram; Mr Pogram glorifies the institutions of the country, and attributes Martin's dissent to British prejudice; Captain Kedgick is surprised to see the travellers return; Mr Pogram holds a le-Vee by request of a committee of the citizens; meeting of Mrs Hominy and Elijah Pogram; Martin and Mark arrive in New York, find Mr Bevan, and learn that the *Screw* is in port, and ready to sail for England the next day; Mark ships as cook, and so pays their passage, enabling them to do without the assistance of Mr Bevan. {35} Arriving in England, they witness the laying of the corner-stone of a new building, at which Mr Pecksniff, as architect, plays a prominent part; Martin recognises the plan of the building as his own, which he designed when studying with Pecksniff. {36} Tom Pinch starts for London to seek his fortune; he takes leave of Mrs Lupin; arrived in London, he calls upon John Westlock at Furnival's Inn, who is delighted to see him, and insists upon his staying with him; Tom goes to see his sister and, finding her subjected to the incivility of servants and the unjust censure of her employers, he expresses his indignation, and takes her away with him; Tom and Ruth find lodgings at Islington. {37} Tom encounters Miss Charity Pecksniff in the street, and goes with her to Mrs Todgers's, where he meets her sister; Mercy gives Tom a message for old Mr Chuzzlewit; Charity introduces Tom to Mr Moddle; Tom tells John Westlock his story, and returns to Ruth. {38} Mr Nadgett prosecutes his inquiries as ordered by Mr Montague; he reports the result of his investigations in writing to his employer; Jonas calls upon Mr Montague, who keeps Nadgett present at their interview, in which he proposes that Jonas should go deeper into their scheme, and draw in his father-in-law also, and gives Jonas, in a whisper, good reason for complying. {39} Tom Pinch and Ruth commence their house-keeping; how Ruth makes a beefsteak pudding, and how John Westlock happens to witness the operation; John narrates the circumstances of a call he had received from a gentleman who offered Tom, through him, a situation as secretary and librarian, with a yearly salary of one hundred pounds; John and Tom call on Mr Fips, the agent of Tom's employer; Mr Fips shows Tom the place where his work is to be, but declines to give his employer's name; John dines with Tom and his sister, and hears Tom's account of his leaving Pecksniff, and of the changes in Pecksniff's family. {40} Tom enters upon his duties and makes considerable progress, but the mystery of his employer is still unsolved; Tom and Ruth, taking a morning walk near the steamboat wharf, encounter Mrs Gamp, anxiously seeking for 'The Ankworks Package'; Mrs Gamp discovers the persons of whom she is in search, and points them out to Tom; Tom is amazed to see Nadgett at his elbow, making inquiries for the same parties; at Nadgett's request Tom carries the man a letter, and is astonished to recognise Jonas Chuzzlewit; effect of the letter upon Jonas, who drags his wife from the steamer, meets Montague upon the wharf, and drives off with him. {41} Montague threatens Jonas with a disclosure of the secret he possesses, unless he accedes to his demands; Montague proposes that Jonas should entice Pecksniff to invest with them and, at Jonas's request, consents to go with him to Pecksniff's; Jonas lunches with Jobling, and questions him in a careless way about the use of his lancets; the doctor narrates the particulars of a remarkable murder. {42} Journey of the two friends to Salisbury during a violent storm; the carriage is overturned, the horses thrown down, and Jonas attempts to force them upon Montague, who is lying senseless in the road, but is stopped by the driver; Bailey, who accompanies them, receives severe injuries from the accident; Montague resolves to travel home alone. {43} Mrs Lupin, sitting alone in her bar, is accosted by a traveller who inquires for Mark Tapley; the traveller proves to be Mark himself who, accompanied by Martin, has just arrived; they learn from Mrs Lupin the changes in Pecksniff's family, and the influence Pecksniff has acquired over old Mr Chuzzlewit; Martin determines to call upon his grandfather, and sends Mark with a letter requesting leave to wait upon him, which Pecksniff receives at the door, and destroys; Martin, accompanied by Mark, gains admission to Pecksniff's house, and appeals to his grandfather, who allows Pecksniff to answer for him; Martin has an interview with Mary, and hears of Pecksniff's suit for her hand; leaving Pecksniff's house, they meet Jonas going there. {44} Mr Pecksniff receives his son-in-law with tender inquiries for his daughters; Jonas informs Pecksniff of big business, introduces him to Montague, and secures the investment of his capital in their concern; Jonas leaves Montague to complete the arrangements with Pecksniff, and returns to London. {45} Ruth Pinch, waiting for Tom in Fountain Court, is joined by John Westlock, who takes Tom and his sister home to his rooms to dine. {46} Tom relates the occurrences of the morning on the wharf, and Jonas suspects foul play; Tom and Ruth, going to call on Mrs Jonas Chuzzlewit, meet Miss Pecksniff and Mr Moddle, who accompany them; Mrs Gamp makes tea for the company, and admonishes Mr Chuffey; Jonas returns home, is incensed to find Tom there, and forces him to leave the house; Jonas retires to a private room, giving orders that he shall not be disturbed, and under cover of the darkness, and in disguise, escapes from the house by an unfrequented way. {47} Jonas returns to Wiltshire, concealed by his disguise, lies in wait for Montague, waylays him as he is passing through a wood, murders him, and returns by night to London; in the morning Jonas is called by his wife, who informs him that Nadgett had called very early to see him. {48} Tom and Ruth are surprised by a call from Martin and Mark; Martin gives Tom an account of his circumstances, and by his advice they go to consult John Westlock, who receives them with some embarrassment on account of having a visitor; Tom and Mark leave Martin with John and, as they walk along, Mark informs Tom of the settlement he proposes to make in life; John introduces Martin to his visitor, Mr Lewsome, who narrates his instrumentality in the death of Anthony Chuzzlewit, and fixes the responsibility upon Jonas, whom he accuses of his father's murder; Martin and John determine what course to pursue. {49} Mrs Gamp entertains Betsey Prig at her apartment in Kingsgate Street, but that lady showing some unpleasant feeling, and venturing to express a doubt of the existence of Mrs Harris, the friends quarrel and part; John and Martin arrive just at this moment, and learn from Mrs Gamp some particulars in regard to Chuffey. {50} Martin accuses Tom Pinch of unfairness, greatly to Tom's surprise; Ruth tells Tom she has discovered his secret love for Mary; Tom's employer at last appears. {51} Jonas Chuzzlewit thinks to carry out his plan for silencing Mr Chuffey; Mrs Gamp arrives, and is soon followed by old Martin and John Westlock, who are followed by Lewsome and Mark Tapley; Lewsome states all the circumstances relating to Jonas's murder of his father, which Chuffey contradicts, by relating how his old master and himself had discovered Jonas's designs, and that Anthony had died from a broken heart, and not from poison; Jonas, thinking himself cleared by this testimony, orders them from the room, when Nadgett enters with officers, and arrests him for the murder of Montague; Jonas attempts to bribe Slyme, who is one of the officers, to allow him to kill himself, but failing in this, he commits suicide by taking poison as they are carrying him to jail. {52} Mark Tapley waits upon old Martin Chuzzlewit by his request, he admits, in turn, Mr John Westlock, Tom Pinch and his sister, young Martin, and Miss Graham and Mrs Lupin; lastly Mr Pecksniff enters, and reproaches them all for taking advantage of the old man, when the old man strikes him down with his staff; Martin compels Pecksniff to listen to his exposure of his meanness, and to witness his reconciliation with young Martin; Mr Pecksniff takes his departure: Mrs Gamp, Mr Poll Sweedlepipe, and the revived Mr Bailey, appear and disappear for the last time. {53} John Westlock declares his love to Ruth, and finds it reciprocated; happiness of old Martin in the joy of the lovers; he entertains them all at dinner; Miss Pecksniff makes arrangements for her wedding. {54} Mr Chuzzlewit calls upon Mercy at Mrs Todgers's, and invites her to place herself under his care; Mark Tapley welcomes home his old neighbours in Eden; how Mr Augustus Moddle deserted his bride, and Miss Pecksniff was not married; what Tom Pinch saw as time passed on.

12

The Chimes

A Goblin Story of some Bells that Rang an Old Year out, and a New Year in

This, the second of the Christmas books, was brought out in 1844 by Bradbury and Evans. It was illustrated with a frontispiece and title on steel by Daniel Maclise, and with woodcuts from drawings by John Leech, Richard Doyle, and Clarkson Stanfield.

[Note – The figures in braces refer to the 'quarters' into which the tale is divided]

CHARACTERS

BOWLEY, Lady – Wife to Sir Joseph Bowley; a very stately lady. {2}

BOWLEY, Master – Her son, a little gentleman aged twelve. {3}

BOWLEY, Sir Joseph – An old and very stately gentleman, who is a member of parliament, and who prides himself upon being the 'poor man's friend and father'. The poor man in his district he considers his business. 'I endeavour,' he says, 'to educate his mind by inculcating on all occasions the one great moral lesson which that class requires; that is, entire dependence on myself. {2, 3}

CHICKENSTALKER, Mrs Anne – A stout old lady keeper of a shop 'in the general line' who, Toby Veck dreams, is married to Tugby, Sir Joseph Bowley's porter. {2, 4}

CUTE, Alderman – A plain man and a practical man; an easy, affable, joking, knowing fellow, up to everything, and not to be imposed on; one who understands the common people, and has not the least difficulty in dealing with them. Being a justice, he thinks he can 'put down' anything among 'this sort of people', and so sets about putting down the nonsense that is talked about want, and the cant in vogue about starvation; and declares his intention of putting down distressed wives, boys without shoes and stockings, wandering mothers, and indeed all young mothers of all sorts and kinds, all sick persons and young children; and, if there is one thing on which he can be said to have made up his mind more than on another, it is to put suicide down. {1, 3}

FERN, Lilian – An orphan; niece to Will Fern. {2–4}

FERN, Will – A poor but honest man, who only wants 'to live like one of the Almighty's creeturs', but has a bad name, and can't. {2–4}

FILER, Mr – A low-spirited gentleman of middle age, of a meagre habit and a disconsolate face, full of facts and figures, and ready to prove anything by tables; a friend of Alderman Cute. {1st, 3rd quarter}

FISH, Mr – Confidential secretary to Sir Joseph Bowley. {2, 3}

LILIAN – *See* **Fern, Lilian**.

RICHARD – A handsome, well-made, powerful young smith, engaged to Meg Veck. {1, 3, 4}

TUGBY – Porter to Sir Joseph Bowley; afterwards married, as Toby Veck dreams, to Mrs Chickenstalker. {2, 4}

VECK, Margaret – *or* **Meg**. Toby Veck's daughter. {1–4}

VECK, Toby – *called* '**Trotty**' from his pace, 'which meant speed, if it didn't make it'. A ticket-porter. Toby has a great liking for the bells in the church near his station. On Christmas Eve, Toby falls asleep by the fireside while reading a newspaper, and dreams that he is called by the chimes, and so goes up into the church tower, which he finds peopled by dwarf phantoms, spirits, elfin creatures of the bells, of all aspects, shapes, characters, and occupations. As he gazes, the spectres disappear, and he sees in every bell a bearded figure, mysterious and awful, of the bulk and stature of the bell – at once a figure and the bell itself. The Great Bell, or the Goblin of the Great Bell, after arraigning him for sundry instances of wrong-doing, puts him in charge of the Spirit of the Chimes, a little child, who shows him various sorrowful scenes of the future, the actors in which he knows, and some of whom are very near and dear to him. But all these scenes point the same moral – 'that we must trust and hope, and neither doubt ourselves, nor the good in one another'. And when Toby breaks the spell that binds him, and wakes up suddenly with a leap that brings him upon his feet, he is beside himself with joy to find that the chimes are merrily ringing in the New Year, and that all the sin and shame and suffering and desperation which he has witnessed is but the baseless fabric of a vision. The lesson is not forgotten, however, and the New Year is made all the happier by his troubled dream.

The little visitor ran into her arms – Hugh Thomson

D. Maclise, R.A. del.

The Chimes frontispeice – Daniel Maclise

13

The Cricket on the Hearth

A Fairy Tale of Home

Published in 1845, inscribed to Lord Jeffrey, and illustrated with a frontispiece and title page by Maclise, and woodcuts from drawings by Doyle, Leech, Clarkson Stanfield, and Landseer.

[Note – The figures in braces refer to the 'chirps' into which the tale is divided]

CHARACTERS

BOXER – John Peerybingle's dog. {1–3}

DOT – *See* **Peerybingle, Mrs Mary.**

FIELDING, May – A friend of Mrs Peerybingle. She is over-persuaded into consenting to bestow her hand upon Tackleton, a surly, sordid, grinding old man; but, on the morning of the day appointed for the wedding, she marries Edward Plummer, a former lover, who suddenly returns after a long absence, and whom she has believed to be dead. {2, 3}

FIELDING, Mrs – Her mother; a little, querulous chip of an old lady, with a peevish face, who is considered to have a most transcendent figure, in right of having preserved a waist like a bedpost. She is very genteel and patronising, in consequence of having once been better off, or of labouring under an impression that she might have been, if something had happened (in the indigo trade) which never did happen, and seemed to have never been particularly likely to happen. {2, 3}

PEERYBINGLE, John – A large, sturdy man, much older than his wife, but 'the best, the most considerate, the most affectionate of husbands' to her. {1–3}

PEERYBINGLE, Mrs Mary – *called* '**Dot**' from her small size. John's wife, a blooming young woman, with a very doll of a baby. {1–3}

PLUMMER, Caleb – A poor toymaker in the employ of Tackleton; a

Well! if you'll believe me they have not been dancing five minutes, when suddenly the Carrier flings his pipe away, takes Dot round the waist, dashes out into the room, and starts off with her, toe and heel, quite wonderfully. Tackleton no sooner sees this, than he skims across to Mrs Fielding, takes her round the waist, and follows suit. Old Dot no sooner sees this, than up he is, all alive, whisks off Mrs Dot in the middle of the dance, and is the foremost there. Caleb no sooner sees this, than he clutches Tilly Slowboy by both hands and goes off at score; Miss Slowboy, firm in the belief that diving hotly in among the other couples, and effecting any number of concussions with them, is your only principle of footing it.

spare, dejected, thoughtful, gray-haired old man, wholly devoted to his blind daughter. {1–3}

PLUMMER, Bertha – His daughter, a blind girl. With her father, she lives in 'a little cracked nutshell of a wooden house, ... stuck to the premises of Gruff and Tackleton like a barnacle to a ship's keel'. Her father deceives her into thinking that the house and furnishing are of quality, and that the dreadful Tackleton is a jolly benefactor. The consequence of this well-meant but ill-judged deception is that Bertha comes secretly to love Tackleton with unspeakable affection and gratitude, and is nearly heartbroken on finding that he means to marry May Fielding. This compels her father to tell her the truth; to confer that he has altered objects, changed the characters of people, invented many things that never have been, to make her happier. The shock to her sensitive nature is great; but instead of losing her confidence in him she clings to him all the more closely, and cherishes him all the more devotedly for his innocent deceit, springing from motives so pure and unselfish. {2, 3}

PLUMMER, Edward – Son to Caleb, and brother to Bertha Plummer. After a long absence in the 'Golden South Americas', he returns to claim the hand of May Fielding, to whom he had been engaged before leaving home. Hearing, when twenty miles away, that she has proved false to him, and is about to marry old Tackleton, he disguises himself as an old man, for the sake of observing and judging for himself, in order to get at the real and exact truth. He makes himself known to Mrs Peerybingle ('Dot'), who advises him to keep his secret close, and not even to let Mr Peerybingle know it, he being much too open in his nature, and too inexperienced in all artifice to keep it for him. She also offers to sound his sweetheart, and to bring them together, which she does, and has the pleasure of seeing them married, and of expressing a hope that Tackleton may die a bachelor. Her mediation, however, becomes known, in part, to her husband, who misconstrues her actions, and suspects her of being untrue to himself. But in the end everything is satisfactorily explained, and everybody is made happy; while even the kettle hums for joy, and the cricket joins the music with its 'Chirp, chirp, chirp'. {1–3}

SLOWBOY, Tilly – Mrs Peerybingle's nurserymaid; a great, clumsy girl, who is very apt to hold the baby topsy-turvy, and who has a habit of mechanically reproducing, for its entertainment, scraps of current conversation, with all the sense struck out of them, and all the nouns changed into the plural number, as when she asks: 'Was it Gruffs and Tackletons the toy makers, then?' and, 'Would it call at pastry-cooks for wedding cakes?' and 'Did its mothers know the boxes when its fathers brought them home?' and so on. {1–3}

TACKLETON – *called* '**Gruff and Tackleton**'. A toy merchant, stern, ill-natured, and sarcastic, with one eye always wide open, and one eye nearly shut. After the marriage of his betrothed, May Fielding, to Edward Plummer, he turns his disappointment to good account by resolving thenceforth to be, and by actually becoming, a pleasant, hearty, kind, and happy man. {1–3}

14

The Battle of Life

A Love Story

Published in 1846, with a frontispiece and title page engraved on wood from drawings by Maclise, and with woodcuts inserted in the text, from designs by Doyle, Leech, and Stanfield.

[Note – The figures in braces refer to the parts of the story]

CHARACTERS

BRITAIN, Benjamin – *called* 'Little Britain'. A small man with an uncommonly sour and discontented face; servant to Doctor Jeddler, afterwards husband of Clemency Newcome, and landlord of The Nutmeg Grater Inn. He gives this summary of his general condition: 'I don't know anything; I don't care for anything; I don't make out anything; I don't believe anything; and I don't want anything'. {1–2}

CRAGGS, Mr Thomas – Attorney-at-law and partner of Jonathan Snitchey. He seems to be represented by Snitchey, and to be conscious of little or no separate existence or personal individuality. {1, 2}

CRAGGS, Mrs – His wife. {2}

HEATHFIELD, Alfred – A young medical student; a ward of Doctor Jeddler, and engaged to his younger daughter Marion. On coming of age, he starts on a three years' tour among the foreign schools of medicine. In the very hour of his return Marion flees from home eloping, as it is supposed, with a young spendthrift named Michael Warden. After a time, her elder sister Grace becomes Alfred's wife; it finally transpires that Marion, though deeply loving him, discovers that Grace also loves him and, deeming herself to be less worthy of such a husband, sacrifices her own happiness to insure her sister's. But, instead of eloping with young Warden, she retires to an aunt's, who lives at a distance, where she remains secluded

This village inn had assumed, on being established, an uncommon sign. It was called the Nutmeg Grater. And underneath that household word, was inscribed, up in the tree, on the same flaming board, and in the like golden characters, By Benjamin Britain. At a second glance, and on a more minute examination of his face, you might have known that it was no other than Benjamin Britain himself who stood in the doorway – reasonably changed by time, but for the better; a very comfortable host indeed.

until after her sister's marriage has taken place. {1–3}

JEDDLER, Doctor Anthony – A great philosopher, the heart and mystery of whose philosophy is to look upon the world as a gigantic practical joke, or as something too absurd to be considered seriously by any practical man. But the loss of his favourite daughter, 'the absence of one little unit in the great absurd account' strikes him to the ground, and shows him how serious the world is, 'in which some love, deep-anchored, is the portion of all human creatures'. {1–3}

JEDDLER, Grace – His elder daughter; married to Alfred Heathfield. {1–3}

JEDDLER, Marion – His younger daughter. {Parts 1–3}

MARTHA, Aunt – Sister to Doctor Jeddler. {Part 3}

NEWCOME, Clemency – Servant to Doctor Jeddler; afterwards married to Benjamin Britain. {Parts 1–3}

SNITCHEY, Jonathan – Attorney-at-law and partner of Thomas Craggs. {1–3}

SNITCHEY, Mrs – His wife. {2}

WARDEN, Michael – A client of Messrs. Snitchey and Craggs; a man of thirty, who has sown a good many wild oats, and finds his affairs to be in a bad way in consequence. He repents, however, and reforms, and finally marries Marion Jeddler, whom he has long loved. {2, 3}

15

Dombey and Son

On 1 October 1846, Messrs Bradbury and Evans issued the first number of a new serial novel under the title of 'Dealings with the Firm of Dombey and Son, Wholesale, Retail, and for Exportation'. Each part was illustrated with two engravings on steel by Phiz. The publication of the work extended over twenty months; and on its completion, in 1848, it was brought out in a single octavo volume, and was 'Dedicated with great esteem to the Marchioness of Normanby'.

CHARACTERS

ANNE – A housemaid at Mr Dombey's, beloved by Towlinson, the footman. {18, 31, 35, 59}

BAGSTOCK, Major Joseph – A retired army officer, wooden-featured and blue-faced, with his eyes starting out of his head. He is a near neighbour of Miss Tox, between whom and himself an occasional interchange of newspapers and pamphlets, and the like Platonic dalliance, is effected through the medium of a dark servant of the major's, whom Miss Tox is content to designate as a 'native', without connecting him with any geographical idea whatever. The Major becomes a friend and companion of Mr Dombey, introduces him to Edith Granger and Mrs Skewton, and plays the agreeable to the mother, while Mr Dombey makes love to the daughter. {7, 10, 20, 21, 26, 27, 31, 36, 40, 51, 59, 60}

BAPS, Mr – Dancing-master at Doctor Blimber's; a very grave gentleman with a slow and measured manner of speaking. {14}

BAPS, Mrs – His wife. {14}

BERINTHIA – *called* 'Berry'. Niece and drudge to Mrs Pipchin, whom she regards as one of the most meritorious persons in the world. She is a good-natured spinster of middle age, but possessing a gaunt and iron-bound aspect, and much afflicted with boils on her nose. {8, 11}

BILER – *See* **Toodle, Robin**.

BITHERSTON, Master – A child boarding at Mrs Pipchin's; a boy of mysterious and terrible experiences. {8, 10, 41, 60}

BLIMBER, Doctor – Proprietor of an expensive private boarding-school for boys, at Brighton, to which Paul Dombey is sent to be educated. {11, 12, 19, 24, 41, 60}

BLIMBER, Mrs – His wife. {11, 12, 19, 24, 41, 60}

BLIMBER, Miss Cornelia – The daughter; a slim and graceful maid. {11, 12, 14, 41, 60}

BLOCKITT, Mrs – Mrs Dombey's nurse; a simpering piece of faded gentility. {1}

BOKUM, Mrs – A friend of Mrs MacStinger's, and her bridesmaid on the occasion of her marriage to Jack Bunsby. {60}

BRIGGS – A pupil of Doctor Blimber's, and the room-mate of Paul Dombey. {12, 14, 41, 60}

BROGLEY, Mr – A sworn broker and appraiser, and second-hand furniture dealer; a friend of Sol Gills. {9}

BROWN, Alice – *alias* **Alice Marwood**. A handsome woman of about thirty years of age; a former mistress of James Carker. After suffering transportation for crime, she comes back to England filled with scorn, hate, defiance, and recklessness. {33, 34, 40, 46, 52, 53, 58}

BROWN, Mrs – *called* (by herself) '**Good Mrs Brown**'. Her mother; a very ugly old woman, with red rims round her eyes, and a mouth that mumbled and chattered of itself when she was not speaking. {6, 27, 34, 40, 46, 52, 58}

BUNSBY, Captain Jack – Master of a vessel called the *Cautious Clara*, and a warm friend of Captain Cuttle, who looks up to him as an oracle. Fearing that the vessel on which her friend Walter Gay has taken passage is lost, Florence Dombey, accompanied by her maid Susan Nipper, goes to Captain Cuttle for advice. Walter's uncle, Sol Gills, is also very much distressed about his nephew; and the captain, being a friend of all parties, tries to reassure them. Not being quite equal to the occasion, however, he fortunately bethinks himself of Jack Bunsby. They accordingly go to see Captain Bunsby and, under the pilotage of Captain Cuttle, board the *Cautious Clara*. He finally consents to go with them, however, and at last delivers his 'opinion'. Notwithstanding his sagacity and independence, Captain Bunsby is finally captured and married, perforce, by his landlady, Mrs MacStinger. {28, 39, 60}

CARKER, Harriet – Sister of John and James Carker; afterwards the wife of Mr Morfin. {22, 33, 34, 53, 62}

CARKER, James – Mr Dombey's head clerk or manager. Enjoying the confidence of his employer, Mr Carker speculates on his own account, and amasses a fortune. When Mr Dombey marries a second time, Carker observes that there is no love or sympathy in the case, and that both parties are of a proud and unyielding disposition; and he secretly takes advantage of the confidence reposed in him by Mr Dombey to increase the constantly widening breach between husband and wife. Goaded to desperation by the conduct of Mr Dombey in making his manager the medium of communicating his directions to her, but equally despising both man and master, Mrs Dombey revenges herself on her husband by eloping with Carker, and on Carker by taunting him with his supposed victory, and leaving him, in the very hour of his anticipated triumph, to the vengeance of her husband, who has pursued them. In trying to avoid Mr Dombey, whom he accidentally encounters at a railway-station, he staggers, slips on to the line, and is killed by a passing train. {13, 17, 22, 24, 26, 27, 31, 33, 36, 37, 40, 42, 45–47, 52–55}

CARKER, Mr John – Brother of James and Harriet Carker, and a junior clerk at Dombey and Son's. When a young man, he had been led astray by evil companions, and had robbed his employers, who had reposed great confidence in him. His guilt was soon discovered ; but the house was merciful and, instead of dismissing him, retained him in a subordinate capacity, in which he made expiation for his crime by long years of patient, faithful service. After the elopement of his brother James with Edith Dombey, he is discharged; but, by the sudden death of his brother, he comes into possession of a fortune, the interest of which, when Mr Dombey becomes a bankrupt, he secretly makes over to him year by year as if it were the repayment of an old lost debt. {6, 19, 22, 33, 34, 53, 58, 62}

CHICK, Mr John – Brother-in-law to Mr Dombey; a stout, bald gentleman with a very large face, and his hands continually in his pockets, and with a tendency to whistle and hum tunes on every sort of occasion. {2, 5, 29, 36}

*Doctor Blimber's young gentlemen as they
appeared when enjoying themselves –*
Hablot K Browne *alias* Phiz

CHICK, Mrs Louisa – His wife; sister to Mr Dombey; a weak, good-natured, self-satisfied woman, very proud of her family and of having always tried, as she puts it, to 'make an effort'. {1, 2, 5–8, 10, 18, 29, 36, 51, 59}

CHICKEN, The Game – *See* **Game Chicken, The**.

CHOWLEY – *See* **MacStinger, Charles**.

CLARK, Mr – A clerk of Mr Dombey's. {6}

CLEOPATRA – *See* **Skewton, Mrs**.

CUTTLE, Captain Edward – Protector of Florence Dombey, friend of Walter Gay, and friend and afterwards partner of Walter's uncle, Sol Gills. His first advent in the story is at the house of the latter at dinner-time. Walter having been selected by his employer to fill a junior situation in the counting-house at Barbadoes, a meeting of a few friends takes place at his uncle's at which Captain Cuttle is present. Old Sol and the Captain accompany the lad on board the ship to see him off, the former with moist eyes, the latter with a very grave face. {4, 9, 10, 15, 17, 19, 23, 25, 32, 39, 48–50, 56, 57, 60, 62}

DAWS, Mary – A young kitchen maid in Mr Dombey's service. {59}

DIOGENES – A dog given by Mr Toots to Florence Dombey 'as a sort of keepsake', he having been a favourite with her brother, little Paul. {14, 18, 22, 23, 28, 30, 31, 35, 41, 41v, 48–50, 56, 62}

DOMBEY, Mrs Edith – Mr Dombey's second wife; daughter of Mrs Skewton, and widow of Colonel Granger She is a woman under thirty, very handsome, very haughty and very wilful; pure at heart, but defiant of criticism. Though she feels neither love nor esteem for Mr Dombey, and does not tempt him to seek her hand, yet she suffers him to marry her, content to be made rich so long as the transaction is understood to be a mere matter of traffic, in which beauty, grace, and varied accomplishments are exchanged for wealth and social position. As might be expected, the alliance proves to be a very unfortunate one. No friendship, no fitness for each other, no mutual forbearance, springs up between the unhappy pair; but indifference gives place to aversion and contempt; arrogance is repaid in kind; opposition arouses opposition. At last, Edith elopes with Mr Carker, a confidential clerk of Mr Dombey's; and this she does with the double motive of revenging herself on her husband, and of befooling and punishing the clerk, who has pursued her from her wedding-day with humiliating solicitations and the meanest stratagems. But she leaves him in the very hour of their meeting, and he is killed by a passing train in trying to escape pursuit. {21, 26–28, 30, 31, 35–37, 40–43, 45, 47, 54, 61}

DOMBEY, Mrs Fanny – Mr Dombey's first wife; mother of Florence and of little Paul. {1}

DOMBEY, Florence – Daughter of Mr Dombey, and sister of little Paul. She is a loving and lovable child but, not having had the good fortune to be born a boy, is of no account in her father's eyes. At first she is merely an object of indifference to him, but by degrees he comes to conceive a positive dislike for her, and at last drives her from his house. She finally marries Walter Gay. {1, 3, 5, 6, 8–12, 14, 16, 18, 19, 22–24, 28, 30, 35–37, 40, 41, 43–45, 47–50, 56, 57, 59, 61, 62}

DOMBEY, Little Paul – Mr Dombey's son and heir. Little Paul's mother dies in giving birth, and he himself is but a weakling. Mr Dombey becomes uneasy about this odd boy, and sends him to Brighton to board with an old lady named Pipchin, who has acquired an immense reputation as a manager of children. But little Paul grows more old-fashioned than ever, without growing any stronger; and his father, bent on his learning everything, and being brought forward rapidly, resolves to make a change, and accordingly enrols him as a student in Dr Blimber's educational establishment, which is conducted on the hothouse or forcing principle. His health continues to fail, however, and at last he is taken home to die. {1–3, 5–8, 10–12, 14, 16}

DOMBEY, Mr Paul – A London merchant, very wealthy, very starched and pompous, intensely obstinate, and possessed by a conviction that the house of Dombey and Son is the central fact of the universe. He has a daughter Florence, who is of no consequence in his eyes; and a son Paul, on whom all his hopes and affections centre, but who dies in childhood. He marries for his second wife a woman whose pride is equal to his own, and who not only has no love to give him, but refuses to render him the deference and submission which he exacts as his due. Goaded to desperation, at last, by his arrogance, and by the slights and affronts he puts upon her, she elopes, upon the anniversary of her marriage, with Mr Carker, Mr Dombey's manager, whom he had chosen as an instrument of her humiliation, content to wear the appearance of an adulteress (though not such in reality), if she can only avenge herself upon her husband. But Mr Dombey, though keenly sensitive to the disgrace she has inflicted upon him, and haunted by the dread of public ridicule, abates no jot of his pride or obstinacy. He drives his daughter from his house, believing her to be an accomplice of his wife, forbids the name of either to be mentioned in his presence, and preserves the same calm, cold, impenetrable exterior as ever. His trouble preys upon his mind, however; his prudence in matters of business deserts him; and the great house of which he is the head soon goes down in utter bankruptcy. But this crowning retribution proves a blessing after all; for it undermines his pride, melts his obstinacy, and sets his injustice plainly before him. His daughter seeks him out, and in her home he passes the evening of his days, a wiser and a better man. {1–3, 5, 6, 8, 10, 11, 13, 16, 18, 20, 21, 26–28, 30, 31, 35, 36, 40–44, 47, 51, 52, 55, 58, 59, 61, 62}

FEEDER, Reverend Alfred, M A – A brother of Mr Feeder, BA. {60}

FEEDER, Mr, B A – An assistant in the establishment of Blimber; afterwards his son-in-law and successor. {11, 12, 14, 41, 60}

FEENIX, Cousin – A superannuated nobleman, nephew to the Honourable Mrs Skewton, and cousin to Edith Dombey. {31, 36, 41, 51, 61}

FLOWERS – Mrs Skewton's maid. {27, 30, 35–37, 40}

GAME CHICKEN, The – A professional boxer and prize-fighter, with very short hair, a broken nose, and a considerable tract of bare and sterile country behind each ear. He is a friend of Mr Toots, whom he knocks about the head three times a week for the small consideration of ten and six per visit. {22, 28, 32, 41, 44, 56}

GAY, Walter – A young man in the employ of Mr Dombey; nephew to Sol Gills. He makes the acquaintance of Florence Dombey, and falls in love with her, but is soon afterward sent to Barbadoes to fill a junior situation in the counting-house there. The ship in which he sails is lost at sea, and it is long thought that he went down with her; but he finally returns and marries Florence. {4, 6, 9, 10, 13, 15–17, 19, 49, 50, 56, 57, 61}

GILLS, Solomon – A nautical instrument maker uncle to Walter Gay. When he hears of the loss of the ship in which his nephew has sailed, he goes abroad in quest of him, leaving his shop in the hands of Captain Cuttle. {4, 6, 9, 10, 15, 17, 19, 22, 23, 25, 56, 57, 62}

GLUBB, Old – An old man employed to draw little Paul Dombey's couch. {12}

GRANGER, Mrs Edith – *See* **Dombey, Mrs Edith**.

HOWLER, The Reverend Melchisedech – A minister 'of the ranting persuasion', who predicts the speedy destruction of the world. He was formerly employed in the West India Docks, but was 'discharged on suspicion of screwing gimlets into puncheons, and applying his lips to the orifice'. {15, 60}

JEMIMA – Mrs Toodle's unmarried sister, who lives with her and helps her take care of the children. {2, 6}

JOE – A labourer. {6}

JOHN – A poor man with no regular employment; father of Martha, a deformed and sickly girl. {24}

JOHNSON – A pupil of Doctor Blimber's. {12, 14}

KATE – An orphan child, visiting Sir Barnet and Lady Skettles, at Fulham, with her aunt, during Florence Dombey's stay them. {25}

MacSTINGER, Alexander – Son of Mrs MacStinger, aged two years and three months. His mother never enters upon any action of importance without previously inverting him to bring him within range of a brisk battery of slaps, and then setting him down on the street pavement; a cool paving-stone being usually found to act as a powerful restorative. {23, 21, 29, 60}

MacSTINGER, Charles – *called* 'Chowley' by his play-mates. Another son of Mrs MacStinger. {39, 60}

MacSTINGER, Juliana – Mrs MacStinger's daughter; the very picture of her mother. 'Another year or two, the captain [Captain Cuttle] thought, and to lodge where that child was would be destruction' {25, 29, 60}

MacSTINGER, Mrs – Captain Cuttle's landlady; a vixenish widow, living at No 9, Brig Place, near the India Docks. She exhibits a disposition to retain her lodgers by physical force, if necessary. The captain stands in mortal fear of her; though, as he says, he 'never owed her a penny', and has 'done her a world of good turns too'. Circumstances, however, occur, that make it absolutely necessary for him to remove to another part of the city; and, as he dare not acquaint her with the fact, he resorts to stratagem to effect his purpose. The brave old salt takes great precautions against discovery and recapture; but Mrs MacStinger finds him out at last, and descends upon him while he is engaged in a consultation with his friend Jack Bunsby. The captain tries to effect his escape, but in vain; for he is stopped by the little MacStingers, who cling to his legs with loud screams of recognition. The gallant captain is relieved, however, by Bunsby, who diverts the widow's attention from his friend, and soothes and softens her by a little delicate flattery, and by offering to 'conwoy' her home, which he does, returning, after some hours, with the captain's chest, which is held to imply a relinquishment of any further claims upon the owner by his late landlady. Mrs MacStinger subsequently marries Captain Bunsby. {9, 17, 23, 25, 39, 56, 60}

MARTHA – The daughter of a poor labouring man, who finds it very difficult to get work to do. She is ugly, misshapen, peevish, ill-conditioned, ragged, and dirty, but dearly loved by her father, John, who makes his own life miserable to add to her comfort. {24}

MARWOOD, Alice – *See* **Brown, Alice**.

'MELIA – A servant-girl at Doctor Blimber's. {12, 14, 41}

MIFF, Mrs – A wheezy little pew-opener; a mighty dry old lady, with a vinegary face, an air of mystery, and a thirsty soul for sixpences and shillings. {31, 57}

MORFIN, Mr – Head clerk to Dombey and Son; a cheerful-looking, hazel-eyed, elderly bachelor, who befriends John Carker, and eventually marries his sister Harriet. {13, 33, 53, 58, 62}

NATIVE, The – A dark servant of Major Bagstock's, so called by Miss Tox, though without connecting him with any geographical idea whatever. He has no particular name, but answers to any vituperative epithet. {7, 10, 20, 21, 26, 27, 29, 58, 59}

NIPPER, Susan – Florence Dombey's maid; a short, brown, womanly girl, with a little snub nose and black eyes like jet beads. Notwithstanding a peculiarly sharp and biting manner, she is, in the main, a good-natured little body, and is wholly devoted to her mistress. She has the audacity to tell Mr Dombey what she thinks of his treatment of his daughter, and is immediately discharged from that gentleman's service. She afterwards marries Mr Toots, who considers her 'a most extraordinary woman'. {3, 5, 6, 13, 15, 16, 18, 19, 22, 23, 28, 32, 43, 44, 56, 57, 60–62}

PANKEY, Miss – A boarder at Mrs Pipchin's; 'select infantine boarding-house', worth 'a good eighty pounds a year' to her. {8, 11}

PAUL, Little – *See* **Dombey, Little Paul**.

PEPS, Doctor Parker – One of the court physicians, and a man of immense reputation for assisting at the increase of great families, on which account his services are secured by Mr Dombey when little Paul is born. {1, 16}

PERCH, Mr – Messenger in Mr Dombey's office, living (when at home) at Balls Pond. {13, 17, 22, 24, 31, 46, 51, 53, 58, 59}

PERCH, Mrs – His wife, always in an interesting condition. {13, 22, 31, 35, 51, 53, 58, 59}

PILKINS, Mr – Mr Dombey's family physician. {1, 8}

PIPCHIN, Mrs – An old lady living at Brighton, with whom little Paul Dombey, accompanied by his sister Florence and a nurse, is sent to board. She afterwards becomes Mr Dombey's housekeeper.

RICHARDS – *See* **Toodle, Polly.**

ROB THE GRINDER – *See* **Toodle, Robin.**

SKETTLES, Lady – The wife of Sir Barnet Skettles. {14, 23, 24, 28, 60}

SKETTLES, Sir Barnet – A member of the House of Commons, living in a pretty villa at Fulham, on the banks of the Thames. It was anticipated that, when he did catch the speaker's eye (which he had been expected to do for three or four years), he would rather touch up the Radicals. His object in life is constantly to extend the range of his acquaintance. {14, 23, 24, 28, 60}

SKETTLES, Barnet, Junior – His son; a pupil of Doctor Blimber's. {14, 24, 28}

SKEWTON, The Hon. Mrs – *called* 'Cleopatra', from the name appended to a sketch of her published in her youth. Aunt to Lord Feenix, and mother to Edith Dombey. An old lady, who was once a belle, and who still retains, at the age of seventy, the juvenility of dress, the coquettishness of manner, and the affectation of speech which distinguished her fifty years before. She parades her fair daughter through all the fashionable resorts in England in order to sell her to the highest bidder. She succeeds in making a very 'advantageous match' for her, but dies soon after of paralysis. {21, 26–28, 30, 35–37, 40, 41}

SOWNDS – A portentous beadle, orthodox and corpulent, who spends the greater part of his time sitting in the sun, on the church steps or, in cold weather, by the fire. {5, 31, 57}

TOODLE, Mr – Husband to Polly Toodle, and father to 'Rob the Grinder'. He is at first a stoker, but afterwards becomes an engine-driver. {2, 15, 20, 59}

TOODLE, Mrs Polly – *called* '**Richards**' by Mr Dombey and his family. His wife; foster-mother of little Paul Dombey; a plump, rosy-cheeked, wholesome, apple-faced young woman with five children of her own, one of them being a nursing infant. {2, 3, 5–7, 15, 16, 22, 38, 56, 59}

TOODLE, Robin – *called by the family* '**Biler**' (in remembrance of the steam-engine), *otherwise styled* '**Rob the Grinder**'. Their son, nominated by Mr Dombey to a vacancy in the establishment of 'The Charitable Grinders'; but the child meets with so much badgering from the boys in the street, and so much abuse from the master of the school, that he runs away. He afterwards becomes the spy and instrument of Mr Carker, and finally enters the service of Miss Tox with a view to his 'restoration to respectability'. {2, 5, 6, 20, 22, 23, 25, 31, 32, 38, 39, 42, 46, 52, 59}

TOOTS, Mr P – The eldest of Doctor Blimber's pupils; a wealthy young gentleman, with swollen nose and excessively large head, of whom people did say that the doctor had rather overdone it with young Toots, and that, when he began to have whiskers, he left off having brains. Having license to pursue his own course of study, he occupies his time chiefly in writing long letters to himself from persons of distinction, addressed 'P Toots, Esq, Brighton, Sussex', which he preserves in his desk with great care. His personal appearance takes a great deal of his attention, and he prides himself especially upon his tailors, Burgess and Co, as being 'fash'nable, but very dear'. His conversational ability is not remarkable; but his deep voice, his sheepish manner, and his stock phrases – of which 'It's of no consequence' is the most usual – are particularly noteworthy. Of his intellectual and social deficiencies he is by no means ignorant, however. 'I am not what is considered a quick sort of a person', he says: 'I am perfectly aware of that. I don't think anybody could be better acquainted with his own – if it was not too strong an expression, I should say with the thickness of his own head than myself'. Mr Toots conceives so strong a passion for Miss Florence Dombey, that he is – to use his own words – 'perfectly sore with loving her'. His attentions however are not encouraged, and he comes very downhearted. 'I KNOW I'm wasting away', he says to Captain Cuttle. 'Burgess and Co. have altered my measure, I'm in that state of thinness. If you could see my legs when I take my boots off, you'd form some idea what unrequited affection is'. He recovers his health and spirits, however, after no long time, and consoles

Rob the grinder reading to Captain Cuttle –
Hablot K Browne *alias* Phiz

himself for the loss of Miss Dombey by marrying her maid, Miss Susan Nipper. The result of this union is a large family of children. After the birth of the third, Mr Toots betakes himself to the 'Wooden Midshipman' to give information of the happy event to his friend Captain Cuttle, whom he always misnames Captain Gills. {11, 12, 14, 18, 22, 28, 31, 32, 39, 41, 45, 48, 50, 56, 57, 60, 62}

TOOTS, Mrs – *See* **Nipper, Susan**.

TOWLINSON, Thomas – Mr Dombey's footman. {5, 18, 20, 28, 31, 35, 44, 51, 59}

TOX, Miss Lucretia – A friend of Mrs Chick's, greatly admired by Major Bagstock. After the death of the first Mrs Dombey, Miss Tox has a modest ambition to succeed her, but, failing of doing so, her regard for Mr Dombey becomes severely platonic. {1, 2, 5–8, 10, 18, 20, 29, 36, 38, 51, 59, 62}

TOZER – A room-mate of Paul Dombey's at Doctor Blimber's; a solemn young gentleman whose shirt-collar curls up the lobes of his ears. {12, 14, 41, 60}

WICKAM, Mrs – A waiter's wife (which would seem equivalent to being any other man's widow), and little Paul Dombey's nurse. {8, 11, 12, 18, 58}

WITHERS – Page to Mrs Skewton; tall, and thin. {21, 25, 27, 30, 37, 40}

PRINCIPAL INCIDENTS

{1} Mr Dombey expresses his gratification at the birth of a son, and receives the congratulations of his sister, Mrs Chick; his sister's friend, Miss Tox, presents her offering; Mrs Dombey, not being able to make the effort urged by Mrs Chick, gradually fails, and dies clinging to her daughter. {2} Mrs Chick exerts herself to provide a wet-nurse for little Paul; Miss Tox also interests herself in the matter, and introduces the Toodle family; Mrs Toodle, as Richards, is engaged. {3} Florence hears from Richards the story of her mother's death; Susan Nipper makes her first appearance; Richards, by a little management, brings the children constantly together. {4} Solomon Gills, on the occasion of his nephew's entering the employ of Dombey and Son, produces a bottle of choice Madeira; Captain Cuttle joins the party, and they drink to Dombey and Son, and Daughter. {5} Mrs Chick and Miss Tox enjoy a social evening in the nursery, to the disgust of Miss Nipper; little Paul is christened, Miss Tox being one of the sponsors; chilling effect of the christening

Mr Toots becomes particular – Diogenes also.
Hablot K Browne *alias* Phiz

collation; Mr Dombey shows his regard for Richards by appointing Biler a 'Charitable Grinder'. {6} Richards and Susan take the children to Staggs's Gardens, the home of the Toodles; returning home, Richards discovers Biler in trouble, and goes to his rescue; an alarm of 'Mad Bull' is raised, and the party gets separated; Florence is picked up by Good Mrs Brown, who robs her of her clothing and turns her into the streets in rags; she is found by Walter Gay, who takes her to his uncle's, and goes to Mr Dombey with the news of her safety, which her father receives quite indifferently; Richards is discharged. {7} Major Joe Bagstock finds himself superseded in the notice of Miss Tox. {8} Little Paul, grown to the age of five years, surprises his father by his questions about money; Paul not being strong and well, the doctor recommends sea-air, and he and Florence are sent to Mrs Pipchin's, at Brighton; Paul is impolite to Mrs Pipchin; Mrs Wickam expresses some superstitions fears in regard to him; Paul asks Florence what the waves are always saying. {9} Walter notices a change in Uncle Sol, and tries to cheer him up; returning from the office one day, he is astonished to find that Mr Brogley, a broker, has taken possession of the stock for debt; Walter looks up Captain Cuttle, whom he has some trouble in coming at on account of the perverseness of his landlady, Mrs MacStinger; the captain takes the matter into consideration, and advises applying to Mr Dombey for a loan, and he and Walter set off to Brighton for that purpose. {10} Major Bagstock traces the cause of Miss Tox's reserve to her devotion to the Dombeys, and goes to Brighton, where he throws himself in Mr Dombey's way, and makes his acquaintance; Walter, supported by Captain Cuttle, makes his application to Mr Dombey; the captain presents his valuables as security; Mr Dombey, through Paul, lends the required amount to Mr Gills. {11} Mr Dombey decides to remove Paul from Mrs Pipchin's to Doctor Blimber's; Doctor Blimber's establishment, and its methods of teaching; Mr Dombey, accompanied by Florence and Mrs Pipchin, takes Paul to Doctor Blimber's, where he is introduced to the family of that learned gentleman, and where he is left to be subjected to the forcing process for which that establishment is celebrated. {12} Miss Blimber takes Paul in hand; Mr Toots shows his good will; Miss Blimber starts Paul in his course of study; Florence obtains the books which contain Paul's lessons, and assists him in their preparation; Mr Toots continues to interest himself in Paul. {13} The deference paid to Mr Dombey by those in and around his office; Mr Carker the manager informs Mr Dombey of a vacancy in their agency at Barbadoes, and he decides to send Walter Gay to fill it; Walter hears a conversation between the brothers James and John Carker, in which the position of the latter is defined; Mr John Carker tells Walter the story of his temptation and fall. {14} Miss Blimber prepares an analysis of Paul's character; Paul grows more and more old-fashioned; he receives his invitation to Doctor and Mrs Blimber's 'early party'; he has a fainting fit in Mr Feeder's room, and by the Doctor's advice is relieved from his studies; Paul collects all his little possessions for taking home; at the Blimbers's party, Paul receives the kindest attentions from all present, and Florence becomes a universal favourite; they all show their fondness for Paul at his departure, and he finally reaches home. {15} Walter makes up his mind to inform his uncle of the Barbadoes project, and goes to Captain Cuttle to get him to break the news to Sol Gills; the captain, in consideration of the matter, 'bites his nails a bit', and finally decides to see Mr Dombey and talk it over with him; Walter, walking about to give the captain time to break the news to Sol Gills, is overtaken by Susan Nipper in a coach, in search of Staggs's Gardens and Mrs Toodle; he helps her to find Richards, and returns with them to Mr Dombey's house, where he is called in. {16} Little Paul, grown more and more feeble, begs to see his old nurse and Walter, and dies with his arms round Florence's neck. {17} Not seeing Mr Dombey at home, Captain Cattle goes to the office of Dombey and Son, and calls on Mr Carker the manager; the captain explains his view of the case to Carker, and his aspirations in connection with Walter and Florence, which Mr Carker takes pains to strengthen, and the captain is fully satisfied that he 'has done a little business for the youngsters'. {18} Funeral of little Paul, and Mr Dombey's indifference to Florence; Mrs Chick and Miss Tox attempt to console Florence; Sir Barnet and Lady Skettles invite Florence to visit them, but she prefers to remain at home; Mr Dombey grows more and more cold towards his daughter; Mr Toots calls upon Florence, and brings Diogenes, the dog of which Paul was so fond at Doctor Blimber's; Susan informs Florence that her father is to leave home on the morrow, in company with Major Bagstock; Florence goes to her father's room, and tries to excite his affection and sympathy, but finds him still cold and reserved. {19} Walter prepares to go away, and is giving his uncle a message for Florence, when she and Susan enter the shop; Florence and Walter take leave of each other, and Florence presents him with a keepsake; John Carker comes to take leave of Walter; Walter goes aboard the *Son and Heir*, and she starts upon her voyage. {20} Mr Dombey breakfasts with Major Bagstock; the major speculates on the matrimonial ambition of Miss Tox; Mr Toodle expresses his sympathy at the death of little Paul, but Mr Dombey does not respond; reflections of Mr Dombey on the road; the major rallies him on his thoughtfulness; they arrive at Leamington. {21} Mr Dombey and Major Bagstock encounter Mrs Skewton and her daughter Mrs Granger; Mrs Skewton expresses her fondness for 'Nature' and 'Heart'; Major Bagstock informs Mr Dombey who these new friends are; Mr Dombey and the major call upon the ladies, and Mrs Granger shows her accomplishments. {22} Mr Carker the manager shows his affection for Mr Carker the junior, and for their sister; Mr Perch informs Mr Carker that Rob the Grinder is seeking employment; Mr Carker has him brought in; Sol Gills comes to pay the instalment due on his debt, and to inquire for news of the *Son and Heir*, which has not been heard from since she sailed; Carker proposes to put Rob into his employ; Carker goes home with Rob, and fully engages to take charge of that young hopeful, whom he places as a spy upon Sol Gills; Carker is witness to the discomfiture of Mr Toots, consequent upon that young gentleman's advances to Susan Nipper. {23} The lonely life of Florence in the deserted house; Florence, anxious at the absence of news from Walter, goes with Susan to see Sol Gills and, not finding him at home, they go to Captain Cuttle's; meeting of Susan Nipper and Mrs MacStinger; Captain Cuttle, at a loss what to say about Walter's ship, consults the oracular Bunsby, who gives an opinion, the 'bearings' of which 'lays in the application on it'. {24} Florence visits the family of Sir Barnet Skettles at Fulham; various incidents remind her of her estrangement from her father; they encounter Carker, who informs Florence that there is no news of the ship. {25} Sudden disappearance of Sol Gills; Captain Cuttle, finding no traces of him, runs away from Mrs MacStinger, and takes possession of the shop. {26} Carker arrives at Leamington; the major and Mrs Skewton encourage the attention of Mr Dombey to Edith; Mrs Skewton accepts for herself and Edith Mr Dombey's invitation to breakfast, and to a ride to Warwick Castle. {27} Carker meets Edith in the grove, and relieves her from the annoyance of Good Mrs Brown; Carker watches Edith closely during the breakfast and the trip to Warwick; Dombey makes an appointment with Mrs Granger 'for a purpose', and she recapitulates to her mother the management they have used in bringing him to a declaration. {28} Florence proposes to return home; how Mr Toots practised boating; returning home, Florence and Susan find the house undergoing extensive alterations; Florence meets Edith and Mrs Skewton for the first time, and hears of the approaching marriage of her father. {29} Mrs Chick calls upon Miss Tox to inform her of Mr Dombey's contemplated marriage; Miss Tox is overcome by the news, and Mrs Chick has her eyes opened to the ambitions hopes of her friend, whom she consequently casts off. {30} Edith shows a warm friendship for Florence; she urges her to remain at home alone after her father's marriage; Mrs Skewton shows her interest in Florence; Edith refuses to allow Florence to remain with Mrs Skewton during her absence. {31} The wedding of Mr Dombey and Edith Granger; the wedding breakfast, where Cousin Feenix makes a speech, and Mr Carker smiles upon the company. {32} Captain Cuttle, keeping close quarters at The Wooden Midshipman, is called upon by Mr Toots and the Game Chicken; Mr Toots is anxious to cultivate Captain Cuttle's acquaintance; he reads from a newspaper an account of the loss of the *Son and Heir* to Captain Cuttle; Captain Cuttle calls again on Mr Carker, who receives him with less politeness than before. {33} Mr James Carker's home near Norwood, with the picture resembling Edith on the wall; Mr John Carker's house on the other side of London; John Carker parts with his sister for the day; she is visited by a stranger gentleman, who is thoroughly acquainted with their history, and who secures her promise to call on him if they ever need assistance; Harriet Carker befriends Alice Brown, a returned convict. {34} Good Mrs Brown welcomes home her daughter; Mrs Brown informs Alice what she knows of Carker, learning that it was his sister who befriended her, she returns to her house, and flings back her gift with curses. {35} Mr and Mrs Dombey are welcomed home after their bridal tour; Mr Dombey, pretending to sleep, watches Florence and Edith, and his heart hardens towards his daughter to find that she has won his wife's love; Florence relates to Edith the story of Walter; Edith warns Florence not to expect to gain through her father's affection. {36} Mr and Mrs Dombey give an entertainment which is not social; Cousin Feenix relates a story; Mr Carker is the only man at ease, and Mrs Chick feels herself slighted; Mr Dombey, in the presence of Carker, makes objections to his wife's conduct. {37} Carker calls upon Mrs Dombey, and insists upon an interview;

Carker assumes the existence of devoted attachment between Mrs Dombey and her husband, and endeavours to establish an influence over her through her fear of injuring Florence; Mrs Skewton is struck with paralysis. {38} Miss Tox, abandoned by Mrs Chick, seeks Richards for information of the Dombeys, and is escorted home by Rob the Grinder. {39} Captain Cuttle bestows on Mr Toots the pleasure of his acquaintance, on condition that Florence must never he named or referred to; Rob the Grinder leaves Captain Cuttle's service; Captain Cuttle, with the approval of his friend Bunsby, opens Sol Gills's packet in the presence of that worthy; Mrs MacStinger and her family suddenly appear on the scene; much to Captain Cuttle's amazement, Bunsby pacifies her and, escorting her home, returns with the captain's box, which he had left at Brig Place on his escape. {40} Mr Dombey expresses to Edith his displeasure at her conduct; she vows her feelings towards him and requests, for the sake of others, mutual forbearance; Mr Dombey insists on his own will; the family, except Mr Dombey, accompany Mrs Skewton to Brighton; Mrs Skewton and her daughter encounter Good Mrs Brown and Alice. {41} Mr Toots, accompanied by Florence, calls at Dr Blimber's; on their return Mr Toots is on the point of making a declaration of his love, which Florence cheeks; death of Mrs Skewton. {42} Rob the Grinder appears in the service of Mr Carker; Mr Dombey and Mr Carker in council; Mr Dombey instructs Carker to act as his agent in expressing to his wife his demands in regard to her conduct; Mr Dombey is thrown from his horse and severely hurt, and Carker carries the news of the accident to Edith. {43} Susan Nipper expresses her opinion of Mr Carker, and of Mrs Pipchin, who has become housekeeper; Florence goes to her father's room, and kisses him in his sleep; Florence finds Edith in a state of great agitation after her interview with Carker. {44} Susan Nipper, watching her opportunity, enters Mr Dombey's room when he is alone, and relieves her mind; Mrs Pipchin gives her warning, and she leaves under the escort of Mr Toots; she destroys his hopes of ever being loved by Florence. {45} Carker requests an interview alone with Edith; he states the position Mr Dombey would have him fill towards her, and declares himself devoted to her service; she denies having any affection for her husband; Carker warns her, for Florence's sake, to withdraw her affection from her. {46} Mr Carker is watched by Good Mrs Brown and her daughter, who afterwards question Rob the Grinder in regard to his master; Mr James Carker again taunts his brother with his disgrace, and sneers at his expressions of good will towards Mr Dombey. {47} Edith avoids Florence, and informs her that they must become estranged; Mr Dombey persists in correcting Edith in the presence of Carker and Florence; Edith answers him, and ask for a separation on his own terms; Mr Dombey rejects the proposition; Carker attempts to conciliate; Edith shrinks from Florence on the stairs; flight of Edith and Carker; Florence is struck down by an angry blow from her father. {48} She flies to the house of Sol Gills, where she is received by Captain Cuttle, from whom she learns of the disappearance of Walter's uncle; the captain provides for the comfort of Florence; Mr Toots calls, and informs Captain Cuttle that a person whom he met at the door that morning is waiting to see him at Mr Brogley's; the captain goes to Brogley's and returns in a state of great excitement. {49} Captain Cuttle takes tender care of Florence, and cheers her by reminding her that 'Wal'r's drownded'; Florence goes shopping with the captain; the captain relates to Florence the story of the ship lost at sea from which one lad was saved; the shadow of a man appears upon the wall, and she welcomes Walter home, while Captain Cuttle 'makes over a little property jintly'. {50} Florence relates the reason of her flight from home; Walter reasons that his uncle is still alive and will return; they discuss the position of Florence, and decide to find out Susan as the best attendant for her; Mr Toots, distracted with the news of Florence's disappearance, is relieved to find she is safe, though in his rival's charge, and promises to devote himself and the Chicken to the recovery of Susan; Florence, pained at Walter's avoiding her, seeks an explanation; their interview results in a mutual profession of love, to the great delight of Captain Cuttle. {51} Mr Dombey warns his sister to be silent on the subject of Florence; Major Bagstock claims the name of Dombey's friend when the time comes for meeting Carker; how the family disaster affects Mr Dombey's clerks. {52} Mr Dombey goes to the abode of Good Mrs Brown to hear news of Carker; from a place of concealment he hears Mrs Brown and her daughter draw from Rob the Grinder, by questions and threats, the secrets of his master's flight with Edith, and their place of destination. {53} John Carker is dismissed; Harriet relates to her brother the appearance of their unknown friend, who proves to be Mr Morfin, of Dombey and Son's house: he relates how he came by a knowledge of their affairs, and promises to assist them; Mr Morfin informs Harriet Carker of the condition of her brother's pecuniary connection with Dombey and Son; Alice Brown relents at her share in the betrayal of Carker and, after relating to Harriet the cause she has to curse him, begs her to warn him that Dombey is on his track. {54} Edith appears alone at the apartment in Dijon; Carker joins her; Edith spares Carker's advances, threatens him with violence if he approaches her, and shows him that her flight with him was in order to avenge the insults she had received from him; she informs him of her husband's presence in the town, and escapes from the apartment, just as Mr Dombey arrives at the door; Carker escapes through an obscure passage. {55} Carker hastens back to England, terrified by the feeling that Mr Dombey is pursuing him; he stops to rest at a remote country station and, as he is about to proceed, he encounters Mr Dombey, in avoiding whom he steps upon the rails, and is cut to pieces by a passing train. {56} Mr Toots returns to The Midshipman with Susan Nipper, and becomes reconciled to the loss of Florence; Mrs Richards becomes housekeeper at The Midshipman; Mr Toots's unhappiness at hearing the banns read in church; return of Sol Gills; his long absence and his silence are explained; the Game Chicken expresses his disgust, and he and Mr Toots part company. {57} Walter and Florence visit the tomb of little Paul; marriage of Walter and Florence, and their departure on a voyage to China. {58} Failure of the house of Dombey and Son; Harriet Carker begs Mr Morfin to give Mr Dombey the interest of the bulk of the fortune left by her brother James; Harriet visits Alice Brown, whom she has rescued from her sinful life, and who now lies very ill, nursed by Mrs Wickam; Mrs Brown informs Harriet of the relationship between her child and Mrs Dombey; death of Alice. {59} Mr Dombey's servants are dismissed and the furniture sold at auction, while Mr Dombey keeps himself unseen in his own apartments; Mrs Pipchin resigns her charge of the house, and is succeeded by Richards; Miss Tox continues to show her sympathy; Mr Dombey wanders through the house by night, and learns to long for Florence; she returns and seeks her father, and takes him home with her; Miss Tox takes Rob the Grinder into her service. {60} Mr Feeder, BA, marries Cornelia Blimber, Mr Toots and his wife, formerly Susan Nipper, being present at the ceremony; Mrs MacStinger leads Bunsby to the altar; Susan returns to Florence. {61} Cousin Feenix takes Florence to his house to meet Edith; the last bottle of the old Madeira is drunk to Walter and his wife. {62} Final disposition of all the characters.

16

The Haunted Man and The Ghost's Bargain

A Fancy for Christmas-Time

Published in 1848, and illustrated with a frontispiece and title-page engraved on wood from drawings by John Tenniel, and with woodcuts in the text from sketches by Stanfield, Leech, and Stone.

CHARACTERS

DENHAM, Edmund – A student, whose true name is Longford. He comes under the evil influence of Mr Redlaw, and loses all sense of the kindness that has been shown him during a dangerous illness. But, when a change falls upon Redlaw, his heart feels the effect also, and glows with affection and gratitude to his benefactress. {2, 3}

LONGFORD, Edmund – *See* **Denham, Edmund**.

REDLAW, Mr – A learned chemist, and a lecturer at an ancient institution in a great city. He is a melancholy but kind-hearted man, whose life has been darkened by many sorrows. As he sits brooding one night over the things that might have been, but never were, Mr William Swidger, the keeper of the Lodge, with his wife Milly, and his father Philip, enter the room to serve his tea and to decorate the apartment with holly in honour of Christmas. The old man reminds Mr Redlaw of a picture of one of the founders of the institution, which hangs in what was once the great dining-hall – a sedate gentleman, with a scroll below him, bearing the inscription 'Lord, keep my memory green!' And then the younger Mr Swidger speaks of his wife's visits to the sick and suffering, and tells how she has just returned from nursing a student who attends Mr Redlaw's lectures, and who has been seized with a fever. After the departure of these humble friends, Redlaw falls back into his train of sorrowful musings and, as he sits before the fire, an awful spectral likeness of himself appears to him. It echoes his mournful thoughts, brings each wrong and sorrow that he has suffered vividly before him, and finally offers to cancel the remembrance of them, destroying no knowledge, no result of study, nothing but the intertwisted chain of feelings and associations, each in its turn dependent on and nourished by the banished recollections. The phantom leaves him bewildered, and with no memory of past wrongs or troubles. He does not know in what way he possesses the power to communicate this forgetfulness to others but, with a vague feeling of having an antidote for the worst of human ills, he goes forth to administer it. Those whom he seeks, and those whom he casually encounters, alike experience the infection of his presence. Charged with poison for his own mind, he poisons the minds of others. Where he felt interest, compassion, sympathy, his heart turns to stone. Selfishness and ingratitude everywhere spring up in his blighting footsteps. There is but one person who is proof against his baneful influence, and that is the ragged child whom Mrs Swidger picked up in the streets. Hardship and cruelty have so blunted the senses of this wretched creature, that it grows neither worse nor better from contact with the haunted man. It is, indeed, already a counterpart of him, with no memory of the past to soften or stimulate it. Shocked by the evil he has wrought, Redlaw awakes to a consciousness of the misery of his condition. Having long taught that in the material world nothing can be spared, that no step or atom in the wondrous structure could be lost without a blank being made in the great universe, he is now brought to see that it is the same with good and evil, happiness and sorrow, in the memories of men. He invokes the spirit of his darker hours to come back and take its gift away – or, at least, to deprive him of the dreadful power of giving it to others. His prayer is heard. The phantom reappears, accompanied by the shadow of Milly, the wife of William Swidger, from whom Redlaw has resolutely kept himself aloof, fearing to influence the steady quality of goodness that he knows to be in her, fearing that he may be 'the murderer of what is tenderest and best within her bosom'. He learns that she, unconsciously, has the power of setting right what he has done, and he seeks her out. Wherever she goes, peace and happiness attend her. The peevish, the morose, the discontented, the ungrateful, and the selfish are suddenly changed, and become their former and

So, resolving with some difficulty where he was, he directed his steps back to
the old college, and to that part of it where the general porch was, and where,
alone, the pavement was worn by the tread of the students' feet.

The keeper's house stood just within the iron gates, forming a part of the
chief quadrangle. There was a little cloister outside, and from that sheltered
place he knew he could look in at the window of their ordinary room, and see
who was within. The iron gates were shut, but his hand was familiar with
the fastening, and drawing it back by thrusting in his wrist between the
bars, he passed through softly, shut it again, and crept up to the window,
crumbling the thin crust of snow with his feet.

Clarkson Stanfield

better selves. Even Redlaw is restored to what he was, and a clearer light shines into his mind, when Milly tells him that, to her, it seems a good thing for us to remember wrong, *that we may forgive it.*

SWIDGER, George – Eldest son of old Philip Swidger; a dying man, repentant of all the wrong he has done and the sorrow he has caused during a career of forty or fifty years, but suddenly changed, by seeing Redlaw at his bedside, into a bold and callous ruffian, who dies with an oath on his lips. {2}

SWIDGER, Milly – Wife of William Swidger; an embodiment of goodness, gentle consideration, love, and domesticity. {1–3}

SWIDGER, Philip – A superannuated custodian of the institution in which Mr Redlaw is a lecturer. He is a happy and venerable old man of eighty-seven years of age, who has a most remarkable memory. When, however, at the bedside of his dying son, he meets Redlaw (who has just closed the bargain with the ghost, in consequence of which he causes forgetfulness in others wherever he goes), he all at once grows weak-minded and petulant; but, when he once more comes within the influence of his good daughter Milly, he recovers all his recollections of the past, and is quite himself again. {1–3}

SWIDGER, William – His youngest son; servant to Redlaw, and husband to Milly; a fresh-coloured, busy, good-hearted man, who, like his father and others, is temporarily transformed into a very different sort of person by coming in contact with his master after 'the ghost's bargain' is concluded. {1–3}

TETTERBY, Mr Adolphus – A newsman, with almost any number of small children – usually an unselfish, good-natured, yielding little race, but changed for a time, as well as himself, into the exact opposite by Mr Redlaw. {2, 3}

TETTERBY, Mrs Sophia – His wife, called by himself his ' little woman'. ' Considered as an individual she was rather remarkable for being robust and portly, but considered with reference to her husband, her dimensions became magnificent'. {2, 3}

TETTERBY, 'Dolphus – Their eldest son, aged ten; he is a newspaper boy at a railway station. {2, 3}

TETTERBY, Johnny – Their second son; a patient, much-enduring child, whose special duty it is to take care of the baby. {2, 3}

TETTERBY, Sally – A large, heavy infant, always cutting teeth. {2, 3}

Mr Tetterby elevated his eyebrows, folded his newspaper afresh, and carried his eyes up it, and down it, and across it, but was wandering in his attention, and not reading it.

John Leech

Haunted – Sir John Tenniel

17

The Personal History of
David Copperfield the Younger

This work was originally brought out under the title: 'The Personal History, Adventures, Experiences, and Observations of David Copperfield the Younger, of Blunderstone Rookery (which he never meant to be published on any account)'. It was issued in twenty monthly parts, with two illustrations by Phiz in each part. The first number appeared 1 May 1849, and the preface was dated October 1850. In it the author spoke thus of his work:

> 'Of all my books, I like this the best. It will be easily believed that I am a fond parent to every child of my fancy, and that no one can ever love that family as dearly as I love them; but, like many fond parents, I have in my heart of hearts a favourite child, and his name is David Copperfield'.

CHARACTERS

ADAMS – Head boy at Doctor Strong's; affable and good-humoured, and with a turn for mathematics. {16, 18}

BABLEY, Richard – *called* **Mr Dick**. A mild lunatic, and a *protégé* of Miss Betsey Trotwood's, who insists that he is not mad. {13–15, 17, 19, 34, 38, 42, 43, 45, 49, 52, 54, 60, 62, 64}

BAILEY, Captain – An admirer of the eldest Miss Larkins. {18}

BARKIS, Mr – A carrier who takes David Copperfield from Blunderstone to Yarmouth, on his first being sent away to school As they jog along, Copperfield asks Mr Barkis if they are going no farther than Yarmouth together. After the death of her mistress, Peggotty becomes 'willin' ' also, and marries Mr Barkis, who makes her a very good husband, save that he is 'rather near', as she expresses it, and jealously guards a box under his bed, which contains his money and valuables; although he persists in telling everybody that it is 'old clothes'. At last he is taken very ill; and David goes down from London to visit him. {2–5, 7, 8, 10, 29, 31}

BARKIS, Mrs – *See* **Peggotty, Clara**.

CHARLEY – A drunken, ugly old dealer in second-hand sailors' clothes and marine stores, to whom David Copperfield sells his jacket for fourpence when travelling on foot to his aunt's. {13}

CHESTLE, Mr – A hop-grower; a plain, elderly gentleman, who marries the eldest Miss Larkins. {18}

CHILLIP, Mr – The doctor who officiates at the birth of David Copperfield. {1, 2, 9, 10, 22, 30, 59}

CLICKETT – An 'orfling' girl from St Luke's Workhouse; servant to the Micawbers. She is a dark-complexioned young woman with a habit of snorting. {11, 12}

COPPERFIELD, Mrs Clara – The mother of David; an artless, affectionate little woman, whom Miss Betsey Trotwood insists upon calling a mere baby. She marries Mr Murdstone, a stern man who, in conjunction with his sister, attempts to teach her 'firmness', but breaks her heart in the experiment. {1–4, 8, 9}

COPPERFIELD, David – The character from whom the story takes its name, or by whom it is supposed to be told. He is a posthumous child, having been born six months after his father's death. His mother, young beautiful, inexperienced, loving, and lovable, not long afterwards marries a handsome and plausible 'but hard and stern man – Mr Murdstone by name – who soon crushes her gentle spirit by his exacting tyranny and by his cruel treatment of her boy. After being for some time instructed at home by his mother, and reduced to a state of dullness and sullen desperation by his stepfather, David is sent from home. He is sent to a villainous school, near London, kept by one Creakle, where he receives more stripes than lessons. Here he is kept until the death of his mother, when his stepfather sends him (he being now ten years old) to London, to be employed in Murdstone and Grimsby's warehouse in washing out empty wine bottles, pasting labels on them when filled, and the like, at a salary of six shillings a week. But such is the secret agony of his soul at sinking into companionship with Mick Walker, 'Mealy Potatoes', and other boys with whom he is forced to associate, that he at length resolves to run away, and throw himself upon the kindness of a great-aunt (Miss Betsey Trotwood), whom he has never seen, but

A stranger calls to see me – Hablot K Browne *alias* Phiz

of whose eccentric habits and singular manner he has often heard. She receives him much better than he has expected, and soon adopts him, and sends him to a school in the neighbouring town of Canterbury. He does well here, and works his way up to the head of the school before leaving. Having made up his mind to become a proctor, he enters the office of Mr Spenlow, in London. Soon after this, his aunt loses the greater part of her property and David, being compelled to look about him for the means of subsistence, learns the art of stenography, and supports himself by reporting the debates in Parliament. In the meantime he has fallen desperately in love with Dora, the daughter of Mr Spenlow, but has been discouraged in his suit by the young lady's father. Mr Spenlow dying, however, he becomes her accepted suitor. Turning his attention soon after to authorship, he acquires a reputation, and obtains constant employment on magazines and periodicals. He now marries Dora, a pretty, captivating, affectionate girl, but utterly ignorant of everything practical It is not long before David discovers that it will be altogether useless to expect that his wife will develop any stability of character, and he resolves to estimate her by the good qualities she has, and not by those which he has not. One night, she says to him in a very thoughtful manner that she wishes him to call her his 'child-wife'. At length Dora falls into a decline, and grows weaker and weaker, day by day. After the death of his wife, David goes abroad, passing through many weary phases of mental distress. When three years have passed, David returns to England, where his few works have already made him famous. But more than all else he values the praise and encouragement he receives from Agnes, whom he has come to think the better angel of his life, and whom he would gladly make his wife, did he not believe that her feeling towards him was merely one of sisterly affection, and that she has formed a deeper attachment for another. He discovers at last, however, that she loves him only, and that she has loved him all her life, though she unselfishly subdued the feelings of her heart so far as to rejoice sincerely in his marriage to Dora. They are soon united, and she then tells him that Dora, on the last night of her life, expressed the earnest wish that she, and she alone, should succeed to her place.

COPPERFIELD, Mrs Dora – *See* **Spenlow, Dora** and **Copperfield, David.**

CREAKLE, Mr – Master of Salem House, the school to which David Copperfield is sent by Mr Murdstone; an ignorant and ferocious brute, who prides himself on being a 'Tartar'. {5–7, 9, 61}

CREAKLE, Mrs – His wife; a thin and quiet woman, ill-treated by her husband. {6, 9}

CREAKLE, Miss – Their daughter; supposed to be in love with Steerforth. {6, 7, 9}

CREWLER, Mrs – Wife of the Reverend Horace Crewler; a very superior woman, who has lost the use of her limbs. She becomes the mother-in-law of Traddles. Whatever occurs to harass her (as the engagement and prospective loss of her daughters) usually settles in her legs, but sometimes mounts to her chest and head, and pervades her whole system in a most alarming manner. {34, 41, 60}

CREWLER, Miss Caroline – Eldest daughter of Mrs Crewler; a very handsome girl, who marries a dashing vagabond, but soon separates from him. {41, 60, 64}

CREWLER, Miss Louisa – Mrs Crewler's third daughter. {41, 60, 64}

CREWLER, Miss Lucy – One of Mrs Crewler's two youngest daughters, educated by her sister Sophy. {41, 60, 64}

CREWLER, Miss Margaret – One of Mrs Crewler's two youngest daughters, educated by her sister Sophy. {41, 60, 64}

CREWLER, Miss Sarah – Mrs Crewler's second daughter. {34, 41, 60, 64}

CREWLER, Miss Sophy – Fourth daughter of Mrs Crewler; always forgetful of herself, always cheerful and amiable, and as much a mother to her mother (who is a confirmed invalid) as she is to her sisters. She becomes the wife of Tommy Traddles, who regards her both before and after marriage as 'the dearest girl in the world'. {27, 28, 34, 41, 43, 59, 61, 62, 64}

CREWLER, The Reverend Horace – A poor Devonshire clergyman, with a large family and a sick wife. {34, 41, 60, 64}

CRUPP, Mrs – A stout woman living in Buckingham Street, in the Adelphi, who lets a set of furnished chambers to David Copperfield when he becomes an articled clerk in the office of Spenlow and Jorkins. She is a martyr to a curious disorder called 'the spazzums', which is generally accompanied with inflammation of the nose, and requires to be constantly treated with peppermint. {23–26, 28, 34, 35, 37}

DARTLE, Rosa – A lady some thirty years old, living with Mrs Steerforth as a companion, and passionately in love with her son, who does not return her affection. She is of a slight, short figure, and a dark complexion; has black hair, and large black eyes, and a remarkable scar on her lip, caused by a wound from a hammer thrown at her by Steerforth, when a boy, in a moment of exasperation. She is very clever, bringing everything, as it were, to a grindstone, and even wearing herself away by constant sharpening, till she is all edge. {20, 21, 24, 29, 32, 36, 46, 50, 56, 64}

DEMPLE, George – A schoolmate of David Copperfield's at Salem House. {5, 7}

DOLLOBY, Mr – A dealer in second-hand clothes, rags, bones, and kitchen-stuff, to whom David Copperfield sells his waistcoat for ninepence when he runs away from Murdstone and Grinby's to seek his aunt. {13}

DORA – *See* **Spenlow, Dora**.

EM'LY, Little – Niece and adopted daughter of Mr Peggotty, and the object of David Copperfield's first love. She is afterwards betrothed to her cousin Ham, but is seduced by Steerforth. {3, 7, 10, 17, 21–23, 30}

ENDELL, Martha – An unfortunate young woman, without money or reputation, who finally discovers 'Little Em'ly', and restores her to her uncle. She is reclaimed, and emigrates to Australia where she marries happily. {22, 40, 46, 47, 50, 51, 57, 63}

FIBBETSON, Mrs – An old woman, inmate of an almshouse. {5}

GEORGE – Guard of the Yarmouth mail. {5}

GRAINGER – A friend of Steerforth's, and a very gay and lively fellow. {24}

GRAYPER, Mr – A neighbour of Mrs Copperfield. {9, 22}

GRAYPER, Mrs – His wife. {2, 22}

GULPIDGE, Mr – A guest of the Waterbrooks, who has something to do at second-hand with the law business of the Bank. {25}

GULPIDGE, Mrs – His wife. {25}

GUMMIDGE, Mrs – The widow of Mrs Peggotty's partner. Her husband dying, poor, Mr Peggotty offers her a home, and supports her for years; and this kindness she acknowledges by sitting in the most comfortable corner by the fireside, and complaining, that she

I am married – Hablot K Browne *alias* Phiz

is a 'lone, lorn creetur, and everythink goes contrary with her'. {3, 7, 10, 21, 22, 31, 32, 40, 51, 57, 63}

HAMLET'S AUNT – *See* **Spiker, Mrs Henry**.

HEEP, Mrs – A very humble widow woman, mother of Uriah Heep, and his 'dead image, only short'. {17, 39, 42, 52, 61}

HEEP, Uriah – A clerk in the law office of Mr Wickfield, whose partner he afterwards becomes. As time runs on, David finds that Uriah is obtaining an unbounded influence over Mr Wickfield, whom he deludes in every possible way, and whose business he designedly perplexes and complicates in order to get it wholly into his own hands; and furthermore, that he looks with greedy eyes upon Mr Wickfield's daughter Agnes, to whom David himself is warmly attached. He even goes so far as to boast of this, and to declare his intention of making her his wife. Uriah goes on weaving his meshes around Agnes and her father until he has them completely in his power. But his rascality is at last unravelled and exposed by Mr Micawber; and Mr Wickfield not only recovers all the property of which he has been defrauded, but is absolved from all suspicion of any criminal act or intent. Uriah pursues his calling in another part of the country, but is finally arrested for fraud, forgery, and conspiracy, and is sentenced to solitary imprisonment. {15–17, 19, 25, 35, 36, 39, 42, 49, 52, 54, 61}

HOPKINS, Captain – A prisoner for debt, in the Bench Prison, at the time that Mr Micawber is also confined there. {11}

JANET – Miss Betsey Trotwood's handmaid. {13–15, 23, 39, 43, 60}

JIP – (a contraction of Gypsy). Dora's pet dog. {26, 33, 36–38, 41–44, 48, 52, 53}

JORAM, Mr – The partner and son-in-law of Mr Omer the undertaker. {9, 21, 23, 30, 51, 56}

JORAM, Mrs – *See* **Omer, Miss**.

JORKINS, Mr – A proctor, partner of Mr Spenlow. {23, 29, 35, 38, 39}

LARKINS, Miss – A tall, dark, black-eyed, fine figure of a woman, of about thirty, with whom David Copperfield fells desperately in love when about seventeen. His passion for her is beyond all bounds; but she crushes his hopes by marrying a hop-grower. {18}

LARKINS, Mr – Her father; a gruff old gentleman with a double chin, and one of his eyes immovable in head. {18}

LITTIMER – Confidential servant of Steerforth. {21–23, 28, 29, 32, 46, 61}

MALDON, Jack – Cousin to Mrs Doctor Strong; an idle, needy libertine, with a handsome face, a rapid utterance, and a confident, bold air. {16, 19, 37, 41, 45, 64}

MARKHAM – A gay and lively fellow of not more than twenty; a friend of Steerforth's. {24, 25}

MARKLEHAM, Mrs – Mother of Mrs Doctor Strong. {16, 19, 36, 42, 45, 64}

MEALY POTATOES – (So called on account of his pale complexion.) A boy employed at Murdstone and Grinby's wine store, with David Copperfield and others, to examine bottles, wash them out, label and cork them, and the like. {11}

MELL, Mr Charles – An under-master at Salem House, Mr Creakle's school. He is a gaunt, sallow young man, with hollow cheeks, and dry and rusty hair. Mr Creakle discharges him because it is ascertained that his mother lives on charity in an almshouse. He emigrates to Australia, and finally becomes Doctor Mell of Colonial Salem House Grammar School. {5–7, 63}

MELL, Mrs – His mother. {5, 7}

MICAWBER, Master Wilkins – Son of Mr Wilkins Micawber. He has a remarkable head voice, and becomes a chorister-boy in the cathedral at Canterbury, At a later date, he acquires a high reputation as an amateur singer. {11, 12, 17, 27, 36, 42, 49, 52, 54, 57, 64}

MICAWBER, Miss Emma – Daughter of Mr Wilkins Micawber; afterwards Mrs Ridger Begs of Port Middlebay, Australia. {11, 12, 17, 27, 36, 42, 49, 52, 54, 57, 64}

MICAWBER, Mr Wilkins – A gentleman – remarkable for his reckless improvidence, his pecuniary involvements, his alternate elevation and depression of spirits, his love of letter-writing, and speech-making, his grandiloquent rhetoric, his shabby devices for eking out a genteel living, and his constantly 'waiting for something to turn up' – with whom David Copperfield lodges while drudging in the warehouse of Murdstone and Grinby. When young Copperfield takes possession of his quarters Mr Micawber's, Windsor Terrace, City Road, he finds the domestic situation of that gentleman beset with difficulties which to any other man would be thoroughly discouraging. His difficulties come to a crisis at last, however; and he is arrested one morning, and carried to the Bench Prison, saying that the God of Day has gone down with him;

but before noon he is seen playing a lively game of skittles. At last he applies for release under the Insolvent Debtors' Act; and in due time is set at liberty. Mrs Micawber's friends being of opinion that his wisest course will be to quit London, he determines to go down to Plymouth, where he thinks something may 'turn up' for him in the custom-house. Before parting from David, he gives him a little friendly counsel. Micawber's first piece of advice is 'never do tomorrow what you can do today. Procrastination is the thief of time'. He then goes on to the oft-quoted admonition: 'Annual income twenty pounds, annual expenditure nineteen nineteen six, result happiness. Annual income twenty pounds, annual expenditure twenty pounds ought and six, result misery.' Some time after this, David – then a pupil of Dr Strong's, at Canterbury – unexpectedly meets Mr Micawber, who has left Plymouth (talent not being wanted in the custom-house) and is invited to dine with him at his inn with him. Mr Micawber next engages in the sale of corn upon commission; but not finding it 'an avocation of a remunerative description', and getting again into 'temporary embarrassments of a pecuniary nature', he accepts an offer from Uriah Heep to become his confidential clerk. But, before leaving London for Canterbury (where Heep is established), he invites David to spend an evening at his house with their common friend Traddles. When the time has nearly come for them to take their leave, Mr Micawber rises to acknowledge a toast proposed by Copperfield. He thanks his friends for their good wishes, and speaks as if he was going 'five hundred thousand miles' away. He hopes to become an ornament to the profession of which he is 'about to become an unworthy member'. Mr Micawber does not find his position in Heep's office as pleasant as his sanguine temperament has led him to anticipate. He soon discovers his employer to be a consummate hypocrite and villain, who is bent upon ruining his partner, Mr Wickfield, and that he himself is being made use of as a tool to aid in furthering the scheme. He therefore sets himself to the task of unravelling the whole tissue of rascality so cunningly woven by Heep; and, when this is done, he denounces and exposes him in a long and characteristic letter which he reads to Copperfield, Traddles, and Miss Betsey Trotwood, who meet by appointment at Mr Wickfield's former office. Miss Trotwood having been made acquainted with Mr Micawber's straitened circumstances, suggests that it might be well

Mrs Micawber and Family – Frank Reynolds

for him to try his fortunes in Australia, and offers to pay his debts, and the passage of himself and family to that country. Mr Micawber is delighted at the idea, and makes immediate preparations for emigrating. In a few days, he informs his kind patron that his 'boat is on the shore', and 'his bark is on the sea'. Many years afterwards, David receives from Peggotty (who went out in the same vessel with Mr Micawber) a copy of an Australian paper containing an account of a public dinner given to 'our distinguished townsman, Wilkins Micawber, Esquire'. {11, 12, 17, 27, 28, 36, 39, 42, 49, 52, 54, 57, 63}

MICAWBER, Miss Emma – Wife of Wilkins Micawber. When her husband's resources are at the lowest ebb, she determines to come to his rescue if she can. In the ease of her temper and the elasticity of her spirits, Mrs Micawber is scarcely surpassed by her husband. Among the striking and praiseworthy characteristics of this remarkable lady, her devoted attachment to her husband is deserving of special mention. {11, 12, 17, 27, 28, 36, 42, 49, 52, 54, 57, 58}

MILLS, Miss Julia – The bosom-friend of Dora Spenlow. {33, 37, 38, 41, 64}

MILLS, Mr – Her father; a terrible fellow to fall asleep after dinner. {33, 37, 38, 41}

MOWCHER, Miss – A dealer in cosmetics, a fashionable hairdresser, &c, who makes herself useful to a variety of people in a variety of ways. She is very talkative, and plumes herself on being 'volatile,' but is thoroughly kind-hearted and honest. {22, 32, 61}

MURDSTONE, Mr Edward – Stepfather of David Copperfield. After the death of David's mother, Mr Murdstone marries for his second wife, a lively young woman, but soon breaks her spirit by his gloom and austerity, and at last reduces her to a state bordering on imbecility. {2–4, 8–10, 14, 33, 59}

MURDSTONE, Miss Jane – Sister to Edward Murdstone; a gloomy-looking severe, metallic lady; dark, like her brother, whom she greatly resembles in face and voice; and with very heavy eyebrows, nearly meeting over her large nose as if, being disabled by the wrongs of her sex from wearing whiskers, she had carried them to that account. She is constantly haunted by a suspicion that the servants have a man secreted somewhere on the premises and, under the influence of this delusion, she dives into the coal-cellar at the most untimely hours, and scarcely ever opens the door of a dark cupboard without clapping it to again in the belief that she has got him. {4, 8–10, 12, 14, 26, 33, 38, 59}

NETTINGALL, The Misses – Principals of a boarding-school for young ladies. {18}

OLD SOLDIER, The – *See* **Markleham, Mrs.**

OMER, Minnie – Daughter of Mr Omer; a pretty, good-natured girl engaged to Mr Joram. {9, 21, 30, 32, 51}

OMER, Mr – A draper, tailor, haberdasher, undertaker, &c., at Yarmouth; a fat, short-winded, merry-looking little old man in black, with rusty little bunches of ribbons at the knees of his breeches, black stockings, and a broad-brimmed hat. {9, 21, 30, 32, 51}

PARAGON, Mary Anne – A servant who keeps house for David Copperfield and Dora. {44}

PASSNIDGE, Mr – A friend of Mr Murdstone's. {2}

PEGGOTTY, Clara – Servant to Mrs Copperfield, and nurse and friend to her son David; a girl with no shape at all, and eyes so dark that they seem to darken their whole neighbourhood in her face, and with cheeks and arms so hard and red, that the birds might peck them in preference to apples. Being very plump, whenever she makes any little exertion after she is dressed, some of the buttons on the back of the gown fly off. After the death of her mistress, Peggotty marries Mr Barkis, a carrier, who has long admired her; but she never forgets her old love for David, whose housekeeper she finally becomes. {1–5, 8–10, 12, 13, 17, 19–23, 27, 30–35, 37, 43, 51, 55, 57, 59, 62, 64}

PEGGOTTY, Mr Daniel – A rough but kind-hearted and noble-souled fisherman; brother to Clara Peggotty. Mr Peggotty's nephew Ham and his adopted niece Emily, a beautiful young woman – both members of his household – are engaged to be married; but before the wedding-day arrives Emily elopes with Steerforth, a brilliant, handsome, plausible fellow, who has succeeded in winning her affections and seducing her. She leaves a letter for Ham, which he gives to David Copperfield to read aloud. Months pass, and Mr Peggotty has been absent – no one know where – the whole time, when suddenly David encounters him in London, and learns the story of his wanderings. At last however, Mr Peggotty finds his niece, and emigrates with her to

Australia. 'No one can't reproach my darling in Australia', he says. 'We will begin a new life over theer'. {2, 3, 7, 10, 21, 30–32, 40, 43, 46, 47, 50, 51, 57, 63}

PEGGOTTY, Ham – Nephew of Daniel Peggotty. He is engaged to little Emily, but on the eve of their marriage, she elopes with Steerforth. Years afterwards he attempts, one night, to rescue some unfortunate passengers from a vessel wrecked in a great storm on Yarmouth beach. One of these passengers proves to be Steerforth, who is returning home from abroad. A mighty wave engulfs them all; and the wronged and wrong-doer perish together on the very scene which had witnessed the triumph of the one and the blighted hopes of the other. {2, 3, 7, 10, 21, 22, 30–32, 40, 46, 51, 55}

QUINION, Mr – A friend of Mr Murdstone's, and chief manager at Murdstone and Grinby's warehouse in London. Mr Murdstone calls on Mr Quinion and Mr Passnidge, at Lowestoft, in company with little David Copperfield, to whose mother he is on the point of being married. {2, 10–12}

SHARP, Mr – First master at Salem House, Mr Creakle's school, near London; a limp, delicate-looking gentleman, with a good deal of nose, and a way of carrying his head on one side, as if it were a little too heavy for him. {6, 7, 9}

SHEPHERD, Miss – A boarder at the Misses Nettingall's Establishment for Young Ladies, with whom David Copperfield is for a time deeply in love. She is a little girl in a spencer, with a round face, and curly flaxen hair. {18}

SPENLOW, Miss Clarissa – The elder of two maiden sisters of Mr Spenlow, with whom his daughter Dora resides after his death. They are both dry little ladies, upright in their carriage, formal, precise, composed, and quiet. {38, 39, 41–43, 53}

SPENLOW, Miss La Vinia – Aunt to Dora, and sister to Miss Clarissa and Mr Francis Spenlow. {38, 39, 41–43, 53}

SPENLOW, Miss Dora – Only daughter of Mr Spenlow; afterwards the 'child-wife' of David Copperfield; a timid, trustful, sensitive, artless little beauty, who is not much more than a plaything, and who dies young. {26, 33, 35, 37, 38, 41–44, 48, 50–53}

SPENLOW, Mr Francis – One of the firm of Spenlow and Jorkins (proctors in Doctors' Commons), and the father of Dora, who is afterwards David Copperfield's wife. {23, 26, 29, 33, 35, 38}

SPIKER, Mr Henry – A guest at a party given by Mr and Mrs Waterbrook. He is solicitor to somebody or something remotely connected with the Treasury, and is so cold a man that his head, instead of being grey, seems to be sprinkled with hoarfrost. {25}

SPIKER, Mrs Henry – His wife; a very awful lady, looking like a near relation of Hamlet – his aunt, say. {25}

STEERFORTH, James – A schoolfellow and friend of David Copperfield's; a young man of great personal attractions and the most easy and engaging manners. Always adapting himself readily to the society he happens to be in, he has no trouble in securing the regard and confidence of simple-hearted Mr Peggotty, whose humble house he visits with David. Here he meets Mr Peggotty's niece and adopted daughter, Emily – a beautiful young woman, betrothed to her cousin Ham – and deliberately sets to work to effect her ruin. In this he is successful; and, on the eve of her intended marriage, she consents to elope with him. They live abroad for some time; but he finally tires of her and, after insultingly proposing that she should marry his valet, a detestable scoundrel cruelly, deserts her. Not long after, he sets sail for England, and meets his death by shipwreck during a fearful gale. {6, 7, 9, 19–25, 28, 29, 31, 55}

STEERFORTH, Mrs – Mother of James Steerforth; an elderly lady, with a proud carriage and a handsome face, entirely devoted to her son, but estranged from him at last; both of them being imperious and obstinate. {20, 21, 24, 29, 31, 36, 46, 56, 64}

STRONG, Doctor – Master of a school at Canterbury attended by David Copperfield; a quiet, amiable old gentleman, who has married a lady many years his junior. The doctor's wife has a cousin, Jack Maldon, who is a pensioner on the bounty of her husband, and who attempts to make love to her, even while enjoying the hospitality of her husband's house. Through very shame, Mrs Strong does not mention this; but there are ready and meddlesome tongues to hint suspicion to the kind old man, and to make him miserable. His faith in his wife never falters, however; and, to prove it, he makes a will, in which he leaves his property unconditionally to her. Hearing of this, and knowing that he has heard a magnified story of her intimacy with her cousin, she resolves to go to her husband and frankly explain all. This she does much to the confusion of those who have hoped to separate them, and to the complete satisfaction of her husband. Mrs Strong had formerly been attached to Mr Jack Maldon; but seeing his course, and having principles and sentiments the exact opposite of his, she concludes that 'there is no disparity in marriage like unsuitability of mind and purpose', and she thanks Heaven for the day she wedded one whom she can esteem and respect and love altogether. {16, 17, 19, 36, 39, 42, 45, 52, 54}

STRONG, Mrs Annie – The wife of Doctor Strong, and daughter of Mrs Markleham (the Old Soldier). She is a beautiful woman, much her husband's junior. {16, 19, 36, 42, 45, 52, 64}

TIFFEY, Mr – An old clerk in the office of Spenlow and Jorkins; a little dry man, wearing a stiff brown wig that looks as if it were made of gingerbread. {23, 26, 33, 35, 38}

TIPP – A carman employed in Murdstone and Grinby's warehouse. {11, 12}

TRADDLES, Thomas – A schoolmate of David Copperfield's at Salem House (Mr Creakle's school). Years afterwards, David meets Traddles in London, and finds him a shy, steady, but agreeable and good-natured young man, with a comic head of hair, and eyes rather wide open, which give a surprised look – not to say a hearth-broomy kind of expression. He is reading for the bar, and fighting his way on in the world against difficulties. He tells David that, at his uncle's death, he got fifty pounds, though he had expected to be handsomely remembered in his will. In due time Traddles is married, and, getting on by degrees in his profession, at last accumulates a competence, becomes a judge, and is honoured and esteemed by all who know him. {6, 7, 9, 25, 28, 34, 36, 38, 41, 43, 44, 48, 49, 51, 54, 57–59, 61, 62, 64}

TROTWOOD, Miss Betsey – The great-aunt of David Copperfield; an austere, hard-favoured, and eccentric, but thoroughly kind-hearted woman. David's father had once been a favourite of hers, but had mortally offended her by marrying 'a wax doll'. On the occasion of the birth of his posthumous son, she pays his widow a visit for the first time. Finding Mrs Copperfield quite ill, she immediately proceeds to take charge of the house, and frightens everybody with her odd manners and abrupt speeches. After the death of his mother, David runs away from the warehouse, in London, where his stepfather has placed him in a menial position, to seek the aunt of whom he has often heard, resolved upon trying to soften her heart and, if need be, to apologise for not having been born a girl. He arrives at last in Dover, ragged, footsore, and weary; ascertains the way to his aunt's house and, on reaching it, sees a figure in the garden which he knows must be that of his kinswoman. After a time, recovering from her astonishment, she begins to consider what she shall do with him, and determines, as a necessary preliminary, to have him well washed. While the bath is heating, she becomes suddenly rigid with indignation, and calls out: 'Janet! Donkeys!' upon which David, to his great surprise, sees his aunt and her servant-girl rush out of doors, and drive off several donkeys and small boys from the green in front of the house. This, he finds, is regularly repeated every hour during the day, and every day during the week, sometimes resulting in a hand-to-hand conflict between his aunt and the bigger boys, in which Miss Betsey always came out victorious. Mr Murdstone, learning the whereabouts of his stepson, calls on Miss Trotwood, and informs her that, if she puts any obstacles in the way of his taking the lad home, his doors will be for ever shut against him. David begs to stay with his aunt, and she tells Mr Murdstone that he can go as soon as he likes, and she will take her chance with the boy. Adopting David as her son, she renames him Trotwood Copperfield; sends him to an excellent school; and afterwards articles him to Spenlow and Jorkins, proctors, London. Finding a new and worthy object for her affection and care, her temper softens by degrees; her oddities of manner diminish; and her solid worth and goodness of heart become more conspicuous from year to year. {2, 8–15, 17, 19, 23–25, 37–40, 43–45, 47–49, 51–55, 57, 59, 60, 64}

TROTWOOD, Husband of Miss Betsey – A handsome man, younger than Miss Betsey, whom he treats so falsely, ungratefully, and cruelly, that she separates from him, and resumes her maiden name. He marries another woman; becomes an adventurer, a gambler, and a cheat; and finally sinks into the lowest depths of degradation. {2, 17, 23, 47, 55}

TUNGAY – Lodge-keeper and tool of Mr Creakle, at Salem House; a stout man with a bull neck, a wooden leg a surly face, overhanging temples, and his hair cut close all round his head. {5–7}

WALKER, Mick – A boy employed at Murdstone and Grinby's, with three or four others (including David Copperfield), to rinse out bottles, cork and label them, &c. {11, 12}

WATERBROOK, Mr – Mr Wickfield's agent in London, a middle-aged gentleman with a short throat and a good deal of shirt-collar, who only wants a black nose to be the portrait of a pug dog. {25}

WATERBROOK, Mrs – His wife; a woman who affects to be very genteel; likes to talk about the aristocracy; and maintains, that, if she has a weakness, it is 'blood'. {25}

WICKFIELD, Agnes – Daughter and housekeeper of Mr Wickfield, and friend and counsellor of David Copperfield, whose second wife she becomes after the death of Dora. {15–19, 24, 34, 35, 39, 42, 43, 52–54, 57, 58, 60, 62–64}

WICKFIELD, Mr – A lawyer at Canterbury, and the agent and friend of Miss Betsey Trotwood. He is nearly ruined by Uriah Heep (at first a clerk in his office, and afterwards his partner) who, by adroit management, the falsification of facts, and various malpractices, acquires a complete ascendancy over him, and obtains control of all his property; but in the end Uriah's machinations are foiled, and his rascality exposed by Mr Micawber, whom he has endeavoured to make use of as an instrument to assist in the accomplishment of his dishonest purposes. {15, 17, 19, 35, 39, 42, 52, 54, 60}

WILLIAM – A waiter in an inn at Yarmouth, who wheedles little David Copperfield out of the greater part of his dinner. {5}

WILLIAM – Driver of the Canterbury coach. {19}

PRINCIPAL INCIDENTS

{1} Mrs Copperfield, sitting by the fire, is startled by the appearance of Miss Betsey Trotwood; their conversation upon the late Mr Copperfield, &c; birth of David, and sudden disappearance of Miss Betsey. {2} David relates some of the incidents of his early childhood; his first meeting with Mr Murdstone; Peggotty remonstrates with Mrs Copperfield against the attentions of Mr Murdstone; David goes to Lowestoft with Mr Murdstone, and reports his conversation to his mother; Peggotty and David go to Yarmouth. {3} David makes the acquaintance of Mr Peggotty and his family, and falls in love with little Em'ly; he returns home, and finds his mother married to Mr Murdstone. {4} Mr Murdstone takes David in hand; arrival of Miss Jane Murdstone, who assumes the place of housekeeper; David falls into disgrace over his lessons; he is beaten by Mr Murdstone, whose hand he bites; he is imprisoned in his room for five days as a punishment, and then sent from home to school. {5} David sends

In Mr Wickfield's Office – Fred Barnard

word to Peggotty that 'Barkis is willin;' the friendly waiter relieves David by eating his dinner; David arrives in London, and is met by Mr Mell of Salem House; they arrive at Salem House, and David has a placard reading 'Take care of him; he bites' attached to his back. {6} Mr Creakle and family return, and the school re-opens; Steerforth takes charge of David's money, and treats the boys in their bedroom therewith. {7} David amuses the boys in his room by repeating the stories he has read; altercation between Steerforth and Mr Mell, and Mr Mell's dismissal from the school; Mr Peggotty and Ham visit David at the school, and are introduced to Steerforth. {8} David goes home for the holidays; Mr Barkis informs him he is expecting an answer from Peggotty; in the absence of Mr Murdstone and his sister, David spends a pleasant evening with his mother and Peggotty; David leads a wretched life during the holidays, and goes back to school. {9} He receives the news of his mother's death; returning home, he makes the acquaintance of Mr Omer; Peggotty relates to David the circumstances of his mother's death. {10} Peggotty receives warning from Miss Murdstone, and she and David go again to Yarmouth; Peggotty accepts Mr Barkis's proposal, and they are married; David returns home, and falls into neglect; he is provided for by a situation in the house with which Mr Murdstone is connected. {11} David begins his life at Murdstone and Grinby's, and also meets Mr Micawber, with whom he is to board; Mr Micawber falls into difficulties, and is taken to the debtors' prison; he petitions the House of Commons for a change in the laws for imprisonment for debt. {12} He is released from confinement, and decides to leave London with his family; David determines to run away from Murdstone and Grinby's, and seek his aunt; his adventures and misfortunes on the road from London to Dover. {13} He introduces himself to Miss Betsey Trotwood; Mr Dick's wise advice is asked and followed; Miss Betsey's indignation at the donkeys. {14} Mr Dick, writing his memorial, finds some difficulty in keeping Charles the First out of it; Miss Betsey tells David Mr Dick's story; she is visited by Mr and Miss Murdstone, who come to claim David; she takes Mr Dick's advice, and decides to keep him, giving him the name of Trotwood. {15} David is taken to Canterbury by his aunt, where he is to be put to school; he makes the acquaintance of Mr Wickfield and Agnes, with whom he is to board, and also of Uriah Heep. {16} David begins his school-life at Dr Strong's; he hears a conversation between Dr Strong and Mr Wickfield about Mr Jack Maldon, and afterwards sees that gentleman at Mr Wickfield's; Uriah Heep explains his 'stumble' character and position; the party at Dr Strong's on the eve of Jack Maldon's departure for India. {17} David hears from Mr Dick the story of the strange man who frightens Miss Trotwood; Mr Dick makes friends with everybody; David takes tea with Uriah and his mother, and Mr Micawber unexpectedly 'turns up'; David enjoys a jovial dinner with the Micawbers, and receives a dismal letter from Mr Micawber directly afterwards. {18} David takes a retrospective view of his school days at Canterbury. {19} After leaving school, his aunt advises a visit to Yarmouth; David first learns from Agnes the influence which Uriah Heep is gaining over Mr Wickfield; he also hears of the illness and probable return of Mr Jack Maldon; David meets Steerforth in London. {20} David goes home with Steerforth; his reception by Mrs Steerforth and Rosa Dartle. {21} His impressions of Littimer; Steerforth accompanies David to Yarmouth; Peggotty's joy at seeing David; Barkis grows a 'little near'; David and Steerforth go to Mr Peggotty's, and hear from him the story of the engagement of Ham and little Em'ly. {22} Steerforth shows David his gloomy side; Steerforth buys a boat which he calls the *Little Em'ly*; they discover Martha following Ham and Em'ly; the 'volatile' Miss Mowcher makes her appearance at the inn; Emily befriends Martha, and sheds tears at the thought of her own unworthiness. {23} David consults Steerforth in regard to his choice of a profession, and decides to become a proctor; Miss Betsey and David, on the way to Doctors' Commons, encounter the strange man who has such an effect upon her: David is articled to Spenlow and Jorkins, and makes his first appearance in court; he takes the lodgings at Mrs Crupp's. {24} He gives a supper at his lodgings to Steerforth and his friends, becomes intoxicated, and goes in that condition to the theatre, where he meets Agnes. {25} His remorse on the following day; by Agnes's invitation he calls upon her, and she warns him against Steerforth; David meets Traddles at the dinner-party at Mr Waterbrook's; David takes Uriah Heep home with him, and hears from him the particulars of the change in his expectations, and his designs in regard to Agnes. {26} David goes home with Mr Spenlow; he meets Miss Dora Spenlow, and falls in love at first sight; Miss Murdstone appears as Dora's 'confidential friend'. {27} David goes to see Traddles, and finds him boarding with Mr and Mrs Micawber. {28} David gives a dinner-party to Traddles and the Micawbers, which is interrupted by the appearance of Littimer; Mr Micawber throws down the gauntlet to society; Steerforth's arrival at David's rooms; he brings news of the illness of Mr Barkis, and David decides to go down to Yarmouth; another gloomy letter from Mr Micawber. {29} David visits Steerforth at his home again. {30} Arriving at Yarmouth he hears from Mr Omer of the unsettled state of little Em'ly; Mr Barkis 'goes out with the tide'. {31} Disappearance of Emily, who is carried away by Steerforth; Mr Peggotty decides to seek his niece, leaving Mrs Gummidge in charge of his house, Ham going to live with his aunt. {32} Miss Mowcher explains her connection with Steerforth's intimacy with Emily, and her determination to do what she can to rescue her; Mr Peggotty and David call upon Mrs Steerforth; passionate conduct of Rose Dartle: Mr Peggotty sets out on his journey. {33} David encounters Mr Murdstone at the office of Mr Spenlow; David attends a party on Dora's birthday, and falls deeper in love; he visits Dora at the house of her friend, Julia Mills, declares his passion, and is accepted; the engagement is to be kept a secret from Mr Spenlow. {34} Traddles gives David some information in regard to the family connections of 'the dearest girl in the world'; with Peggotty's assistance he redeems his household goods, taken in execution by Mr Micawber's creditors; David, returning home, is astonished to find his aunt and Mr Dick in his rooms, and to hear from her of the loss of her property. {35} David makes an ineffectual attempt to cancel his articles; David's joy at unexpectedly meeting Agnes, who goes with him to see Miss Betsey, and they hear from her an account of her losses; Uriah Heep shows his increasing influence over Mr Wickfield. {36} David becomes amanuensis to Dr Strong, who has removed to London; he meets Mr Jack Maldon, who has returned from India; David determines to learn shorthand, and he and Traddles find employment for Mr Dick; Mr Micawber, about to leave London for Canterbury as the confidential clerk of Uriah Heep, entertains David and Traddles, and settles his pecuniary obligations to the latter by presenting him his IOU. {37} David informs Dora of the change in his fortunes and prospects. {38} Traddles delivers parliamentary speeches, and David reports him; Mr Spenlow discovers, through Miss Murdstone, the attachment of David and Dora, and forbids the engagement; sudden death of Mr Spenlow, and the disordered state in which his affairs are found; Dora goes to live with her maiden aunts at Putney. {39} David finds Mr Micawber installed as confidential clerk to Wickfield and Heep, and not altogether easy in the position, he consults Agnes on the state of his engagement to Dora, and by her advice writes to Dora's aunts; Uriah forces his company upon David, and intimates his designs in regard to Agnes; effect upon Mr Wickfield of the knowledge of these designs. {40} David encounters Mr Peggotty, who relates his travels in search of Emily, and is overheard by Martha Endell. {41} David and Traddles go to Putney to see the Misses Spenlow, who consent, on certain conditions, to receive David's visits. {42} Agnes's first meeting with Dora; Uriah Heep attempts to convince Dr Strong of the faithlessness of his wife, and the noble answer of the doctor to his aspersions; David gives Uriah a blow; David receives a singular letter from Mrs Micawber. {43} Marriage of David and Dora. {44} Some account of their housekeeping. {45} Mr Dick suspects the cause of the unhappiness of Mrs Strong, and determines to 'set things right'; a convenient opportunity offering, he brings about the desired explanation. {46} David, passing by Mrs Steerforth's house, is called in by Rose Dartle, who makes Littimer repeat to him the story of Steerforth and Emily, their separation, and Emily's flight; David repeats the story to Mr Peggotty, and advises him to put Martha upon the watch for Emily, if she should return to London. {47} David and Mr Peggotty follow Martha to the riverside, and save her from suicide, and then secure her promise to devote herself to the task of saving Emily; David meets again the strange man who has such an influence over Miss Betsey, and learns from her that he is her husband. {48} Some further account of David's housekeeping, and the start of Dora's decline. {49} David receives a mysterious letter from Mr Micawber; Traddles has one equally mysterious from Mrs Micawber; they meet Mr Micawber by appointment, and find him in very low spirits; they take him home to Miss Trotwood's, where he is overcome by the cordiality of Mr Dick; commits sundry strange blunders in his favourite occupation of making punch, and finally relieves his mind by a frantic denunciation of Uriah Heep. {50} Martha brings David news of Emily; going to Martha's lodging, they see Rosa Dartle enter the room, and from an unoccupied room they witness the interview between Rosa Dartle and Emily; Peggotty returns, and meets Emily. {51} Peggotty relates to David and Miss Betsey the story of Emily's escape from Littimer, how she was befriended by a poor cottager, and finally, reaching London, was rescued by Martha; he also informs them of his plan of emigrating with Emily to Australia; David calls upon Mr Omer, and finds him in good spirits; Ham gives David a parting message for Emily, Mrs Gummidge insists on going with Mr Peggotty. {52} Miss Betsey, Mr Dick, Traddles, and David go down to Canterbury to keep their appointment with Mr Micawber; interview in the office of Wickfield and Heep, where Micawber exposes the villainy of Uriah, and Traddles, acting for Mr Wickfield, makes certain demands with which Uriah thinks it best to comply; Miss Betsey and David witness the reconciliation of Mr and Mrs Micawber; Miss Betsey proposes to them emigration, with an offer of pecuniary assistance. {53} Dora's increasing weakness, and her death. {54} Mr Micawber's preparations for emigrating; Traddles explains the condition of Mr Wickfield's affairs, and the recovery of Miss Trotwood's property; they arrange Micawber's money matters; Miss Betsey tells David the reason of her recent trouble, and he accompanies her to the funeral of her husband; David writes to Emily, communicating Ham's last message, and receives her reply. {55} The great storm at Yarmouth; David goes down to the shore to see the wrecked schooner, with the active figure conspicuous among her people; Ham attempts to reach the wreck, and is killed by the waves, and the body of the active seaman is washed ashore, and proves to be Steerforth. {56} David bears the news to Mrs Steerforth; passionate manner of Rosa Dartle towards Mrs Steerforth. {57} The emigrants complete their preparations, and set sail, Mr Peggotty taking Martha with him. {58} David goes abroad, and remains for three years. {59} On his return he seeks Traddles, finds him married and living in chambers, with five of Sophy's sisters for visitors; David encounters Mr Chillip, and hears news of the Murdstones. {60} He returns to Dover; Miss Betsey gives him a hint that Agnes's affections are engaged; David's interview with Agnes and her father, and Mr Wickfield's story of her care and kindness. {61} A glimpse at the happy life of Traddles and Sophy; David and Traddles find Mr Creakle a respected magistrate; under his escort they visit a model prison, and find Littimer and Uriah Heep among its inmates. {62} Miss Betsey strengthens David's belief in the attachment that Agnes has formed; questioning Agnes, David finds that he is himself the object of it. {63} Marriage of David and Agnes; ten years after, they receive a visit from Mr Peggotty, who brings good accounts of all the emigrants. {64} A last retrospect, showing what has happened to the principal personages of the story.

18

Bleak House

In the preface to *David Copperfield*, Dickens promised to renew his acquaintance with the public by putting forth again 'two green leaves once a month'. This he did by bringing out, in 1852, in the familiar serial form, the first number of a new novel, called *Bleak House*. It was published by Bradbury and Evans, was illustrated by *Phiz*, and ran through the usual twenty numbers. The preface was dated August 1853; the dedication was to the author's 'companions in the guild of literature and art'. The work was aimed chiefly at the vexatious delays of the Court of Chancery, and the enormous expense of prosecuting suits therein. At the time of publication there was a suit before the court which had started nearly twenty years before; in which from thirty to forty counsel had been known to appear at one time, and in which costs had been incurred to the amount of seventy thousand pounds; it was a *friendly suit*, which was said to be no nearer to its termination then than when it was begun.

CHARACTERS

BADGER, Mr Bayham – A medical practitioner in London, to whom Richard Carstone is articled. Mr Badger is noted principally for his enthusiastic admiration of his wife's former husbands; he being the third. {8, 17, 50}

BADGER, Mrs Bayham – A lady of about fifty, who dresses youthfully, and improves her fine complexion by the use of a little rouge. She is not only the wife of Mr Badger, but the widow of Captain Swosser of the Royal Navy, and of Professor Dingo, to the loss of whom she has become inured by custom, combined with science – particularly science. {8, 17}

BAGNET, Matthew – *called* '**Lignum Vitæ**'. An ex-artilleryman, 'tall and upright, with shaggy eyebrows, and whiskers like the fibres of a coconut, not a hair upon his head, and a torrid complexion'. On leaving the service he goes into 'the musical business', and becomes a bassoon-player. Of his wife's judgement he has a very exalted opinion; though he never forgets the apostolic maxim that 'the head of the woman is the man'. {27, 34, 18, 53, 66}

BAGNET, Mrs – His wife; a soldierly-looking woman, usually engaged in washing greens. {27, 34, 49, 53, 55, 66}

BAGNET, Malta – Their elder daughter; so called in the family from the place of her birth in barracks. {27, 34, 49, 56}

BAGNET, Quebec – Their younger daughter; so called in the family from the place of her birth in barracks. {27, 34, 49, 56}

BAGNET, Woolwich – Their son; so called in the family from the place of his birth in barracks. {27, 34, 49}

BARBARY, Miss – Aunt and godmother to Esther Summerson. {3}

BLINDER, Mrs – A good-natured old woman, with a dropsy, or an asthma, or perhaps both; a friend of the Necketts. {15, 23}

BOGSBY, James George – Landlord of The Sol's Arms tavern. {33}

BOODLE, Lord – A friend of Sir Leicester Dedlock's; a man of considerable reputation with his party, and who has known what office is. {7}

BOYTHORN, Lawrence – A friend of Mr Jarndyce's. {9, 12, 13, 15, 18, 23, 43, 66}

BUCKET, Mr Inspector – A detective officer, wonderfully patient, persevering, affable, alert, imperturbable, and sagacious; a stoutly built, steady-looking, sharp-eyed man in black, of about the middle age. {22, 24, 25, 49, 53, 55, 56, 57, 59, 61, 62}

BUCKET, Mrs – Wife of Mr Inspector Bucket; a lady of a natural detective genius, which, if it had been improved by professional exercise, might have done great things, but which has paused at the level of a clever amateur. {53, 54}

BUFFEY, The Right Honourable William, MP – A friend of Sir Leicester Dedlock's. {7, 28, 53, 58, 66}

CARSTONE, Richard – A ward of John Jarndyce, and a suitor in Chancery; a handsome young man with an ingenuous face and a most engaging laugh, afterwards married to Ada Clare. Though possessed of more than ordinary talent, and of excellent principles, he yet lacks tenacity of purpose, and becomes successively a student of law, a student of medicine, and a soldier. Ever haunted by the long-pending Chancery suit, and always basing his expenditures and plans on the expectation of a speedy and favourable decision of the case, he at last becomes very restless, leaves the army, and devotes all his energies to the suit. When the case is finally closed, and the whole estate is found to have been swallowed up in costs, the blow proves too much for him, and quickly results in his death. {3–6, 8, 9, 12, 14, 17, 18, 20, 23, 24, 35, 37, 39, 43, 45, 51, 60, 61, 64, 65}

CHADBAND, The Reverend Mr – A large yellow man, with a fat smile, and a general appearance of having a good deal of train-oil in his system. Visiting Mrs Snagsby's with his wife one day, he salutes the lady of the house, and her husband, which may serve as a specimen of his usual style of delivering himself. {19, 25, 55}

CHADBAND, Mrs – *formerly*, **Mrs Rachael**. Wife of the Reverend Mr Chadband; a stern, severe-looking, silent woman. {3, 19, 25, 29, 54}

CHARLEY – *See* **Neckett, Charlotte**.

CLARE, Ada – A ward of Mr John Jarndyce, and a friend of Esther Summerson; afterwards wife of Richard Carstone. {3–6, 8, 9, 13–15, 16, 17, 30, 31, 35, 37, 43, 45, 50, 51, 59, 60–62, 64, 67}

COAVINSES – *See* **Neckett, Mr**.

DARBY – A constable who accompanies Mr Bucket to Tom-all-Alone's. {22}

DEDLOCK, Sir Leicester – Representative of one of the great county families of England. {2, 7, 9, 12, 29, 40, 41, 43, 48, 53–56, 58, 63, 66}

DEDLOCK, Lady Honoria – Mother of Esther Summerson by Captain Hawdon, a gay rake, to whom she is engaged, but whom she never marries. She afterwards becomes the wife of Sir Leicester Dedlock, who knows nothing of this portion of her history but, fascinated by her beauty and wit, marries her solely for love, for she has not even 'family'. Being a proud and ambitious woman, she assumes her new position with dignity, and holds it with cold composure, hiding in her heart, however, her disgraceful secret. She flies from home upon the eve of its discovery and dies miserably, from the combined effects of shame, remorse, and exposure, at the gate of a wretched graveyard, in which the father of her child lies buried, in one of the worst and filthiest portions of London. {2, 7, 9, 12, 16, 18, 28, 29, 33, 36, 39–41, 48, 53–58}

DEDLOCK, Volumnia – A cousin of Sir Leicester Dedlock's, from whom she has an annual allowance, on which she lives at Bath, making occasional visits to the country house of her patron. She is a young lady of sixty, of high standing in the city in which she resides, but a little dreaded elsewhere, in consequence of an indiscreet profusion in the article of rouge, and persistency in wearing an obsolete pearl necklace, like a rosary of little bird's eggs. {28, 40, 53, 54, 56, 58, 66}

DONNY, Miss – Proprietor of a boarding-school, called 'Greenleaf', at Reading, where Esther Summerson spends six years. {3}

FLITE, Miss – A half-crazed little old woman, who is a suitor in Chancery, and attends every sitting of the court, expecting judgement in her favour. {3, 5, 11, 14, 20, 24, 33, 35, 46, 47, 50, 60, 65}

GEORGE – *See* **Rouncewell, George**.

GRIDLEY, Mr – called 'The Man From Shropshire'. A ruined suitor in Chancery, who periodically appears in court, and breaks out into efforts to address the Chancellor at the close of the day's business, and can by no means be made to understand that the Chancellor is legally ignorant of his existence after making it desolate for a quarter of a century. Badgered and worried and tortured by being knocked about from post to pillar and from pillar to post, he gets violent and desperate, threatens the lawyers, and pins the Chancellor like a bulldog, and is sent to the Fleet Prison over and over again for contempt of court. At last he becomes utterly discouraged and worn out, and suddenly breaks down, and dies in a shooting gallery, where he is trying to hide from the officers. {1, 15, 24}

GRUBBLE, W – Landlord of 'The Dedlock Arms', a pleasant-looking, stoutish, middle-aged man, who never seems to consider himself cosily dressed for his own fireside without his hat and top-boots, but who never wears a coat except at church. {37}

GUPPY, Mrs – Mother of William Guppy; a wayward old lady, in a large cap, with rather a red nose and rather an unsteady eye, but always smiling all over. {38, 64}

GUPPY, William – A lawyer's clerk, in the employ of Kenge and Carboy, Mr Jarndyce's solicitors; usually spoken of as 'the young man of the name of Guppy'. He conceives a passion for Esther Summerson, the heroine of the story, and declares his love ('files a declaration', as he phrases it) in a very amusing manner. At a later day, on receiving a business call from Miss Summerson and

Coavinses – Hablot K Browne *alias* Phiz

discovering that, from the effects of illness, she has lost her former beauty, he fancies that she has come to hold him to his proposal, and becomes, in consequence, very confused and apprehensive. Although she assures him that such is not the case, he nevertheless asks her to make a full and explicit statement, before a witness, whose name and address he carefully notes with legal precision, that there has never been any engagement or promise of marriage between them. {3, 4, 7, 9, 13, 19, 20, 24, 29, 32, 33, 38, 39, 44, 54, 55, 60, 63, 64}

GUSTER – (*by some supposed to have been christened* **Augusta**). Maid-servant of the Snagsbys; a lean young woman of some three or four and twenty, subject to fits. Taken originally from the workhouse, she is so afraid of being sent back there that, except when she is found with her head in the pail, or the sink, or the copper, or the dinner, or anything else that happens to be near her at the time of her seizure, she is always at work. {10, 11, 19, 22, 25, 42, 59}

GUSHER, Mr – A friend of Mrs Pardiggle's; a flabby gentleman, with a moist surface, and eyes so much too small for his moon of a face that they seem to have been originally made for somebody else. {15}

HAWDON, Captain – A law-writer who lodges at Mr Krook's, and gives himself the name of Nemo; formerly a rakish military officer, and a lover of a young lady (afterwards Lady Dedlock), who gives birth to a child (Esther Summerson) of which he is the father. He dies in a garret, and is buried in a miserable graveyard at the gate of which Lady Dedlock is found lying lifeless, after her flight from her husband's house. {5, 10, 11}

HORTENSE, Mademoiselle – Lady Dedlock's waiting-woman, and the murderess of Mr Tulkinghorn. {12, 18, 22, 23, 42, 44, 54}

JARNDYCE, John – Guardian of Richard Carstone and Ada Clare, and friend and protector of Esther Summerson. He is an unmarried man of about sixty, upright, hearty, and robust, with silvered iron-grey hair; a handsome, lively, quick face, full of change and motion; pleasant eyes; a sudden, abrupt manner; and a very benevolent heart. He affects to be subject to fits of ill humour, and has a habit of saying, when deceived or disappointed in any person or matter, that 'the wind is in the east'; and of taking refuge in his library, which he calls 'The Growlery'. Mr Jarndyce is one of the parties in the celebrated Chancery suite of 'Jarndyce and

Jarndyce'. And Mr Jarndyce does not allow himself to think of it, if he can possibly help doing so. With the warning example of so many of his kinsmen, living or dead, always before him, he refuses to enter the court, or have anything whatever, of his own accord, to do with the case; but he deeply pities and benevolently assists those of his relatives who have thrown themselves into it, and make it the object of their lives. It is found, however, that the whole estate has been absorbed in costs; and thus the suit lapses and melts entirely away. {1, 3, 6, 8, 9, 13–15, 17, 18, 23, 24, 30, 31, 35–37, 39, 43–45, 47, 50–52, 56, 60–62, 64, 65, 67}

JELLYBY, Caroline – *called* '**Caddy**'. Mrs Jellyby's eldest daughter, and her amanuensis; a pretty and industrious but sadly neglected and overworked girl. Becoming heartily disgusted and tired with copying never-ending letters to innumerable correspondents concerning the welfare of her species, she resolves that she won't be a slave all her life, and accordingly marries Prince Turveydrop, who makes her very happy. {4, 5, 14, 18, 23, 30, 38, 50, 65, 67}

JELLYBY, Mrs – A very pretty, very diminutive, plump woman, of from forty to fifty, with handsome eyes, though they have a curious habit of looking a long way off. She is a lady of remarkable strength of character, who has devoted herself to an extensive variety of public subjects, at various times, and especially to the subject of Africa, with a view to the general cultivation of the coffee-berry, *and* the natives, and the happy settlement of a portion of our superabundant home population in Borrioboola-Gha, on the left bank of the Niger. Her energies are so entirely devoted to this philanthropic project that she finds no time to consider the happiness or welfare of her own family, and the result is that her children grow up dirty, ignorant, and uncared-for; her house is disgracefully cold, cheerless, and untidy; and her husband becomes a dejected and miserable bankrupt. {4, 5, 19, 23, 30, 38, 50, 67}

JELLYBY, Mr – The husband of Mrs Jellyby; a mild, bald, quiet gentleman in spectacles, who is completely merged in the more shining qualities of his wife. {4, 5, 14, 23, 30, 38, 67}

JELLYBY, '**Peepy**' – (so self-named). A neglected and unfortunate son of Mr and Mrs Jellyby. {4, 5, 14, 23, 30, 38, 67}

JENNY – Wife of a drunken brickmaker. {8, 22, 31, 35, 46, 57}

JO – *called* '**Toughey**'. A street-crossing sweeper. A stranger who has died very suddenly has been seen speaking to Jo, who is brought before the coroner's jury. His evidence is set aside. Questioned apart, however, and privately, Jo tells his story with directness, and a touching and simple pathos. Becoming accidentally and unfortunately possessed of information which involves the secret of Lady Dedlock, poor Jo is driven away from London by officers in the service of Mr Tulkinghorn, and is always being told to 'move on', no matter where he may seek a resting-place. Worn out at last, he steals into the city, avoiding even those who would befriend him, but is finally found and taken in charge by a kind physician (Mr Woodcourt), who knows a portion of his story, and in the illness which follows is properly cared for. Jo desires to be laid in the strangers' burying-ground, near his unknown friend. {11, 16, 19, 20, 25, 29, 32, 46, 47}

JOBLING, Tony – *otherwise* 'Weevle'. A friend of Mr Guppy's, and a law writer for Mr Snagsby. 'He has the faded appearance of a gentleman in embarrassed circumstances; even his light whiskers droop with something of shabby air'. {7, 20, 32, 33, 39, 54, 55, 65}

KENGE, Mr – *called* 'Conversation Kenge'. Senior member of the firm of Kenge and Carboy, solicitors; a portly, important-looking gentleman dressed in black, with a white cravat, large gold watch seals, a pair of gold eye-glasses, and a large seal ring upon his little finger. {3, 4, 13, 17–20, 23, 24, 37, 39, 62, 65}

KROOK, Mr – Proprietor of a rag and bottle shop, and dealer in marine stores, bones, kitchen-stuff, waste paper, &c; landlord to Miss Flite and Captain Hawdon; and only brother to Mrs Smallweed. He is unmarried, old, eccentric, and much given to the use of intoxicating drinks. In person he is short, cadaverous, and withered; with his head sunk sideways between his shoulders, and the breath issuing in visible smoke from his mouth, as if he were on fire within. His only companion is a large grey cat, of a fierce disposition, which is accustomed to sit on his shoulder. With this man Mr Jobling has an appointment for twelve o'clock on a certain night. Going into the room at the hour agreed upon, he finds it full of smoke, the window-panes and furniture covered with a dark, greasy deposit, more of which is discovered lying in a small heap of ashes on the floor before the fire. The explanation is that Krook has perished, a victim to spontaneous combustion. This incident excited much controversy at the time of the publication of *Bleak House*; the possibility of spontaneous combustion being vehemently denied by the miscellanist G H Lewes (1817–78) and others. In his preface, Dickens maintains his ground, and brings forward a number of 'notable facts' in support of his position. {5, 10, 11, 14, 19, 20, 29, 32}

LIZ – A brickmaker's wife. {8, 22, 31, 46, 57}

THE MAN FROM SHROPSHIRE – *See* **Gridley, Mr.**

MELVILLESON, Miss M – A 'noted siren', or vocalist, advertised under that name, though she has been married a year and a half, and has her baby clandestinely conveyed to The Sol's Arms every night to receive its natural nourishment during the entertainments. {32, 33, 39}

MERCURY – A footman in the service of Sir Leicester Dedlock. {2, 16, 29, 33, 40, 48, 53, 54}

MOONEY – A beadle. {11}

NECKETT, Charlotte – *called* '**Charley**'. Elder daughter of Mr Neckett, a sheriff's officer. She is a womanly, self-reliant girl of about thirteen or fourteen, who, after the death of her father, goes out to work to earn a livelihood for herself and a younger brother and sister. {15, 21, 23, 30, 31, 35–37, 44, 45, 51, 61, 62, 64, 67}

NECKETT, Emma – Infant daughter of Mr Neckett. {15, 23, 67}

NECKETT, Mr – A sheriff's officer. {6, 15}

NECKETT, Tom – Mr Neckett's only son; brother to Charley and Emma. {15, 23, 67}

NEMO – *See* **Hawdon, Captain**.

PARDIGGLE, Mr O A, FRS – Husband of Mrs Pardiggle; an obstinate-looking man, with a large waistcoat and stubbly hair, always talking in a loud bass voice about his mite, or Mrs Pardiggle's mite, or their five boys' mites. {8, 30}

PARDIGGLE, Mrs – One of those charitable people who do little and make a great deal of noise. She is a School lady, a Visiting lady, a Reading lady, a Distributing lady, and on the Social Linen Box Committee, and many general committees. {8, 15, 30}

PARDIGGLE, Alfred – Youngest son of Mr and Mrs Pardiggle, aged five years. He voluntarily enrols himself in the 'Infant Bonds of Joy', and is pledged never, through life, to use tobacco in any form. {8}

PARDIGGLE, Egbert – Eldest son of Mr and Mrs Pardiggle, aged twelve years. He sends out his pocket money, to the amount of five and threepence, to the Tockahoopo Indians. {8}

PARDIGGLE, Felix – Fourth son of Mr and Mrs Pardiggle, aged seven years; contributor of eightpence to the 'Superannuated Widows'. {8}

PARDIGGLE, Francis – Third son of Mr and Mrs Pardiggle, aged nine years; a contributor of one and sixpence halfpenny to the 'Great National Smithers Testimonial'. {8}

PARDIGGLE, Oswald – Second son of Mr and Mrs Pardiggle, aged ten and a half. He gives two and ninepence to the 'Great National Smithers Testimonial'. {8}

PERKINS, Mrs – An inquisitive woman living near The Sol's Arms; neighbour to Mr Krook. {11, 20, 32, 33, 39}

PIPER, Mrs – A woman who lives near Krook's rag and bottle shop, and who leads the court. {11, 20, 32, 33, 39}

PRISCILLA – Mrs Jellyby's servant girl; 'always drinking'. {4, 5}

QUALE, Mr – A friend of Mrs Jellyby's; a loquacious young man with large shining knobs for temples, and his hair all brushed to the back of his head. He is a philanthropist, and has a project for teaching the coffee colonists of Borrioboola-Gha to teach the natives to turn pianoforte legs, and establish an export trade. {4, 5, 15, 23}

RACHAEL, Mrs – Servant to Miss Barbary; afterwards the wife of the Reverend Mr Chadband.

ROSA – Lady Dedlock's maid; a dark-haired, shy village beauty, betrothed to Watt Rouncewell. {7, 12, 16, 18, 28, 40, 48, 63}

ROUNCEWELL, Mrs – Sir Leicester Dedlock's housekeeper at Chesney Wold; a fine old lady, handsome, stately, and wonderfully neat. {7, 12, 16, 28, 34, 52, 55, 56, 58}

ROUNCEWELL, Mr – Her son; an iron master; father of Watt Rouncewell. {7, 28, 40, 48, 63}

ROUNCEWELL, George – *called* '**Mr George**'. Another son; a wild young lad, who enlists as a soldier, and afterwards becomes keeper of a shooting gallery in London. {7, 21, 24, 26, 27, 34, 47, 49, 52, 55, 56, 58, 63, 66}

ROUNCEWELL, Watt – Her grandson, betrothed to Rosa. {7, 12, 18, 28, 40, 48, 63}

SHROPSHIRE, The Man from – *See* **Gridley, Mr.**

SKIMPOLE, Arethusa – Mr Skimpole's blue-eyed 'Beauty' daughter, who plays and sings odds and ends, like her father. {43}

SKIMPOLE, Harold – A protégé of Mr John Jarndyce; a sentimentalist, brilliant, vivacious, and engaging, but thoroughly selfish and

The appointed time – Hablot K Browne *alias* Phiz

unprincipled; a genial caricature – so far as mere external peculiarities and mannerisms are concerned – of Leigh Hunt. The likeness was instantly recognised; and Dickens, while admitting that he had 'yielded to the temptation of too often making the character speak like his old friend', felt himself called upon to declare, that 'he no more thought, God forgive him! that the admired original would never be charged with the imaginary vices of the fictitious creature, than he has himself ever thought of charging the blood of Desdemona and Othello on the innocent Academy model who sat for Iago's leg in the picture'. Mr Skimpole is constantly getting into debt, and as constantly being helped out by somebody whom he never seriously thanks. Mr Skimpole is arrested for debt. He turns the matter over to his friends, completely washing his hands of the entire affair, and smiles benevolently on them as they pay him out. His furniture is seized. He remonstrates with his landlord, informing him that the articles are not paid for, and that his friend Jarndyce will have to suffer if they are taken. No attention being paid to this, he is greatly amused at 'the oddity of the thing', not understanding how a man can wish to pay himself 'at another man's expense'. {4, 8, 9, 15, 18, 31, 37, 43, 46, 57, 61}

SKIMPOLE, Mrs – Wife of Harold Skimpole; a delicate, high-nosed invalid, suffering under a complication of disorders. {43}

SKIMPOLE, Kitty – Mr Skimpole's 'Comedy' daughter, who sings a little, but don't play. {43}

SKIMPOLE, Laura – Mr Skimpole's 'Sentiment' daughter, who plays a little, but don't sing. {43}

SMALLWEED, Bartholomew – *jocularly called* '**Small**' and '**Chick Weed**'. Grandson of Mr and Mrs Smallweed, twin brother of Judy, and a friend of Mr William Guppy, on whom he sponges for dinners as often as he can. {20, 21, 33, 39, 55, 63}

SMALLWEED, Grandfather – An old man who has been in the 'discounting profession', but has become superannuated, and nearly helpless. His mind, however, is unimpaired, and still holds, as well as it ever did, the first four rules of arithmetic, and a certain small collection of the hardest facts. His favourite amusement is to throw at the head of his venerable partner a spare cushion, with which he is provided, whenever she makes an allusion to money – a subject on which he is particularly sensitive. The exertion this requires has the effect of always throwing him back into his chair like a broken puppet, and makes it necessary that he should undergo the two operations, at the hands of his granddaughter, of being shaken up like a great bottle, and poked and punched like a great bolster. {21, 26, 27, 33, 34, 54, 55, 63}

SMALLWEED, Grandmother – His wife; so far fallen into a childish state as to have regained such infantine graces as a total want of observation, memory, understanding and interest, and an eternal disposition to fall asleep over the fire, and into it. {21, 26, 27, 33, 34, 63}

SMALLWEED, Judy – Granddaughter of Mr and Mrs Smallweed, and twin sister of Bartholomew. She is so indubitably his sister that the two kneaded into one would hardly make a young person of average proportions. {21, 26, 27, 33, 34, 63}

SNAGSBY, Mr – A law stationer in Cook's Court, Cursitor Street; a mild, bald, timid man, tending to meekness and of black obesity, with a shining head and a scrubby clump of black hair sticking out at the back. Being a timid man, he is accustomed to cough with a variety of expressions, and so to save words. {10, 11, 19, 20, 22, 25, 33, 42, 47, 54, 59}

SNAGSBY, Mrs – His wife; a short shrewish woman something too violently compressed about the waist, and with a nose, like a sharp autumn evening, inclining to be frosty towards the end. {10, 11, 19, 20, 22, 25, 33, 42, 47, 54, 59}

SQUOD, Phil – A man employed in Mr George's shooting gallery. {21, 24, 26, 34, 47, 56, 66}

STABLES, The Honourable Bob – Cousin to Sir Leicester Dedlock. {2, 28, 40, 58}

SUMMERSON, Esther – Protégée of Mr Jarndyce; afterwards the wife of Allan Woodcourt. She is the narrator of a part of the story, and is represented as a prudent, wise little body, a notable housewife, a self-denying friend, and a universal favourite. She proves to be an illegitimate daughter of Lady Dedlock and Captain Hawdon. {3–6, 8, 9, 13–15, 17–19, 23, 24, 29–31, 35–38, 43–45, 47, 54, 56, 57, 59–65, 67}

SWILLS, Little – A red-faced comic vocalist, engaged at the Harmonic meetings at The Sol's Arms. {11, 19, 32, 33, 39}

TANGLE, Mr – A lawyer who knows more about the case of Jarndyce and Jarndyce than anybody, and is supposed never to have read anything else since he left school. {1}

THOMAS – Sir Leicester Dedlock's groom. {1}

TOUGHEY – *See* Jo.

TULKINGHORN, Mr – An attorney-at-law, and a solicitor of the Court of Chancery, who is the legal adviser to Sir Leicester Dedlock. Becoming acquainted with the early history of Lady Dedlock, he quietly informs her of the fact, and of his intention to reveal it to her husband, which causes her eventually to flee from home, and results in her death. Shortly after this disclosure, he is murdered in his room by a French waiting maid, whom he has made use of to discover certain family secrets, and whom he refuses to reward to the amount she desires. {2, 7, 10–12, 15, 16, 22, 24, 27, 29, 33, 34, 36, 40–42, 44, 47, 48}

TURVEYDROP, Mr – 'A very gentlemanly man, celebrated almost everywhere for his deportment'. {14, 23, 30, 38, 50, 57}

TURVEYDROP, Prince – His son; so named in remembrance of the Prince Regent, whom Mr Turveydrop the elder adored on account of his deportment. He is a little blue-eyed fair man, of youthful appearance, with flaxen hair parted in the middle, and curling at the ends all round his head. He marries Miss Caddy Jellyby. {14, 17, 23, 30–38, 50, 57}

VHOLES, Mr – Richard Carstone's solicitor; a man who is always 'putting his shoulder to the wheel', without any visible results, and is continually referring to the fact that he is a widower, with three daughters and an aged father in the Vale of Taunton, who are dependent on him for their support. {37, 39, 45, 51, 61, 62, 65}

WEEVLE, Mr – See Jobling, Tony.

WISK, Miss – A friend of Mrs Jellyby's, betrothed to Mr Quale. Her 'mission' is to show the world that woman's mission is man's mission, and that the only genuine mission of both man and woman is to be always moving declaratory resolutions about things in general at public meetings. {30}

WOODCOURT, Allan – A young surgeon, who afterwards marries Esther Summerson. {11, 13, 14, 17, 30, 35, 46, 47, 50–52, 59–61, 64, 65, 67}

WOODCOURT, Mrs – His mother; a handsome old lady, small, sharp, upright, and trim, with bright black eyes; very proud of her descent from an illustrious Welsh ancestor, named Morgan-ap-Kerrig. {17, 30, 60, 62, 64}

PRINCIPAL INCIDENTS

{1} The High Court of Chancery in session, with the suit of Jarndyce and Jarndyce; the Lord Chancellor postpones the hearing. {2} Mr Tulkinghorn reports some new proceedings in the case to Sir Leicester and Lady Dedlock; Lady Dedlock asks who copied an affidavit he reads; she swoons. {3} Esther Summerson narrates the history of her childhood, under the care of her godmother; she is informed of the stain upon her birth; she is introduced to Mr Kenge; Miss Barbary dies, and Esther learns she was her aunt; Mr Jarndyce's offer to educate Esther; on her journey to Reading, Esther is roughly befriended by a gentleman in the coach; she spends six years in Miss Donny's establishment, when she is summoned to London by Mr Jarndyce as a companion for his ward; Esther meets Ada Clare and Richard Carstone, and they go before the Lord Chancellor; Miss Flite bestows her blessing. {4} Esther, Ada, and Richard go to Mrs Jellyby's to spend the night, and find her very busy with African matters; Caddy Jellyby complains to Esther of the African business, and falls asleep with her head on Esther's lap. {5} The young people encounter Miss Flite again, who invites them to her lodgings, over Mr Krook's, to whom she introduces them; Mr Krook relates the story of Tom Jarndyce and his suicide; Miss Flite shows her birds; old Krook surprises Esther by writing out 'Jarndyce' and 'Bleak House' letter by letter. {6} On the road to Bleak House the young people receive notes of welcome from Mr Jarndyce; Esther recognises in Mr Jarndyce her stage-coach friend of six years before; description of Bleak House; Esther receives the housekeeping keys; Mr Skimpole is presented and his character described; Skimpole is arrested for debt, and released by Esther and Richard, who pay the debt; Mr Jarndyce cautions them against Mr Skimpole's weaknesses; Mr Jarndyce experiences sudden changes in the wind. {7} Mrs Rouncewell, house-keeper at Chesney Wold, conversing with her grandson, receives a call from Mr Guppy, who desires to see the house; he knows Lady Dedlock's picture, but don't know how he knows it; Mrs Rouncewell relates to her grandson and Rosa the story of the Ghost's Walk. {8} Mr Skimpole discourses on the bee; Mr Jarndyce introduces Esther to the Growlery, and explains the Chancery business; Esther finds her advice sought in everything; Mrs Pardiggle calls with her family; she explains her mission and her energy in it; Esther and Ada accompany Mrs Pardiggle on her visit to the brickmaker's; Jenny's infant dies; sympathy of Jenny's friend, and Esther, and Ada. {9}

Richard's reasoning to prove that he makes money; Mr Boythorn arrives at Bleak House; his account of his lawsuit with Sir Leicester Dedlock; Mr Guppy calls upon Mr Boythorn on business from Kenge and Carboy; he asks to see Esther alone, and 'makes an offer', which she declines. {10} Mr Tulkinghorn calls on Mr Snagsby to ascertain who copied an affidavit in Jarndyce and Jarndyce; Mr Snagsby conducts him to Krook's house, where the copyist lodges. {11} Gaining admission to the lodger's room, Mr Tulkinghorn finds him dead from an overdose of opium; Mr Snagsby relates what he knows of the deceased; Mr Tulkinghorn suggests a search for papers, but none is found; the coroner sets aside Jo's evidence; Jo watches the dead man's grave. {12} Sir Leicester and Lady Dedlock, on the road home from Paris, receive Mr Tulkinghorn's message that he had seen the person who copied the affidavit; Lady Dedlock takes notice of Rosa, which gives Hortense offence; Mr Tulkinghorn arrives at Chesney Weld, and gives them an account of the dead copyist. {13} Richard, choosing a profession, decides to become a surgeon; Mr Kenge recommends Mr Bayham Badger, and Richard is placed with him; Esther is worried by Mr Guppy's attentions; Mr Jarndyce and his wards dine at Mr Bayham Badger's; Ada confides to Esther her engagement to Richard; and they all consult Mr Jarndyce. {14} Richard begins to trust to the success of the suit in Chancery; Caddy Jellyby calls upon Esther and Ada; she informs them of her engagement; Esther accompanies her to Mr Turveydrop's academy, and is introduced to Prince Turveydrop; Mr Turveydrop, senior, exhibits his 'Deportment'; Caddy shows a desire to learn housekeeping; going to Miss Flite's room to meet Mr Jarndyce and Ada, Esther learns of the suicide of Mr Krook's lodger; Mr Allan Woodcourt appears as Miss Flite's medical attendant; Miss Flite receives a pension from an unknown source; Krook repeats the names of Miss Flite's birds; his attempts to teach himself to read. {15} Mr Skimpole's method of paying his debts; he informs Esther of the death of 'Coavinses'; they all visit Bell Yard to find Neckett's children; how Charley takes care of her brother and sister; Mrs Blinder explains the situation of the family; Mr Gridley's suit in Equity; Mr Skimpole's commentary on this state of things. {16} Jo, sweeping his crossing, is accosted by a lady to whom, at her request, he points out the places associated with the dead copyist, and is rewarded with a sovereign. {17} Richard becomes languid in the profession he has chosen; he argues to Esther that it is of little consequence, being only a kind of probation until their suit is decided; he thinks 'the law is the boy for him'; Mr Jarndyce tells Esther all he knows of her early history; Mr Woodcourt comes to take leave before going to India; Caddy Jellyby brings the flowers left by Mr Woodcourt for Esther. {18} Richard shows his careless disposition in money-matters; Mr Skimpole's idea of property; they visit Mr Boythorn, and receive a characteristic welcome; Esther experiences peculiar emotions on seeing Lady Dedlock in church; the same feelings return on meeting her in a lodge where they take shelter from the rain; how the pride of Hortense was wounded, and how she revenged herself. {19} Mr and Mrs Chadband take tea with the Snagsbys; Mr Chadband discourses; a constable brings Jo to Mr Snagsby's because he won't 'move on'; Mr Guppy appears on the scene; Jo tells the story of the lady and the sovereign; Mr Chadband improves the occasion, and Jo 'moves on'. {20} Mr Guppy invites his friends Smallweed and Jobling to dine with him; Mr Guppy proposes to Jobling to apply for copying to Snagsby, and also to take the vacant lodgings at Krook's; Mr Guppy presents his friend to Krook under the name of Weevle, and he takes possession of the room. {21} The Smallweed family introduced; Mr George calls to pay the interest on a loan from Mr Smallweed's 'friend in the City'; their talk concerning Captain Hawdon; returning to his shooting-gallery, George is received by Phil Squod. {22} Mr Snagsby, repeating to Mr Tulkinghorn Jo's story of the sovereign, is surprised to find Mr Bucket in company; Mr Bucket and Snagsby go to 'Tom-all-Alone's' in search of Jo; they find Jenny and her friend; finding Jo, they return with him to Mr Tulkinghorn's rooms, where Jo recognises the dress of the lady who bestowed the sovereign, but not the lady herself, she being personated by Mademoiselle Hortense. {23} Mr Jarndyce and his wards return to Bleak House; Hortense offers herself to Esther as lady's maid; Richard is again unsettled, and now makes choice of the army; Caddy consults Esther on breaking the news of her engagement to Mr Turveydrop and Mrs Jellyby; Mr Turveydrop is overcome, but soon recovers; Mrs Jellyby is too much absorbed in Borrioboola-Gha to show any interest in her daughter; Esther returns home and finds Charley engaged as her maid. {24} Mr Jarndyce desires Richard and Ada to cancel their engagement before Richard joins his regiment; Mr George calls to teach Richard fencing, and thinks he has seen Esther before; Esther and Richard visit the Court of Chancery; Mr Guppy introduces Mrs Chadband, formerly Mrs Rachael; Mr George appears in search of Miss Flite, whom Gridley, who is hiding at George's to avoid arrest, wants to see; Esther and Richard accompany them to George's; Mr Bucket obtains admittance in disguise; death of Gridley. {25} Mrs Snagsby becomes suspicious and jealous; Mr Chadband 'improves a tough subject'; Jo is fed by Guster, Mr Snagsby's servant, and dismissed by Snagsby with the gift of half-a-crown. {26} Mr George and Phil Squod converse about the country; Phil's account of his early life; Mr George is visited at his gallery by Grandfather Smallweed and Judy; Mr Smallweed wants to obtain a specimen of Captain Hawdon's writing for a lawyer; Mr George accompanies him to the lawyer, who proves to be Mr Tulkinghorn. {27} Mr Tulkinghorn offers him a reward for the writing he possesses; Mr George declines, but proposes to take a friend's advice; the 'old girl' gives George Mr Bagnet's opinion, which confirms his own; Mr George returns to Mr Tulkinghorn's, who uses high words to him in the presence of a clerk. {28} Sir Leicester and Lady Dedlock, after their visitors retire, give audience to Mrs Rouncewell's son; he speaks of the attachment of his son for Rosa and requests to be allowed to remove her from Chesney Wold; Sir Leicester declines; Lady Dedlock invites Rosa's confidence, and promises to make her happy if she can. {29} The young man of the name of Guppy calls on Lady Dedlock; he mentions the remarkable resemblance of Esther Summerson to my lady, relates what he has discovered of her history – that her real name is Hawdon, and that he has found that the deceased law-writer's was the same; he promises to bring my lady Mr Hawdon's papers, of which he will gain possession that night; Lady Dedlock's secret agony for her child. {30}. Mrs Woodcourt visits Bleak House; Caddy Jellyby spends three weeks at Bleak House, preparing for her wedding; Caddy and Prince are married. {31} Charley informs Esther of the return of Jenny and Liz, and a sick boy with them; Esther and Charley go to Jenny's, and find Jo; he is terrified at Esther's resemblance to the lady who gave him the sovereign; they take Jo home, where they find Mr Skimpole, who advises turning him into the street; Jo disappears in the night; Esther nurses Charley through a dangerous illness, and falls ill herself. {32} Mr Snagsby, passing through Cook's Court at night, calls Mr Weevle's attention to a peculiar smell about the place; Mr Guppy and Mr Weevle, waiting the appointed time for receiving the packet of Captain Hawdon's letters from Krook, are disgusted by the taint in the atmosphere;

keeping his appointment, they find Krook dead by spontaneous combustion. {33} Mr Snagsby is followed to The Sol's Arms by his wife, who takes him home again; Mr Guppy recommends Weevle to remain in Krook's house, and keep possession of the property; unexpected appearance of heirs to the estate in the persons of the Smallweed family; Mr Guppy carries the news of Krook's death, and the probable destruction of the papers, to Lady Dedlock; retiring, he meets Mr Tulkinghorn. {34} George receives due notice of the maturity of his loan from Grandfather Smallweed; Mr Bagnet and his wife, coming in to renew his draft, find Mr George in this dilemma: Mr Bagnet gives his opinion, through the 'old girl', that they had better see Mr Smallweed at once; Mr Smallweed refuses to renew the loan, and breaks the pipe of peace; they go to Mr Tulkinghorn's, where they meet Mrs Rouncewell coming out; to free himself from Smallweed's claims, Mr George sells Mr Tulkinghorn the specimen of Captain Hawdon's writing; George advises Woolwich to honour his mother. {35} Esther's recovery; her first interview with Mr Jarndyce; she receives a call from Miss Flite; Miss Flite's account of her case in Chancery, and her warning about Richard; the story of Mr Woodcourt's heroic bravery. {36} Esther and Charley go to Mr Boythorn's; Esther first sees the reflection of her face scarred by the disease; Esther, resting in the wood, is met by Lady Dedlock, who owns her as her child, but tells her they must never meet again; Esther's first meeting with Ada since her recovery. {37} Richard sends for Esther to meet him at The Dedlock Arms; Mr Skimpole appears as Richard's artless friend; Esther has an interview with Richard, who shows increasing dislike for Mr Jarndyce, and increasing confidence in the early decision of the suit; Ada writes to Richard, praying him to relinquish his hope from the suit; Esther tries to give Mr Skimpole an idea of responsibility; Mr Vholes, Richard's new legal adviser, appears, Mr Skimpole showing how he introduced him to Richard; Mr Vholes informs Richard that his cause is coming on the next morning, and they return to town immediately. {38} Esther goes to London; she calls on Caddy Jellyby, and dances with the apprentices: Esther and Caddy call on Mr Guppy; Esther requests a private interview with Mr Guppy, and cures that gentleman's passion by showing her face; she requests him to give up all idea of serving her through any discovery relating to her parentage. {39} Mr Vholes's respectability; interview between Vholes and Richard, in which Vholes appears with 'his shoulder to the wheel'; Mr Guppy and Mr Weevle go to Krook's house to remove Mr Weevle's effects; they find Mr Tulkinghorn looking on as the Smallweeds examine Krook's papers; Mr Guppy declines to explain to Mr Tulkinghorn the business he had with Lady Dedlock. {40} Sir Leicester and his retinue return to Chesney Wold; Sir Leicester discusses with Volumnia the pending elections; Mr Tulkinghorn arrives with the news of the defeat of Sir Leicester's party, and that Mr Rouncewell and his son were very active in aiding that result; Mr Tulkinghorn tells a story bearing on Rosa's position as Lady Dedlock's maid. {41} Mr Tulkinghorn, on retiring to his room, is sought by Lady Dedlock; she asks how long he has known her secret, and how far it is known to others; she informs him of her design to leave Chesney Wold at once; he counsels her to remain just as before in all respects, and promises to take no steps to expose her without warning. {42} Mr Snagsby complains to Mr Tulkinghorn of the persecutions of Mademoiselle Hortense; Mr Tulkinghorn threatens to have Hortense put in confinement if she continues her importunities. {43} Esther suggests to her guardian that Mr Skimpole is not a safe adviser for Richard; they visit Mr Skimpole at his home; Mr Skimpole introduces his family; he returns with Mr Jarndyce to Bleak House; they receive a call from Sir Leicester Dedlock; Esther's agitation in his presence; Esther tells her guardian of the relationship between herself and Lady Dedlock. {44} Mr Jarndyce sends Esther a letter, with her permission, asking her to become the mistress of Bleak House; Esther destroys the flowers sent her by Mr Woodcourt; she answers yes to Mr Jarndyce's letter. {45} Mr Vholes calls upon Mr Jarndyce, and reports the sad state of Richard's affairs; Esther decides to go and see Richard at Deal, where he is stationed, and she sets out with Charley for her companion; she finds Richard looking worn and haggard; Richard grows more and more angry with Mr Jarndyce as the cause of his trials, and convinces Esther of the necessity of his withdrawing from the army; Esther recognises Allan Woodcourt among some gentlemen landing from an Indiaman just arrived; she has an interview with him, and requests him to befriend Richard, which he promises to do. {46} Going through Tom-all-Alone's, Mr Woodcourt finds Jenny with a bruised head, which he dresses for her; they pursue and overtake Jo, and Allan hears from Jenny the story of his having been taken in at Bleak House, and Esther catching his disease; Jo gives the reason of his escaping from Bleak House, and Allan takes charge of him. {47} Jo tells Allan the story of the lady in the veil; Woodcourt consults Miss Flite to find a place of refuge for Jo, and she recommends George; Mr George takes him in; George expresses to Mr Woodcourt his feelings towards Tulkinghorn; Jo sends a message to Mr Snagsby, who calls to see him; Jo makes his last request, and dies. {48} Lady Dedlock dismisses Rosa; Mr Rouncewell calls, by Lady Dedlock's appointment, and she relinquishes Rosa to his care; Mr Tulkinghorn, who is present at the interview, warns Lady Dedlock that he considers her course a departure from her promise, and that he shall soon undeceive Sir Leicester; Mr Tulkinghorn goes home to his rooms, and in the morning is found murdered lying on the floor. {49} Mr Bagnet prepares a feast on his wife's birthday; George joins them in dull spirits, which he accounts for by Jo's death; Mr Bucket adds himself to the party, and makes himself friendly; Bucket arrests George for the murder of Mr Tulkinghorn. {50} Caddy Jellyby, who has an infant, and is ill, sends for Esther, and Mr Jarndyce and Ada go with her to London; Caddy recovers under Mr Woodcourt's medical care; Esther notices a change in Ada's manner towards her; Mr Woodcourt applies to Vholes for Richard's address. {51} He finds him next door; Esther and Ada visit Richard at his rooms; Ada acknowledges her secret marriage to Richard, and Esther returns alone; Esther tells Mr Jarndyce. {52} Mr Woodcourt tells Mr Jarndyce and Esther of the murder of Mr Tulkinghorn and the arrest of Mr George; the three visit him in prison; George is determined to stand by the exact truth, and have no lawyer; Mr and Mrs Bagnet also come to see George; George mentions the resemblance of Esther to a figure he saw on Mr Tulkinghorn's stairs at the time of the murder. {53} Mrs Bagnet reasons that George's mother is alive, and sets off for Lincolnshire in search of her; Mr Bucket watches his wife and their lodger; Bucket receives anonymous letters containing Lady Dedlock's name; he informs Sir Leicester that he has the case nearly worked up. {54} Next morning, Mr Bucket informs Sir Leicester that the case is complete; he proceeds to relate the conduct of Lady Dedlock, and her fear of Tulkinghorn, when they are interrupted by the arrival of Smallweed, the Chadbands, and Mrs Snagsby, who demand to be paid for suppressing what they have learnt of Lady Dedlock's story; Bucket dismisses them, and admits Mademoiselle Hortense, whom he accuses of the murder, and shows how he has worked up the evidence. {55} Mrs Bagnet brings Mrs Rouncewell, Mr George's mother, to London; the mother and son in prison; Mrs

Rouncewell informs Lady Dedlock that she has found her son, and appeals to her for pity; Mr Guppy requests an interview with Lady Dedlock, and informs her that Mr Smallweed and others, probably, know all she would have; concealed; flight of Lady Dedlock. {56} Sir Leicester is struck with paralysis; Mr Bucket interprets his signs, and sets off in pursuit of Lady Dedlock; he goes to Mr Jarndyce's house, and gets Esther to accompany him. {57} Bucket tracks Lady Dedlock to the brickmaker's at St Albans; they are bold she went north, while Jenny went to London, and they follow on northward in search of her; Bucket at fault. {58} He decides to follow the other one, and returns to London; what rumour says of Lady Dedlock; Sir Leicester insists on seeing Mr Rouncewell's son George; they watch through the day and night for Lady Dedlock's return; Esther and Mr Bucket reach London. {59} They trace the person they are following to Mr Snagsby's, meeting Mr Woodcourt by the way; they find a letter for Esther, written by Lady Dedlock; following Guster's directions, they find Lady Dedlock lying dead at the gate of the burying-ground. {60} Esther learns from her guardian that Mr Woodcourt has decided to remain in England; Miss Flite makes Richard her executor; Mr Vholes discusses Richard's interests with Esther; Ada confides her secret to Esther. {61} Esther requests Mr Skimpole not to go to Richard's any more, and attempts to remonstrate with him for betraying Jo to Bucket; Mr Skimpole drops from this history; Allan Woodcourt declares his love to Esther. {62} Esther fixes the day for becoming mistress of Bleak House; Mr Bucket introduces Mr Smallweed, with a newly discovered will in Jarndyce. {63} George makes the acquaintance of his brother and his family. {64} Mr Jarndyce goes to Yorkshire to look after Mr Woodcourt's business, and sends for Esther to follow him; he shows her the house he has prepared for Allan, which he has named Bleak House, and relinquishes her to Woodcourt; Mr Guppy, backed by his mother and Mr Jobling, renews his proposal. {65} Jarndyce and Jarndyce is over for good; Richard is reconciled to Mr Jarndyce, and 'begins the world'. {66} Sir Leicester's life at Chesney Wold. {67} Esther closes her narrative.

19

Hard Times

For these Times

This tale was originally published in *Household Words*; the first chapter making its appearance in No 210 (April 1851), and the last in No 229 (12 August 1854). In the same year it was brought out, independently, in one octavo volume of 352 pages, and was inscribed to Thomas Carlyle.

'My satire is against those who see figures and averages, and nothing else – the representatives of the wickedest and most enormous vice of this time; the men who, through long years to come, will do more to damage the really useful truths of political economy than I could do (if I tried) in my whole life; the addled heads who would take the average of cold in the Crimea during twelve months as a reason for clothing a soldier in nankeen on a night when he would be frozen to death in fur, and who would comfort the labourer, in travelling twelve miles a day to and from his work, by telling him that the average distance of one inhabited place from another on the whole area of England is not more than four miles.'

CHARACTERS

BITZER – A light-haired and light-eyed pupil of Mr M'Choakumchild's, in Mr Gradgrind's model school; crammed full of hard
facts, but with all fancy, sentiment, and affection taken out of him.
After he leaves school, Bitzer is employed as light porter and clerk
at Mr Bounderby's bank. When Mr Gradgrind's son, after robbing
the bank, endeavours to escape, he starts in pursuit, and pounces on
him just as he is about to start for Liverpool. {Book 1: ch 2, 5; Book
2: ch 1, 4, 6, 8, 9, 11; Book 3: ch 7–9}

BLACKPOOL, Mrs – Wife of Stephen Blackpool. Soon after her
marriage, she takes to drinking, and goes on from bad to worse,
until she becomes a curse to her husband, to herself, and to all
around her. {Book 1: ch 10–13; Book 3: ch 9}

BLACKPOOL, Stephen – A simple, honest power-loom weaver, in Mr Bounderby's factory. A rather stooping man, with a knitted brow, a pondering expression of face, and a hard-looking head, sufficiently capacious, on which his iron-grey hair lay long and thin. His lot is a hard one. Tied to a miserable, drunken wife, who has made his home a desolation and a mockery, and for whom he has long ceased to feel either respect or love, he finds himself unable to marry – as he would like to do – a woman (Rachael) who has been a kind and dear friend to him for many years; and he goes to Mr Bounderby for advice. When the Coketown operatives enter into a combination against their employers, and establish certain 'regulations', Stephen refuses to join them, and they all renounce and shun him. And when Mr Bounderby questions him about the association (styled the 'United Aggregate Tribunal'), calling the members 'a set of rascals and rebels', he earnestly protests that they are acting from a sense of duty, and is angrily told to finish what he's at, and then look elsewhere for work. Stephen leaves Coketown in search of employment, but soon after returns, being falsely accused of complicity in the robbery at Mr Bounderby's bank and, on his way, he falls into an abandoned coal shaft ('Old Hell Shaft') hidden by thick grass, where he remains for some days, when he is accidentally discovered and is rescued, alive, but dreadfully bruised, and so injured that he dies soon after being brought to the surface. {Book 1: ch 10–13; Book 2: ch 4–6, 9; Book 3: ch 4–6}

BOUNDERBY, Josiah – A wealthy Coketown manufacturer, who marries the daughter of Mr Gradgrind. {Book 1: ch 3–9, 11, 14–16; Book 2: ch 1–12; Book 3: ch 2–9}

BOUNDERBY, Mrs Louisa – *See* **Gradgrind, Louisa**.

CHILDERS, Mr E W B – A young man who is a member of Sleary's Circus Troupe, and is celebrated for his daring vaulting act as the Wild Huntsman of the North American Prairies. {Book 1: ch 6; Book 3: ch 7, 8}

GORDON, Emma – A member of Sleary's Circus Troupe, and a friend to Sissy Jupe. {Book 1: ch 6; Book 3: ch 7}

GRADGRIND, Mr Thomas – A retired wholesale hardware merchant. Mr Gradgrind's residence is a very matter-of-fact place called Stone Lodge, situated on a moor within a mile or two of the great manufacturing town of Coketown. Mr Gradgrind marries his eldest daughter, according to a mathematical plan which he has

Stephen Blackpool recovered – Fred Walker

adopted, to his friend Mr Bounderby, who is not only twenty years her senior, but is in every respect unsuited to her. The result of this ill-assorted union is unhappiness not only to the wife but to her father as well, for whom a still sharper trial is in store. His eldest son, whom he has carefully trained, becomes dissipated, robs his employer, Mr Bounderby, and brings disgrace on the hitherto unblemished name of Gradgrind. In his sore trouble, Mr Gradgrind is consoled and strengthened by two of the most unpractical people in the world – Mr Sleary, the manager of a circus, and Sissy Jupe, the daughter of a clown – both of whom he has repeatedly lectured on their utter want of worldly wisdom and practicality. Forced to admit that much of his misfortune is attributable to his own hard system of philosophy, he becomes a humbler and a wiser man, bending his hitherto inflexible theories to appointed circumstances; making his facts and figures subservient to Faith, Hope, and Charity, and no longer trying to grind that heavenly trio in his dusty little mills. {Book 1: ch 1–9, 14–16; Book 2: ch 1–3, 7, 9, 11, 12; Book 3: ch 1–9}

GRADGRIND, Mrs – Wife of Mr Thomas Gradgrind. {Book 1: ch 4, 9, 15; Book 2: ch 9}

GRADGRIND, Adam Smith – A younger son of Mr Gradgrind. {Book 1: ch 4}

GRADGRIND, Jane – Mr Gradgrind's younger daughter. (Book 1: ch 4, 16; Book 2: ch 9; Book 3: ch 1}

GRADGRIND, Louisa – Eldest child of Mr Gradgrind. {Book 1: ch 3, 4, 6–9, 14–16; Book 2: ch 1–3, 5–12; Book 3: ch 1–9}

GRADGRIND, Malthus – A son of Mr Gradgrind. {Book 1: ch 4}

GRADGRIND, Thomas – Mr Gradgrind's youngest son; a selfish, ill-natured, sensual, mercenary whelp. He is employed as a clerk in Bounderby's Bank and, being a dissipated and extravagant idler, robs it of some hundred and fifty pounds. For a time he succeeds in throwing suspicion upon an innocent factory operative, Stephen Blackpool; but his own guilt is soon established, and he flees from the country to avoid arrest and imprisonment. {Book 1: ch 3, 4, 7–9, 14, 16; Book 2: ch 1–3, 5–8, 10–12; Book 3: ch 2–9}

HARTHOUSE, Mr James – A friend of Mr Gradgrind's; a thorough gentleman, made to the model of the time, weary of everything, and putting no more faith in anything than Lucifer. He is 'five-and-thirty, good looking, good figure, good teeth, good voice, dark hair, bold eyes'. {Book 2: ch 1– 3, 5, 7–12; Book 3: ch 2, 3}

JUPE, Cecilia – *or* **Sissy**. The daughter of a clown. She has been kindly permitted to attend the school controlled by Mr Gradgrind; but Mr Bounderby thinks that she has a bad influence over the other children, and advises that the privilege should be withdrawn. The two gentlemen accordingly visit The Pegasus' Arms, at Pod's End, to inform her father of their intention; but they find that Signor Jupe – always a half-cracked man – having got old and stiff in the joints, so that he cannot perform his parts satisfactorily, and having got his daughter into the school, and therefore, as he seems to think, got her well provided for, has run off to parts unknown. Under these circumstances, Mr Gradgrind decides to take charge of the girl, and educate and support her. She accompanies him home, and makes herself very useful and companionable in his family. When Louisa is about to fall into the meshes of Mr Harthouse, Sissy visits that gentleman, and persuades and shames him into leaving the neighbourhood; and when Mr Gradgrind's son is about to be arrested for the robbery of Bounderby's Bank, she sends him to her father's old employer, Mr Sleary, who conceals him and gets him safely abroad. {Book 1: ch 2, 4–9, 14, 15; Book 2: ch 9; Book 3: ch 1, 2, 4–9}

JUPE, Signor – A clown in Sleary's circus; father of Sissy Jupe, and owner of the 'highly-trained performing dog Merrylegs'. {Book 1: ch 2, 3, 5, 6, 9; Book 3: ch 2, 8}

KIDDERMINSTER, Master – A member of Sleary's Circus Troupe; a diminutive boy, with an old face, who assists Mr Childers in his daring vaulting act as the Wild Huntsman of the North American Prairies; taking the part of his infant son, and being carried upside down over his father's shoulder, by one foot, and held by the crown of his head, heels upwards, in the palm of his father's hand, according to the violent paternal manner in which wild huntsmen may be observed to fondle their offspring. {Book 1: ch 6; Book 2: ch 7}

M'CHOAKUMCHILD, Mr – Teacher in Mr Gradgrind's model school. {Book 1: ch 1–3, 9, 14}

MERRYLEGS – Signor Jupe's trained performing dog. {Book 1: ch 3, 5–8; Book 3: ch 8}

PEGLER, Mrs – Mother of Josiah Bounderby; a mysterious old woman, tall and shapely, though withered by time. Her son, growing rich, becomes ashamed of her, and gives her thirty pounds a year to keep away from him, and not claim any relationship with him; but the secret is at last divulged, under the most ridiculous circumstances, through the agency of the inquisitive Mrs Sparsit. {Book 1: ch 12; Book 2: ch 6, 8; Book 3: ch 4, 5}

RACHAEL – A factory hand; a friend of Stephen Blackpool's. {Book 1: ch 10–13; Book 2: ch 4, 6; Book 3: ch 4–6, 9}

SCADGERS, Lady – Great-aunt to Mrs Sparsit; an immensely fat old woman with an inordinate appetite for butcher's meat, and a mysterious leg, which has refused to get out of bed for fourteen years. {Book 1: ch 7; Book 2: ch 8; Book 3: ch 9}

SLACKBRIDGE – A trades-union agitator and orator. {Book 2 ch 4; Book 3: ch 4}

SLEARY, Josephine – Daughter of a circus proprietor; a pretty, fair-haired girl of eighteen, noted for her graceful Tyrolean flower act. {Book 1: ch 6; Book 2: ch 7}

SLEARY, Mr – Proprietor of a 'Horse-riding', or circus; a stout man, with one fixed eye and one loose eye, a voice (if it can be called so) like the efforts of a broken old pair of bellows, a flabby surface, and a muddled head, which is never sober, and never drunk. He is troubled with asthma, and his breath comes far too thick and heavy for the letter 's'. {Book 1: ch 6, 9; Book 3: ch 7, 8}

SPARSIT, Mrs – Mr Bounderby's housekeeper; an elderly lady, highly connected, with a Coriolanian style of nose and dense black eyebrows. Mr Bounderby gives her a hundred a year, disguising the payment under the name of an 'annual compliment'. {Book 1: ch 7, 11, 16; Book 2: ch 1, 3, 6, 8–11; Book 3: ch 3, 5, 9}

PRINCIPAL INCIDENTS

BOOK 1 – {1} Mr Thomas Gradgrind discourses on fact to the schoolchildren. {2} He examines Sissy Jupe, and expresses his dissatisfaction at the business of her father; Mr Gradgrind and his friend, addressing the school, insist upon the supremacy of fact. {3} Mr Gradgrind's horror at finding his children peeping at the circus. {4} Mr Bounderby gives Mrs Gradgrind an account of his bringing up; Mr Gradgrind enters with the children, and he and Bounderby decide that the presence of Sissy Jupe in the school has produced a bad effect, and that she should be dismissed. {5} Mr Gradgrind and Mr Bounderby go to Coketown to carry out this design, when they

Mr Harthouse and Tom Gradgrind in the garden –
F. Walker and Maurice Greiffenhagen

meet Sissy in the street, and go with her to the house where her father is staying. {6} Jupe is missing, and Sissy goes in search of him; Mr E W B Childers suspects Jupe has run away, and so explains his absence; finding Jupe does not return, Gradgrind offers Sissy a home under certain conditions, which she accepts. {7} Mrs Sparsit appears as Mr Bounderby's housekeeper; Mr Gradgrind completes his plan of befriending Sissy Jupe, and takes her home with him to Stone Lodge. {8} Sympathy between Tom and Louisa, and Tom's plan of managing Bounderby through her influence. {9} Sissy's account of her progress in school; she tells Louisa about her father and his occupation; Sissy's continued disappointment at bearing nothing from her father. {10} Stephen Blackpool, watching for Rachael as the hands leave the factories, misses her, but afterwards overtakes her on the way home; leaving her, he proceeds home, and finds his drunken wife come back. {11} Stephen consults Mr Bounderby how he can get rid of his wife by law, and is more than ever convinced that it 'is a' a muddle'. {12} After leaving Mr Bounderby's house, Stephen encounters a mysterious old woman, who is greatly interested in that gentleman's welfare. {13} Stephen finds Rachael tending his wife; Rachael prevents her from poisoning herself; Rachael's influence over Stephen. {14} Sissy Jupe is removed from school; Mr Gradgrind becomes sensible that Louisa has grown quite a young woman; Tom gives Louisa a hint of how she may be useful to him. {15} Mr Gradgrind informs Louisa that Mr Bounderby has offered to make her his wife, and she accepts him. {16} Mr Bounderby informs Mrs Sparsit of his approaching marriage, and provides for her removal to the bank; Mr Bounderby makes a speech at his wedding breakfast.

BOOK 2 – {1} Bitzer informs Mrs Sparsit of his suspicions of Mr Tom; Mr James Harthouse calls at the bank to make inquiries for Mr Bounderby. {2} Mr Harthouse presents his letters of introduction to Mr Bounderby, and is introduced to Mrs Bounderby; Mr Harthouse, watching for something to move Louisa, finds it in the appearance of Tom. {3} Harthouse draws from Tom some particulars in regard to his sister and her education. {4} Slackbridge harangues the Coketown operatives; Stephen declines to enter into the proposed regulations of the workmen, and is shunned by all his old friends. {5} Bounderby sends for Stephen, who expresses to him and Harthouse his opinion of the action of the workmen, who Stephen justifies, though he does not join them; Bounderby becomes angry with him, and discharges him. {6} Stephen is surprised to meet Rachael in company with Mrs

Pegler, the mysterious old woman whom he had met before; he informs them of his discharge, and invites them to accompany him home; Mrs Pegler speaks of the son whom she has lost, and shows great fear of meeting Mr Bounderby; Louisa calls upon Stephen, accompanied by Tom, to express her sympathy, and to offer him assistance; Tom, under promise of doing him a service, asks Stephen to hang about the bank each evening before he leaves Coketown; Stephen leaves Coketown in search of work. {7} Harthouse goes to Mr Bounderby's country-house, and finds Louisa alone; he assumes an interest in Tom for the purpose of securing an influence over her; Harthouse accuses Tom of ingratitude to his sister, and he promises amendment. {8} The robbery of Bounderby's Bank, and the effect of the news upon Louisa; Stephen Blackpool is suspected of the crime on the evidence of Mrs Sparsit and Bitzer, by whom he was seen hanging about the bank; Mrs Sparsit shows her determination to pity Bounderby, and keeps her eye on Harthouse and Louisa; Louisa goes to Tom's room, and bogs him to confide in her. {9} Mrs Sparsit's action throws Harthouse and Louisa more together; sickness and death of Mrs Gradgrind; Mrs Sparsit watches the growing intimacy of Harthouse with Louisa. {10} Harthouse tries to convince Louisa of Blackpool's guilt. {11} Mrs Sparsit, learning from Tom that he has an appointment to meet Mr Harthouse at Coketown, suspects this is a plan to keep Tom out of the way, while Harthouse goes to meet Louisa alone in the absence of Mr Bounderby; hastening off to the country-house, she finds them together, and overhears Harthouse's declaration of love; Mrs Sparsit follows Louisa, through a drenching storm, to Coketown, and there loses sight of her. {12} Louisa goes home to her father, tells him her story, and begs him to save her.

BOOK 3 – {1} Mr Gradgrind begins to suspect some defect in his system of education; Sissy comforts Louisa. {2} Mr Harthouse, in doubt of what may happen next, receives a call from Sissy Jupe, who informs him he can never see Louisa again, and asks him, as the only reparation he can make, to leave the place immediately, which he decides to do. {3} Mrs Sparsit informs Bounderby of her discoveries, and he takes her to Mr Gradgrind's, where he learns what has become of Louisa; at Mr Gradgrind's suggestion that Louisa should remain there for a time, Bounderby determines to leave her there altogether. {4} Bounderby offers a reward for the apprehension of Stephen Blackpool; Rachael appeals to Louisa to confirm her story of Louisa's visit to Stephen, and promises that he shall be there in two days; Stephen fails to appear, and cannot be found. {5} Mrs Sparsit captures old Mrs Pegler, and takes her to Bounderby's house; she proves to be Bounderby's mother, and all his stories of his childhood are falsehoods. {6} Sissy and Rachael, walking in the fields, discover Stephen's hat at the mouth of an abandoned coal shaft; help gathers, and Stephen is raised from the pit, still alive; he recognises Rachael, and asks Mr Gradgrind to clear his name, as his son can tell him how; Stephen dies. {7} Tom vanishes at a hint from Sissy; Louisa and Sissy inform Mr Gradgrind of their previous suspicions of Tom, and that Sissy had sent him to Mr Sleary to be hidden; Mr Gradgrind, Louisa and Sissy go to Mr Sleary, then exhibiting not far from Liverpool, and arrange for Tom's escape from the country, in disguise, when their plan is interrupted by Bitzer. {8} Mr Sleary, through the aid of his trained horse and dog, helps Tom to escape. {9} Mrs Sparsit takes leave of Mr Bounderby; fate of the characters.

He drew up a placard offering twenty pounds reward for Stephen Blackpool – Harry French

20

The Seven Poor Travellers

[Published in *Household Words*, 1854]

In the ancient city of Rochester, in Kent, is an ancient house with this inscription over its quaint old door:

RICHARD WATTS, ESQ.
BY HIS WILL, DATED 22 AUG 1579,
FOUNDED THIS CHARITY
FOR SIX POOR TRAVELLERS
WHO, NOT BEING ROGUES, OR PROCTORS,
MAY RECEIVE GRATIS FOR ONE NIGHT
LODGING, ENTERTAINMENT,
AND FOURPENCE EACH

On a certain Christmas eve, the narrator of the story – who describes himself as being a traveller, and withal as poor as he hopes to be – visits the Charity, and makes inquiries of the matron concerning the institution and its management. He finds that the prescribed number of travellers is forthcoming every night from year's end to year's end, but that they are not lodged in the house itself, occupying two little galleries at the back instead; neither are they provided with entertainment, as might be supposed, but buy what they can with their fourpences, and prepare their own suppers, a fire and cooking utensils being furnished them for this purpose. Of the whole revenue of the establishment, only about a thirtieth part is expended for the objects commemorated in the inscription over the door; the rest being handsomely laid out in chancery, law-expenses, collectorship, receivership, poundage, and other appendages of management highly complimentary to the importance of the Six Poor Travellers, and essential to the dignity of the Board of Trustees. Having ascertained these facts, the narrator becomes desirous of treating the travellers on that night to a supper and a glass of hot wassail at his own expense. Consent being granted, he sets before them a most substantial and excellent meal, and after it is ended tells them

THE STORY OF RICHARD DOUBLEDICK

CHARACTERS INTRODUCED

BEN – A waiter.

DOUBLEDICK, Richard – A young man who has run wild, and has been dismissed by the girl to whom he was betrothed. Made reckless by this well-deserved stroke, he enlists in a regiment of the line under an assumed name, becomes more dissipated than ever, and is constantly getting punished for some breach of discipline. Under the influence of the captain of his company, however, he becomes an altered man, rises rapidly from the ranks, and gains the reputation of being one of the boldest spirits in the whole army. At Badajos the captain falls, mortally wounded by a French officer; and from that moment Doubledick devotes himself to avenging the death of his friend, in case he should ever meet that French officer again. At Waterloo he is among the wounded, and for many long weeks his recovery is doubtful; but he is tenderly nursed by Mrs Taunton, the mother of his lost friend, and by the young lady (Mary Marshall) to whom he had been engaged, and who now marries him. Three years afterwards, he has occasion to visit the South of France, to join Mrs Taunton (who has gone thither for her health), and escort her home. He finds her the unwitting guest of the very officer who killed her son, and whose life he has vowed to have in return. But the frank and noble demeanour of the Frenchman, the innocent happiness of his pleasant home, and the warm regard which Mrs Taunton has come to feel for him – all combine to suggest better thoughts, and feelings; and Captain Doubledick secretly forgives him in the name of the divine Forgiver of injuries.

MARSHALL, Mary – A beautiful girl, betrothed to Richard Doubledick; afterwards estranged from but finally married to him.

TAUNTON, Captain – The captain of the company in which Private Richard Doubledick enlists.

TAUNTON, Mrs – His mother.

21

The Holly Tree

Published in Household Words, *December 1855*

This is the story of a gentleman who, imagining himself to have been supplanted in the affections of a young lady, resolves to go straight to America – on his 'way to the Devil.' Before starting, however, he finds occasion to make a visit to a certain place on the farther borders of Yorkshire, and on the way thither he gets snowed in for a week at The Holly-Tree Inn, where he finds himself the only guest. Sitting by the fire in the principal room, he reads through all the books in the house; namely, a 'Book of Roads,' a little song-book terminating in a collection of toasts and sentiments, a little jest-book, an odd volume of *Peregrine Pickle*, and *The Sentimental Journey*, to say nothing of two or three old newspapers. These being exhausted, he endeavours to while away the time by recalling his experience of inns, and his remembrances of those he has heard or read of. He further beguiles the days of his imprisonment by talking, at one time or another, with the whole establishment, not excepting the 'Boots' who, lingering in the room one day, tells him a story about a young gentleman not eight years old, who runs off with a young lady of seven to Gretna Green, and puts up at The Holly-Tree. When the roads are at last open, and just as the disconsolate traveller is on the point of resuming his journey, a carriage drives up, and out jumps his (as he supposes) successful rival, who is running away to Gretna too. It turns out, however, that the lady he has with him is not the one with whom the traveller is in love, but her cousin. The fugitives are hastened on their way; and the traveller retraces his steps without delay, goes straight to London, and marries the girl whom he thought he had lost for ever.

CHARACTERS

BOOTS – *See* **Cobbs**.

CHARLEY – Guest at The Holly-Tree Inn; a self-supposed rejected man; in love with Angela Leath.

COBBS – The 'Boots' at The Holly-Tree Inn formerly under-gardener at Mr Walmers's.

EDWIN – Supposed rival of Charley the guest at The Holly-Tree; betrothed to Emmeline.

EMMELINE – Cousin to Angela Leath. She elopes with her lover, Edwin, and is married to him at Gretna Green.

GEORGE – Guard of a coach.

LEATH, Angela – The lady-love and afterwards the wife of Charley (The Holly-Tree guest), who for a time deludes himself into thinking that she prefers his friend Edwin.

NORAH – Cousin to Master Harry Walmers, junior, with whom she runs away from home, intending to go to Gretna Green and be married to him. She is, however, overtaken and carried home, and long afterwards becomes the wife of a captain; and finally dies in India.

WALMERS, Master Harry, Junior – A bright boy, not quite eight years old, who falls in love with his cousin, a little girl of seven, and starts with her for Gretna Green, to get married. Stopping at The Holly-Tree Inn on their journey, they are recognised by the 'Boots', who had been in the service of the young gentleman's father. The landlord immediately sets off for York to inform the parents of the two little runaways of their whereabouts. They return late at night.

WALMERS, Mr – The father of Master Harry; a gentleman living at the 'Elmses', near Shooter's Hill, six or seven miles from London.

22

Little Dorrit

The first number of this tale was issued on the first day of December 1856, and the twentieth and last number made its appearance in June 1857. The work was illustrated by Phiz, and on its completion it was dedicated to the late Clarkson Stanfield, the eminent landscape-painter.

CHARACTERS

AUNT, Mr F's – *See* **Mr F's Aunt.**

BANGHAM, Mrs – A charwoman and messenger; nurse of Mrs Dorrit in the Marshalsea Prison. {Book 1: ch 6, 7; Book 2: ch 19}

BARNACLE, Clarence – *called*, '**Barnacle, Junior**'. Son of Mr Tite Barnacle; an empty-headed young gentleman employed in the Circumlocution Office. {Book 1: ch 10, 17, 34, 35}

BARNACLE, Lord Decimus Tite – Uncle of Mr Tite Barnacle; a windy peer, high in the Circumlocution Office. {Book 1: ch 17, 25, 34; Book 2: ch 7, 24, 28}

BARNACLE, Ferdinand – Private secretary to Lord Decimus Tite Barnacle; a gracious, well-looking, well-dressed, agreeable young fellow, on the more sprightly side of the family. Arthur Clennam, wishing to investigate Mr Dorrit's affairs, with the view of releasing him, if possible, from the Marshalsea, inquires of Barnacle how he can obtain information as to the real state of the case. {Book 1: ch 10, 34; Book 2: ch 12, 28}

BARNACLE, Mr Tite – A man of family, a man of place, and a man of gentlemanly residence, who usually coaches or crams the statesman at the head of the Circumlocution Office. {Book 1: ch 9, 10, 34; Book 2: ch 12}

BEADLE, Harriet – *called* '**Tattycoram**'. A girl taken from the Foundling Hospital by Mr Meagles to be a maid to his daughter Minnie. She is a handsome girl, but headstrong and passionate. Mr Meagles takes great pains to improve her disposition and character, and always advises her, when she is not in a good temper, to 'take a little time', and to 'count five-and-twenty'. She proves insensible, however, to all his goodness and kind consideration, runs away after a time; and places herself under the protection of a certain Miss Wade; but in the end she returns, humble and penitent, to her benefactor's house. {Book 1: ch 2, 16, 27, 28; Book 2: ch 9, 10, 20, 33}

BLANDOIS – See **Rigaud**.

BOB – Turnkey of the Marshalsea Prison; godfather to Little Dorrit. {Book 1: ch 6, 7; Book 2: ch 19}

CASBY, Christopher – Landlord of Bleeding Heart Yard; a selfish, crafty impostor, who likes to be thought a benefactor to his species, and who grinds his tenants by proxy. {Book 1: ch 12, 13, 23, 24, 35; Book 2: ch 9, 23, 32}

CALVETTO, John Baptist – A fellow-prisoner with Rigaud at Marseilles; afterwards in Arthur Clennam's employ. {Book 1: ch 1, 11, 23, 25, 29; Book 2: ch 12, 22, 23, 28, 30}

CHIVERY, John – A non-resident turnkey of the Marshalsea Prison. {Book 1: ch 18, 19, 22, 25, 31, 35, 36; Book 2: ch 18, 26, 27, 29, 31, 34}

CHIVERY, Young John – His son; a lover of Little Dorrit. This sentimental youth, before ever he had told his love, had often meditated on the happiness that would result from his marriage to Little Dorrit, and on the loving manner in which they would 'glide down the stream of time in pastoral and domestic happiness'. He finally musters up the courage to approach Miss Dorrit in relation to the subject that is so near to the heart. She, however, not only gives him no encouragement, but requests him very plainly (though with the utmost delicacy and consideration) never to refer to the matter again. John does not easily recover from the blow he has received and when, long afterwards, he learns that Little Dorrit is to be married to Arthur Clennam, he is made very wretched, though he endeavours to bear the intelligence with manly fortitude. {Book 1: ch 18, 19, 22, 25, 31, 35, 36; Book 2: ch 18, 19, 26, 27, 29, 31, 33, 34}

CHIVERY, Mrs – Wife of John Chivery, and keeper of a small tobacco-shop round the corner of Horsemonger Lane. {Book 1: ch 18, 22, 25}

CLENNAM, Arthur – Reputed son, but really the adopted son of Mrs Clennam. At the age of twenty he had been sent to China to join his father, a merchant, who had been living in that country for some years, taking care of the business there, while his mother managed the business at home. He stays there till he is forty and, his father then dying, he returns to London to see his mother; but she receives him very coldly, as does her old servant and confidential adviser, Flintwinch. Finding a young woman in the house who is called 'Little Dorrit', and who is employed by his mother to do needlework, and feeling a growing interest in her, he ascertains her history, and is the means of her father's release from the Marshalsea. Being afterwards unfortunate in business, he is arrested for debt, and is thrown into the same prison; but he finds a fast friend in Little Dorrit and, when he at last gains his liberty, she marries him. {Book 1: ch 2, 3, 5, 7–10, 12–17, 22, 24–28, 31, 32, 34–36; Book 2: ch 3, 4, 8–11, 13, 20, 22, 23, 26–34}

CLENNAM, Mrs – The supposed mother of Arthur Clennam, who turns out, however, to have been the child of another woman whom his father had known before marrying Mrs Clennam. She is a hard, stern woman, with cold grey eyes, cold grey hair, and an immovable face. Though an invalid, who has lost the use of her limbs, and is confined to a single room, she retains the full vigour of her mind and is still, as she has always been, a thorough woman of business. An austere moralist, a religionist whose faith is in a system of gloom and darkness, of vengeance and destruction, she yet does not hesitate to suppress a will, by virtue of which two thousand guineas were to go to Little Dorrit on her coming of age. Finding that her guilt has been discovered, and is certain to be made known, she throws herself on the mercy of the girl she has so grievously wronged, and is freely forgiven. {Book 1: ch 3–5, 8, 15, 29, 30; Book 2: ch 10, 17, 23, 28, 30, 31}

CRIPPLES, Master – A white-faced boy, son of Mr Cripples. {Book 1: ch 9}

CRIPPLES, Mr – Teacher of an academy for 'evening tuition'. (Book 1: ch 9)

DAWES – A rosy-faced, gay, good-humoured nurse, who is Miss Wade's special antipathy.

DORRIT, Amy – *called* '**Little Dorrit**'. Daughter of Mr William Dorrit. She becomes the wife of Arthur Clennam. {Book 1: ch 3, 12–16, 18–25, 27, 29, 31, 32, 35, 36; Book 2: ch 1–8, 11, 14, 15, 19, 24, 26, 27, 29–31, 33, 34}

DORRIT, Edward – *called* 'Tip'. The brother of Little Dorrit; a spendthrift and an idler, for whom his sister is always calculating and planning. {Book 1: ch 6–8, 12, 18, 20, 22, 24, 31, 35, 36; Book 2: ch 1, 3, 5, 11, 15, 19, 24, 29, 33, 34}

DORRIT, Fanny – Daughter of Mr William Dorrit, and elder sister of Amy, or 'Little Dorrit'. She is, for a time, a ballet-dancer, but finally marries Mr Edmund Sparkler, and rules him with a rod of iron. {Book 1: ch 6–9, 18, 20, 31, 35, 36; Book 2: ch 1–3, 5–7, 11, 14–16, 18, 19, 24, 33, 34}

DORRIT, Mr Frederick – Brother to Mr William Dorrit. {Book 1: ch 7–9, 19, 20, 26; Book 2: ch 1, 4, 5, 19}

DORRIT, Mr William – A prisoner for debt in the Marshalsea; a shy, retiring man, well-looking, though in an effeminate style, with a mild voice, curling hair, and irresolute hands. His young wife joins him with their two children; and in a few months another child is born to them, a girl, from whom the story takes its name. When this child is eight years old, the wife dies. Years pass by, and Dorrit becomes gray-haired and venerable, and is known in the prison as the Father of the Marshalsea – a title he grows to be very vain of. From an early period his daughter devotes herself to the task of being his support and protection, becoming, in all things but precedence, the head of the fallen family, and bearing in her own heart its anxieties and shames. After twenty-five years spent within the prison walls, Mr Dorrit proves to be heir-at-law to a great estate that has long remained unknown of, unclaimed, and accumulating. He leaves the Marshalsea a rich man; but that quarter of a century behind its bars has done its work; and he leaves it with a failing intellect, and makes himself ridiculous by his pride, by the lofty airs he gives himself, and by his unwillingness to recall at any time the old days of his poverty and confinement. He declines slowly but surely, and at last dies in a palace at Rome, fancying it to be the Marshalsea. {Book 1: ch 6–9, 18, 19, 22, 23, 31, 32, 35, 36; Book 2: ch 5–7, 12, 13, 15–19}

DOYCE, Daniel – An engineer and inventor, who becomes the partner of Arthur Clennam. {Book 1: ch 10, 12, 16, 17, 23, 26, 28, 34; Book 2: ch 8, 13, 22, 26, 34}

F'S AUNT, Mr – *See* **Mr F's Aunt**.

FINCHING, Mrs Flora – Daughter of Christopher Casby; a wealthy widow of some thirty-eight or forty years of age, sentimental and affected, but thoroughly good-hearted. She talks with the most disjointed volubility, pointing her conversation with nothing but commas, and very few of them. {Book 1: ch 13, 23, 24, 25; Book 2: ch 9, 17, 23, 34}

FLINTWINCH, Affery – An old servant of Mrs Clennam's, wife of Jeremiah Flintwinch She is apt to fall into a dreamy sleep-waking state, much to the displeasure of her husband, who tells her, 'If you ever have a dream of this sort again it'll be a sign of your being in want of physic, and I'll give you such a dose, old woman – such a dose!' {Book 1: ch 3–5, 15, 29, 30; Book 2: ch 10, 17, 23, 30, 31}

FLINTWINCH, Ephraim – Jeremiah's 'double' and confederate. {Book 1: ch 4; Book 2: ch 30}

FLINTWINCH, Jeremiah – Servant and afterwards partner of Mrs Clennam. He is a short, bald old man, bent and dried, with a one-sided crab-like manner of locomotion.

GENERAL, Mrs – A widow-lady of forty-five, whom Mr Dorrit engages to 'form the mind' and manners of his daughters. Observing that Amy Dorrit calls Mr Dorrit 'father', Mrs General informs her that 'papa' is a preferable mode of address. {Book 2: ch 1–5, 7, 11, 15, 19}

GOWAN, Henry – An artist, who marries Miss Minnie Meagles. {Book 1: ch 17, 26, 28, 33, 34; Book 2: ch 1, 3–8, 11, 14, 17, 20, 24, 33}

GOWAN, Mrs – His mother; a courtly old lady, a little lofty in her manner. {Book 1: ch 17, 26, 33, 34; Book 2: ch 5, 8}

GOWAN, Mrs, Henry – *See* **Meagles, Minnie**.

HAGGAGE, Doctor – A poor debtor in the Marshalsea; a hoarse, puffy, red-faced, dirty, brandy-drinking, medical scarecrow, who assists Little Dorrit into the world. {Book 1: ch 6, 7}

JENKINSON – A messenger at the Circumlocution Office. {Book 1: ch 10}

LAGNIER – *See* **Rigaud**.

MAGGY – A granddaughter of Mrs Bangham's, and a *protégée* of Little Dorrit's; afterwards an assistant to Mrs Plornish. {Book 1: ch 9, 14, 20, 22, 24, 31, 32, 35, 36; Book 2: ch 3, 4, 13, 29, 33, 34}

MAROON, Captain – One of Mr Edward Dorrit's creditors. {Book 1: ch 12}

MARSHALSEA, Father of The – *See* **Dorrit, Mr William**.

MEAGLES, Mr – A retired banker, good-natured and benevolent, and always priding himself on being a practical man. {Book 1: ch 2, 10, 12, 16, 17, 23, 26–29, 33, 34; Book 2: ch, 8–10, 33, 34}

MEAGLES, Mrs – His wife; a comely and healthy woman, with a pleasant English face which, like her husband's, has been looking at homely things for five-and-fifty years or more, and shines with a bright reflection of them. {Book 1: ch 2, 16, 17, 28, 33, 34; Book 2: ch 8, 9, 33, 34}

MEAGLES, Minnie – *called* 'Pet'. Their daughter, afterwards the wife of Mr Henry Gowan. {Book 1: ch 2, 16, 17, 26, 28, 34; Book 2: ch 1, 3, 4–8, 11, 28, 33}

MERDLE, Mr – A London banker, who, after a remarkably successful career, becomes a bankrupt and commits suicide. {Book 1: ch 24, 33; Book 2: ch 5, 7, 12–16, 18, 19, 24, 25, 28}

MERDLE, Mrs – His wife, and mother of Mr Edmund Sparkler; a very fashionable lady. {Book 1: ch 20, 24, 33; Book 2: ch 3, 5, 7, 12, 14–16, 19, 24, 25, 33}

MR F'S AUNT – A singular old lady, who is a legacy left to Mrs Flora Finching by her deceased husband. {Book 1: ch 13, 23, 24, 35; Book 2: ch 9, 34}

NANDY, John Edward – Father to Mrs Plornish; an old man with a weak, piping voice, though his daughter considers him 'a sweet singer'. {Book 1: ch 13; Book 2: ch 13, 26, 27}

PANCKS, Mr – Mr Casby's collector of rents. Though the agent of the man who, despite his benevolent and patriarchal air, is a hard, avaricious old sinner, and though, in accordance with his instructions, he periodically squeezes and harasses his employer's tenants, he is by no means a cruel or ungenerous man. Indeed, he is so chafed and exasperated by the disagreeable nature of his work, and by the hypocrisy of his 'proprietor', that he makes up his mind to seek some other occupation. {Book 1: ch 12, 13, 23–25, 27, 29, 32, 34, 35; Book 2: ch 9, 11, 13, 17, 20, 22, 26, 28–30, 32, 34}

PET – *See* **Meagles, Minnie**.

PLORNISH, Mr – A plasterer living in Bleeding Heart Yard, one of Mr Casby's tenants, and a friend of Little Dorrit's; a smooth-cheeked, fresh-coloured, sandy-whiskered man of thirty, long in the legs, yielding at the knees, foolish in the face, flannel-jacketed, lime-whitened. {Book 1: ch 6, 9, 12, 23, 24, 31, 36; Book 2: ch 4, 13, 27, 29}

Little mother – Hablot K Browne *alias* Phiz

PLORNISH, Mrs – His wife; a young woman, made somewhat slatternly in herself and her belongings by poverty; and so dragged at by poverty and the children together, that their united forces have already dragged her face into wrinkles. {Book 1: ch 6, 12, 23, 31; Book 2: ch 4, 13, 26, 27, 29, 30}

RIGAUD – *alias* **Blandois** *alias* **Lagner**. A *chevalier d'industrie*, with polished manners, but a scoundrel's heart. Having murdered his wife, and been lodged in a French jail, he contrives to effect his escape, and flees to England. Gaining a knowledge of Mrs Clennam's frauds, he tries to wring from her a very large amount of hush-money, but is killed by the sudden falling of the house in which he is waiting for her. {Book 1: ch 1, 11, 29, 30; Book 2: ch 1, 3, 6, 7, 9, 10, 17, 20, 22 23, 28, 30, 31, 33}

RUGG, Miss Anastasia – Daughter of Mr Rugg. She has little nankeen spots, like shirt buttons, all over her face; and her yellow tresses are scrubby rather than luxuriant. {Book 1: ch 25; Book 2: ch 26, 28}

RUGG, Mr – A general agent, accountant, and collector of debts, who is Mr Pancks's landlord. He has a round white visage – as if all his blushes had been drawn out of him long ago – and a ragged yellow head like a worn-out hearth-broom. {Book 1: ch 25, 32, 35, 36; Book 2: ch 26, 28, 34}

SPARKLER, Mr Edmund – Son of Mrs Merdle by her first husband. He marries Fanny Dorrit, considering her to be 'a young lady with no nonsense about her'. {Book 1: ch 20, 31, 33; Book 2: ch 3, 6, 7, 12, 14–16, 18, 24, 33}

SPARKLER, Mrs Edmund – *See* **Dorrit, Fanny**.

STILTSTALKING, Lord Lancaster A gray old gentleman of dignified and sullen appearance, whom the Circumlocution Office had maintained for many years as a representative of the Britannic majesty abroad. {Book 1: ch 26}

TATTYCORAM – See Beadle, Harriet.

TICKIT, Mrs – Mr Meagle's cook and housekeeper. She makes Buchan's *Domestic Medicine* her constant *vade mecum*, though she is believed never to have consulted it to the extent of a single word in her life. {Book 1: ch 16, 34; Book 2: ch 9, 33}

TINKLER, Mr – William Dorrit's valet. {Book 2: ch 3, 5, 15, 19}

TIP – *See* **Dorrit, Edward**.

WADE, Miss – A woman with a sullen and ungovernable temper, a self-tormentor, who fancies that wrongs and insults are heaped upon her on every side. Finding a kindred spirit in Tattycoram, the adopted child of Mr Meagles, she entices the girl to leave that excellent couple, and live with her and, when she has done so, makes and keeps her as miserable, suspicious, and tormenting as herself. But Tattycoram grows tired of such a life, and at length returns, repentant and grateful, to her old master and mistress. {Book 1: ch 2, 16, 27, 28; Book 2: ch 9, 10, 20, 24, 33}

WOBBLER, Mr – A clerk in the secretarial department of the Circumlocution Office. {Book 1: ch 10}

PRINCIPAL INCIDENTS

Book 1 – {1} Rigaud and Cavalletto, in prison in Marseilles, have their food brought them by the jailer and his little daughter; Rigaud gives Cavalletto the reason of his imprisonment; Rigaud is carried out to his trial. {2} Mr Meagles is impatient at the detention in quarantine; Mr Meagles gives Arthur Clennam an account of Tattycoram, and how they adopted her; confidence between Mr Meagles and Mr Clennam, in which some of the circumstances in the history of each are narrated; Miss Wade's indifference at parting with her fellow-travellers; her influence over Tattycoram, who shows signs of discontent. {3} Arthur Clennam arrives home on a dismal Sunday evening, after an absence of twenty years; he is received without any emotion by the old serving-man, Jeremiah Flintwinch, and as coldly welcomed by his mother; Affery gives Arthur some hints of the relations existing between his mother and Flintwinch, and tells him how she came to marry Jeremiah; Arthur has his memory of an old sweetheart revived. {4} Mrs Flintwinch sees, 'in a dream', Jeremiah and his 'Double', whom he entrusts with an iron box, and dismisses from the house. {5} Arthur Clennam consults with his mother in regard to the business of the house; he intimates his suspicions that his father had unhappily committed a wrong against someone without making reparation; she threatens to renounce him if he ever renews the theme; Arthur relinquishes his share of the business, which the widow bestows upon Jeremiah; Little Dorrit appears in attendance on Mrs Clennam; Arthur resolves to watch her, and know more of her story. {6} Mr Dorrit and his family enter the Marshalsea; Little Dorrit is born; death of Mrs Dorrit; Mr Dorrit becomes the Father of the Marshalsea. {7} Little Dorrit becomes the pet of the prison and, as she grows older, the principal support of her father, and the head of the fallen family; Tip, after repeated failures to succeed in business, comes back to the Marshalsea as a prisoner; Arthur traces Little Dorrit to the Marshalsea. {8} He encounters Frederick Dorrit, who takes him into the prison, and introduces him to Mr Dorrit; Mr Dorrit gives him the history of a delicate action; Mr Clennam is locked in, and spends the night in prison. {9} Arthur sends Little Dorrit a request to meet him at his uncle's lodgings; he questions her about the family reverses in the hope of releasing Mr Dorrit; they meet Maggy in the street, and who Maggy is. {10} The Circumlocution Office, and its principle of HOW NOT TO DO IT; Arthur Clennam makes inquiries at the Circumlocution Office about Mr Dorrit's creditors, but gets no information; he encounters Mr Meagles and Daniel Doyce; who Daniel Doyce is, and how he came in the Circumlocution Office; the party go to Bleeding Heart Yard. {11} Rigaud, released by the law, arrives in Chalons, and stops at a cabaret, where he hears his character discussed, and his crime denounced, by the guests going to bed, he recognises in the man who shares his room his old companion, Cavalletto; Cavalletto escapes from him in the morning. {12} Clennam finds Mr and Mrs Plornish, friends of Little Dorrit; through Mr Plornish he compromises for Tip's debts, and secures his release. {13} Arthur renews his acquaintance with Mr Casby; meets Mr Pancks, Mr Casby's agent, and has the Flora of his early love and after recollections destroyed by an interview with the actual Flora; Arthur's introduction to 'Mr F's Aunt', who makes some very pertinent remarks; Arthur and Mr Pancks return to the city together; leaving Pancks, Arthur encounters Cavalletto, borne on a litter, his leg broken, and accompanies him to a hospital; Arthur's sorrowful meditations are interrupted by the entrance of Little Dorrit and Maggy. {14} She tells him Tip is released, and how she would thank his benefactor if allowed to know him; her suspicions that Flintwinch has watched her, and followed her home; she begs Arthur not to bestow any gift upon her father; Little Dorrit and Maggy spend the night in the street. {15} Mrs Flintwinch dreams again, and hears an angry conversation between her husband and Mrs Clennam. {16} Mr Clennam goes to Twickenham to renew his acquaintance with the Meagleses, and over takes Daniel Doyce going there also; Mr Meagles shows them his house and curiosities; Arthur questions whether he should allow himself to fall in love with Pet, and decides

At Mr John Chivery's tea-table – Hablot K Browne alias Phiz

in the negative; Tattycoram relates her interview with Miss Wade; Clennam proposes to Mr Meagles to recommend him as a partner to Daniel Doyce. {17} Clennam meets Henry Gowan at the Ferry, and afterwards at Mr Meagles's house; Mr Gowan proposes to introduce a friend; Arthur inquires of Doyce who Gowan is; Barnacle junior appears as Gowan's friend; Arthur does not like the intimacy between Henry Gowan and Minnie. {18} Young John Chivery forms an attachment for Little Dorrit; he presents a little testimonial to the Father of the Marshalsea, he follows Amy in her walk, and is on the point of making a declaration, when she checks him, and disappoints his hopes. {19} Contrast between the brothers William and Frederick Dorrit; Mr Chivery's vexation; Mr Dorrit explains to Amy the cause of Chivery's vexation; he becomes despondent, and she comforts him. {20} Little Dorrit seeks her sister at the theatre, where she is engaged as a dancer, during a rehearsal; Fanny introduces her to Mrs Merdle, the lady who gave her a bracelet; Mrs Merdle gives Little Dorrit the circumstances of her son's attachment to Fanny, and the understanding she and Fanny have upon the subject. {24} Who the Merdles were, and their position in society; a dinner-party at Mr Merdle's, and that gentleman's complaint. {22} Mr Clennam does not find favour with the Father of the Marshalsea; Mrs Chivery shows Arthur her son's despondency, and explains the cause; Arthur and Little Dorrit meet on the bridge, and Maggy joins them with notes from Mr Dorrit and Tip, requesting loans. {23} Clennam becomes a partner in Mr Doyce's business; Flora and 'Mr F's Aunt' visit him in his counting-room; they are followed by Mr Casby and Pancks; Flora takes an interest in Little Dorrit; 'Mr F's Aunt' makes a demonstration, and is taken out by Mr Pancks; Mr Pancks shows an absorbing interest in the Dorrit family, and questions Arthur about them; Mr Pancks goes through Bleeding Heart Yard collecting rents, but does not satisfy his proprietor. {24} Little Dorrit goes to work for Flora; Flora gives her the history of her old attachment to Arthur; Mr Pancks surprises Little Dorrit by his skill in fortune-telling; Amy tells Maggy the story of the beautiful princess, and the little woman who had a secret. {25} Mr Pancks, Mr Rugg, and young John Chivery dine together, and appear to be engaged in a conspiracy which interests Little Dorrit; Mr Pancks calls upon Cavalletto, and Mrs Plornish acts as interpreter. {26} Doyce and Clennam discuss the intimacy of Henry Gowan at the cottage; Mr Gowan expresses his opinion of the world; Arthur visits, at her son's request, Mrs Gowan at Hampton Court; she questions him about the Meagleses, and he assures her that they are not pleased by her son's attentions to Pet, and have hoped to break off the engagement. {27} Mr Meagles informs Clennam of Tattycoram's sudden disappearance; their thoughts both turn to Miss Wade as the probable cause; they seek Miss Wade, and find Tattycoram with her, but cannot induce her to return home with Mr Meagles. {28} Mr Clennam encounters Minnie alone and, as they walk home through the avenue, he anticipates her confidence, invokes a blessing on her marriage with Gowan, and promises to be a friend to her father when she is away; Mr Meagles delicately intimates to Arthur his suspicion of the hopes he once cherished in regard to Pet. {29} Mr Pancks calling at Mrs Clennam's, she understands that it is to see Little Dorrit, who is there; Mrs Clennam is unusually gentle towards Amy; Affery, shut out in the street, is accosted by a traveller, who climbs into the window, and opens the door for her. {30} The stranger announces himself to Jeremiah as Blandois, and produces a letter of introduction to Clennam and Co; Mr Blandois, having dined at a neighbouring tavern, returns to pay his respects to Mrs Clennam; the visitor shows particular interest in Mrs Clennam's watch, with its peculiar monogram; at his request he is shown through the old house; he appears delighted with the house, and takes singular freedoms with Jeremiah. {31} Mr John Edward Nandy is introduced; Little Dorrit takes him with her to the Marshalsea, to the indignation of Miss Fanny and the grief of her father; the father becomes reconciled, and bestows his patronage upon Nandy; Tip and Miss Fanny show 'a proper spirit' in their conduct towards Arthur. {32} Arthur secures an interview alone with Little Dorrit, and confides to her the story of the love he had overcome; he urges her to entrust to him any secret grief or care she may have; Mr Pancks appears in a state of great excitement, which half frightens Amy, but which Clennam understands; Mr Pancks imparts his discovery to Clennam. {33} Mrs Merdle advises Mrs Gowan on the requirements of society in regard to her son's marriage; Mrs Merdle complains to her husband that he carries his business too much with him. {34} Mr Henry Gowan explains to Clennam the disappointment he has suffered; marriage of Henry Gowan and Minnie Meagles, attended by all the Barnacles. {35} Mr Dorrit proves heir-at-law to a great estate, Mr Pancks having traced out the evidence; Pancks narrates all the particulars to Arthur, who carries the news immediately to Little Dorrit ; her first thought is of her father, and they go to tell him; emotion with which Mr Dorrit receives the news of his good fortune. {36} Mr Dorrit and family prepare for leaving the prison, and Mr Dorrit gives an entertainment to the collegians; at the moment of departure, the family is disgraced by Amy, who has fainted in her shabby dress, and is carried to the carriage in that condition by Arthur.

Book 2 – {1} The Dorrit party, Mr and Mrs Henry Gowan, and Blandois meet at the Convent of the Great St Bernard; Mrs Gowan, having received an injury on the road, faints away, and her husband carries her to her room; Amy seeks Minnie Gowan in her room, and gives her a letter from Clennam; leaving the room, Amy encounters Blandois in the dark gallery; Blandois registers his name under the others in the Travellers' Book. {2} Who Mrs General was, and how Mr Dorrit engaged her to 'form the minds' of his daughters. {3} Mr Dorrit and Fanny are indignant at Amy for seeking the acquaintance of a friend of Clennam; the Dorrit party leave the convent, watched in their descent by Blandois; at Martigny, Mr Dorrit has an altercation with the innkeeper, who has allowed one of the rooms engaged for him to be used by other travellers; the travellers prove to be Mrs Merdle and Mr Sparkler, and the lady appeases Mr Dorrit by her apology; the party moves on to Venice. {4} Amy writes to Clennam, and relates her interview with Minnie Gowan. {5} Mr Dorrit takes the liberty to suggest to Mrs General that there is something wrong in Amy; Mr Dorrit begs Amy to accommodate herself better to the circumstances of her station; he speaks of the old days in the Marshalsea, and accuses her of always recalling them by her manner; the Gowans being in Venice, Mr Dorrit, after consulting Mrs General, consents to recognise their acquaintance; Mr Frederick is moved to protest against the way in which Amy is treated. {6} Mr Gowan decides to encourage the acquaintance of Blandois, who has accompanied them to Venice; Fanny and Amy call upon the Gowans; in Gowan's studio, Blandois is attacked by Gowan's dog; returning home, they are attended by Mr Sparkler, and Fanny tells Amy how she means to receive attentions; Mr Dorrit decides to bestow his patronage upon Henry Gowan, and engages him to paint his portrait; Gowan loses his dog. {7} Fanny suspects Mrs General of matrimonial designs on Mr Dorrit; Gowan accepts, in his deprecating way, Mr Dorrit's commission; Blandois prevents the confidence between Amy and Mrs Gowan; the family goes to

Rome, and Mrs Merdle renews the acquaintance 'begun at Martigny'. {8} Doyce explains to Clennam the invention he has cherished for years, and Arthur determines to urge its claims at the Circumlocution Office; the dowager Mrs Gowan calls upon the Meagleses, and reminds them that, considering the sacrifice her son has made, 'it never does' for people of such different antecedents to try to get on together. {9}. Mr Meagles informs Arthur of his intention to go abroad and see Pet, and Arthur urges him to do so; Mrs Tickit sees Tattycoram; soon after, Arthur himself sees her in company with Miss Wade and Blandois; Blandois leaves them, and Arthur sees them enter Mr Casby's house, but on gaining admission to the house, and inquiring for them, Casby gives him vague answers. {10} Arthur, on the way to see his mother, is jostled in the street by Blandois, and is greatly astonished, on following him, to find him seeking admittance to Mrs Clennam's house; Arthur objects to his presence there, but Mrs Clennam informs him that Blandois has business with them; Blandois hints darkly at the feeling existing between Clennam and Co. {11} Little Dorrit writes again to Arthur, with further intelligence of the Gowans and of her own family. {12} A dinner is given at Mr Merdle's, attended by Bar, Bishop, &c, and the Barnacles, the object being to secure a meeting for five minutes between Mr Merdle and Lord Decimus, the consequence of which is the appointment of Edmund Sparkler, Esquire, as one of the lords of the Circumlocution Office. {13} Everybody talks of Mr Merdle and of his enterprises; Mr Pancks calls at Mr Plornish's shop after a trying day; singular performances of Cavalletto, consequent on his seeing Rigaud, and trying to avoid him; Clennam calls at the Plornishes on his return home; Pancks accompanies Clennam home, and argues in favour of the Merdle enterprises, in which he has himself invested. {14} How the news of Mr Sparkler's appointment was received by his friends in Italy; Fanny 'takes Amy's advice' as to the end of her intercourse with Mr Sparkler and decides, for the sake of securing a more defined position, and of asserting herself against his mother, that she will encourage him; Fanny, attended by Mr Sparkler, informs Amy of their engagement. {15} Mr Dorrit finds Mrs Merdle charmed with Mr Sparkler's choice; Fanny expresses herself tired of Mrs General; Mr Dorrit remonstrates, and insists upon the engagement being announced to her; Fanny 'looks to Amy' for advice in regard to the time of her marriage, and decides that it shall be soon; Fanny is married, and leaves for England; Mr Dorrit joins her at Florence, and Amy and Mrs General are left at Rome. {16} Mrs Sparkler is established in the rooms of Mrs Merdle; Mr Merdle calls upon Mr Dorrit at his hotel, and offers to assist Mr Dorrit in investing his money. {17} Mrs Finching calls upon Mr Dorrit, and informs him of the disappearance of Blandois, who has never been seen since he entered the house of Mrs Clennam, and asks him to look out for him on his return to Italy; Mr Dorrit goes to Mrs Clennam's to ask about Blandois; Mrs Affery is again frightened by the noises. {18} Young John Chivery calls to pay his respects to Mr Dorrit, much to that gentleman's indignation; passing through Paris, Mr Dorrit selects two little gifts for a lady. {19} Mr Dorrit arrives at Rome late in the evening, and finds his brother and Amy alone; he thinks his brother greatly broken; they receive an invitation to Mrs Merdle's farewell assembly; Mr Dorrit begins an important conversation with Mrs General, the conclusion of which, at her request, he postpones; at Mrs Merdle's party, Mr Dorrit's mind wanders; he fancies himself again the Father of the Marshalsea, and welcomes the company to that institution; his brother and Amy got him home and, after ten days of wandering, Mr Dorrit dies; Mr Frederick Dorrit dies by the bedside of his dead brother. {20} Arthur Clennam gains an interview with Miss Wade at her lodgings in Calais; he seeks news of Blandois, but she will give him none; her hatred of the Gowans; her influence over Tattycoram. {21} Miss Wade's history, as written out by herself for Mr Clennam's perusal; Doyce receives an appointment as engineer from a foreign power. {22} Before leaving England, Clennam gives him a statement of their business, and Doyce cautions him against speculating; Doyce's departure; Clennam, unconsciously repeating the tune he had heard Blandois sing, is surprised to hear Cavalletto continue it; Cavalletto tells Arthur where he knew Rigaud, and who he was, and Arthur despatches him in search of the missing man. {23} Arthur informs his mother what he has heard regarding Blandois; Arthur secures an opportunity of speaking privately to Affery, who tells him the house is full of mysteries, but will say no more until he bids her 'tell her dreams' before his mother and Jeremiah. {24} Mrs Sparkler passes a long day with her husband; they receive a call from Mr Merdle; who, on leaving, borrows Fanny's penknife. {25} Mr Merdle is found dead in a bath, having committed suicide with Fanny's knife; the chief butler gives notice; Mr Merdle's 'complaint' proves to be forgery and robbery. {26} Clennam finds his firm ruined by the failure of

Merdle's Bank, resigns everything into the hands of their creditors, and exonerates Doyce from blame; Arthur is arrested and taken to the Marshalsea; young John Chivery conducts him into the old room, but declines to shake hands with him. {27} Young John invites Arthur to take tea with him, and opens his eyes in regard to Little Dorrit's feelings for him; young John composes his final epitaph. {28} Ferdinand Barnacle calls upon Arthur in prison; Rugg calls, but is unable to move Arthur's decision to remain where he is; Rigaud enters Arthur's room, followed by Cavalletto and Pancks; Cavalletto relates how he found him; Rigaud gives his reasons for disappearing; he sends a note to Mrs Clennam, naming a time for the adjustment of their business; Flintwinch comes in person to answer the note. {29} Arthur's health fails in the prison; Little Dorrit comes to him, having just returned to London, and heard of his misfortunes; she offers him all her wealth to free him from embarrassment, but he declines, and requests her to avoid him; young John brings Little Dorrit's parting-message to Arthur. {30} Rigaud, closely followed by Cavalletto and Pancks, keeps his appointment with Clennam and Co; Pancks calls upon Affery in Arthur's name to 'tell her dreams'; partly by Rigaud relating what he knows, and partly through Affery's 'dreams', it is told that Mrs Clennam is not Arthur's mother; that he is her husband's child by a woman whom he loved, but was forced by his uncle to give up; that Mrs Clennam forced her husband to give up to her the object of his love, whom she also forced to relinquish her child, to be reared as, and believed to be, Mrs Clennam's own son; that Mrs Clennam had suppressed a codicil to Gilbert Clennam's will, by which Little Dorrit would have received two thousand guineas; that Jeremiah had entrusted the papers establishing these facts to his brother's keeping, and that they had fallen into Rigaud's hands; Rigaud threatens, if his terms for silence are not accepted, to put copies of these papers in Arthur's hands; Mrs Clennam starts up regardless of her paralytic state, and rushes out of the house, followed by Affery and Jeremiah. {31} Mrs Clennam's interview with Little Dorrit in the prison; fall of the old house, burying Blandois in its ruins. {32} Mr Pancks exposes his patron to the Bleeding Hearts. {33} Mr Meagles sets himself to hunting up the box containing the papers Rigaud had stolen, his interview with Miss Wade, who denies all knowledge of them; he returns to England unsuccessful, but is followed by Tattycoram, who brings the missing box, and begs to be taken back; Mr Meagles starts off again in search of Doyce. {34}

Little Dorrit informs Arthur that her father's property was all lost by Mr Merdle's failure, and he now will share her fortune with her; Flora's last act of friendship, and the crowning defiance of 'Mr F's Aunt'; Doyce returns with Mr Meagles, exonerates Arthur, and offers to renew the partnership; Little Dorrit gives Arthur a folded paper to burn, Arthur and little Dorrit are married.

Mr Dorrit feels jealous – Marcus Stone

23

A Tale of Two Cities

The first portion of this story was published in the first number of *All the Year Round*, 30 April 1859. It was concluded in No 31, 26 November 1859. It was also issued in eight monthly parts, with two Phiz illustrations in each. On its completion, it was published as an independent volume by Chapman and Hall, and was inscribed to Lord John Russell 'in remembrance of many public services and private kindnesses'.

CHARACTERS

BARSAD, John —See Pross, Solomon.

CARTON, Sydney – A dissipated, reckless drudge for Mr Stryver; a man of good abilities and good emotions, incapable of their directed exercise, incapable of his own help and his own happiness, sensible of the blight on him, and resigning himself to let it eat him away. {Book 1: ch 2–6, 11, 13, 20, 21; Book 3: ch 8, 9, 11, 12, 13, 15}

CLY, Roger – An Old Bailey spy, partner of Solomon Pross, and formerly servant to Charles Darnay. {Book 2: ch 3, 14; Book 3: ch 8, 15}

CRUNCHER, Jerry – An odd-job-man at Tellson's Bank, in London, who is also a resurrection-man (or body snatcher). His wife, a pious woman, is greatly distressed by her knowledge of the horrible nature of his nightly occupation; and, as her remonstrances prove to be unavailing, she resorts to prayers and supplications to Heaven to aid her in the reformation of her husband. This is very distasteful to Mr Cruncher – so much so, indeed, that he sometimes resorts to violence to prevent it. {Book 1: ch 2, 3; Book 2: ch 1–3, 6, 14, 24; Book 3: ch 7–9, 14}

CRUNCHER, Young Jerry – His son and assistant. {Book 2: ch 1, 2, 14; Book 3: ch 9}

CRUNCHER, Mrs – Wife of Jerry Cruncher; called by him

'Aggerawayter'. (Book 2: ch 1, 2, 14; Book 3: ch 9, 14} *See* **Cruncher, Jerry**.

DARNAY, Charles – *See* **St Evrémonde, Charles**.

DARNAY, Mrs Lucie – *See* **Manette, Lucie**.

DEFARGE, Madame Thérèse – Wife of Monsieur Defarge, and leader of the Saint Antoine rabble of women in the Revolution. She is a well-made woman, with a watchful eye that seldom seems to look at anything, a steady face, strong features, and great composure of manner. She is killed in an encounter with Miss Manette's maid, Miss Pross, who refuses to admit her into a room in which her mistress is supposed to be. {Book 1: ch 5, 6; Book 2: ch 7, 15, 16, 21, 21; Book 3: ch 3, 5, 6, 8–10, 12, 14, 15}

DEFARGE, Monsieur Ernest – Keeper of a wine-shop in the suburb of Saint Antoine, in Paris, and ringleader of the revolutionists in that quarter of the city. At his house, Doctor Manette is temporarily placed after being released from the Bastille; and it is he who finds the record, which the old man had written and secreted in the prison, and who produces it in court against Darnay. {Book 1: ch 5, 6; Book 2: ch 7, 15, 16, 21, 22; Book 3: ch 1, 3, 6, 9, 10, 12, 14, 15}

EVRÉMONDE, Charles – *See* **St Evrémonde, Charles**.

GABELLE, Monsieur Théophile – A combined postmaster and some kind of taxing functionary united. {Book 2: ch 8, 9, 23, 24; Book 3: ch 1, 6}

GASPARD – Assassin of the Marquis St Evrémonde. {Book 1: ch 5; Book 2: ch 7, 15, 16}

JACQUES ONE – A prominent assistant of Defarge in the French Revolution. {Book 1: ch 5; Book 2: ch 15, 21, 23}

JACQUES TWO – Another revolutionist, who is also an assistant of Defarge. {Book 1: ch 5; Book 2: ch 15, 21, 23}

JACQUES THREE – An associate of Defarge, and a member of the revolutionary jury; a cannibal-looking, bloody-minded man. {Book 1: ch 5; Book 2: ch 15, 2123; Book 3: ch 12, 14}

JACQUES FOUR – A name given to himself by Monsieur Defarge as one of the Saint Antoine revolutionists.

JACQUES FIVE – An associate of Defarge; a mender of roads, afterwards a wood-sawyer. {Book 2: ch 8, 9, 15, 16, 23; Book 3: ch 5, 9, 14, 15}

JOE – A coachman. {Book 1: ch 2}

LORRY, Mr Jarvis – A confidential clerk at the banking house of Tellson and Company, in London. He is a friend of the Manettes, and their companion during the terrible scenes of the Revolution in Paris. {Book 1: ch 2–6; Book 2: ch 2–4, 6, 12, 16–21, 24; Book 3: ch 2–6, 8, 9, 11–13, 15}

MANETTE, Doctor Alexander – A physician of Paris confined for eighteen years in the Bastille because, in his professional capacity, he had become acquainted with the secret crimes of a noble family. Released just before the outbreak of the Revolution, he goes to England, whither his wife and daughter had preceded him, and where the former had died. Restored to his child, who nurses him with tender solicitude, he gradually recovers the use of his faculties, which had become greatly impaired during his long imprisonment. About this time a young French nobleman, disgusted with the tyranny of the class to which he belongs, renounces his title and fortune, expatriates himself, and settles in England, where he passes under the name of Charles Darnay. He there becomes acquainted with and marries the daughter of Doctor Manette. Having been summoned back to Paris at the outbreak of the Revolution, to release from prison, by his testimony, an old and faithful servant of his family, he is himself thrown into La Force immediately upon his arrival, as a proscribed emigrant. His wife and her father follow him, however, and Doctor Manette, whose popularity is very high, succeeds in securing his acquittal. Yet in a few days he is re-accused and rearrested, the charge against him being that he is aristocrat, one of a family of tyrants, denounced enemies of the Republic; and the evidence against him is a paper written by Doctor Manette, when a prisoner in the Bastille, and secreted by him in a hole in the chimney of his cell. This document, which had been discovered at the capture of the prison, recites the story of the good doctor's sufferings, details the abominable iniquities of the St Evrémonde family (to which Darnay belongs), and ends by denouncing them and their descendants, to the last of the race, to the times when all such things shall be answered for. Darnay is condemned to death; but, through the heroic self-devotion of Sydney Carton, he is saved from such a fate, and is taken to England by his wife and her father, where they all lead a peaceful, prosperous, and happy life, and pass at last to a tranquil death. {Book 1: ch 2–4; Book 2: ch 2, 6, 9, 10, 12, 13, 16–21, 24; Book 2: ch 2–7, 9–12, 14, 15}

MANETTE, Lucie – His daughter; afterwards the wife of Charles Darnay. {Book 1: ch 4–6; Book 2: ch 2–6, 9–13, 16–21, 24; Book 3: ch 3–7, 9–12, 14, 15}

PROSS, Miss – Miss Lucie Manette's maid; sister of Solomon Pross. She is a grim, wild-looking woman, with red face and hair, brawny arms, abrupt manners, and singular habits. When the Manettes escape from Paris, Miss Pross remains behind to conceal their flight and, in trying to do so, gets involved in a hand-to-hand conflict with Madame Defarge, a ruthless and desperate woman, who is on their track. In the struggle, Madame Defarge draws a pistol and attempts to shoot her antagonist; but Miss Pross strikes it at the moment of firing, and the charge takes effect on the French woman, killing her instantly. Miss Pross hurries from the house, closely veiled; takes a carriage which has been in waiting for her, and succeeds in escaping safely to England. {Book 1: ch 4; Book 2: ch 6, 10, 17–19, 21; Book 3: ch 2, 3, 7, 8, 14}

PROSS, Solomon – *called also* '**John Barsad**'. A heartless scoundrel, who strips his sister of everything she possesses, as a stake to speculate with, and then abandons her in her poverty to support herself as she can. He becomes a spy and secret informer in the service of the English Government, and afterwards a turnkey in the Conciergerie in Paris. {Book 1: ch 3, 6; Book 2: ch 16; Book 3: ch 8, 9, 11, 13–15}

ST EVRÉMONDE, Marquis – Uncle of Charles Darnay; twin brother, joint inheritor, and next successor of the elder marquis. {Book 2: ch 7–9; Book 3: ch 10}

ST EVRÉMONDE, Marquis – Twin brother of the younger marquis, and father of Charles Darnay. {Book 3: ch 10}

ST EVRÉMONDE, Marquise – His wife; a young lady, handsome, engaging, and good, but not happy in her marriage. {Book 3: ch 10}

ST EVRÉMONDE, Charles – *called* 'Charles Darnay'. His son; a French émigré, afterwards married to Lucie Manette. {Book 2: ch 2–6, 9, 10, 16–18, 20, 21, 24; Book 3: ch 1–7, 9–15}

ST EVRÉMONDE, Lucie – His daughter. {Book 2: ch 21; Book 3: ch 2, 3, 5–7, 11, 13, 14}

STRYVER, Mr – A London barrister; counsel for Charles Darnay, and patron of Sydney Carton. {Book 2: ch 2–5, 11, 21, 24}

TELLSON AND COMPANY – An old and eminent banking firm in London. {Book 1: ch 3, 4; Book 2: ch 1, 3, 7, 9}

A Tale of Two Cities frontispiece – Hablot K Browne *alias* Phiz

TOM – Coachman of the Dover mail. {Book 1: ch 2}

VENGEANCE, The – One of the leading Revolutionists among the Saint Antoine women; lieutenant to Madame Defarge. {Book 2: ch 22; Book 3: ch 9, 12, 14, 15}

PRINCIPAL INCIDENTS

Book 1 – {1} Social condition of England and France in 1775. {2} The Dover Mail climbing Shooter's Hill; a messenger overtakes it with a despatch for Mr Jarvis Lorry; he receives a very singular message to carry back; his perplexity over it. {3} Mr Lorry's dream as he rode through the night. {4} How he looked, and what he did at The Royal George, at Dover; Miss Manette comes; he tells her, as 'a matter of business', that her father, whom she supposed dead, has been imprisoned many years, but is now free at Paris; she is stunned by the intelligence. {5} A wine-cask bursts in Saint Antoine, and a crowd tries to secure the wine; Defarge, the wine-shop keeper, leads Mr Lorry and Miss Manette to the garret where her father is making shoes. {6} Doctor Manette's appearance and voice; how he came to understand shoemaking; Lucie tries to recall to his mind long-forgotten incidents; they take him from the garret, and out of France.

Book 2 {1} Tellson's Bank a triumph of inconvenience; Jerry Cruncher at home; is greatly disturbed by Mrs Cruncher's 'flopping'; with young Jerry goes to his station near Tellson's, and chews straws till called to go on an errand. {2} He is sent to the Old Bailey, where Charles Darnay is put on trial for treason. {3} The attorney-general's speech; testimony of John Barsad and Roger Cly of Mr Lorry, of Miss Manette, of Doctor Manette; strange likeness of Sydney Carton, the barrister, to the prisoner; Darnay is acquitted. {4} Receives his friends' congratulations; Carton and Darnay dine together. {5} Stryver as lion, and Carton as jackal; Carton 'works up', two cases for Stryver. {6} Doctor Manette's house near Soho Square; Mr Lorry goes there one fine Sunday; talks with Miss Pross; the doctor and Lucie come home; Mr Darnay calls, and tells of a curious fact he heard while confined in the Tower, by which the doctor is much startled; Carton calls; their conversation before and during a thunderstorm. {7} Monseigneur, a French lord, takes his chocolate; character of the people who frequented his rooms; Marquis St Evrémonde drives over and kills Gaspard's child; Defarge comes, and a stout woman, knitting. {8} The marquis goes to his country seat; the poverty-stricken village near it; a road-mender tells the marquis of seeing a spectral-looking man swinging by the carriage-drag; a poor woman, whose husband has died of want, petitions the marquis for a bit of stone or wood to mark his grave. {9} He reaches the chateau, and soon his nephew, Charles Darnay, comes; their conversation; the sleepless night and the waking morning; the marquis is found assassinated. {10} Charles Darnay teaches in England; tells Doctor Manette his love for Lucie. {11} Conversation between Stryver and Carton about Stryver's plan to marry Miss Manette. {12} Stryver, on his way to tell her his intention, stops at Tellson's, communicates his plan to Mr Lorry, who advises him not to do it; Mr Lorry, after seeing Miss Manette, reiterates his advice, and is astounded by the nonchalance of Stryver. {13} Sydney Carton confesses to Miss Manette that she is the last dream of his life, and that even her

The accomplices – Hablot K Browne *alias* Phiz

influence cannot redeem him from the ruin he has brought on his career and character. {14} The funeral of Roger Cly, first followed, then managed, by a fierce mob; Jerry, having notified his wife that he shall 'work' her for 'flopping', if ill success attend his efforts, goes out 'fishing' after midnight; young Jerry follows; sees him, joined by two other men, enter a graveyard; they raise a coffin, and young Jerry flees home in deadly fear, fancying himself closely pursued by the coffin; Cruncher, returning unsuccessful, takes his wife to task for it; next morning, on their way to Tellson's, young Jerry asks his father about the business of a 'resurrection-man'. {15} Wine-drinking at Defarge's, madame keeping shop; Defarge and the road-mender enter, and soon follow the three Jacques to the garret once occupied by Doctor Manette; the road-mender tells of Gaspard, the assassin of Marquis St Evrémonde; his arrest eleven months after the murder; his imprisonment in the marquis's castle; his execution; Defarge and madame go with the road-mender on Sunday to Versailles to see the king and nobility; the road-mender is enthusiastic in his loyal demonstrations. {16} Defarge tells madame that John Barsad has been commissioned as government spy for Saint Antoine, and describes him; madame reassures Defarge's failing courage; Barsad comes to the wine-shop; madame puts a rose in her hair, and the customers all go out, leaving him talking with her; he feigns much sympathy for Gaspard; addresses Defarge – who comes in – as *Jacques*, but is corrected; he tells them that Miss Manette is going to marry Charles Darnay. {17} Doctor Manette and Lucie under the plane-tree the evening before her marriage; he assures her of his entire satisfaction that she is to be married: tells her the thoughts and fancies he had of her while in prison. {18} Mr Lorry gives her his parting bachelor-blessing; the marriage; Darnay and Lucie leave for Warwickshire; something Darnay had told the doctor just before the marriage brings back his old bewilderment, and he returns to making shoes; expedients adopted by Mr Lorry to restore him, and not to mar Lucie's wedding-tour. {19} The tenth morning, Mr Lorry finds the doctor recovered; has a long conversation with him on the cause of his malady, and obtains his consent to remove the shoemaker's bench and tools during his absence. {20} Carton asks and obtains permission of Darnay to come to his house occasionally; tells Darnay that Carton is better at heart than he seems, and begs for kind and generous treatment of him. {21} Echoes of little feet in Lucie's life; Carton's manner when visiting the Darnays; Stryver shoulders himself into wealth, marries a rich widow, takes her three sons to be taught by Darnay, who declines the patronage; Mr Lorry calls at Darnay's one July evening, quite irritated by his unusual day's work; the same day the people of Saint Antoine rise in revolution; Defarge leads them in repeated furious assaults on the Bastille; when it is taken, he forces the turnkey to conduct him to North Tower, where Doctor Manette had been confined; apparently finds nothing; the governor is stabbed by the mob, and Madame Defarge hews off his head. {22} Foulon, who had once told the famished people to eat grass, is taken, briefly tried, and hanged. {23} A grim, shaggy man comes where the road-mender is at work, learns the situation of the castle, then falls asleep; that night, the castle is burned; the villagers refuse to aid in extinguishing the fire, but ring the bell, and illuminate their houses. {24} Monseigneur, representative of the French nobility escaped from Paris, at Tellson's; Mr Lorry announces to Darnay his plan of going to Paris to secure from Tellson's Paris Bank some important books and papers; Darnay sees a letter addressed to him by his real name (Evrémonde); the depreciating remarks of Monseigneur, and the coarse bullying remarks of Stryver; letter from Gabelle in prison at Paris, imploring Darnay's assistance; Darnay resolves to go to Paris; sees Mr Lorry off, writes letters to Lucie and Doctor Manette, and next night starts on his journey.

Book 3 {1} He meets obstacles constantly from citizen patriots; finally is furnished with escorts; just escapes with life from the mob at Beauvais; arrives at Paris; is at once consigned to the prison of La Force; Defarge accompanies him, asking some questions, but declaring that he will do nothing for him; at the prison, a company of refined and courteous prisoners welcomes him; he is put in a cell, and left to his maddening thoughts. {2} Tellson's Bank at Paris; Doctor Manette and Lucie rush into Mr Lorry's room, to his utter surprise; he tells Lucie that he knows of no harm having befallen Darnay; puts her in a safer room, then looks out of a window with Doctor Manette on a yard where scores of fierce men and women are grinding weapons dulled by murdering prisoners; Doctor Manette, safe because he has himself been a Bastille prisoner, rushes into the crowd, makes himself known, and is hurried away to La Force to save Darnay. {3} Mr Lorry procures lodgings for Lucie, her daughter and Miss Pross; Defarge brings him a note from the doctor, stating that

Darnay is safe; Madame Defarge and The Vengeance look carefully at Lucie and her child, but give little heed to her plea for kindness to Darnay. {4} What the doctor said and heard while trying to save Darnay; his perfect self-possession and resolution; the sharp female called La Guillotine; Lucie's steady devotion to her household duties. {5} She goes daily to a spot where the doctor had told her Darnay could see her, though she could not see him; the horrible dance of the Carmagnole. {6} Darnay is summoned before the Tribunal; his answers; the testimony of Gabelle, Doctor Manette, and Mr Lorry; he is acquitted; the crowd carry him home in triumph. {7} Miss Pross and Cruncher prepare for an unusually elaborate marketing in honour of the release of Darnay; he is again arrested on the accusation of Defarge, madame, and another. {8} Miss Pross, marketing with Jerry, meets her brother Solomon in The Good Republican Brutus of Antiquity; he goes with her into the street, and is just getting rid of her, when Jerry half-recognises him, and Sydney Carton calls him by name, 'Barsad'; by a half-threat, Carton induces Barsad to go with him to Mr Lorry's; convinces him that he knows so much of his villainy as to have him in his power; Barsad declares Cly dead, and Jerry vehemently denies it. {9} Mr Lorry questions Jerry as to his knowledge of Cly's being alive, and learns that Jerry is an 'Agricultooral character'; Carton tells Mr Lorry he has arranged with Barsad, who is one of the turnkeys at the Conciergerie, to be admitted to Darnay at once if it should go ill with him; the talk of Lucie, of the days when they were children at their mothers' knees; Carton talks with a wood-sawyer about the guillotine; procures some drugs from a chemist; walks the streets all night, repeating again and again the words read at his father's grave; Darnay again before the Tribunal; the prosecutor states that Darnay is denounced by Monsieur and Madame Defarge, also by Doctor Manette; the doctor, denying the statement, is stopped, and obliged to sit down; Defarge testifies to having found in North Tower a paper written by Doctor Manette in prison in 1767. {10} in which the doctor sets forth how, in December 1757, he was overtaken by two men; was compelled to go with them to a country seat two miles out of Paris, where he found a young patient female, who in her delirium, at regular intervals, shrieked and said; 'My husband, my father, and my brother', then counted twelve; how, in the same place, he found another patient, a boy of seventeen dying of a sword-wound, who told the doctor in the presence of the two unfeeling St Evrémonde brothers, how brutally these nobles treat their tenants, that the delirious young woman is his sister, that her husband was worked to death in order that the younger brother might obtain possession of her; that he had hidden his younger sister, then tried to kill the younger noble, and was mortally wounded; the young woman dies; the doctor writes all the circumstances to the minister; the wife of Marquis St Evrémonde calls on the doctor, and expresses her great desire to do what she can to atone for the gross wrongs of her husband and his brother; the doctor is imprisoned. On this testimony, Darnay is swiftly condemned to die within twenty-four hours. {11} Darnay and Lucie meet a few moments in the court-room; Carton carries Lucie to a carriage, thence to her room; arranges to have Doctor Manette make another effort to save Darnay, and meet him at Mr Lorry's at nine o'clock that night. {12} Carton goes to Defarge's wine-shop; hears Madame Defarge, Jacques Three, and The Vengeance urge the utter extermination of all the family of Evrémonde; Defarge opposes this for the doctor's sake; Madame declares herself the younger sister of the woman and boy killed by the Evrémondes; at midnight, the doctor enters Mr Lorry's room crazy, demanding his bench again; Carton finds a passport in his case; tells Mr Lorry what he heard Madame Defarge say; arranges with him to have everything ready to start for England next day at two pm; then bids him 'Good-bye'. {13} Darnay's last night in the Concièrgerie; he becomes composed; writes letters to Lucie, Doctor Manette, and Mr Lorry; dreams of his happy home near Soho Square; wakes, and counts the hours calmly; at one o'clock Sydney Carton comes in; Carton dictates a letter for Darnay to write and, with drugs procured at the chemist's, renders him unconscious; changes clothes with him; then Barsad carries Darnay out as if overcome with grief; Carton meets a sweet-faced seamstress in the hall where the day's victims are gathered, and promises to hold her hand as they ride to execution; the carriage, with Mr Lorry, Doctor Manette, Darnay, Lucie, and the child, reaches the Barrier; the papers are examined; they drive as fast as they dare, not to excite suspicion, but are not pursued. {14} Madame Defarge, The Vengeance, and Jacques Three determine that Lucie shall be denounced; having directed The Vengeance to reserve for her a seat at the execution, Madame Defarge goes to see Lucie, to be able to bear witness that she impeached the justice of the Republic; Jerry and Miss Press consult as to the best place for them to start from; Jerry goes; Madame Defarge enters the house, and demands to see Lucie; Miss Pross defiant; neither understands a word the other says; at last they grapple, and in the struggle madame is shot by her own pistol; Miss Press locks the door, throws the key into the river, joins Jerry, and they start for England, the crash of the pistol-shot ringing in her ears, and to ring there for ever. {15} Sydney Carton's ride in a tumbril to the guillotine; The Vengeance is greatly excited because Madame Defarge does not come; Carton cheers and comforts the seamstress, they kiss, and are executed; the prophetic thoughts Carton may have had of the future of his friends and foes.

24

Hunted Down

This tale was written specially for *The New York Ledger*, in which paper it appeared in the numbers for 20 & 27 August and 3 September 1859 (Vol 15, No 24–26), illustrated with seven woodcuts. It was republished in 1860 in *All the Year Round*, 4 & 11 August (First series, Nos 67 and 68).

CHARACTERS

ADAMS, Mr – Clerk in the life assurance office of which Mr Sampson is the chief manager.

BANKS, Major – A character assumed by Mr Meltham in furtherance of his plans against Mr Slinkton.

BECKWITH, Mr Alfred – *See* **Meltham, Mr**.

MELTHAM, Mr – Actuary of the Inestimable Life Assurance Company. He falls in love with one of Mr Julius Slinkton's nieces, a lovely girl, whose life is insured in his office. She soon dies from the effects of a slow poison secretly administered to her by her uncle, and Mr Meltham, having become thoroughly assured of the villain's guilt, devotes himself thenceforth to the single object of hunting him down. Resigning his situation, he causes a report of his death to be put into circulation, assumes the name of Mr Alfred Beckwith, takes rooms in the Middle Temple, opposite those of Mr Slinkton – to whom he is personally unknown – and makes them a trap for him. Affecting to be a confirmed drunkard, he deludes the murderer into thinking that it would be an easy thing to obtain an insurance on his life for two thousand pounds, and then to do him to death with brandy – or, brandy not proving quick enough, with something quicker. Slinkton's plotting, however, is well understood all along, and he is gradually led on to his ruin. The fitting time having arrived, he is confronted with the evidences of his guilt when, finding himself brought to bay, he swallows some of the powerful poison which he always carries with him, and falls down a dead man.

NINER, Miss Margaret – Mr Slinkton's niece. She is saved from falling a victim to the wickedness of her uncle by the efforts of Mr Sampson and Mr Meltham, who reveal to her his real character, and induce her to leave him for ever.

SAMPSON, Mr – Chief manager of a life assurance company, and narrator of the story, in which he is also one of the actors.

SLINKTON, Mr Julius – A gentleman – educated, well-bred and agreeable – who professes to be on the point of going into orders, but who is, in reality, a consummate hypocrite and villain. He effects an insurance for two thousand pounds on the life of Mr Alfred Beckwith, and then attempts to poison him in order to get the money but, being foiled in his object, he destroys himself.

25

Uncommercial Traveller

In December 1860, 17 papers on a variety of topics, which had previously appeared at intervals in *All the Year Round*, were published in a collective form by Chapman and Hall under the above title. A cheap edition in 1865 added a further 11 pieces, and an 1871 edition, with illustrations, carried 36 pieces. Finally, the Gadshill edition of 1890 at last presented all the 37 pieces.

The Uncommercial Traveller introduces himself to the reader in these words:

> 'I am both a town traveller and a country-traveller, and am always on the road. Figuratively speaking, I travel for the great house of Human Interest Brothers, and have rather a large connection in the fancy goods way. Literally speaking, I am always wandering here and there from my rooms in Covent Gardens, London – now about the city streets, now about the country byroads – seeing many things, and some great things, which, because they interest me, I think may interest others.'

The titles of the 17 pieces in the first edition are as follows:

1   His General Line of Business
2   The Shipwreck
3   Wapping Workhouse
4   Two Views of a Cheap Theatre
5   Poor Mercantile Jack
6   Refreshments for Travellers
7   Travelling Abroad
8   The Great Tasmania's Cargo
9   City of London Churches
10 Shy Neighbourhoods
11 Tramps
12 Dullborough Town (Rochester)
13 Night Walks

14   Chambers
15   Nurse's Stories
16   Arcadian London
17   The Italian Prisoner

The 11 pieces added in the 1865 edition are:

18   The Calais Night-mail
19   Some Recollections of Mortality
20   Birthday Celebrations
21   Bound for the Great Salt Lake
22   The City of the Absent
23   An Old Stage-Coaching House
24   The Boiled Beef of New England
25   Chatham Dockyars
26   In the French-Flemish Country
27   Medicine-Men of Civilisation
28   Titbull's Alms-houses

The eight pieces added to the Illustrated Library Edition (1875):

29   Among the Short-timers
30   The Ruffian
31   Aboard Ship
32   A Small Star in the East
33   A Little Dinner in an Hour
34   Mr Barlow
35   On an Amateur Beat
36   A Plea for Total Abstinence.

Finally, the Gadshill Edition of 1890 contained a piece omitted from the earlier collections:

37   A Fly-leaf in a Life.

CHARACTERS

ANDERSON, John – A tramp, whose only improvidence appears to have been that he has spent the last of his little all upon soap. {11 *Tramps*}

ANDERSON, Mrs – His wife; a woman spotless to behold. {11 *Tramps*}

ANTONIO – A swarthy young Spanish guitar-player. {5 *Poor Mercantile Jack*}

BATTENS, Mr – A virulent old pensioner at Titbull's. {27 *Titbull's Almshouses*}

'This is a sweet spot, ain't it? A lovelly spot' – G J Pinwell

BONES, Mr Banjo – A comic Ethiopian minstrel, with a blackened face and a limp sugar-loaf hat. {5 *Poor Mercantile Jack*}

BONES, Mrs Banjo – His wife; a professional singer. {5 *Poor Mercantile Jack*}

CARLAVERO, Giovanni – Keeper of a small wine-shop, in a certain small Italian town on the Mediterranean. He had been a political offender, sentenced to imprisonment for life, but was afterwards released through the zealous intervention of a generous English nobleman. Desirous of testifying his gratitude to his benefactor, whom he has not seen since his liberation, he sends him by Mr Dickens an immense demijohn of wine, the first produce of his little vineyard. With infinite difficulty this frail and enormous bottle, holding some half-dozen gallons, is safely carried to England; but the wine turns to vinegar before it reaches its destination. Yet 'the Englishman,' says Mr Dickens, 'told me, with much emotion in his face and voice, that he had never tasted wine that seemed to him so sweet and sound; and long afterwards the bottle graced his table.'. {17 *The Italian Prisoner*}

CHIPS – A shipwright who sells himself to the Devil for half a ton of copper, a bushel of tenpenny nails, an iron pot, and a rat that can speak. He gets disgusted with the rat, and tries to kill it, but does not succeed, and is punished by being subjected to a swarm and plague of rats, who finally compass his destruction 'by eating through the planks of a ship in which he has been 'pressed' for a sailor. {15 *Nurse's Stories*}

CLEVERLY, Susannah – A Mormon emigrant; a young woman of business. {21 *Bound for the Great Salt Lake*}

CLEVERLY, William – Her brother; also a Mormon emigrant. {21 *Bound for the Great Salt Lake*}

DIBBLE, Mr Sampson – A Mormon emigrant; a very old man, who is stone-blind. {21 *Bound for the Great Salt Lake*}

DIBBLE, Mrs Dorothy – His wife, who accompanies him. {21 *Bound for the Great Salt Lake*}

FACE-MAKER, Monsieur The – A corpulent little man with a comical face. He is heralded as 'the great changer of countenances, who transforms the features that Heaven has bestowed upon him into an endless succession of surprising and extraordinary visages, comprehending all the contortions, energetic and expressive, of which the human face is capable, and all the passions of the human heart, as love, jealousy, revenge, hatred, avarice, despair.'. {26 *In the French-Flemish Country*}

FLANDERS, Sally – A former nurse of the Uncommercial Traveller, and widow of Flanders, a small master-builder. {27 *Medicine-Men of Civilization*}

FLIPFIELD, Mr – A friend of the Uncommercial Traveller's. {20 *Birthday Celebrations*}

FLIPFIELD, Mrs – His mother. {19 *Birthday Celebrations*}

FLIPFIELD, Miss – His elder sister. She is in the habit of speaking to new acquaintances, in pious and condoning tones, of all the quarrels that have taken place in the family from infancy. {20 *Birthday Celebrations*}

FLIPFIELD, Mr Tom – *called* **'The Long Lost'**. A brother of Mr Flipfield's. After an absence of many years in foreign parts, he returns home, and is warmly welcomed by his family and friends; but he proves to be an 'antipathetical being, with a peculiar power and gift of treading on everybody's tenderest place' and everybody wishes that he could be instantly transported back to the foreign parts which have tolerated him so long. {20 *Birthday Celebrations*}

GLOBSON, Bully – A schoolmate of the Uncommercial Traveller's; a big fat boy, with a big fat head, and a big fat fist. {20 *Birthday Celebrations*}

GRAZINGLANDS, Mr Alexander – A midland county gentleman, of a comfortable property, on a visit to London. {6 *Refreshments for Travellers*}

GRAZINGLANDS, Mrs Arabella – His wife; the pride of her division of the county. {6 *Refreshments for Travellers*}

JACK, Dark – A Negro sailor. {5 *Poor Mercantile Jack*}

JACK, Mercantile – A representative of the sailors employed in the merchant marine. {5 *Poor Mercantile Jack*}

JOBSON, Jesse, Number Two – A Mormon emigrant, the head of a family of eight persons. {21 *Bound for the Great Salt Lake*}

KING, Horace – An inmate of the King's Bench Prison, where he dies. {13 *Night Walks*}

KINDHEART, Mr – An Englishman of an amiable nature, great enthusiasm, and no discretion. {27 *Medicine-Men of Civilization*}

KLEM, Mr – A weak old man, meagre and mouldy, who is never to be seen detached from a flat pint of beer in a pewter pot. {16 *Arcadian London*}

KLEM, Mrs – His wife; an elderly woman, labouring under a chronic sniff, and having a dejected consciousness that she is not justified in appearing on the surface of the earth. {16 *Arcadian London*}

KLEM, Miss – Their daughter, apparently ten years older than either her father or mother. {16 *Arcadian London*}

MELLOWS, Mr J – Landlord of The Dolphin's Head. {23 *An Old Stage-Coaching House*}

MERCY – A nurse who relates diabolical stories to the Uncommercial Traveller, when a child, with a fiendish enjoyment of his terrors. {15 *Nurse's Stories*}

MITTS, Mrs – A pensioner at Titbull's; a tidy, well-favoured widow, with a propitiatory way of passing her hands over and under one another. {28 *Titbull's Almshouses*}

MURDERER, Captain – A diabolical wretch, admitted into the best society, and possessing immense wealth. His mission is matrimony, and the gratification of a cannibal appetite with tender brides. {15 *Nurse's Stories*}

OAKUM-HEAD – A refractory female pauper, who 'would be very thankful to be got into a place, or got abroad'. {3 *Wapping Workhouse*}

ONOWENEVER, Mrs – Mother of a young lady ardently loved by the Uncommercial Traveller in his youth. {20 *Birthday Celebrations*}

PANGLOSS – An official friend of the Uncommercial Traveller's lineally descended from the learned doctor of the same name, who was tutor to Candide. {8 *The Great Tasmania's Cargo*}

PARKLE, Mr – A friend of the Uncommercial Traveller's. {14 *Chambers*}

QUICKEAR – A policeman. {5 *Poor Mercantile Jack*}

QUINCH, Mrs – The oldest pensioner at Titbull's; a woman who has 'totally lost her head'. {28 *Titbull's Almshouses*}

REFRACTORY, Chief – A surly, discontented female pauper, with a voice in which the tonsils and uvula have gained a diseased ascendancy. {3 *Wapping Workhouse*}

REFRACTORY, Number Two – Another pauper of the same character. {3 *Wapping Workhouse*}

SAGGERS, Mrs – One, of the oldest pensioners at Titbull's, who has split the small community in which she lives into almost as many parties as there are dwellings in the precinct, by standing her pail outside her dwelling. {28 *Titbull's Almshouses*}

SALCY, P, Family – A troupe of fifteen dramatic artists, under the management of Monsieur P Salcy. {26 *In the French-Flemish Country*}

SHARPEYE – A policeman. {5 *Poor Mercantile Jack*}

SPECKS, Joe – An old schoolfellow of the Uncommercial Traveller; afterwards a physician in Dullborough (where most of us come from who come from a country town). {12 *Dullborough Town*}

SPECKS, Mrs – His wife, formerly Lucy Green; an old friend of the Uncommercial Traveller's. {12 *Dullborough Town*}

SQUIRES, Olympia – An old flame of the Uncommercial Traveller's. {20 *Birthday Celebrations*}

STRAUDENHEIM – A shopkeeper at Strasburg; a large-lipped, pear-nosed old man, with white hair and keen eyes, though near-sighted. {7 *Travelling Abroad*}

SWEENEY, Mrs – A professional laundress, in figure extremely like an old family umbrella. {14 *Chambers*}

TESTATOR, Mr – An occupant of a very dreary set of chambers, in Lyons Inn, which he furnishes with articles he finds locked up in one of the cellars, and having no owner, so far as is known to anyone. He is afterwards visited, late at night, by a man considerably sodden with liquor, who examines every article, claims them all as his own, and promises to call again the next morning, punctually at ten o'clock, but who fails to do so. {14 *Chambers*}

TRAMPFOOT – A policeman. {5 *Poor Mercantile Jack*}

VENTRILOQUIST, Monsieur The – A performer attached to a booth at a fair. He is a thin and sallow man of a weakly aspect. {26 *In the French-Flemish Country*}

VICTUALLER, Mr Licensed – Proprietor of a singing-house frequented by sailors; a sharp and watchful man, with tight lips, and a complete edition of Cocker's Arithmetic in each eye. {5 *Poor Mercantile Jack*}

WEEDLE, Anastasia – A pretty Mormon emigrant, elected by universal suffrage the beauty of the ship. {21 *Bound for the Great Salt Lake*}

WILTSHIRE – A simple, fresh-coloured farm labourer of eight-and-thirty. {21 *Bound for the Great Salt Lake*}

26

Great Expectations

This tale originally appeared in *All the Year Round*, starting on 1 December 1860. On its completion in 1861, it was published by Chapman and Hall in three volumes, with illustrations by Marcus Stone, and was 'affectionately inscribed to Chauncy Hare Townshend' (1798–1868; poet).

CHARACTERS

AGED, The – *See* **Wemmick, Mr, Senior**

AMELIA – One of Mr Jaggers's clients. {20}

AVENGER, The – *See* **Pepper**.

BARLEY, Clara – Daughter of Old Bill Barley; a very pretty, slight, dark-eyed girl of twenty or so, of natural and winning manners, and a confiding and amiable disposition. She is betrothed to Herbert Pocket, whom she afterwards marries. {46, 55, 58, 59}

BARLEY, Old Bill – A bedridden purser; a sad old rascal, always more or less drunk, and tormented by the gout in his right hand – and everywhere else. {46, 58}

BIDDY – An orphan; second cousin to Mr Wopsle, being his 'great-aunt's granddaughter'. She is a good, honest girl, poor in purse and condition, but with a wealth of true womanliness which makes Joe Gargery, whose second wife she becomes, very rich indeed. {7, 16–19, 35, 58, 59}

BRANDLEY, Mrs – A widow-lady at Richmond, with whom Estella is placed by Miss Havisham. {38}

CAMILLA, Mr John or Raymond – A relative of Miss Havisham; a toady and a humbug. {11, 25}

CAMILLA, Mrs – His wife; sister to Mr Pocket. She professes a great deal of love for Miss Havisham, and calls on her husband to testify that her solicitude for that lady is gradually undermining her to the extent of making one of her legs shorter than the other. {11, 25}

CLARRIKER – A young merchant or shipping broker. {52, 58}

COILER, Mrs – A toady neighbour of Mr and Mrs Pocket's; a widow-lady of that highly sympathetic nature, that she agrees with everybody, blesses everybody, and sheds smiles or tears on everybody, according to circumstances. {23}

COMPEYSON – A convict, and 'the worst of scoundrels'. He proves to be the man who professed to be Miss Havisham's lover. He is at length committed for felony, is sentenced to seven years' imprisonment; and is finally killed in a struggle with Magwitch. {3, 5, 42, 45, 47, 50, 53–56}

DRUMMLE, Bentley – called '**The Spider**'. A sulky, old-looking young man of a heavy order of architecture; idle, proud, niggardly, reserved, and suspicious. He is a fellow-boarder with Pip at Mr Pocket's, and his rival for the hand of Estella whom he marries and treats with great cruelty. {23, 25, 38, 43, 44, 48}

ESTELLA – The adopted daughter of Miss Havisham, and the heroine of the story. She proves to be the daughter of Abel Magwitch (or Provis), Pip's benefactor. Her foster-mother tells Pip that she had wished for a little girl to rear, and to save from her own fate (see **HAVISHAM, Miss**); and that Mr Jaggers had accordingly brought her such a child – an orphan of about three years. Not content with moulding the impressionable child into the form that her own wild resentment, spurned affection, and wounded pride find vengeance in, she marries her to an ill-tempered, clumsy, contemptible booby (Bentley Drummle), who has nothing to recommend him but money and a ridiculous roll of addle-headed predecessors. After leading a most unhappy life, she separates from her husband, who subsequently dies from an accident consequent on his ill-treatment of a horse. Some two years after this event, she happens to meet Pip (who has always loved her) on the very spot where their first meeting had been when they were children. {7, 9, 11–16, 18, 22, 27, 29, 30, 32, 33, 38, 39, 43, 44, 48–51, 56, 57, 59}

FLOPSON – A nurse in Mr Pocket's family. {22, 23}

GARGERY, Joe – A blacksmith, married to Pip's sister, who is an out-and-out termagant. When Pip is a small boy, he is harshly treated by his sister (with whom he lives, both his parents being dead); but his kind-hearted brother-in-law befriends him as much as is possible, and makes quite a companion of him. In the course of conversation, one night, when they happen to be left by themselves, Joe gives him some account of his early history, of the circumstances attending his marriage, and of the principles on which he regulates his domestic conduct. After the death of his wife Joe marries Biddy, a sweet-tempered woman, who makes him an excellent wife, and with whom he lives happily for many years, ever doing the duty that lies before him with a strong hand, a quiet tongue, and a gentle heart. {2–7, 9, 10, 12–20, 27, 35, 57–59} *See* **Gargery Mrs Joe**.

GARGERY, Mrs Georgiana Maria – His wife; sister to Pip, and a thorough shrew. When Pip grows up, he goes out into the world, and his experiences of his sister's tender mercies come to an end; but poor Joe continues to bear his cross with exemplary patience, until death relieves him of it by opening a grave for Mrs Gargery. {2, 4–7, 9, 10, 12–18, 24, 25} *See* **Orlick, Dolge**

GEORGIANA – A cousin of Mr Pocket's, and a relative of Miss Havisham's; an indigestive single woman, who calls her rigidity religion, and her liver love. {11, 25, 57}

HAVISHAM, Miss – Estella's foster-mother. In her youth she had been a beautiful heiress, and looked after as a great match. She was pursued in particular by a certain showy man (Compeyson), who professed to be devoted to her. She received a letter from him, however, when she was dressing for church, that most heartlessly broke the marriage off. When she recovered from a bad illness that she had, she laid waste the whole place where she resided (Satis House), stopped all the clocks at twenty minutes to nine – the time of her receiving the letter – and never afterwards looked upon the light of day. Filled with bitterness towards all mankind, Miss Havisham adopts a beautiful orphan girl (Estella) and rears her in the midst of all this desolation, educating her to steel her heart against all tenderness, but to lead young men on to love her, that she may break their hearts. {8, 9, 11–14, 19, 22, 29, 38, 44, 49, 57} *See* **Estella**.

HUBBLE, Mr – A wheelwright, who is a friend of Mrs Joe Gargery; a tough, high-shouldered, stooping old man, of a sawdusty fragrance, with his legs extraordinarily wide apart. {4, 5, 35}

HUBBLE, Mrs – His wife; a little, sharp-eared person, who holds a conventionally juvenile position, because she married Mr Hubble when she was much younger than he. {4, 5, 35}

JACK – A grizzled, slimy man, with a slushy voice, who is employed on a little causeway on the Thames. {54}

A rubber at Miss Haversham's – Marcus Stone

JAGGERS, Mr – A criminal lawyer of Little Britain, employed by Pip's unknown patron to inform him of his 'great expectations', and to act as his guardian until he comes into full possession of his fortune. Mr Jaggers has an air of authority that is not to be disputed, and a manner expressive of knowing something secret about everybody that would effectually do for each individual if he chose to disclose it. His clerk tells Pip that it always seems to him as if his master had set a man-trap and was watching it. When he is not biting his large forefinger, he is in the habit of throwing it, in a half-bullying sort of way, at the person he is talking with. He never laughs; but he wears great bright creaking boots, and in poising himself on these, with his large head bent down, and his eyebrows; joined together, awaiting an answer, he sometimes causes the boots to creak as if *they* laughed in a dry and a suspicious way. {11, 18, 20, 21, 24, 26, 29, 36, 40, 48, 49, 51, 56}

MAGWITCH, Abel – *alias* **Provis**. A convict who escapes from the Hulks and, meeting Pip, terrifies the boy into supplying him with food and a file to enable him to file off his fetters. Though very soon captured, and transported to New South Wales, he retains a grateful remembrance of Pip, and after some years, growing wealthy in the business of sheep-farming, sets him up as a gentleman, making Mr Jaggers his guardian and banker. He does this privately, however; and Pip supposes himself to be indebted to Miss Havisham for his good fortune – a mistake which that lady, for reasons of her own, does not trouble herself to correct. Magwitch at last returns to England under the assumed name of Provis, and makes himself known to Pip, who endeavours to save his benefactor from recapture, but in vain. In spite of every precaution, Magwitch is discovered and taken; but he dies in prison, and thus escapes execution. {1, 3, 5, 29–42, 46, 54–56}

MARY ANNE – A neat little girl who is Wemmick's servant. {25, 45}

MIKE – A one-eyed client of Mr Jaggers. {20, 51}

MILLERS – A nurse in Mr Pocket's family. {22–23}

MOLLY – Mr Jaggers's housekeeper, and a former mistress of Abel Magwitch, by whom she is the mother of Estella. {24, 26}

ORLICK, Dolge – A journeyman employed by Joe Gargery. He secretly strikes a blow, which results in the death of Mrs Gargery ; and he afterwards attempts the life of Pip. {15–17, 29, 30, 53}

PEPPER – called '**The Avenger**'. Pip's boy. {27}

PIP – *See* **Pirrip**, Philip.

PIRRIP, Philip – called 'Pip'. The narrator and the hero of the story; 'a good fellow, with impetuosity and hesitation, boldness and diffidence, action and dreaming, curiously mixed in him'. His father and mother being dead, Pip is brought up 'by hand' by his sister, Mrs Joe Gargery, who is more than twenty years older than he. She is something of a shrew, and does not treat him very kindly; but her husband, being a fellow-sufferer, makes an equal and companion of him, and they are 'ever the best of friends'. When Pip is old enough, he is apprenticed to Joe, to learn the blacksmith's trade; but, before he is out of his time, he is informed that, through the generosity of an unknown friend, he will one day come into a handsome property; and in accordance with the wish of his benefactor, he removes to London to be brought up as a gentleman. Elated by his good fortune, he looks down upon the humble friends of his earlier days, and treats them with condescending kindness when he sees them, which is but seldom. At last, to his astonishment and disgust, he discovers his patron to be Abel Magwitch, the convict for whom he had done a favour when a child. Transported for crime, this man has retained a grateful sense of the kindness Pip had shown him and, accumulating wealth, has determined to educate and provide for him, and ultimately to make him his heir. Though sentenced for life, such is his desire to see the gentleman he has made that he runs the risk of detection, returns to England, makes himself known to Pip, and avows himself his benefactor. This declaration is a staggering blow to Pip, who has always supposed himself to be a *protégé* of Miss Havisham, and the intended husband of her adopted daughter, Estella, with whom he is deeply in love. The young lady is married to another, and to add to his troubles, Magwitch is recognised, denounced, arrested, tried, and sentenced to death – he dies in prison before the day of execution arrives. His possessions being, under the law, forfeited to the Crown, Pip finds himself suddenly reduced to poverty and arrested for debt. He is on the point of being thrown into jail, when he is seized with a malignant fever, becomes delirious and suffers greatly. When he begins to recover, he finds his old friend Joe by his bedside. When he gets about again, Pip sells all he has, and puts aside as much as he can for a composition with his creditors, becomes a clerk and, after some years, a partner, in the house of Clarriker and Co, and finally marries Estella, who has been left a widow.

POCKET, Herbert – A son of Matthew Pocket, who becomes a warm friend of Pip's. He has 'great expectations' as well as Pip, whom he quite astonishes with the grandeur of his ideas, and his plans for making money. Pip's lavish habits lead Herbert into expenses that he cannot afford, corrupt the simplicity of his life, and disturb his peace with anxieties and regrets. At a later date Herbert becomes a partner in the house of Clarriker and Co, through the kind assistance of Pip, which is secretly rendered, and is not discovered for many a year. He marries Clara Barley. {11, 21–27, 30, 31, 34, 36–42, 45–47, 49, 50, 52–55, 58}

POCKET, Alick – One of Mr Pocket's children, who makes arrangements, while still wearing a frock, for being married to a suitable young person at Kew. {22, 23}

POCKET, Jane – A little daughter of Mr Pocket's ; a mere mite, who has prematurely taken upon herself some charge of the others. Her desire to be matrimonially established is so strong that she might be supposed to have passed her short existence in the perpetual contemplation of domestic bliss. {22, 23}

POCKET, Joe – Another child. {23}

POCKET, Fanny – Another child. {23}

POCKET, Mr Matthew – A relative of Miss Havisham's, living at Hammersmith, with whom Pip studies for a time. He is a gentleman with a rather perplexed expression of face, and with his hair disordered on his head, as if he didn't quite see his way to putting anything straight. {22–24, 33, 39}

POCKET, Mrs Belinda – His wife. {22, 23, 33}

POCKET, Sarah – A relative of Miss Havisham; a little, dry, brown, corrugated old woman, with a blandly-vicious manner, a small face that might have been made of walnut shells, and a large mouth like a cat's, without the whiskers. {11, 15, 19, 29}

POTKINS, William – A waiter at The Blue Bear. {58}

PROVIS – *See* **Magwitch, Abel**.

PUMBLECHOOK, Uncle – A well-to-do corn chandler and seedsman; uncle to Joe Gargery, but appropriated by Mrs Joe. He is a large, hard-breathing, middle-aged, slow man, with a mouth like a fish, dull, staring eyes, and sandy hair standing upright on his head; so that he looks as if he had been choked, and had just come to. Pumblechook is the torment of Pip's life, for the bullying old fellow is in the habit of coming to Mrs Gargery's house, where Pip lives, and discussing his character and prospects in his presence. When Pip comes, most unexpectedly, into property and great expectations' and about to depart for London, obsequiousness of Pumblechook is equal to his former assumption of authority. When Pip is reduced to poverty by the death of his patron, Mr Pumblechook again changes his manner and conduct, becoming as ostentatiously compassionate and forgiving as he had been meanly servile in the time of Pip's new prosperity. {4–9, 12, 13, 15, 19, 35, 58}

SKIFFINS, Miss – A lady of an uncertain age and a wooden appearance, but 'a very good sort of fellow'. She stands possessed of 'portable property', which is so strong a recommendation in the eyes of Mr Wemmick, that he makes her his wife. {37, 55}

SOPHIA – A housemaid in Mr Pocket's service. {23}

SPIDER, The – *See* **Drummle, Bentley**.

STARTOP, Mr – A lively, bright young man, with a woman's delicacy of feature, who is a fellow-boarder with Pip at Pocket's. {23, 25, 26, 34, 52–54}

TRABB, Mr – A prosperous old bachelor, who is a tailor and undertaker in the quiet old town where Pip lives during his boyhood. He has a shop-boy who is one of the most audacious young fellows in all that countryside. When Pip comes into a handsome property, and people stare after him, and are excessively polite if he happens to speak to them, the only effect upon Trabb's boy is to make him more independent and impudent than before. As Pip is returning, on one occasion, to The Blue Boar from Satis House, to take the coach back to London, fate throws him in the way of 'that unlimited miscreant'. {19, 35}

WALDENGARVER, Mr – *See* **Wopsle, Mr**.

WEMMICK, Mr John – Mr Jaggers's confidential clerk. He is a dry man, rather short in stature, with a square wooden face, whose expression seems to have been imperfectly chipped out with a dull-edged chisel. He has glittering eyes – small, keen, and black – and thin, white mottled lips, and has had them, apparently, from forty to fifty years. His guiding principle, and his invariable advice to his friends is, to take care of portable property, and never on any account to lose an opportunity of securing it. Although his business relations to Mr Jaggers are of the most intimate nature, their acquaintance and fellowship goes no further, and each pretends to the other that he is made of the sternest and flintiest stuff. But notwithstanding their hard exterior and their fear of showing themselves to one another in a weak and unprofessional light, they are kindly men at heart – Wemmick especially, who has a pleasant home at Walworth, where he devotes himself to the comfort of his venerable father, and refreshes his business life in many pleasant and playful ways, the latest and most important of them being the transformation of Miss Skiffins into Mrs Wemmick. {20, 21, 24–26, 32, 36, 37, 45, 48, 51, 55} *See* **Skiffins, Miss**

WEMMICK, Mr Senior – called 'The Aged'. Mr John Wemmick's father; a very old man, clean, cheerful, comfortable, and well cared for, but intensely deaf. {25, 37, 45, 48, 51, 55}

WEMMICK, Mrs – *See* **Skiffins, Miss.**

WHIMPLE, Mrs – A lodging-house keeper at Mill Pond Bank, Chinks's Basin; an elderly woman of a pleasant and thriving appearance, who is the best of housewives. {46}

WILLIAM – *See* **Potkins, William**

WOPSLE, Mr – A friend of Mrs Joe Gargery's; at first parish clerk, afterwards an actor in London under the stage-name of Mr Waldengarver. {4–7, 10, 13, 15, 18, 31, 47}

PRINCIPAL INCIDENTS

{1} Pip, in the churchyard, is frightened by the appearance of a fearful man with a great iron on his leg, who makes him promise to bring him, the next morning, a file and some food. {2} Pip, with some difficulty, conceals the food Mrs Joe gives him for supper, and early in the morning robs the pantry, and runs for the marshes. {3} Pip meets a convict, who is not the one he seeks, and afterwards finds the right one, who eagerly devours his food. {4} Mrs Joe's preparations for Christmas; Pip's sufferings during the Christmas dinner for fear his theft should be discovered; Pip starts to run away, and runs into a party of soldiers at the door. {5} Joe mends a pair of handcuffs for the sergeant, and the party start in search of the escaped convicts on the marshes; they find the two convicts struggling together in a ditch, and Pip's convict claims to have taken and given up the other one; Pip's convict confesses to having stolen the food taken by Pip from Mrs Gargery's pantry. {6} Pip's fear of confessing to Joe. {7} Pip's education is attended to, and he indites a letter to Joe; Joe's delight at finding his name in print; Joe's account of his father's goodness of heart, and of his marriage to Pip's sister; Pip goes to play at Miss

Uncle Pumblechook – Charles Pears

Havisham's. {8} Pip breakfasts at Mr Pumblechook's, and proceeds to Miss Havisham's, where he is received by Estella: singular appearance of Miss Havisham, and of everything around her; Estella and Pip play cards for Miss Havisham's amusement; Estella sends Pip home. {9} Pip gives his sister and Pumblechook an account of Miss Havisham's and his visit there, the falsity of which he afterwards acknowledges to Joe. {10} Pip goes to The Three Jolly Bargemen to meet Joe, and see there a stranger, by a sign from whom he knows he has seen his convict; the stranger gives Pip a shilling, wrapping it in two one-pound notes. {11} Pip goes again to Miss Havisham's, and finds her friends have come to see her on her birthday; Pip meets the pale young gentleman, who challenges him to fight and, being victorious, he is rewarded by a kiss from Estella. {12} Pip having grown old enough to be apprenticed to Joe, Miss Havisham sends for Joe, to whom she gives twenty five guineas as a premium with Pip. {13} Joe gives the money to his wife, with a message from Miss Havisham, and Pip is 'bound out of hand' by Mr Pumblechook. {14} Pip desires to go and see Miss Havisham, and Joe gives him and Orlick a half-holiday. {15} Orlick calls Mrs Gargery names, and is beaten by Joe; Pip goes to Miss Havisham's in the hope of seeing Estella, but is disappointed; Mrs Gargery receives a severe injury from an unknown hand. {16} Pip forms a theory in regard to the assailant of his sister, and is surprised that she does not denounce Orlick. {17} Pip pays a visit to Miss Havisham on his birthday; Pip expresses on cases to Biddy, who has become Joe's house- keeper, his desire to be a gentleman. {18} Mr Wopsle, reading at The Three Jolly Bargemen the account of a murder, is cross-questioned by Mr Jaggers; Jaggers requests a private conference with Joe and Pip, and informs them that Pip has GREAT EXPECTATIONS, and must henceforth be brought up as a gentleman; Jaggers informs them that the conditions imposed are that Pip shall always bear that name, and that he is never to ask or seek to know the name of his benefactor; Jaggers advises Pip what to do, and offers Joe compensation for the loss of Pip's time, which he refuses; Joe tells the news at home. {19} Biddy gives Pip her idea of good manners; Pip waits upon Mr Trabb, and orders his new clothes; Mr Pumblechook entertains Pip, and congratulates him on his good fortune, of which he claims to be the instrument; Pip takes a final leave of Miss Havisham; Pip starts on his journey to London. {20} Arriving in London, Pip calls on Mr Jaggers, and witnesses that gentleman's manner of bullying his clients; Wemmick accompanies

Pip from Jaggers's office to young Mr Pocket's. {21} Pip's impressions of Barnard's Inn; Pip is welcomed by Herbert Pocket, in whom he recognises the pale young gentleman he had fought with at Miss Havisham's. {22} Herbert informs Pip of his former expectations from Miss Havisham, and their disappointment; Herbert gives Pip the name of Handel; Pip learns from Herbert the history of Miss Havisham, interspersed with some hints for the improvement of his own manners; Pip is introduced to Mr Matthew Pocket and his family. {23} Some account of Mr and Mrs Pocket, their lodgers, and their domestic mismanagement. {24} Pip begins to do business with Mr Jaggers, and is shown that gentleman's office arrangements by Mr Wemmick. {25} Pip accompanies Wemmick home to Walworth, where he is introduced to the Aged, and spends the night. {26} Pip and his friends dine with Mr Jaggers; singular appearance of that gentleman's housekeeper; quarrel between Bentley Drummle and Pip, at Mr Jaggers's table. {27} Pip receives a letter from Biddy, announcing a visit from Joe, and soon after Joe himself arrives; Miss Havisham sends word by Joe that Estella has returned, and would be glad to see Pip. {28} Pip goes down to the old town, by stage, and recognises, in a convict who is being taken to the hulks, the man from whom he bad received the two one-pound notes. {29} Pip is surprised to find Orlick occupying the place of porter at Miss Havisham's; meeting of Pip and Estella, and their walk together in the garden; Miss Havisham's passionate appeal to Pip to love Estella, and the sudden appearance of Mr Jaggers in the room. {30} How Trabb's boy met Pip in the street, and attended him from the town; Pip acknowledges to Herbert his love for Estella and his doubts of ever winning her; Herbert returns the confidence by informing Pip of his own engagement. {31} Mr Wopsle's appearance as Hamlet; Pip receives a note from Estella informing him of her approaching visit to London. {32} He accompanies Wemmick to Newgate, and witnesses the estimation in which Jaggers is held in that institution. {33} Pip receives Estella on her arrival, and escorts her to her destination at Richmond. {34} Effect produced upon Pip by his expectations, and the way in which he and Herbert 'looked into their affairs'; Pip receives notice of the death of his sister, and goes down to attend the funeral. {35} He has a conversation with Biddy, who understands him better than he understands himself. {36} Jaggers congratulates Pip on his coming of age, and presents him with five hundred pounds from his unknown benefactor, but does not disclose the name of the person. {37} Wemmick makes a distinction between his opinions in the office and at Walworth; Pip spends Sunday at Wemmick's, and witnesses his care of his aged parent, and his attentions to Miss Skiffins; Pip, with Wemmick's assistance, sets Herbert up in business. {38} Pip pays frequent visits to Estella at Mrs Brandley's, and escorts her home to Miss Havisham's; some harsh words are exchanged between Miss Havisham and Estella; Drummle offends Pip by toasting Estella; Pip remonstrates with Estella for encouraging Drummle's attentions. {39} Pip, sitting alone in his room at a late hour of the night, is interrupted by a strange visitor, in whom he recognises his convict, and from whom he learns that this man himself is the unknown patron whose money he has been spending; he also learns the risk at which the convict has returned to England. {40} Pip stumbles over a man on his staircase, and learns from the watchman that his convict was followed by another person; satisfaction of Provis in seeing 'the gentleman he has made'; Pip engages rooms for Provis, whom he represents as his uncle; Pip verifies by reference to Mr Jaggers, his knowledge that Provis is his sole benefactor. {41} Herbert returns and, taking the oath demanded by Provis, is told the whole secret of his connection with Pip; aversion of the young men for Pip's patron. {42} Provis relates the story of his life, and his connection with Compeyson, the other convict who had been retaken with him on the marshes; Herbert recognises in Compeyson the man who professed to be Miss Havisham's lover. {43} Having decided to go abroad with Provis, Pip goes down to see Miss Havisham and Estella before leaving England; he encounters Bentley Drummle at The Blue Boar. {44} Pip calls upon Miss Havisham, informs her of his discovery that she is not his patron, as he had always supposed, and begs her to continue to Herbert the assistance he had begun to render; he confesses to Estella his love for her, and learns that she is soon to be married to Drummle; returning to London, Pip is warned by Wemmick not to go home. {45} Pip goes down to Warwick to consult Wemmick, and learns from him that Provis and himself had been watched, that Compeyson is in London, and that, with Herbert's assistance, Provis had been taken to a place of greater safety. {46} Pip accompanies Herbert to Mrs Whimple's, meets Clara Barley, and becomes acquainted with the peculiarities of old Bill Barley; they arrange a plan for the escape of Magwitch by water. {47} Pip seeks to divert his mind by going to the play, and after the performance learns from Wopsle that the second of the two convicts of the marshes was in the audience. {48} Pip receives through Jaggers a message from Miss Havisham, requesting to see him; he suspects Jaggers's house-keeper to be Estella's mother, and questions Wemmick in regard to her story. {49} Pip goes down again to Miss Havisham's, and receives from her the assistance he had asked for Herbert; he confirms his belief that Molly is the mother of Estella; Pip walks round the place before leaving, and returning to Miss Havisham's room, sees her clothes in flames, and rescues her. {50} Pip learns from Herbert that portion of Provis's history relating to some trouble he had with a woman, and knows from the facts that the convict is Estella's father. {51} Pip informs Jaggers of his discovery of Estella's parentage; Jaggers and Wemmick discover something unprofessional in each other's character. {52} Pip receives notice from Wemmick that the attempt to get Provis off may safely be made, and arranges accordingly; he also receives a singular letter, requesting his presence by night at the lime kiln on the old marshes. {53} Obeying this call, he goes to the place designated, where he is set upon and bound by old Orlick, who is about to kill him, when he is rescued by Herbert and Startop; how Herbert came to rescue Pip. {54} Pip, Herbert, and Startop take Provis down the river in order to get him aboard a foreign steamer; as they are about to accomplish this purpose, another boat joins them, and they are summoned to give up Magwitch; as the two boats lie side by side, Magwitch grasps Compeyson, who is in the officer's boat; they are run down by the approaching steamer, Compeyson drowned, and Magwitch severely injured. {55} Herbert leaves London to take charge of a branch house of his business in Cairo; Wemmick's regret at the sacrifice of Magwitch's 'portable property'; marriage of Wemmick and Miss Skiffins. {56} Trial and conviction of Magwitch; he gradually sinks under the injuries he had received, and is tenderly nursed by Pip until his death. {57} Delirious illness of Pip, from which he recovers to find Joe at his bedside; Joe informs him of Miss Havisham's death and the conditions of her will; Pip recovers his strength, and Joe leaves him. {58} Pip resolves to return to the forge and to offer himself to Biddy; Pumblechook puts in his claim to be the founder of Pip's fortune, for the last time; Pip goes to the forge in search of Biddy and Joe, and finds them celebrating their wedding day; Pip joins Herbert, and remains abroad eleven years, at the end of which time he revisits Satis House, where he meets Estella, who is now a widow, and sees 'no shadow of another parting from her'.

27

Somebody's Luggage

Published in All the Year Round, in December 1862

This Christmas tale contains an amusing description, given by a head waiter named Christopher, of the struggles, trials, and experiences of the class to which he belongs, and also an account of his purchasing a quantity of luggage left more than six years previously in Room 24B by a strange gentleman who had suddenly departed without settling his bill, which amounted to £2 16s 6d. Christopher pays Somebody's bill, and takes possession of Somebody's luggage, consisting of a black portmanteau, a black bag, a desk, a dressing-case, a brown-paper parcel, a hat-box, and an umbrella strapped to a walking-stick. These articles are in great part filled with manuscripts. 'There was writing in his dressing-case, writing in his boots, writing among his shaving tackle, writing in his hat-box, writing folded away down among the very whalebones of his umbrella'. The writing found in the boots proves to be a very pretty story; and it is disposed of, together with the other documents, to the conductor of *All the Year Round* (Mr Dickens) on the most satisfactory terms. The story is put in type; and a young man is sent with 'The Proofs' to Christopher, who does not understand that they are intended to receive any corrections he may wish to make, but supposes that they are the proofs of his having illegally sold the writings. In a few days, the strange gentleman suddenly reappears at the hotel; and Christopher, overcome with terror and remorse, makes a full confession of what he has done, lays 'The Proofs' before him, and offers any gradual settlement that may be possible. To his amazement, the unknown grasps his hand, presses him to his breastbone, calls him 'benefactor' and 'philanthropist', forces two ten pound notes upon him, and explains, that, 'from boyhood's hour', he has 'unremittingly and unavailingly endeavoured to get into print'. Sitting down with several new pens, and all the inkstands well filled, he devotes himself, the night through, to the task of correcting the proofs, and is found the next morning to have smeared himself and the proofs to that degree, that 'few could have said which was them, and which was him, and which was blots'.

CHARACTERS

BEBELLE – (*a playful name for* **Gabrielle**). A little orphan girl, very pretty and very good; the protégée of Corporal Théophile, and afterwards adopted by Mr Langley.

BOUCLET, Madame – Mr Langley's landlady; a compact little woman of thirty-five or so, who lets all her house overlooking the place in furnished flats, and lives up the yard behind.

CHRISTOPHER – Head waiter at a London coffee-house; born as well as bred to the business. He dedicates his introductory essay on 'waitering' to Joseph, 'much respected head-waiter at the Slamjam Coffee House, London, EC, than which, an individual more eminently deserving of the name of man, or a more amenable honour to his own head and heart, whether considered in the light of a waiter, or regarded as human being, do not exist'.

GABRIELLE – *See* **Bebelle**.

LANGLEY, Mr – *called* '**Mr The Englishman**'. A lodger at Madame Bouclet's, in the Grande Place of a dull old fortified French town. He is a very unreasonable man, given to grumbling, moody, and somewhat vindictive. Having had a quarrel with his erring and disobedient daughter, he has disowned her and gone abroad to be rid of her for the rest of his life. But becoming acquainted with Corporal Théophile and his orphan charge Bebelle, and witnessing their strong affection for each other, and the deep grief of the child at the death of her friend, his heart is penetrated and softened. He adopts the forlorn little one as a trust providentially committed to him, and goes back with her to England, determined on a reconciliation with his daughter.

MARTIN, Miss – A young lady at the bar of the hotel where Christopher is head-waiter, who makes out the bills.

MUTUEL, Monsieur – A friend of Madame Bouclet's; a Frenchman with an amiable old walnut-shell countenance.

PRATCHETT, Mrs – Head-chambermaid at the hotel where Christopher is head-waiter; 'a female of some pertness, though acquainted with her business'. Her husband is in Australia, and his address there is 'The Bush'.

THÉOPHILE, Corporal – A brave French soldier, beloved by all his comrades; friend and protector of little Bebelle.

28

Mrs Lirriper's Lodgings

Published in All The Year Round *in December 1863*

This Christmas tale purports to be the reminiscences of a Mrs Lirriper, a lodging-house keeper of No 81 Norfolk Street, Strand. It sets forth the circumstances in which she has carried it on for eight-and-thirty years, including her trials with servant-girls, and her troubles with an opposition establishment. The chief interest of the story, however, centres around the child of Mrs Edson, a delicate young woman, who is cruelly deserted by her husband within a few months of their marriage. She dies, heart-broken, in giving birth to a little boy, who is adopted by Mrs Lirriper, and who is brought up under the joint guardianship of herself, and her friend and lodger Major Jemmy Jackman.

CHARACTERS

BOBBO – Friend and schoolfellow of the hero of an extravagant story that Jemmy Lirriper tells his grandmother and godfather.

EDSON, Mr – A gentleman from the country who takes lodgings for himself and wife at Mrs Lirriper's and, after staying there for three months, cruelly deserts her under pretence of being suddenly called by business to the Isle of Man. *See further in 'Mrs Lirriper's Legacy'.*

EDSON, Mrs Peggy – His wife; a very pretty and delicate young lady. When she discovers that her husband has abandoned her, she attempts to end her own life, and that of her unborn infant, by throwing herself into the Thames; but she is prevented by Mrs Lirriper and Major Jackman, who watch and follow her, but conceal their knowledge of her intention. Desolate and heart-broken, however, she dies not long afterwards in giving birth to a little boy, who is adopted and brought up by Mrs Lirriper.

JACKMAN, Major Jemmy – A gentleman who leaves Miss Wozenham's lodging-house in a rage, because 'she has no appreciation of a gentleman', and takes the parlours at Mrs Lirriper's. He becomes a warm friend of his new landlady, who reciprocates his regard. The Major becomes the godfather of Mrs Edson's little boy, who is named for him; and he takes it upon himself to cultivate his mind on a system of his own, which Mrs Lirriper thinks 'ought to be known to the throne and lords and commons'.

JANE – A housemaid in Miss Wozenham's service.

LIRRIPER, Jemmy Jackman – The son of Mrs Edson, who dies in giving birth to him. He is named after Mrs Lirriper, who adopts him, and after Major Jackman, who becomes his godfather. He grows up to be a bright, blithe, and good boy, delighting the hearts of both his guardians, who agree that he 'has not his like on the face of the earth'. **LIRRIPER, Mrs Emma** – The narrator of the story; a lodging-house keeper at No 81 Norfolk Street, Strand, 'situated midway between the City and St James's, and within five minutes' walk of the principal places of public amusement'.

MAXEY, Caroline – One of Mrs Lirriper's servant-girls; a good-looking, black-eyed girl, with a high temper, but a kind and grateful heart.

PERKINSOP, Mary Anne – A girl in Mrs Lirriper's service, who is enticed away by an offer from Miss Wozenham of one pound per quarter more in the way of wages. Mrs Lirrpier regards her as 'worth her weight in gold' for overawing her lodgers, without driving them away.

SERAPHINA – The heroine of an extravagantly fanciful story related by Master Jemmy Jackman Lirriper to his 'grand-mother' and his godfather. She was a schoolmaster's daughter, and the most beautiful creature that ever was seen.

SOPHY – *called* '**WILLING SOPHY**'. A poor, half-starved creature, whom Mrs Lirriper takes her into her house as a servant, and who is 'down upon her knees, scrubbing, early and late, and ever cheerful, but always smiling with a black face'.

WOZENHAM, Miss – A lodging-house keeper in Norfolk Street, not far from Mrs Lirriper's, but on the other side of the way. There is a considerable rivalry between the two establishments, and Mrs Lirriper conceives a strong dislike to Miss Wozenham, on account of her advertising in Bradshaw's 'Railway Guide', her systematic underbidding for lodgers, her enticing servant-girls away by the offer of higher wages, and her doing various other ill-natured and unfriendly acts. *See 'Mrs Lirriper's Legacy'.*

Mrs Lirriper's Legacy

Published in All The Year Round *in December 1864*

This is a sequel to 'Mrs Lirriper's Lodgings' (1863), which met with a very warm reception from the public, and excited a general desire to know more of the old lady's experiences. The legacy is left to Mrs Lirriper by the Mr Edson who is introduced in the former part of the story as deserting his young wife shortly after marrying her, and who dies repentant, many years after, in France, whither she goes to take care of him in his last moments, accompanied by his son Jemmy (whom he has never seen), and by her friend and adviser, Major Jackman. The benevolent conduct of this good soul to her good-for-nothing brother-in-law, Doctor Joshua Lirriper; to the obnoxious collector of assessed taxes, Mr Buffle, on the night when his house is burnt down; and to Miss Wozenham, when that lady was in danger of having her chattels taken from her on execution – forms the subject of the remainder of the story.

CHARACTERS

BUFFLE, Mr – Collector of the assessed taxes. His manners when engaged in his business are not agreeable; and he has a habit of looking about, as if suspicious that goods are being removed in the dead of night by a back door. Major Jackman knocks his hat off his head twice for keeping it on in Mrs Lirriper's presence, when he calls at her house in the discharge of his regular duties. But when his house catches fire and burns to the ground, he and his family are taken by the Major to Mrs Lirriper's for shelter; and from this kindness an intimacy springs up between the two households, which is very agreeable to all parties, Mr Buffle even going so far as to call the Major his 'preserver' and 'best friend'.

BUFFLE, Mrs – His wife; a woman who gives herself airs because her husband keeps 'a one-horse pheayton'.

BUFFLE, Miss Robina – Their daughter; a thin young lady with a very small appetite. She looks favourably on her father's articled young man, George, in opposition to the wishes of her parents, though they finally give their consent to the match.

EDSON, Mr – A former lodger of Mrs Lirriper's, and the husband of a young woman whom he cruelly deserted after living with her for a few months. Years pass by; and he is taken dangerously ill at a town in France. Finding that his recovery is impossible, he leaves all that he has to Mrs Lirriper, who had been very kind to his poor wife, and who has brought up their child as if it were her own. On learning from the French consul in London that an unknown Englishman is lying at the point of death in Sens, and that her name is mentioned in a communication to the authorities, which is found among his papers, she sets out at once for that place with her adopted child and her friend Major Jackman. Recognising Mr Edson in the sick stranger, and finding him truly penitent for the grievous wrong he had done, she forgives him, and causes the boy – who does not know who the dying man is – also to say; 'May God forgive you!'

GEORGE – A rather weak-headed young man, articled to Mr Buffle, and enamoured of his daughter.

GRAN, Mrs – (*ie*, **Mrs Lirriper**). A highly respected and beloved lady who resides within a hundred miles of Norfolk Street, and who figures in Jemmy Lirriper's imaginary version of the story of Mr Edson's life.

JACKMAN, Major Jemmy – A lodger at Mrs Lirriper's; her warm personal friend, and the godfather of her adopted child Jemmy.

LIRRIPER, Doctor Joshua – Youngest brother of Mrs Lirriper's deceased husband. He is a dissipated scapegrace, and a systematic sponger upon his benevolent and unsuspecting sister-in-law.

LIRRIPER, Mrs – *See i*ntroductory remarks, **Edson (Mr), Wozenham (Miss)**, and **'Mrs Lirriper's Lodgings'**.

LIRRIPER, Jemmy Jackman – Son of Mr Edson, adopted by Mrs Lirriper, and brought up under the joint guardianship of herself and Major Jackman, who is at once his godfather and his 'companion, guide, philosopher, and friend'. As he develops a taste for engineering, the Major assists him in the construction and management of a railway, which they name 'The United Grand Junction Lirriper and Jackman Great Norfolk Parlour Line', which is kept on the Major's sideboard, and dusted with his own hands every morning. The young gentleman accompanies Mrs Lirriper to Sens, and is present at the death of Mr Edson; though he does not know him to be his father, and is ignorant of the facts in regard to his cruel desertion of his wife soon after marriage. Being in the habit of composing and relating stories for the amusement of his 'grandmother' and godfather, and his mind dwelling on the death-bed scene he has witnessed, he frames an imaginary version of his father's history, which is woefully unlike the fact.

MADGERS, Winifred – A servant-girl at Mrs Lirriper's; a 'Plymouth sister', and a remarkably tidy young woman.

RAIRYGANOO, Sally – One of Mrs Lirriper's domestics, suspected to be of Irish extraction, though professing to come of a Cambridge family. She absconds, however, with a bricklayer of the Limerick persuasion, and is married to him in pattens, being too impatient to wait till his black eye gets well.

WOZENHAM, Miss – A neighbour of Mrs Lirriper's in Norfolk Street, and the keeper of a rival lodging-house. For many years, Mrs Lirriper has been strongly prejudiced against Miss Wozenham; but on hearing that she has been 'sold up', she feels so much sympathy for her, that she goes to her without delay or ceremony, expresses her regret for the unpleasantness there has been between them in the past, and cheers her up with true womanly tact and kindliness.

Our Mutual Friend

Like most of its predecessors, this novel made its first appearance in twenty monthly parts. The first part was issued 1 May 1864, and the last in November 1865. The illustrations were on wood from drawings by Marcus Stone. On its completion, the work was published in two octavo volumes by Chapman and Hall, with a dedication to the late Sir James Emerson Tennent.

CHARACTERS

AKERSHEM, Miss Sophronia – An acquaintance of the Veneerings; a fast young lady of society, with raven locks, and a complexion that lights up well when well powdered. She marries Mr Alfred Lammle. {Book 1: ch 2, 10, 11; Book 2: ch 4, 5, 16; Book 3: ch 5, 12, 14, 17; Book 4: ch 2, 8}

BLIGHT, Young – A dismal boy, who is Mr Mortimer Lightwood's clerk and office boy. {Book 1: ch 8; Book 3: ch 17; Book 4: ch 9, 16}

BOFFIN, Mrs Henrietta – Wife of Mr Boffin, a stout lady, of a rubicund and cheerful aspect, described by her husband as 'a high-flyer at fashion'. {Book 1: ch 5, 9, 15–17; Book 2: ch 8–10, 14; Book 3: ch 4, 5, 15; Book 4: ch 2, 12–14, 16}

BOFFIN, Nicodemus – *called* 'Noddy', *also* '**The Golden Dustman**'. A confidential servant of the elder Mr Harmon, who at death leaves him all his property, in case his son refuses to marry a certain young lady named in his will. This son has quarrelled with his father, and parted from him and, at the time of Mr Harmon's death, is a resident of Cape Colony. He returns to England on hearing of that event but disappears immediately on his arrival, and a body, supposed to be his, is subsequently found floating in the Thames, in an advanced state of decomposition, and much injured. Mr Boffin, therefore, as residuary legatee, comes into possession of the whole property, amounting to upwards of one hundred thousand pounds, standing in the books of the Bank of England.

Mr Boffin closes his interview with Mr Lightwood by authorising him to offer a reward of ten thousand pounds for the arrest of the murderer of John Harmon the younger. John Harmon, however, is not dead, though he has but barely escaped being murdered. Learning of the condition in his father's will, under which he is to inherit, it occurs to him to take advantage of the false report of his death to make the acquaintance of the young lady (Miss Bella Wilfer) and, if he likes her, to try to win her without disclosing. himself. He accordingly assumes the name of John Rokesmith, and hires a room at her father's house, which gives him an opportunity of thus seeing and speaking to her. He also succeeds in making an engagement to act as secretary and man of business to Mr Boffin, who shortly afterwards adopts Miss Wilfer, who is thus brought daily into contact with Mr Rokesmith. She treats him with great disdain; but he comes, in time, to love her devotedly. At last his features, which have long attracted and puzzled Mrs Boffin, betray him; and he is forced to acknowledge the truth about himself. The discovery is kept a profound secret from Miss Wilfer, however, and Mr Boffin comes to Harmon's assistance, and endeavours to win her love for him by first exciting her sympathy. He therefore pretends to become very miserly, and grows so anxious about the management of his estate that he shamefully abuses his factotum for not taking better care of it. In the end this strategy proves successful, and Bella marries the poor secretary, who still retains the name of Rokesmith. Meanwhile Mr Boffin has discovered, secreted in an old Dutch bottle, a later will than the one he has proved, and under which he has entered upon possession of the estate. By this document, everything is given to him absolutely, excluding and reviling the son by name. But, with rare disinterestedness and munificence, Mr Boffin transfers the entire property to the rightful heir, reserving for himself only the house occupied by his late master, which is popularly called 'Harmon's Jail', on account of his solitary manner of life, or 'Harmony Jail', on account of his never agreeing with anybody; but which Mrs Boffin renames Boffin's Bower'. {Book 1: ch 5, 8, 9, 15–17; Book 2: ch 7, 8, 10, 14; Book 3: ch 4–7, 14, 15; Book 4: ch 2, 3, 12–14, 16} *See* **Harmon (John), Wegg (Silas).**

BOOTS, Mr and Brewer, Mr – Fashionable toadies; friends of the Veneerings. {Book 1: ch 2, 10; Book 2: ch 3, 16; Book 3: ch 17; Book 4: ch 16}

Bibliomania of the Golden Dustman – Marcus Stone

CHERUB, The – *See* **Wilfer**, *Reginald*.

CLEAVER, Fanny – *called* '**Jenny Wren**'. A doll's dressmaker. Lizzie Hexam, after her father's death, has temporary lodgings with her; and one day Charley Hexham, Lizzie's brother, calls to see her. {Book 2: ch 1, 2, 5, 11, 15; Book 3: ch 2, 3, 10, 13; Book 4: ch 8–11, 15}

CLEAVER, Mr – *called* '**Mr Dolls**'. Her father; a good workman at his trade, but a weak, wretched trembling creature, falling to pieces, and never sober. {Book 2: ch 2; Book 3: ch 10, 17; Book 4: ch 8, 9}

DOLLS, Mr – *See* **Cleaver**, **Mr**.

FLEDGEBY, Mr – *called* '**Fascination Fledgeby**'. A dandified young man, who is a dolt in most matters, but sharp and tight enough where money is concerned. He is an acquaintance of Mr Lammle, who unsuccessfully endeavours to marry him to Miss Georgiana Podsnap, Fledgeby having given him his note for one thousand pounds in case he effects the arrangement. Fledgeby is a money broker, and has an office kept by an aged Jew in his service, known under the name of Pubsey & Co. Under the pretence of using his influence with Pubsey & Co, he pretends to plead with the Jew for an extension on the overdue bills of some of his acquaintances. The old man watches his face for some sign of permission to do so, which is never given; yet Fledgeby habitually reviles him and his race for not granting the accommodation that he has himself forced him to deny. {Book 2: ch 4, 5, 16; Book 3: ch 1, 7, 8, 17; Book 4: ch 8, 9, 16} *See* **Riah**, **Mr**.

GLAMOUR, Bob – A customer at The Six Jolly Fellowship Porters. {Book 1: ch 6; Book 3: ch 3}

GLIDDERY, Rob – Potboy at The Six Jolly Fellowship Porters. {Book 1: ch 6, 13; Book 3: ch 3}

GOLDEN DUSTMAN, The – *See* **Boffin**, **Nicodemus**.

HANDFORD, Julius – *See* **Harmon**, **John**.

HARMON, John – *alias* **Julius Handford**, *alias* **John Rokesmith**. Heir to the Harmon estate. On the death of his father, he returns to England from South Africa, where he has been living for a good many years. On his arrival, he is invited into a waterside inn by a pretended friend named George Radfoot, with whom he has made the passage, and is drugged, robbed, and thrown into the Thames. This pretended friend had previously changed clothes with

Harmon, at the request of the latter, who desired to avoid recognition until he had seen a certain young lady whom he is required by his father's will to marry. The would-be assassin falls into a quarrel with a confederate over the money obtained by the robbery, and is himself murdered and thrown into the river. The cold water into which Harmon is plunged restores him to consciousness and, swimming to the shore, he escapes. The body of his assailant is found by a boatman named Hexam, and is taken in charge by the authorities. The clothes and the papers on the body having been identified, it is supposed that the body itself is that of young Harmon who, finding himself reported dead, resolves to take advantage of the circumstance to further his own plans, and assumes the name of **Julius Handford**, which he afterwards changes to **John Rokesmith**. {Book 1: ch 2–4, 8, 9, 15–17; Book 2: ch 7–10, 12–14; Book 3: ch 4, 5, 9, 15, 16; Book 4: ch 4, 5, 11–14, 16} *See* **Boffin, Nicodemus**.

HARMON, Mrs John – *See* **Wilfer, Miss Bella**.

HEADSTONE, Bradley – A master in a school in that district of the flat country tending to the Thames, where Kent and Surrey meet. He falls passionately in love with Lizzie Hexam and, finding that she loves Mr Eugene Wrayburn, dogs his footsteps, and attempts to kill him. Believing that he has done so, he flies, but is followed by one Riderhood, a desperate character, who has discovered his plans, and who compels him to pay liberally for keeping the secret. At last, Riderhood's demands and persecution become so unendurable, that Headstone determines to get rid of him once and for all. {Book 2: ch 1, 6, 11, 14, 15; Book 3: ch 10, 11; Book 4: ch 1, 6, 7, 11, 15}

HEXAM, Jesse – *called* 'Gaffer'. A Thames 'waterside character'; a strong man with ragged, grizzled hair and a sun-browned face, whose principal occupation is recovering dead bodies from the Thames. He is falsely accused of the murder of John Harmon. {Book 1: ch 1, 3, 6, 12–14, 16} *See* **Hexam, Lizzie**.

HEXAM, Charley – His son; a pupil of Bradley Headstone's, and a curious mixture of uncompleted savagery and completed civilisation. He is tenderly loved and cared for by his sister, but renounces her because she refuses his friend Headstone. Always utterly selfish and empty-hearted, and always bent on rising in the social scale, and increasing his 'respectability', he renounces Headstone with equal readiness when he finds good reason to think him guilty of the murder of his sister's favoured lover, Eugene Wrayburn, and that his own name is therefore likely to be dragged into injurious notoriety. {Book 1: ch 3, 6; Book 2: ch 1, 6, 15; Book 4: ch 7}

HEXAM, Lizzie – Daughter of Jesse or 'Gaffer' Hexam. She is in the habit of rowing with her father on the Thames, and on one occasion, while thus engaged, they find the body of a man, afterwards identified as John Harmon. Through the jealousy of Rogue Riderhood, suspicion is cast upon her father; and the officers undertake to arrest him as being concerned in the murder, but they find him in the river, drowned, and attached to his own boat by a cord, in which he had apparently become entangled when he fell overboard. A young barrister, Eugene Wrayburn, who accompanies the officers, becomes interested in the daughter, manifests much sympathy with her in her affliction, and aids her in obtaining an education. Her brother's teacher, Bradley Headstone, falls deeply in love with her, and makes an offer of marriage. This she refuses, and to escape his importunities, and also to save Wrayburn from his vengeance (for Headstone believes him to be the cause of his rejection), she leaves London, and obtains employment in a paper-mill in the country. After much fruitless search, Wrayburn ascertains where she is, and follows, bent on having an interview with her. He is, in turn, followed by Headstone, who comes upon them while they are engaged in conversation. Waiting until they part, the schoolmaster stealthily follows his rival, and deals him a murderous blow as he stands for a moment looking into the river. Lizzie hears the blows, a faint groan, and a fall into the water. Brave by nature and by habit, she runs towards the spot from which the sound had come. Seeing a bloody face turned up to the moon, and drifting away with the current, she jumps into a boat near by, puts out into the stream and, when she has rescued the sufferer, finds that it is her lover. She tenderly nurses him through the dangerous illness that follows. When consciousness returns, he asks to be married to his preserver without delay, though no hope of his recovery is entertained by anyone. Lizzie becomes his wife, and he grows stronger and better by slow degrees, and is at last restored to perfect health. {Book 1: ch 1, 3, 6, 13, 14; Book 2: ch 1, 2, 5, 11, 14–16; Book 3: ch 1, 2, 8, 9; Book 4: ch 5, 10, 11, 16, 17}

HIGDEN, Mrs Betty – A poor woman who keeps a 'minding-school', and also a mangle, in one of the complicated back settlements of Brentford. {Book 1: ch 16; Book 2: ch 9, 10, 14; Book 3: ch 8}

INSPECTOR, Mr – A police officer who investigates the Harmon murder. {Book 1: ch 3; Book 4: ch 7}

JOEY, Captain – A bottle-nosed regular customer at The Six Jolly Fellowship-Porters. {Book 1: ch 6; Book 3: ch 3}

JONATHAN – A customer at The Six Jolly Fellowship Porters. {Book 1: ch 6; Book 3: ch 3}

JOHNNY – An orphan, grandson of Betty Higden. The Boffins propose to adopt him, but he dies before the plan is carried into effect. {Book 1: ch 16; Book 2: ch 8, 9, 14; Book 3: ch 9}

JONES, George – A customer at The Six Jolly Fellowship Porters. {Book 1: ch 6}

KIBBLE, Jacob – A fellow-passenger of John Harmon's on his voyage from Cape Colony to England. {Book 2: ch 8; Book 4: ch 12}

LAMMLE, Alfred – A mature young gentleman with too much nose in his face, too much ginger in his whiskers, too much torso in his waistcoat, too much sparkle in his studs, his eyes, his buttons, his talk, and his teeth. He is an adventurer and a fortune-hunter; he marries Miss Sophronia Akershem, supposing her to be a lady of wealth, while she marries him also for money; each being deceived by Mr and Mrs Veneering, who really know next to nothing about either of them. This precious pair of entrapped impostors determine to revenge themselves on Veneering for his part in the matter, but fail in their plans, and after an attempt (which is also a failure) to supplant Rokesmith in the house of Mr Boffin, leave the country. {Book 1: ch 2, 10, 11; Book 2: ch 5, 16; Book 3: ch 1, 5, 12, 17; Book 4: ch 2, 8}

LAMMLE, Mrs Alfred – *See* **Akershem, Miss Sophronia**.

MORTIMER – A young solicitor and attorney employed by Mr Boffin. He is an intimate friend of Eugene Wrayburn. {Book 1: ch 2, 3, 8, 10, 12, 16; Book 2: ch 6, 14, 16; Book 3: ch 10, 11, 17; Book 4: ch 9–12}

MARY ANNE – Miss Peecher's assistant and favourite pupil, so imbued with the class-custom of stretching out an arm, as if to hail a cab or omnibus, whenever she finds she has an observation on hand to offer to Miss Peecher, that she often does it in their domestic relations. {Book 1: ch 1, 11; Book 4: ch 7}

MILVEY, Mrs Margaretta – Wife of the Reverend Frank; a pretty, bright little woman, something worn by anxiety, who has repressed many pretty tales and bright fancies and substituted, in their stead, schools, soup, flannel, coals, and all the weekday cares and Sunday coughs of a large population, young and old. {Book 1: ch 9, 16; Book 2: ch 10; Book 3: ch 9; Book 4: ch 11}

MILVEY, The Reverend Frank – A young curate. {Book 1: ch 9, 16; Book 2: ch 10; Book 3: ch 9; Book 4: ch 11}

MULLINS, Jack – A frequenter of The Six Jolly Fellowship Porters. {Book 1: ch 6}

PEECHER, Miss Emma – A teacher in the female department of the school in which Bradley Headstone is a master. {Book 1: ch 11, 15; Book 3: ch 11; Book 4: ch 7}

PODDLES – The pet name of a little girl in Mrs Betty Higden's 'minding-school' (Book 1: ch 16}

PODSNAP, Miss Georgiana – A shy, foolish, affectionate girl of nearly eighteen in training for 'society'. (Book 1: ch 11, 17; Book 2: ch 4, 5, 16; Book 3: ch 1, 17; Book 4: ch 2}

PODSNAP, Mr John – Her father; a member of 'society' and a pompous self-satisfied man, swelling with patronage of his friends and acquaintances. {Book 1: ch 2, 10, 11, 17; Book 2: ch 3–5, 16; Book 3: ch 1, 17; Book 4: ch 17}

PODSNAP, Mrs – His wife; a 'fine woman for Professor Owen, quantity of bone, neck and nostrils like a rocking-horse, hard features', and a majestic presence. {Book 1: ch 2, 10, 11, 17; Book 2: ch 3, 4; Book 3: ch 1, 17; Book 4: ch 17}

POTTERSON, Miss Abbey – Sole proprietor and manager of a well-kept tavern called The Six Jolly Fellowship Porters; a woman of great dignity and firmness, tall, upright, and well-favoured, though severe of countenance, and having more the air of a schoolmistress than mistress of a public house. {Book 1: ch 6, 8; Book 3: ch 2, 3; Book 4: ch 12}

POTTERSON, Job – Her brother; steward of the ship in which John Harmon is a passenger. {Book 1: ch 3; Book 2: ch 8; Book 4: ch 7}

PUBSEY AND CO – The name of a fictitious firm of money-brokers in Saint Mary Axe, used by 'Fascination' Fledgeby to conceal his sharp practices.

RIAH, Mr – An aged Jew, of venerable aspect and a generous and noble nature, who befriends Lizzie Hexam, and obtains

Eugene's bedside – Marcus Stone

employment for her. He is the agent of 'Fascination' Fledgeby, who directs all his proceedings, while keeping himself in the background. {Book 2: ch 5, 15; Book 3: ch 1, 2, 10, 12, 13; Book 4: ch 8, 9, 16}

RIDERHOOD, Pleasant – Daughter of Roger Riderhood, finally married to Mr Venus, after rejecting him more than once. {Book 2: ch 12, 13; Book 3: ch 4, 7; Book 4: ch 14}

RIDERHOOD, Roger – *called* '**Rogue**'. A desperate 'waterside character', in whose house an attempt is made on John Harmon's life. Quarrelling with Gaffer Hexam, who had been his partner, and anxious to obtain the reward offered by Mr Boffin for the arrest of the supposed murderer, he goes to Mortimer Lightwood's office, and accuses Hexam of having done the deed. Search being made for Hexam, he is discovered drowned; and the reward is consequently not paid. Riderhood finally becomes a deputy lock keeper at Plashwater Weir Mill, and is cognisant of Bradley Headstone's attack on Eugene Wrayburn. He uses his knowledge as a means of extorting money from Headstone and at last, by his continued demands, drives him to desperation. A quarrel ensues, which results in the death of both. {Book 1: ch 1, 6, 12–14; Book 2: ch 12–14, 16; Book 3: ch 2, 3, 8, 11; Book 4: ch 1, 7, 15} *See* **Headstone, Bradley**.

ROKESMITH, John – *See* **Harmon, John**.

ROKESMITH, Mrs John – *See* **Harmon, Mrs John**.

SAMPSON, George – A young man who is very intimate with the Wilfer family. At first he hovers round Miss Bella but, on her betrothal to Mr John Harmon, transfers his affections to her sister, Lavinia, who keeps him – partly in remembrance of his bad taste in having overlooked her in the first instance – under a course of stinking discipline. {Book 1: ch 4, 9; Book 2: ch 14; Book 3: ch 4, 16; Book 4: ch 5, 16}

SLOPPY – A love-child, found in the street, brought up in the poor-house, and adopted by Betty Higden, who keeps him employed in turning a mangle. He is afterwards taken into Mr Boffin's service. {Book 1: ch 16; Book 2: ch 9, 10, 14; Book 3: ch 9; Book 4: ch 3, 14, 16}

SNIGSWORTH, Lord – First cousin to Mr Twemlow; a nobleman with gout in his temper. {Book 1: ch 2, 10; Book 2: ch 3, 5, 16; Book 4: ch 16}

SPRODGKIN, Mrs – A portentous old parishioner of the Reverend Frank Milvey, and the plague of his life. She is constantly wishing to know who begat whom, or wanting some information concerning the Amorites. {Book 4: ch 11}

TAPKINS, Mrs – A fashionable woman, who calls at the door of the 'eminently aristocratic' mansion to which the Boffins remove from the 'Bower', and leaves a card for herself, Miss Tapkins, Miss Malvina Tapkins, and Miss Euphemia Tapkins; also the card of Mrs Henry George Alfred Swoshle, *née* Tapkins; also the card, 'Mrs Tapkins at home Wednesdays, Music, Portland Place'. (Book 1: ch 17}

TIPPINS, Lady – A friend of the Veneerings, and a member of 'society'; relict of the late Sir Thomas Tippins, knighted by mistake for somebody else, by his Majesty King George the Third. She is a charming old woman, with an immense, obtuse, drab, oblong face, like a face in a tablespoon, and a dyed long walk up the top of her head, as a convenient public approach to the bunch of false hair behind. She affects perennial youth in her dress and manners, and exerts herself to fascinate the male sex, especially the unmarried portion of it. {Book 1: ch 2, 10, 17; Book 2: ch 3, 16; Book 3: ch 17; Book 4: ch 17}

TODDLES – The pet name of a little boy in Mrs Betty Higden's 'minding-school'. (Book 1: ch 16}

TOOTLE, Tom – A frequenter of The Six Jolly Fellowship Porters. {Book 1: ch 6; Book 3: ch 2, 3}

TWEMLOW, Mr Melvin – A friend of the Veneerings, and a member of 'society'. He is poor, and lives over a livery-stable-yard in Duke Street, St James's; but, being first cousin to Lord Snigsworth, he is in frequent requisition at many houses. His noble relative allows him a small annuity on which he lives ; and takes it out of him, as the phrase goes, in extreme severity; putting him, when he visits at Snigsworthy Park, under a kind of martial law; ordaining that he shall hang his hat on a particular peg, sit on a particular chair, talk on particular subjects to particular people, and perform particular exercises, such as sounding the praises of the family varnish (not to say pictures), and abstaining from the choicest of the family wines, unless expressly invited to partake. {Book 1: ch 2, 10, 17; Book 2: ch 3, 16; Book 3: ch 13; Book 4: ch 16, 17}

VENEERING, Mr Hamilton – A *parvenu*, tolerated by 'society' on account of his wealth. Formerly traveller or commission-agent of Chicksey and Stobbles, druggists, but afterwards admitted into the firm, of which he becomes the supreme head, absorbing both his partners. He is a man of forty, wavy-haired, dark, tending to corpulence, sly, mysterious, filmy – a kind of sufficiently well-looking veiled prophet, not prophesying. By a liberal expenditure of money, he gets himself returned to the House of Commons from the Borough of Pocket-Breaches. {Book 1: ch 2, 10, 11, 17; Book 2: ch 3, 16; Book 3: ch 17; Book 4: ch 17}

VENEERING, Mrs Anastasia – His wife; a fair woman, aquiline-nosed and fingered, not so much light hair as she might have, gorgeous in raiment and jewels, enthusiastic, propitiatory. {Book 1: ch 2, 10, 11, 17; Book 2: ch 3, 16; Book 3: ch 17; Book 4: ch 17}

VENUS, Mr – A preserver of animals and birds, and articulator of human bones. He becomes a confederate of Mr Wegg's in his plan of blackmailing Mr Boffin; but being, on the whole, a very honest man, and repenting of what he has done, he makes amends by confidentially disclosing the whole plot. {Book 1: ch 7; Book 2: ch 7; Book 3: ch 6, 7, 14; Book 4: ch 3, 14}

WEGG, Silas – A balladmonger, who also keeps a fruit stall near Cavendish Square. Mr Boffin thinking himself too old 'to begin shovelling and sifting at alphabeds and grammar-books', and wanting to engage someone to read to him, is attracted by Mr Wegg's collection of ballads displayed on an unfolded clothes-horse. He enters into conversation with the proprietor and, when he finds that 'all print is open to him', is filled with admiration of him as being 'a literary man *with* a wooden leg'. After some further conversation, and some ciphering, Mr Boffin offers Mr Wegg half-a-crown a week to read to him two hours every evening. Mr Wegg turns out to be a rascal. Not resting satisfied with the salary which he receives from Mr Boffin, he tries to better his condition by knavery. Prying everywhere about the premises, he at last discovers a will in which the elder Mr Harmon leaves all his property to the Crown. Ascertaining that this will is of later date than the one in Mr Boffin's favour, which has been admitted to probate, he conspires with an acquaintance (Mr Venus), either to oust Mr Boffin, or to compel him to buy them off. He finds, to his astonishment, however, that there is a still later will in the possession of Mr Boffin, who has suppressed it because it leaves him all the property; while the one which has been proved leaves it to the testator's son on the condition of his marrying Miss Bella Wilfer. Discomfited and crestfallen, the avaricious Wegg returns, perforce, to his old trade of selling ballads, gingerbread, and the like. {Book 1: ch 5, 7, 15, 17; Book 2: ch 7, 10; Book 3: ch 6, 7, 14; Book 4: ch 3, 14}

WILFER, Miss Bella – Daughter of Reginald Wilfer, and *protégée* of the Boffins; afterwards the wife of John Harmon. {Book 1: ch 4, 9, 16, 17; Book 2: ch 8–10, 13; Book 3: ch 4, 5, 7, 9, 15, 16; Book 4: ch 4, 5, 11–13, 16} *See* **Boffin, Mr Nicodemus**.

WILFER, Miss Lavinia – Youngest of Mr Wilfer's children; a sharp, saucy, and irrepressible girl. {Book 1: ch 4, 9; Book 2: ch 1, 9, 8; Book 3: ch 4, 16; Book 4: ch 5, 16}

WILFER, Reginald – *called* '**The Cherub**'. A poor hen-pecked clerk in the house of Chicksey, Veneering, and Stobbles. {Book 1: ch 4; Book 2: ch 8, 13; Book 3: ch 4, 16; Book 4: ch 4, 5, 16}

WILFER, Mrs Reginald – His wife; a tall, angular woman, very stately and impressive. {Book 1: ch 4, 9, 16; Book 2: ch 1, 9, 13; Book 3: ch 4, 16; Book 4: ch 5, 16}

WILLIAMS, William – A frequenter of The Six Jolly Fellowship Porters. {Book 1: ch 6; Book 3: ch 3}

WRAYBURN, Eugene – A briefless barrister, who hates his profession. He is a gloomy, indolent, unambitious, and reckless young man. Becoming interested in Lizzie Hexam, he assists her to obtain education; and, though he seeks her society, he does so with no definite aim in view. Lizzie saves Wrayburn's life, nurses him tenderly through a long and dangerous sickness, is married to him, and finds that, transformed by the power of love, he has a mine of purpose and energy which he turns to the best account. {Book 1: ch 2, 3, 8, 10, 12–14; Book 2: ch 1, 3, 6, 11, 14–16; Book 3: ch 10, 11, 17; Book 4: ch 1, 6, 9–11, 16, 17}

WRAYBURN, Mrs Eugene – See **Hexam, Lizzie**.

WREN, Jenny – See **Cleaver, Fanny**.

PRINCIPAL INCIDENTS

Book 1 – {1} Jesse Hexam and his daughter finds a body in the Thames; he rejects Riderhood's offer to share his luck. {2} Description of the Veneering dinner, where Mortimer Lightwood relates the story of John Harmon and his will, and receives the news of the death of the heir by drowning. {3} Mortimer and Eugene go to

Hexam's house to make inquiries about the body, and encounter Mr Julius Handford; they all go to the police station to view the body, and Mr Handford lays himself open to suspicion; Lizzie Hexam shows Charley the pictures in the fire; verdict of the coroner's jury. {4} John Rokesmith engages lodgings at the house of Mr Wilfer. {5} Silas Wegg, tending his stall at the street corner, is accosted by Mr Boffin, and Mr Boffin engages him to read *The Decline and Fall*; Mr Wegg visits Boffin's Bower, and commences his readings. {6} Mr Abbey Potterson forbids Rogue Riderhood to visit The Six Jolly Fellowship Porters; Miss Abbey informs Lizzie Hexam of the suspicions against her father, and counsels her to leave him; Lizzie refuses to do this, and Miss Abbey forbids him also the house; Charley Hexam leaves home for school without his father's knowledge. {7} Mr Wegg calls upon Mr Venus to 'look after himself'; Mr Venus puts a low value on the amputated leg of Wegg, and also explains to that gentleman the reason of his low spirits. {8} Mr Boffin visits Lightwood at his office in the Temple, and instructs him to offer a reward of £10,000 for the discovery of the murderer of Harmon; he is introduced to Eugene Wrayburn; John Rokesmith applies to Mr Boffin for the situation of secretary. {9} Mr and Mrs Boffin in consultation decide to 'go in strong' for fashion, to invite Miss Bella Wilfer to live with them, and to adopt an orphan-child and give him John Harmon's name; Mr and Mrs Boffin visit the Revd Frank Milvey in search of an orphan, and also the Wilfers to tender their invitation to Miss Bella; Mr Rokesmith's agitation at unexpectedly bearing John Harmon's name. {10} The Veneerings plan the marriage of Mr Alfred Lammle and Miss Sophronia Akershem, and Twemlow gives away the bride; finding they have been mutually imposed upon, they enter into a new 'marriage contract' to deceive the world. {11} What constitutes 'Podsnappery'; Mr and Mrs Podsnap give a party on Miss Georgiana's birthday; Mrs Lammle begins her friendship with Georgiana. {12} Riderhood goes to Lightwood's office, and accuses Hexam of the Harmon murder; Lightwood, Wrayburn, and the inspector go to The Fellowship Porters, while Riderhood tracks Hexam. {13} Eugene discovers Lizzie Hexam through the window, watching by the fire. {14} They find Hexam's boat and his drowned body. {15} John Rokesmith enters upon his duties as Mr Boffin's secretary; Mr Boffin places

Wegg in charge of the Bower; Mrs Boffin sees the faces of old Harmon and the children; Rokesmith objects to meeting Mr Lightwood. {16} Mrs Boffin and the secretary go to see the orphan at Betty Higden's. {17} Charley Hexam asking permission to go and see his sister, his schoolmaster decides to go with him.

Book 2 – {1} Miss Peecher catechises Mary Anne on the parts of speech; Charley Hexam and Bradley Headstone make the acquaintance of Miss Jenny Wren, who gives them an account of her occupation; first meeting of Bradley Headstone and Lizzie Hexam; leaving Lizzie, they encounter Wrayburn. {2} Eugene calls upon Lizzie, and persuades her to receive instruction at his expense; Jenny's fancies; Jenny's father comes home intoxicated, and she reprimands him. {3} Veneering's friends 'rally round him', and he is elected to Parliament. {4} The Lammles improve the acquaintance of Miss Georgiana Podsnap, and introduce her to Fascination Fledgeby. {5} Mr Lammle breakfasts with Fledgeby at his rooms and, not liking that gentleman's manner, threatens to pull his nose; Fledgeby apologises, and reconciliation follows; Fledgeby goes to the house at St Mary Axe, where he does business under the name of Pubsey and Co, and meets Riah, his Jewish agent; Riah shows him Lizzie Hexam and Jenny Wren on the housetop. {6} Eugene and Mortimer, in their private chambers, are visited by the schoolmaster and Charley Hexam; Hexam reproaches Eugene for his attentions to Lizzie; Eugene exasperates them by his coolness, and gives up Mortimer's riddle, 'What is to come of it?' {7} Mr Wegg and Mr Venus enter into a 'friendly move' in regard to the dust-mounds. {8} Miss Bella Wilfer visits her father's house; Mr Boffin sends her a purse containing £50, and she spends it for the benefit of her father. {9} Sickness of Johnny, the adopted orphan; his removal to the Children's Hospital, where he 'makes his will', and dies. {10} Mr and Mrs Boffin decide to provide for Sloppy. {11} Bradley Headstone appeals to Lizzie Hexam to renounce Wrayburn's attentions; Lizzie tells Jenny what the lady 'in the hollow down by the flare' says of Eugene. {12} Rokesmith, in disguise, goes to Rogue Riderhood's house; his interviews, first with Miss Pleasant and then with her father. {13} Rokesmith removes his disguise, and repeats to himself the circumstances attending the supposed death of John Harmon, and decides still to retain his assumed character; as the secretary, he offers himself to Bella, and is rejected. {14} Betty Higden develops to the secretary her plan for running away; Rokesmith completes his plan of forcing from Riderhood a recantation of his testimony against Hexam, and sends the same to Lizzie; and Betty Higden completes her arrangements for running away. {15} Bradley Headstone, seconded by Charley Hexam, seeks Lizzie again, offers himself, and is rejected; Charley's indignation, and renunciation of his sister; Lizzie is met by Riah, and afterwards by Eugene, who take her home. {16} The Lammles celebrate the anniversary of their wedding by a breakfast; Lightwood continues his story by relating the disappearance of Lizzie Hexam; Mrs Lammle begs Twemlow to warn Podsnap against Fledgeby.

Book 3 – {1} Riah goes to Fledgeby's chambers; Lammle also calls there, and informs Fledgeby that their game is up; Fledgeby cautions Lammle against Riah, and tries to draw from Riah the secret of Lizzie Hexam's retreat. {2} Riah and Jenny Wren go to The Six Jolly Fellowship Porters to show Miss Abbey Potterson Riderhood's declaration of Hexam's innocence of the Harmon murder; Riderhood is run down by a steamer, and – {3} – is barely saved from drowning. {4} Mr and Mrs Wilfer celebrate their wedding anniversary; Bella tells her father four secrets. {5} Mr Boffin defines Rokesmith's position; he begins to collect 'The Lives of Misers'; Mrs Lammle improves Bella's acquaintance, and Bella confides to her secret of the secretary's proposal. {6} Wegg and Venus, discussing their friendly move at the Bower, are visited by Boffin with a load of books on misers; Mr Boffin, with a dark lantern, makes the tour of the mounds, the friends watching him; he digs up and carries away a glass bottle. {7} Wegg imparts to Venus the secret of his having found a will of the late John Harmon in the pump; they carry this will to Mr Venus's place to examine it, and Venus insists upon keeping it; they discuss the course to be pursued. {8} Betty Higden on her travels; her fainting-fit in the market-place; and the second one, in which she is relieved by Riderhood, serving as deputy lock-keeper; her discovery by Lizzie Hexam, and her death. {9} Lizzie tells Bella her story, and the reason of her concealment; Bella and the secretary on better terms; Eugene Wrayburn tries unsuccessfully to obtain Lizzie's address from Jenny Wren. {10} Mr Dolls promises to obtain the direction for him; Eugene informs Lightwood of his being watched by the schoolmaster, and they indulge in the pleasures of the chase. {11} Headstone and Riderhood meet at the Temple gate. {12} Mr and

Mrs Lammle, having broken down in their scheme against the Podsnaps, turn their attention to the Boffins; Mrs Lammle begs Fledgeby to use his influence with Riah. {13} He acts accordingly; Fledgeby also intercedes for Twemlow, and opens the eyes of Jenny Wren. {14} Venus makes known to Mr Boffin the friendly move of Silas Wegg; Mr Boffin, concealed by Venus, hears Wegg's plan for bringing his nose to the grindstone; interview between Mrs Lammle and Mr Boffin. {15} Mr Boffin denounces Rokesmith, and sees Bella righted; Bella's indignation at Mr Boffin, and her apology to the secretary; Bella relinquishes all she has received from the Boffins, and secretly leaves the house. {16} She goes to her father's office, where Rokesmith follows her, whose love she now accepts. {17} Mrs Lammle reminds Twemlow of their confidence; Mr Dolls brings Wrayburn the desired address.

Book 4 – {1} Eugene in his boat passes Plashwater Weir Mill Lock, kept by Riderhood; he is followed by Bradley Headstone in the disguise of a bargeman; Bradley witnesses the meeting of Eugene with Lizzie Hexam, and returns to the lock; Riderhood confirms his suspicion that the schoolmaster is copying his dress in his disguise. {2} Mr and Mrs Lammle breakfast with the Boffins; their plot is understood, and their plans frustrated. {3} Wegg 'drops down' on Mr Boffin and, after showing him the will, sees him home. {4} John Rokesmith and Bella are married; how Mrs Wilfer receives the news. {5} Bella's housekeeping. {6} Eugene and Lizzie meet by appointment on the river-bank; he urges his suit, but Lizzie firmly declines to encourage him, on account of the difference of their positions in society, and begs him to leave her; Eugene, walking by the river after their interview, is assaulted by Headstone, and his body thrown into the water; he is rescued by Lizzie. {7} Bradley Headstone returns to the lock-house; he is dogged by Riderhood, who sees him resume his own dress, and throw his disguise into the river; Charley Hexam upbraids Headstone, and drops his acquaintance; Rogue Riderhood catches his fish. {8} Fledgeby attempts to learn from Jenny Wren the place of Lizzie Hexam's retreat; Fledgeby is caned by Lammle, and has his wounds dressed by Jenny. {9} Jenny comes to an understanding of Riah's true character; Fledgeby sends Riah his discharge; death of Jenny's father; Mortimer desires Jenny's presence at the bedside of Eugene. {10} Jenny divines that Eugene wishes to marry Lizzie. {11} Bradley Headstone's meeting with the Revd Mr Milvey, and agitation at the news of Lizzie's approaching marriage; the marriage of Eugene and Lizzie. {12} Rokesmith encounters Lightwood, and is recognised as Julius Handford; John goes with the inspector of police and Bella to The Fellowship Porters on a matter of identification; John takes Bella to their new home in London. {13} Mrs Boffin relates to Bella the story of her husband's identity, how she had found him out, and how they had planned to test her love for him. {14} Wegg finds Venus in improved spirits, and appoints a time for bringing Boffin to the grindstone; Wegg finds his friendly move checkmated, and is finally disposed of by Sloppy. {15} Riderhood visits Headstone in his school; Headstone goes to Riderhood's lock, and refuses his demands; finding he cannot get rid of him he seizes him, forces him into the lock, and both are drowned. {16} Mrs Wilfer, with Miss Lavinia and George Sampson, visit Bella in her new home; first interview between Sloppy and Jenny Wren; Mr and Mrs Wrayburn visit Mr and Mrs John Harmon. {17} Mortimer takes a final look at society.

31

Doctor Marigold

Originally published as part of the collection of tales entitled 'Doctor Marigold's Prescriptions', which formed the Christmas number of *All the Year Round* for 1865. The story takes its name from a 'Cheap Jack', who relates the history of his life.

CHARACTERS

MARIGOLD, Doctor – The narrator of the story. He describes himself 'as a middle-aged man, of a broadish build, in cords, leggings, and a sleeved waistcoat, the strings of which is always gone behind', with a white hat, and a shawl round his neck, worn loose and easy. He is a ' Cheap Jack', born on the highway, and named 'Doctor' out of gratitude and compliment to his mother's accoucheur. He marries, and has one child, a little girl, but loses both daughter and wife, and continues his travels alone. Coming across a deaf-and-dumb child, however, who he fancies resembles his lost daughter, he adopts her, and sends her to a school for deaf mutes to be educated; but she falls in love with a young man who is also deaf and dumb, and Marigold is forced to give her up. She sails for China with her husband, but returns after an absence of a few years bringing with her a little daughter who can both hear and talk; and the measure of the Doctor's happiness is once more full.

MARIGOLD, Mrs – Wife of Doctor Marigold; a young Suffolk woman whom he courted from the footboard of his cart. At such times, she does not spare her little daughter, but treats her with great cruelty. When, however, the child dies, she takes to brooding, and tries to drown remorse in liquor; but one day, seeing a woman beating a child unmercifully, she stops her ears, runs away like a wild thing, and the next day she is found in the river.

MARIGOLD, Little Sophy – Their daughter; a sweet child, shamefully abused by her mother, but dearly loved by her father, to whom she is quite devoted. She takes a bad low fever, and dies in his arms while he is convulsing a rustic audience with his jokes and witty speeches.

MARIGOLD, Willum – Doctor Marigold's father; a 'lovely one, in his time', at the 'Cheap Jack' work.

MIM – A showman, who is a most ferocious swearer, and who has a very hoarse voice. He is master to Pickleson, and stepfather to Sophy, whom he disposes of to Doctor Marigold for half-a-dozen pairs of braces.

PICKLESON – *called* 'Rinaldo di Velasco'. An amiable though timid giant, let out to Mim for exhibition by his mother, who spends the wages he receives.

SOPHY – A deaf-and-dumb girl adopted by Doctor Marigold after the death of his own daughter Sophy. She becomes greatly attracted to her new father, who loves her fervently in return, and is very kind and patient with her, trying at first to teach himself to read, and then sending her to an institution for deaf mutes to be educated. She subsequently marries a man afflicted like herself; goes abroad with him; and, after an absence of over five years, returns home with a little daughter.

32

Barbox Brothers and Barbox Brothers & Co.

This story – for 'Barbox Brothers and Co' is merely a pendant or sequel to 'Barbox Brothers' – is one of a number of tales included in 'Mugby Junction', the extra Christmas number of *All the Year Round* for 1866. The hero of the story, who is also the narrator of it, is at first a clerk in the firm of Barbox Brothers, then a partner, and finally the firm itself. From being a moody, self-contained, and unhappy person, made so by the lumbering cares and the accumulated disappointments of long monotonous years, he is changed, in circumstances that awaken and develop his better nature, into a thoroughly cheerful man, with eyes and thoughts for others, and a hand ever ready to help those who need and deserve help; and thus, taking, as it were, thousands of partners into the solitary firm, he becomes Barbox Brothers and Co'.

CHARACTERS

BARBOX BROTHERS – *See* **Jackson, Mr.**

BEATRICE – A careworn woman, with her hair turned gray, whom 'Barbox Brothers' had once loved and lost. She is the wife of Tresham. *See* **Jackson (Mr), Tresham**.

JACKSON, Mr – A former clerk in the public notary and bill-broking firm of Barbox Brothers who, after imperceptibly becoming the sole representative of the house, at length retires, and obliterates it from the face of the earth, leaving nothing of it but a name on two portmanteaus, which he has with him one rainy night when he leaves a train at Mugby Junction. With a bitter recollection of his lonely childhood; of the enforced business, at once distasteful and oppressive, in which the best years of his life have been spent; of the double faithlessness of the only woman he ever loved and the only friend he ever trusted; his birthday, as it annually recurs, serves but to intensify his ever-present sense of desolation; and he resolves to abandon all thought of a fixed home, and to pass the rest of his days in travelling, hoping to find relief in a constant change of scene. It is after three o'clock of a tempestuous morning when, acting on a sudden impulse, he leaves the train at Mugby Junction. At that black hour, he cannot obtain any conveyance to the inn, and willingly accepts the invitation of 'Lamps', a servant of the railway company, to try the warmth of his little room for a while. He afterwards makes the acquaintance of Lamps's daughter Phœbe, a poor bedridden girl; and their happy disposition, strong mutual affection, peaceful lives, modest self-respect, and unaffected interest in those around them, teach him a lesson of cheerfulness, contentment, and moral responsibility which the experience of years had failed to impart. On a visit, one day, to a distant town, he is suddenly accosted by a very little girl, who tells him she is lost. He takes her to his hotel and, failing to discover who she is, or where she lives, he makes arrangements for her staying for the night, and amuses himself with her childish prattle, and her enjoyment of her novel situation. The little one's mother at last appears, and proves to be the woman he had loved, and who had so heartlessly eloped with his most trusted friend years before. She tells him that she has had five other children, who are all in their graves; that her husband is very ill of a lingering disorder, and that he believes the curse of his old friend rests on the whole household. Will Mr Jackson forgive them? The injured man – now so changed from what he once was – responds by taking the child to her father, placing her in his arms, and invoking a blessing on her innocent head. 'Live and thrive, my pretty baby!' he says, 'live and prosper, and become, in time, the mother of other little children, like the angels who behold the Father's face'.

'LAMPS' – A railway servant employed at Mugby Junction father of Phœbe. He is a very hard-working man being on duty fourteen, fifteen, or eighteen hours a day, and sometimes even twenty-four hours at a time. But he is always on the bright side and the good side. He has a daughter who is bed-ridden, and to whom he is entirely devoted. Besides supplying her with books and newspapers, he takes to composing comic songs for her amusement, and – what is still harder, and at first goes much against his grain – to singing them also.

PHŒBE – His daughter; crippled and helpless in consequence of a fall in infancy. She supports herself by making lace, and by teaching a few little children. Notwithstanding her great misfortune, she is always interested in others, of all sorts. She makes the acquaintance of Mr Jackson ('Barbox Brothers'); and her pure and gentle life becomes the guiding star of his.

POLLY – Daughter of Beatrice and Tresham; a little child found by 'Barbox Brothers' in the streets of a large town. *See* **Jackson, Mr.**

TRESHAM – A former friend of 'Barbox Brothers', who advances him in business, and takes him into his private confidence. In return, Tresham comes between him and Beatrice (whom 'Barbox Brothers' loves), and takes her from him. This treachery after a time receives its fitting punishment in poverty, and loss of health and children; but 'Barbox Brothers', whose awakened wrath had long seemed unappeasable, is made better at last by the discipline and experience of life, and generously forgives those who had forced him to undergo so sharp a trial.

The Boy at Mugby

This tale as originally published, formed the third portion of 'Mugby Junction', the extra Christmas number of *All the Year Round* for 1866. It is a satirical description of the ordinary English railway refreshment-room, as it was at that time, with its wretched tea and coffee, as compared with the excellent provision made in France for the entertainment and comfort of travellers. The proprietress of the refreshment-room at Mugby Junction crosses the Channel for the express purpose of looking into the French method of conducting such establishments.

CHARACTERS

EZEKIEL – 'The boy at Mugby'; an attendant in the refreshment-room at Mugby Junction, whose proudest boast is that 'it never yet refreshed a mortal being'.

PIFF, Miss – One of the 'young ladies' in the same refreshment-room.

SNIFF, Mr – 'A regular insignificant cove' employed by the mistress of the refreshment-room.

SNIFF, Mrs – His wife; chief assistant of the mistress of the refreshment-room.

WHIFF, Miss – An attendant in the refreshment-room.

Two Ghost Stories

THE TRIAL FOR MURDER

The first of the two stories reprinted under the above title was originally published as a portion of 'Doctor Marigold's Prescriptions', the extra Christmas number of *All the Year Round* for 1865. It was the sixth of the 'Prescriptions', and was labelled 'To be taken with a grain of salt'. It is supposed to have been written by 'a literary character' whom the doctor discovers in travelling about the country, and to have intended (as well as the tales accompanying it) for the amusement of his adopted deaf-and-dumb daughter Sophy. It purports to be an account of circumstances preceding and attending a certain noted trial for murder. The narrator – who is summoned to serve on the jury – is haunted, from the time he first hears of the deed until the close of the trial, by the apparition of the murdered man. Though seen by no one else, it mingles with the jury and the officers of the court, looks at the judge's notes over his shoulder, confronts the defendant's witnesses, and stands at the elbow of the counsel, invariably causing some trepidation or disturbance on the part of each and, as it were, dumbly and darkly overshadowing their minds.

'Finally the Jury returned into Court at ten minutes past twelve. The murdered man at that time stood directly opposite the jury-box, on the other side of the Court. As I took my place, his eyes rested on me with great attention; he seemed satisfied, and slowly shook a great gray veil, which he carried on his arm for the first time, over his head and whole form. As I gave in our verdict; 'Guilty', the veil collapsed, all was gone, and his place was empty'.

Besides those above mentioned (the names of none of whom are given), the following are the only

CHARACTERS

DERRICK, John – Valet to the haunted juryman.

HARKER, Mr – An officer in charge of the jury, and sworn to hold them in safe keeping.

THE SIGNALMAN

The second Ghost Story is an account of an incident occurring on one of the branch lines leading from Mugby Junction. It forms the fourth division of the extra Christmas number bearing that name, which was published in 1866, in connection with *All the Year Round*. It is supposed to be related by 'Barbox Brothers', who makes a careful study of the Junction and its vicinity, and communicates to his poor bedridden friend Phœbe the substance of what he sees, hears, or otherwise picks up on the main line and its five branches. Exploring Branch Line No 1, he visits a signalman who is stationed in a deep cutting near the entrance of a tunnel. He is a cool, vigilant, clear headed, and educated man, who had been, when young, a student of natural history, and had attended lectures, but had run wild, misused his opportunities, gone down, and never risen again. Notwithstanding his intelligence, and his freedom from any taint of superstition, he is continually haunted by a strange apparition, which, just before any fatal accident, stands by the red light at the mouth of the tunnel and with one hand over its eyes, as if to shut out the frightful scene about to take place, cries: 'Holloa! Below there! Look out! For God's sake clear the way!' Twice has this occurred, and been followed by accident and death; and now the figure has been seen and heard again. The visitor goes away, hardly knowing how he ought to act in view of his knowledge of the man's state of mind; but he finally resolves to offer to accompany him to a wise medical practitioner, and to take his opinion.

35

Holiday Romance

This story was written expressly for *Our Young Folks* (a juvenile magazine published in America), and appeared during the months of January, March, April, and May 1868. It was also brought out in England, in *All the Year Round*, in January, February, and March of the same year. The story is in four parts of which the first, supposed to be written by a young gentleman of eight years of age, explains 'how what comes after came to be written'. It contains an account of two small boys, who 'make believe' that they are married to two little girls, and that they are all high and mighty personages, with relatives and friends of the same stamp. Finding, however, that the 'grown-up people won't do what they ought to do', and refuse to allow their claims, they agree that, during the approaching holidays, they will 'educate the grown-up people' by hinting to them how things ought to be, veiling their meaning under a mask of romance. They accordingly write three stories, in which the children act the part of men and women, while the men and women are treated as if they were children.

CHARACTERS

ALICIA, Princess – The heroine of Miss Alice Rainbird's romance; eldest child of King Watkins the First, and god-daughter of the good fairy Grandmarina, who gives her a magic fish-bone, which can only be used once, but which is warranted to bring her, that once, whatever she wishes for, provided she wishes for it at the right time. The princess is a notable housewife, and is also a very motherly girl, taking sole charge of her eighteen brothers and sisters. She has great good sense, and refrains from using her magic present until some great exigency shall arise. But when at last her father informs her that his money is all gone, and that he has no means of getting any more, though he has tried very hard, and has tried all ways, she thinks the right time must have come for testing the virtue of her godmother's gift, and she therefore wishes it were quarter day; and immediately it *is* quarter day, and the king's quarter's salary comes rattling down the chimney. Moreover, her godmother appears, changes the coarse attire of the princess into the splendid raiment of a bride, and whisks her off to church, where she is married to Prince Certainpersonio, after which there is a magnificent wedding-feast.

ALICUMPAINE, Mrs – One of the characters in Miss Nettie Ashford's romance; a little friend of Mr and Mrs Orange, whom she invites to 'a small juvenile party' of grown-up people. *See* **Ashford, Miss Nettie**.

ASHFORD, Miss Nettie – A child of seven; pretended bride of William Tinkling, Esquire (aged eight), and author of a romance, the scene of which is laid in 'a most delightful country to live in', where 'the grown-up people are obliged to obey the children, and are never allowed to sit up to supper, except on their birthdays'. *See* **TINKLING, William, Esquire**.

BLACK, Mrs – One of Mrs Lemon's pupils in Miss Nettie Ashford's romance. She is a grown-up child, who is always at play, or gadding about and spoiling her clothes, besides being 'as pert and as flouncing a minx as ever you met with in all your days'.

BOLDHEART, Captain – Hero of Master Robin Redforth's romance. He is master of the schooner *Beauty*, and greatly distinguishes himself by various valiant exploits, notably his capture of the *Scorpion*, commanded by an old enemy, the Latin-grammar Master, whom he turns adrift in an open boat, with two oars, a compass, a bottle of rum, a small cask of water, a piece of pork, a bag of biscuit, and a Latin grammar. He afterwards finds him on a lonely island, and rescues him from the hands of the natives, who are cannibals; but, when he subsequently discovers him plotting to give him up to the master of another vessel (*the Family*), he incontinently hangs the traitor at the yard-arm.

BOOZEY, William von – One of the crew of the *Beauty*, rescued from drowning by Captain Boldheart, and ever afterwards his devoted friend.

BROWN – A vicious (grown-up) boy, greedy, and troubled with the gout, in Miss Nettie Ashford's romance. *See* **Ashford, Miss Nettie**.

CERTAINPERSONIO, Prince – A young gentleman who becomes the husband of the Princess Alicia. *See* **Alicia, Princess**.

DROWVEY, Miss – A schoolmistress in partnership with Miss Grimmer. The opinion of their pupils is divided as to 'which is the greatest beast'.

GRANDMARINA, Fairy – Godmother of the Princess Alicia. *See* **ALICIA, Princess**.

GRIMMER, Miss – A schoolmistress. *See* **Drowvey, Miss**.

LATIN-GRAMMAR MASTER, The – An old teacher and enemy of Captain Boldheart. *See* **Boldheart**.

LEMONY Mrs – The proprietress of a preparatory school for grown-up pupils, who figure in Miss Nettie Ashford's romance. *See* **ASHFORD, Miss Nettie**.

ORANGE, Mr James – The 'husband' of Mrs Orange.

ORANGE, Mrs – A character in Miss Nettie Ashford's romance; 'a truly sweet young creature', who has the misfortune to be sadly plagued by a numerous family of grown-up 'children', including two parents, two intimate friends of the one godfather, two godmothers, and an aunt. *See* **Ashford, Miss Nettie**.

PEGGY – Lord Chamberlain at the Court of King Watkins the First, in Miss Alice Rainbirds romance.

PICKLES – A fishmonger in the same story.

RAINBIRD, Alice – The 'bride' of Robin Redforth, and the author of the romance of which the Princess Alicia is the heroine. *See* **Alicia (Princess)**, *and* **Redforth (Lieutenant-Colonel Robin)**.

REDFORTH, Lieutenant-Colonel Robin – Cousin to William Tinkling, Esq. He is a young gentle, aged nine, who assumes the part of a Pirate, and affects to be peculiarly lawless and bloodthirsty. The romance which contains the story of Captain Boldheart is from his pen. *See* **Boldheart, Captain**.

TINKLING, William, Esquire – Author of the introductory portion of the romance, and editor of the other portions. He is eight years old; and to him Miss Nettie Ashford is 'married' in the right-hand closet in the corner of the dancing-school where they first met, with a ring (a green one) from Wilkingwater's toy-shop. His bride, and the bride of his friend Lieutenant-Colonel Robin Redforth, being in captivity at the school of Drowvey and Grimmer, the two young gentlemen resolve to cut them out on a Wednesday, when walking two and two. The plan fails, however, and Tinkling's bride brands him as a coward. He demands a court-martial, which is granted and assembles; the Emperor of France, the President of the United States, and a certain admiral being among the members of it. The verdict of 'Not guilty' is on the point of being rendered, when an unlooked-for event disturbs the general rejoicing. This is no other than the Emperor of France's aunt catching hold of his hair. The proceedings abruptly terminate, and the court tumultuously dissolves.

TOM – Cousin to Captain Boldheart; a boy remarkable for his cheekiness and unmannerliness.

WATKINS THE FIRST, King – A character in Miss Alice Rainbird's romance; the manliest of his sex, and husband of a queen who is the loveliest of hers. *See* **Alicia, Princess**.

WHITE – A pale bald child (a grown-up one) with red whiskers, who is a pupil in Mrs Lemon's preparatory school.

36

George Silverman's Explanation

This tale was written expressly for *The Atlantic Monthly*, and was published in that magazine in the months of January, February and March 1868. It was republished, the same year, in *All the Year Round*.

CHARACTERS

FAREWAY, Adelina – Pupil of George Silverman, who falls in love with her, and finds his love reciprocated, but resigns her to another out of pure self-depreciation and unworldliness.

FAREWAY, Lady – Her mother; widow of the late Sir Gaston Fareway Baronet; a penurious and managing woman, handsome, well-preserved, of somewhat large stature, with a steady glare in her great round eyes. She presents Mr George Silverman to a living of two hundred a year in North Devonshire, but imposes the condition that he shall help her with her correspondence, accounts, and various little things of that kind, and that he shall gratuitously direct her daughter's studies.

FAREWAY, Mr – Her second son; a young gentleman of abilities much above the average, but idle and luxurious, who for a time reads with Mr Silverman.

GIMBLET, Brother – An elderly drysalter; a man with a crabbed face, a large dog's-eared shirt collar, and a spotted blue neckerchief, reaching up behind to the crown of his head. He is an expounder in Brother Hawkyard's congregation.

HAWKYARD, Mr Verity – of West Bromwich. George Silverman's guardian or patron; a yellow-faced, peak-nosed man, who is an exhorter in a congregation of an obscure denomination, among whom he is called Brother Hawkyard. He is given to boasting, and has a habit of confirming himself in a parenthesis, as if, knowing himself, he doubted his own word.

SILVERMAN, George – The narrator of the story; born in a cellar in Preston. While still a small child, George loses his father and mother, who die miserably of a fever; is taken from the cellar in a half-starved state; and is handed over by the authorities to Brother Hawkyard who, as it seems, has accepted a trust in behalf of the boy from a rich grandfather who has just died at Birmingham. After being disinfected, comfortably fed, and furnished with new clothes, he is sent to an old farmhouse at Hoghton Towers, where he remains for a considerable time, and where he begins to form a shy disposition, to be of a timidly silent character under misconstruction, to have an inexpressible and even a morbid dread of becoming sordid or worldly. He is afterwards put to school, told to work his way and, as time goes on, becomes a Foundation Boy on a good foundation, and is preached at on Sundays by Brother Hawkyard and other expounders of the same kidney. Working still harder, he at last obtains a scholarship at Cambridge, where he lives a secluded life, and studies diligently. Knowing himself to be 'unfit for the noisier stir of social existence', he applies his mind to the clerical profession, and at last is presented by Lady Fareway to a living worth two hundred a year. Adelina, the only daughter of Lady Fareway, pursues her studies under his direction, and a strong but undeclared affection springs up between them. But the young clergyman, conscious that her family and fortune place him far beneath her, and feeling that her merits are far greater than his, resolves upon self-sacrifice, and quietly sets to work to turn the current of her love into another channel. For this purpose he introduces to her Mr Granville Wharton, another pupil of his, and contrives, in various ways, to interest them in each other. The object is accomplished and, in little more than a year, they come before him, hand in hand, and ask to be united in marriage. As they are both of age, and as the young lady has come into possession of a fortune in her own right, he does not hesitate to do so; but the consequences to himself are disastrous. Lady Fareway has had ambitious projects for her daughter, and indignantly charges George Silverman with taking a percentage upon Adelina's fortune as a bribe for putting Mr Wharton in possession of it. With the old cry of; 'You worldly wretch!' she demands that he should resign his living, contumeliously dismisses him from her presence, and pursues him for many years with bitter animosity. But Adelina and her husband stand by him, and at length he obtains a college living in a sequestered place, lives down the suspicions and calumnies that have dogged his steps, and pens his 'Explanation'.

SYLVIA – A girl at the farmhouse of Hoghton Towers, where George Silverman is placed by Mr Hawkyard, after the death of his father and mother.

WHARTON, Mr Granville – Pupil of George Silverman, and married by him to Adelina Fareway.

37

New Uncommercial Samples

Published in All The Year Round *in 1869*

A SMALL STAR IN THE EAST

JOHN – A boiler-maker, living in the neighbourhood of Ratcliffe and Stepney, who obtains employment but fitfully and rarely, and is forced to live on the work of his wife.

POODLES – A comical mongrel dog, found starving at the door of the East London Children's Hospital, and taken in and fed, since when he has made it his home. On his neck he wears a collar presented him by an admirer of his mental endowments, and bearing the legend; 'Judge not Poodles by external appearances'.

A LITTLE DINNER IN AN HOUR

BULLFINCH – A gentleman who, having occasion to go to the seaside resort of Namelesston with a friend for the transaction of some business, proposes that they should dine at The Temeraire. They accordingly drive to that house and order a little dinner, which is to be ready punctually in one hour. They return promptly, but try in vain to eat and drink what is set before them, and come to the conclusion that no such ill-served, ill-appointed, ill-cooked, nasty little dinner could be got for the money anywhere else under the sun.

COCKER, Mr Indignation – A dissatisfied diner at the same house, who disputes the charges in his bill.

MR BARLOW

BARLOW, Mr – An irrepressible instructive monomaniac, who knows everything, didactically improves all sorts of occasions, and presents himself in all sorts of aspects and under all kinds of disguises; so named from an all-knowing tutor in Thomas Day's juvenile story of 'Sandford and Merton'.

ON AN AMATEUR BEAT

POODLES – A mongrel dog attached to the East London Children's Hospital. *See* **A Small Star in the East**.

38

The Mystery of Edwin Drood

This first number of this work, which closes the series of Dickens's novels, was issued by Messrs Chapman and Hall on 1 April 1870, with two illustrations on wood from drawings by S L Fildes. The story was to be completed in twelve monthly parts, but Dickens died soon after the third part was published. He left three more parts for publication, so half the story did appear in print.

CHARACTERS

BAZZARD, Mr – Clerk to Mr Grewgious, over whom he possesses a strange power. He is a pale, puffy-faced, dark-haired person of thirty, with big, dark eyes wholly wanting in lustre, and with a dissatisfied, doughy complexion, that seems to ask to be sent to the baker's. {11, 20}

BILLICKIN, Mrs – A widowed cousin of Mr Bazzard's, who lets furnished lodgings in Southampton Street, Bloomsbury Square. Personal faintness and an overpowering candour are the distinguishing features of her organisation. With this lady Mr Grewgious obtains rooms for his ward, Miss Rosa Bud. Having concluded the bargain, he writes and signs a few lines of agreement, and requests Mrs Billickin to put her signature to the document also, 'Christian and surname' in full. {22}

BUD, Miss Rosa – *called* '**Rosebud**'. A wonderfully pretty, childish, and whimsical young lady, who is an orphan, and the ward of Mr Grewgious. While yet a mere child, she is betrothed to Edwin Drood; her father and his having been very dear and firm and fast friends, and desiring that their only children should be to one another. But as Rosa and Edwin grow up they find that they are not truly happy in their engagement, and that each resents being thus married by anticipation. They accordingly agree to break off the engagement, and to 'change to brother and sister' thenceforth. Shortly after this event, Edwin Drood disappears, and is supposed to have been murdered. {3, 7, 9, 13, 19–22} *See* **Tartar, Lieutenant**.

CRISPARKLE, The Reverend Septimus – One of the minor canons of Cloisterham Cathedral; a model clergyman, and a true Christian gentleman. {2, 6–8, 10, 12, 14–17, 21–23}

CRISPARKLE, Mrs – *called* 'The China Shepherdess'. His mother; a pretty old lady, with bright eyes, a calm and cheerful face, and a trim and compact figure. {6, 7, 10}

DATCHERY, Dick – A mysterious white-haired man, with black eyebrows, who presents himself in Cloisterham shortly after the death of Edwin Drood, and who takes lodgings overlooking the rooms of Mr Jasper. Who or what he is does not appear; but it is plain that he takes up his abode in Cloisterham for the sole purpose of watching Jasper. {18, 23}

DEPUTY – A hideous small boy, hired by Durdles to pelt him home if he catches him out too late. He explains to Jasper that he is a 'man-servant up at The Traveller's Twopenny', a crazy wooden inn near the cathedral. As a caution to Durdles to stand clear if he can, or to betake himself home, the young imp always chants a note of preparation before beginning to fling stones. {5, 7, 18, 23}

DROOD, Edwin – The character from whom the story takes its name; a young man left an orphan at an early age and betrothed, in accordance with his father's dying wish, to Miss Rosa Bud, the daughter of an old and very dear friend. At the time the story opens, the young lady is attending the school of Miss Twinkleton, at Cloisterham, and the young gentleman is studying engineering in London. Neither of them is reconciled to the thought that their destiny in life has, in a most important respect, been predetermined for them; yet the thought of questioning the arrangement has not occurred to either; and Edwin runs down to Cloisterham every now and then both to see his intended and to visit his uncle, Mr Jasper, who is but little older than himself, and is his most intimate friend and companion. On one of these occasions, he meets at the Reverend Mr Crisparkle's a young man named Neville Landless, and his sister Helena, who are pursuing their studies – the one under Mr Crisparkle's direction, the other at Miss Twinkleton's establishment. The young men take a strong dislike to each other. Edwin thinks Neville's sister vastly superior to her brother; while the latter is disgusted by the air of proprietorship with which Edwin treats Rosa. They escort the young ladies home for the night, and then repair at the invitation of Mr Jasper to his lodgings to have a glass of wine. The drink is mixed for them by their host; and, although they take only a moderate quantity, it seems to madden them; for from sarcastic remarks they soon come to open violence, when they are separated by Jasper, who takes young Neville home and reports his conduct to Mr Crisparkle. In the morning, Edwin departs for London, and Mr Crisparkle is consequently unable to bring about an immediate reconciliation; but he resolves to do so on the first opportunity that offers. He talks about the matter to Neville, who expresses himself willing to make an apology; and Mr Jasper writes to Edwin who replies that he shall be glad to make any amends for his hasty display of temper. It is therefore arranged that the young men shall meet again at Mr Jasper's rooms and 'shake hands, and say no more about it'. Before revisiting Cloisterham, Edwin calls on Rosa's guardian, Mr Grewgious, who gives him a wedding-ring which belonged to her departed mother, and charges him to look carefully into his own heart before making Rosa his wife; for, although the marriage was a wish dear both to his own father and to hers, he ought not to commit himself to such a step for no higher reason than because he has long been accustomed to look forward to it. Edwin departs and, deeply pondering the injunction of Mr Grewgious, becomes convinced that the marriage ought not to take place. He resolves to have a frank conversation with Rosa, feeling well assured that her views will coincide with his own. Repairing to the Nuns' House, he seeks her with this intention, but finds himself anticipated; for she enters at once upon the subject herself. The result is that, although they agree to remain the best of friends, they cease to be lovers, and resolve to send at once for Mr Grewgious, and communicate their determination to him, but to be quite silent upon the subject to all others until his arrival. Edwin's sole anxiety, as he tells Rosa, is for his uncle, whom he dearly loves, and who, as he believes, has set his heart on the union. Although Rosa does not declare her thoughts, she yet believes that breaking off the match will not be so great a disappointment to Mr Jasper as Edwin thinks, having good reason to know that he is himself deeply in love with her. They separate for the night, the young man going to his uncle's to meet Neville Landless who, after promising Mr Crisparkle that he will curb his impetuous temper, directs his steps to the same place. The next morning, Edwin Drood is nowhere to be found; and young Landless sets out early for a two-weeks' ramble through the neighbouring country. Mr

Jasper, becoming alarmed at the disappearance of his nephew, arouses the town. He says that the young men, after meeting at his room, went out together for a walk near the river. The feud between them is well known; and dark suspicions are entertained of foul play. Young Landless is followed and arrested. The river is dragged and no body is discovered; but a watch, identified as Edwin's, is found; and a jeweller testifies that he wound and set it for him at twenty minutes past two on the afternoon of his arriving and that it had run down before being cast into the water. Further than this, nothing can be discovered and, as there is not evidence enough to warrant Neville's detention, he is set at liberty. So strong is the popular feeling against him, however, that he is forced to leave the town, and takes up his residence in an obscure part of London. Here he is visited by Mr Crisparkle, who firmly believes in his innocence; and here he is watched and dogged by Mr Jasper, who has taken a solemn oath to devote his life to ferreting out the murderer. Although the reader is left in the dark, by the abrupt termination of the novel, as to who is the guilty party, he is led to believe that Mr Jasper is the real assassin. He is desperately in love with Rosa though she thoroughly dislikes and despises him. After the death of Edwin, he visits her, and declares his love, promising to forego his pursuit of young Landless, in whom she is deeply interested, if she will give him some encouragement. He shows himself at least to be fully capable of the crime; and he is suspected by Rosa herself and by Mr Grewgious. {2, 7, 8, 11, 13, 14}

DURDLES – A stonemason; chiefly in the gravestone, tomb, and monument way, and wholly of their colour from head to foot. Mr Jasper visits the cathedral one night with Durdles, whom he plies with liquor until he falls asleep; and he improves the opportunity to make an extended examination of the crypt, using the keys of his companion to obtain admission into its locked-up recesses. For what purpose this exploration is made does not appear, but probably, for the sake of finding a safe hiding-place for the body of Edwin Drood, whom Jasper, as the reader is led to infer, has made up his mind to put out of the way. {4, 12, 14} *See* **Deputy**.

FERDINAND, Miss – A pupil at Miss Twinkleton's school. {9, 13}

GIGGLES, Miss – Another pupil at the same school. {9, 13}

GREWGIOUS, Hiram, Esquire – Miss Rosa Bud's guardian, and a 'particularly angular man', After the disappearance of Edwin

Drood, Mr Grewgious has an interview with Jasper, whose appearance and conduct are such as to excite the strongest suspicions of his being the murderer of that young gentleman. Mr Grewgious keeps his thoughts to himself however; but when Rosa, pursued by Jasper, goes to London to throw herself on her guardian's protection, he astonishes his little ward by his indignation, exclaiming with a sudden rush of amazing energy: 'Damn him!' he immediately sets about making his ward comfortable, procures lodgings for her, makes arrangements for Miss Twinkleton's staying with her as a companion and friend, and devotes himself to investigating the mystery of Edwin Drood's sudden disappearance.

HONEYTHUNDER, Mr Luke – Chairman of the Convened Chief Composite Committee of Central and District Philanthropists, and guardian of Neville and Helena Landless. He is a large man, with a tremendous voice, and an appearance of being constantly engaged in crowding everybody to the wall. {6, 17}

JASPER, John – A music-master who is employed as choirmaster in Cloisterham Cathedral; uncle to Edwin Drood, for whom he professes the strongest affection. Jasper is addicted to the use of opium, and resorts every now and then to a miserable hole in

Up the River – Sir Luke Fildes

London, where the drug is prepared in a peculiar form by an old hag, and where he smokes himself into the wildest dreams. He goes to this place after the disappearance of Edwin Drood and is followed, when he leaves, by the old woman, who thus ascertains who and what he is. The two are, in turn, watched by Mr Datchery, who appears well satisfied on discovering the connection between them. {1, 2, 4, 5, 7–10, 12, 14–16, 18, 19, 22, 23}

JENNINGS, Miss – A pupil at Miss Twinkleton's Seminary for Young Ladies. {9}

JOE – Driver of an omnibus, which is the daily service between Cloisterham and external mankind. {6, 15, 20}

LANDLESS, Helena – A native of Ceylon, but the child of English parents; a ward of Mr Honeythunder's, who sends her to Miss Twinkleton's School for Young Ladies in Cloisterham, where she becomes the friend and confidante of Rosa Bud. She is an unusually handsome, lithe girl, very dark and rich in colour – almost of the gypsy type with – something untamed about her, as there is, also, about her twin brother Neville. {6, 7, 10, 12, 14, 22}

LANDLESS, Neville – Her brother, studying with the Reverend Mr Crisparkle, and suspected of the murder of Edwin Drood. {6–8, 10, 12, 14–17}

LOBLEY, Mr – A boatman in the Service of Mr Tartar – 'the dead image of the sun in old woodcuts', his hair and whisker answering for rays all around him. {22}

REYNOLDS, Miss – A pupil at the Nuns' House, Miss Twinkleton's Seminary for Young Ladies. {9}

RICKITTS, Miss – Another pupil at the same establishment.

THOMAS – An auctioneer, afterwards Mayor of Cloisterham.

SAPSEA, Mr Thomas – An auctioneer, afterwards Mayor of Cloisterham. Having lost his wife, Mr Sapsea determines to compose an epitaph for her tombstone, that shall strike all ordinary minds with awe and confusion. When this literary thunderbolt is forged, he calls in Mr Jasper to get his opinion of it. Not to astound the young man immediately launching this masterpiece of scholastic workmanship at him, Mr Sapsea considerately begins by explaining how he came, first by his extensive knowledge, secondly by his wife. The lady thus honoured was a Miss Brobity, the mistress of a school in Cloisterham. {4, 12, 14–16, 18}

TARTAR, Lieutenant – An ex-officer of the Royal Navy, who has come into possession of a fortune, and has retired from the service. He becomes the friend of Neville Landless, and makes the acquaintance of Rosa Bud, whose husband, it is probable, Mr Dickens intended him to become. {17, 21, 22}

TISHER, Mrs – A deferential widow, with a weak back, a chronic sigh, and a suppressed voice, who looks after the young ladies' wardrobes at the Nuns' House, Miss Twinkleton's seminary at Cloisterham. {2, 7, 9, 8}

TOPE, Mr – Chief verger of Cloisterham Cathedral. {2, 6, 12, 14, 16, 18, 23}

TOPE, Mrs – His wife. {2, 12, 14, 16, 18, 23}

TWINKLETON, Miss – Mistress of a boarding-school for young ladies in Cloisterham, attended by Rosa Bud and Helena Landless. {3, 6, 7, 9, 13, 22}

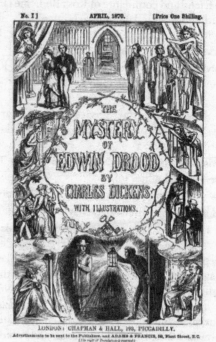

No. I]   APRIL, 1870.   [Price One Shilling.

THE MYSTERY OF EDWIN DROOD. BY CHARLES DICKENS. WITH ILLUSTRATIONS.

LONDON: CHAPMAN & HALL, 193, PICCADILLY.
Advertisements to be sent to the Publishers, and ADAMS & FRANCIS, 59, Fleet Street, E.C.
[The right of Translation is reserved.]

Wrapper design for the monthly parts of Edwin Drood –
Charles Allston Collins

39

Reprinted Pieces

Under this name, thirty-one sketches, all of them originally published in *Household Words*, between the years 1850 and 1856, were first brought together in 1858, and published in the twelfth volume of the 'Library Edition' of Dickens's works, issued jointly by Messrs Chapman and Hall, and Messrs Bradbury and Evans. In the pages here devoted to these 'Reprinted Pieces', several are wholly left out of view; the characters in them being nameless, and therefore not falling within the scope of this Dictionary.

CHARACTERS
THE LONG VOYAGE

(Containing recollections of various incidents of travel)

BLIGH, Captain – Master of the *Bounty*, turned adrift on the wide ocean in an open boat.

BRIMER, Mr – Fifth mate of the *Halsewell*, an East-Indiaman wrecked on the island of Purbeck.

CHRISTIAN, Fletcher – One of the officers of the *Bounty*; a mutineer.

CHRISTIAN, Thursday October – A native of Pitcairn's Island; son of Fletcher Christian by a savage mother.

MACMANUS, Mr – A midshipman on board of the *Halsewell*.

MANSEL, Miss – A passenger on the same ship.

MERITON, Mr Henry – Second mate of the *Halsewell*.

PIERCE, Captain – Master of the *Halsewell*.

PIERCE, Miss Mary – His daughter.

ROGERS, Mr – Third mate of the *Halsewell*.

SCHUTZ, Mr – A passenger in the same ship.

THE BEGGING-LETTER WRITER

SOUTHCOTE, Mr – One of the many aliases of a professional swindler, who writes letters soliciting money for the relief of his necessities.

SOUTHCOTE, Mrs – His wife.

OUR ENGLISH WATERING-PLACE

MILLS, Miss Julia – A sentimental novel-reader, who figures also in *David Copperfield* as the bosom friend of Dora Spenlow.

PEEPY, The Honourable Miss – The beauty of her day, but long deceased.

OUR FRENCH WATERING-PLACE

LOYAL DEVASSEUR, M – Citizen, town-councillor, and landlord. He is an old soldier, and a staunch admirer of the great Napoleon.

FÉROCE, M – A gentleman 'in the bathing line'; immensely stout, of a beaming aspect, and of very mild and polished manners.

BIRTHS. MRS MEEK, OF A SON

BIGBY, Mrs – Mother of Mrs Meek, and a most remarkable woman.

MEEK, Augustus George – Infant son of Mr George Meek.

MEEK, Mr George – The narrator of the story; a quiet man, of small stature, a weak voice, and a tremulous constitution. He is made utterly miserable by the manner in which his infant child is smothered, and rasped, and dosed and bandaged by the nurse, aided and abetted by his wife's mother; and he is betrayed into expressing himself warmly on the subject, notwithstanding his wish to avoid giving rise to words in the family.

MEEK, Mrs – His wife.

PRODGIT, Mrs – Mrs Meek's nurse; considered by Mr Meek to be 'from first to last a convention and a superstition', whom the medical faculty ought to take in hand and improve.

LYING AWAKE

WINKING, Charley – A sturdy vagrant in one of Her Majesty's jails who, like Her Majesty, like the author, like everybody else, has had many astonishing experiences in dreams.

THE POOR RELATION'S STORY

(one of the tales in 'A Round of Stories by the Christmas Fire', the Christmas number of *Household Words*, 1852)

CHILL, Uncle – An avaricious, crabbed old man; uncle to Michael.

CHRISTIANA – An old sweetheart of Michael's, to whom he imagines that he is married.

FRANK, Little – A cousin of Michael's; a diffident boy, for whom he has a particular affection.

MICHAEL – The 'poor relation', and the narrator of the story, which hinges upon a fancy of *what might have been*. Premising that he is not what he is supposed to be, he proceeds in the first place, to state what he *is* supposed to be, and then goes on to tell what his life and habits and belongings really are. He is thought to be very poor; in fact, he is rich. He is thought to be friendless; but he has the best of friends. He is thought to have been refused by a lady whom he loved: it is a mistake; he married the lady, and has a happy family around him. He is thought to live in a lodging in the Clapham Road: in reality, he lives in a castle – *in the air*.

SNAP, Betsey – Uncle Chill's only domestic; a withered, hard-favoured, yellow old woman.

SPATTER, John – Michael's clerk, and afterwards partner.

THE CHILD'S STORY

(One of the tales in 'A Round of Stories by the Christmas Fire', the Christmas number of *Household Words*, 1852)

FANNY – One of the prettiest girls that ever was seen, in love with 'Somebody'.

THE SCHOOL-BOY'S STORY

CHEESEMAN, Old – A poor boy at a boarding-school, who is a general favourite with his fellows, until he is made second Latin master; when they all agree in regarding him as a spy and a deserter, who has sold himself for gold (two pounds ten a quarter, and his washing). After this his life becomes very miserable; for the master and his wife look down upon him, and snub him; while the boys persecute him in many ways, and even form a society for the express purpose of making a set against him. One morning he is missed from his place, and it is thought at first by the pupils that, unable to stand it any longer, he has got up early and drowned himself. It turns out, however, that he has come into a large fortune, a fact which puts a very different face upon matters, making the master obsequious, and the scholars afraid for the consequence of what they have done. But 'Old Cheeseman' is not in the least puffed up or changed by his sudden prosperity, addressing them as 'his dear companions and old friends', and gives them a magnificent spread in the dining-room.

PITT, Jane – A sort of wardrobe-woman to the boys. Though a good friend to the boys, she is also a good friend to 'Old Cheeseman'; and the more they go against him the more she stands by him. It is therefore only a natural thing and one to be expected, that when 'Old Cheeseman' succeeds to his grandfather's large property, he should share it with her by making her his wife.

TARTAR, Bob – The 'first boy' in the school, and president of the 'Society' formed for the purpose of annoying 'Old Cheeseman'.

NOBODY'S STORY

BIGWIG FAMILY, The – A large household, composed of stately and noisy people, professed humanitarians, who do nothing but blow trumpets, and hold convocations, and make speeches, and write pamphlets, and quarrel among themselves.

NOBODY – otherwise '**Legion**'. The narrator of the story which, under the guise of an allegory, contains an appeal to the governing classes on behalf of the poor, and an argument for their proper instruction and rational amusement as a means of preventing drunkenness, debauchery, and crime.

THE GHOST OF ART

(A satire on the conventionalities of Art)
PARKINS, Mrs – A laundress who invariably disregards all instructions.

OUT OF TOWN

(A description of a little town named Pavilionstone, which has become a favourite seaside resort)

Within a quarter of a century, it was a little fishing town; and they do say that the time was when it was a little smuggling town... Now, gas and electricity run to the very water's edge, and the South Eastern Railway Company screech at us in the dead of night... We are a little mortary and limy at present; but we are getting on capitally. Indeed, we were getting on so fast, at one time, that we rather overdid it, and built a street of shops, the business of which may be expected to arrive in about ten years. We are sensibly laid out in general and, with a little care and pains (by no means wanting, so far), shall become a very pretty place. We ought to be; for our situation is delightful; our air is delicious; and our breezy hills and downs, carpeted with wild thyme, and decorated with millions of wild flowers are, on the faith of a pedestrian, perfect.

OUT OF THE SEASON

BLOCKER, Mr – A grocer.

WEDGINGTON, Mr B – A singer and clog-dancer who gives an exhibition at a watering-place, after the 'season' is over.

WEDGINGTON, Mrs B – His wife ; a singer and pianist.

WEDGINGTON, Master B – Her infant son, aged ten months; nursed by a shivering young person in the boxes, while his mother is on the stage.

A POOR MAN'S TALE OF A PATENT

BUTCHER, William – A Chartist; friend to John.

JOHN – The narrator of the story; a poor man, a smith by trade, who undertakes to obtain a patent on an invention which he has been twenty years in perfecting. He succeeds in doing so only after going through thirty-five distinct stages of obeying forms and paying fees, at a cost of ninety-six pounds, seven and eightpence, though nobody opposes his application.

JOY, Thomas – A carpenter with whom John lodges in London.

A FLIGHT

COMPACT ENCHANTRESS, The – A French actress.

DIEGO, Don – Inventor of the last new flying-machine.

ZAMIEL – A tall, grave, melancholy Frenchman, with whom (and with other passengers) the writer takes a flying trip from London to Paris.

THE DETECTIVE POLICE

CLARKSON – Counsel for Shepherdson and other thieves, traced out and arrested by Sergeant Mith.

DORNTON, Sergeant – A detective police-officer; a man about fifty years of age, with a ruddy face and a high sunburnt forehead. He is famous for steadily pursuing the inductive process, working on from clue to clue until he bags his man.

DUNDEY, Doctor – A man who robs a bank in Ireland, and escapes to America, whither he is followed and captured by Sergeant Dornton.

FENDALL, Sergeant – A detective police officer; a light-haired, well-spoken, polite person, and a prodigious hand at pursuing private inquiries of a delicate nature.

FIKEY – A man accused of forgery; taken prisoner by Inspector Field.

MESHECK, Aaron – A Jew, who gets acceptances from young men of good connections (in the army chiefly) on pretence of discount, and decamps with the same. He is finally found by Sergeant Dornton in the Tombs prison in New York City.

MITH, Sergeant – A detective police-officer; a smooth-faced man with a fresh, bright complexion, and a strange air of simplicity. He is a dab at housebreakers.

PIGEON, Thomas – *See* **Thompson, Tally-Ho**.

SHEPHERDSON, Mr – A thief, who informs Detective Mith (who, under the disguise of a young butcher from the country, gained his confidence) that he is going 'to hang out for a while' at The Setting Moon, in the Commercial Road, where he is afterwards found, and is taken into custody.

STALKER, Mr Inspector – A detective police-officer; a shrewd, hard-headed Scotchman; in appearance not at all unlike a very acute, thoroughly-trained schoolmaster from the Normal Establishment at Glasgow.

STRAW, Sergeant – A detective; a little wiry man of meek demeanour and strong sense, who would knock at a door, and ask a series of questions in any mild character you choose to prescribe to him, from a charity-boy upward; and seem as innocent as an infant.

THOMPSON, Tally-Ho – *alias* **Thomas Pigeon**. A famous horse-stealer, couper, and magsman, tracked to a lonely inn in Northamptonshire by Sergeant Witchem who, single-handed, arrests him, and takes him to London; though he has two big and ugly-looking companions with him at the time.

WIELD, Mr Inspector – A detective police-officer; a middle-aged man, of a portly presence, with a large, moist, knowing eye, a husky voice, and a habit of emphasising his conversation by the aid of a corpulent forefinger which is constantly in juxtaposition with his eyes and nose.

WITCHEM – A detective; a short, thickset man, marked with the smallpox, and having something of a reserved and thoughtful air, as if he were engaged in deep arithmetical calculations. He is renowned for his acquaintance with the swell mob.

THREE 'DETECTIVE' ANECDOTES

GRIMWOOD, Eliza – *called* '**The Countess**'. A handsome young woman, found lying dead, with her throat cut, on the floor of her bedroom, in the Waterloo Road.

PHIBBS, Mr – A haberdasher.

TATT, Mr – A gentleman formerly in the public line; quite an amateur detective in his way. He loses a diamond pin in a scrimmage, which is recovered by his friend Sergeant Witchem who sees the man who took it, and while they are all down on the floor together, knocking about, touches him on the back of his hand, as his 'pal' would; and he thinks it *is* his pal, and gives it to him.

TRINKLE, Mr – A young man suspected of the murder of Eliza Grimwood, but proved innocent.

ON DUTY WITH INSPECTOR FIELD

BARK, Bully – A lodging-house keeper, and a receiver of stolen goods, who lives in the innermost recesses of the worst part of London.

BLACK – A constable who, with his fellow-constable Green, accompanies Inspector Field to Wentworth Street to unveil its midnight mysteries.

BLACKEY – An imposter, who has stood soliciting charity near London Bridge for five-and-twenty years, with a painted skin, to represent disease.

CLICK, Mr – A vagabond.

FIELD, Inspector – A detective officer, who accompanies the writer, by night, to the lowest parts of London, visiting Rats' Castle (a dark, close cellar, a lodging house for thieves, near St Giles's Church), the old Farm House near the Old Mint, the sailors' dance-houses in the region of Ratcliffe Highway, the low haunts of Wentworth Street, and revealing the worst mysteries of the great city.

GREEN – A constable who, with another constable, named Black, acts as an escort to Inspector Field on his visiting Wentworth Street.

MILES, Bob – A vagabond and jail-bird.

PARKER – A constable who attends Inspector Field on the occasion of his visit to the Old Mint.

ROGERS – A constable who goes with Inspector Field to Rats' Castle.

WARWICK, The Earl of – A thief, so called.

WHITE – A constable who shows Inspector Field and his visitor the lodging-houses in Rotten Gray's Inn Lane.

WILLIAMS – A constable who pilots Inspector Field and his visitor to the sailors' dance-houses in the neighbourhood of Ratcliffe Highway.

DOWN WITH THE TIDE

PEA, or PEA COAT – A river policeman, with whom the writer goes down the Thames, at night, on a tour of inspection.

WATERLOO – A toll-taker, so called, at the bridge of that name.

PRINCE BULL: A FAIRY TALE

BEAR, Prince – An enemy of Prince Bull; intended as a person-ification of Russia.

BULL, Prince – A powerful prince, married to a lovely princess named Fair Freedom, who brought him a large fortune, and has borne him an immense number of children. Under this name the English Government is satirised, with especial reference to its bungling, inefficient prosecution of the Crimean war, and its obstinate adherence, under all circumstances, to mere official routine and formality.

TAPE – A malicious old beldame; godmother to Prince Bull.

OUR HONOURABLE FRIEND

TIPKISSON – A saddler; a plain, hard-working man, and an opponent of 'Our Honourable Friend', who is returned to Parliament as the member for Verbosity – the best represented place in England.

OUR SCHOOL

BLINKINS, Mr – Latin master; a colourless, doubled-up, near-sighted man, with a crutch, who is always cold, and always putting onions into his ears for deafness, and always disclosing ends of flannel under all his garments, and almost always applying a ball of pocket-handkerchief to some part of his face with a screwing action round and round.

DUMBLEDON, Master – A parlour-boarder; an idiotic, goggle-eyed boy, with a big head, and half-crowns without end; rumoured to have come by sea from some mysterious part of the earth, where his parents rolled in gold; and said to feed in the parlour on steaks and gravy, likewise to drink currant wine.

FROST, Miss – A schoolgirl.

MAWLS, Master – A schoolboy, with manners susceptible of much improvement.

MAXBY, Master – A day-pupil, favoured by the usher, who is sweet upon one of his sisters.

PHIL – A serving-man, with a sovereign contempt for learning.

OUR VESTRY

(A satire on the proceedings of Parliament)

BANGER, Captain – (of Wilderness Walk). A vestryman, and an opponent of Mr Tiddypot, with whom he has a Pickwickian altercation.

CHIB, Mr – (of Tucket's Terrace). A hale old gentleman of eighty-two, who is the father of the vestry.

DOGGINSON, Mr – A vestryman who is regarded as 'a regular John Bull'.

MAGG, Mr – (of Little Winkling Street). One of the 'first orators' of 'Our Vestry'.

TIDDYPOT, Mr – (of Gumtion House). A vestryman. *See* **Banger, Captain**.

WIGSBY, Mr – (of Chumbledon Square). A vestryman, who is a debater of great eminence.

40

Some Uncollected Pieces

THE STRANGE GENTLEMAN

This is a comic burletta, in two acts. It was first performed at the St James's Theatre on Thursday, 29 September 1836; was well received; and ran until December, when it was withdrawn for 'The Village Coquettes', a comic opera by the same author. 'The Strange Gentleman' was acted by J P Harley. In 1837, the piece was published, under the pseudonym of 'Boz', by Chapman and Hall, in a small octavo pamphlet of forty-six pages, illustrated with an etched frontispiece by Phiz.

The play is a dramatised version of the story of 'The Great Winglebury Duel', in 'The Sketches by Boz', with some few changes in the plot, and some alterations of the names of places and persons. Thus 'Great Winglebury' becomes a small anonymous town on the road to Gretna 'The Winglebury Arms' is turned into 'The St James's Arms'; 'Stiffun's Acre' (the scene of the proposed duel) is renamed 'Corpse Common'; instead of Mr Horace Hunter and Mrs Williamson, we have Mr Horatio Tinkles and Mrs Noakes; Miss Julia Manners turns her surname into Dobbs; and Mr Joseph Overton, his christian name into Owen; while Mr Alexander Trott figures as the Strange Gentleman, and is at last discovered to be Mr Walker Trott.

CHARACTERS

BROWN, Miss Emily – A young lady beloved by both Mr Trott (the Strange Gentleman) and Mr Tinkles, but married to the latter.

DOBBS, Miss Julia – A wealthy woman, formerly engaged to be married to a Mr Woolley, who died leaving her his property free from all encumbrances; the encumbrance of himself as a husband not being among the least Being desperately in want of a young husband, she falls in love with a certain wild and not very strong-minded nobleman, Lord Peter, who engages to run away with her to Gretna and be married. He fails to keep the appointment, however; and she gives her hand to Mr Trott (the Strange Gentleman) instead.

JOHN – A waiter at The St James's Arms.

JOHNSON, John – A hare-brained madcap, enamoured of Miss Mary Wilson, with whom he starts for Gretna Green, but is temporarily detained at The St James's Arms by his thoughtless liberality to the postboys, which leaves him absolutely penniless. A timely loan, however, enables him to continue his journey.

NOAKES, Mrs – Landlady of The St James's Arms.

OVERTON, Mr Owen – An attorney, who is mayor of the small town in which is The St James's Arms.

PETER, Lord – A sprig of nobility, very wild, but not very sagacious or strong-minded, who is in love with Miss Julia Dobbs – or her handsome fortune.

SPARKS, Tom – 'Boots' at The St James's Arms.

STRANGE GENTLEMAN, The – *See* **Trott, Mr Walker**.

TOMKINS, Charles – A young gentleman in love with Miss Fanny Wilson. He has arranged to run away with her to Gretna Green, and meets her for this purpose at The St James's Arms. As he has agreed not to disclose his name, she imagines that the Strange Gentleman staying at that house, and rumoured to be insane, but whom she has not seen, is her lover. When she meets Mr Tomkins, therefore, she acts upon the presumption that he is actually mad; and her conduct seems to him so strange, that he suspects her of playing him false, and works himself up into a tempest of jealousy, which only serves to confirm her belief in his lunacy. They are both, however, disabused at last, and set off without delay for their original destination.

TROTT, Mr Walker – *called* '**The Strange Gentleman**'. A young man desirous of marrying Miss Emily Brown, but deterred by the hostile attitude of Mr Horatio Tinkles, who challenges him to mortal combat (on Corpse Common) for daring to think of such a thing. He accepts the challenge in a bloodthirsty note, but immediately sends another, and an anonymous one, to the mayor, urging that a Strange Gentleman at The St James's Arms be forthwith arrested, as he is bent upon committing a rash and sanguinary act. By a ludicrous blunder, he is mistaken for Lord Peter, who is expected at the same house for the purpose of meeting Miss Julia Dobbs, his intended; and who is to be seized and carried off as an insane person, in order that his relatives may not discover him. As he is being forced into the carriage, however, the lady discovers that he is unknown to her; and she refuses to accompany him. At the same moment, a letter from his rival is put into his hands, saying that the challenge was a *ruse*, and that the writer is far on his way to Gretna to be married to Miss Emily Brown. Determined not to be thus balked of a wife, Mr Trott offers himself to Miss Dobbs on the spot, is accepted, and starts *instanter* for the same place in a post-chaise and four.

WILSON, Fanny – A young lady affianced to Mr Charles Tomkins.

WILSON, Mary – The *inamorata* of Mr John Johnson.

THE VILLAGE COQUETTES

This 'comic opera in two acts', for which Mr John Hullah composed the music, was written in 1835, and was brought out at the St James's Theatre, in London, on Tuesday evening, 6 December 1836. The libretto of the opera was published by Bentley in 1836, in a pamphlet of seventy-one pages, the dedication, to James Pritt Harley, being dated 15 December. The scene is laid in an English village, and the time is supposed to be the autumn of 1729.

BENSON, Lucy – A beautiful village girl betrothed to George Edmunds, a humble but worthy man. Squire Norton, a man much her superior in social station, tries to lead her astray, and for a time she coquettes with him; but she sees her error before it is too late, rejects the elopement he urges, and returns to her discarded lover.

BENSON, Old – Her father; a small farmer.

BENSON, Young – His son ; Lucy's brother.

EDMUNDS, George – A young man m love with Lucy Benson.

FLAM, The Honourable Sparkins – Friend to Squire Norton; fascinated by Rose, a village beauty, whom he ineffectually endeavours to lead from the path of virtue; though she is at first flattered by his attentions.

MADDOX, John – A young man attached to Rose.

NORTON, Squire – A country gentleman who attempts – but unsuccessfully – to seduce the fair Lucy Benson.

ROSE – Cousin to Lucy Benson; a lovely village maiden, whom the Honourable Sparkins Flam vainly seeks to ruin.

STOKES, Mr Martin – A very small farmer with a very large circle of particular friends.

IS SHE HIS WIFE? OR, SOMETHING SINGULAR

An unedited comic burletta, in one act, played at the St James's Theatre, on Monday, 6 March 1837. The part of the principal character, Mr Felix Tapkins, was taken by James Pritt Harley.

JOHN – Servant to Mr Lovetown.

LIMBURY, Mr Peter – A friend of Mr Felix Tapkins's; made furiously jealous by the attentions his wife receives from Mr Lovetown.

LIMBURY, Mrs – A vain, conceited woman, who carries on a flirtation with Mr Lovetown for the double purpose of assisting him in curing his wife of her self-tormenting suspicions, and of teaching her husband the misery of the jealous fears he has been accustomed to harbour.

LOVETOWN, Mr Alfred – A newly-married man perpetually yawning, and complaining of *ennui*. His wife, chagrined by his seeming indifference, determines to remove it, if she can, by wounding his vanity, and arousing his jealousy. She accordingly carries on a flirtation with a gay young bachelor (Mr Tapkins), which perfectly effects her object. Lovetown, stung to the quick, affects a passion for Mrs Limbury, which he does not feel, and to which she never really responds, with the double motive of obtaining opportunities of watching his wife, and of awaking any dormant feelings of affection for himself that may be slumbering in her bosom. In the carrying on of these intrigues, many amusing misunderstandings occur; but in the end mutual explanations remove all suspicions, and re-establish the confidence and affection which have temporarily been driven away.

LOVETOWN, Mrs – His wife.

TAPKINS, Mr Felix – A gay, good-hearted bachelor, who has a sufficient share of vanity, and who plumes himself on his gallantry. He resides at Rustic Lodge (near Reading), a remarkable cottage, with cardboard chimneys, Grecian balconies, Gothic parapets, and a thatched roof. Such a model of compactness is this house, that even the horse can't cough without his owner's hearing him; the stable being close to the dining-room windows. *See* **Lovetown, Mr Alfred.**

PUBLIC LIFE OF MR TULRUMBLE (Once Mayor of Mudfog)

(From *Bentley's Miscellany*, January, 1837)

JENNINGS, Mr – A gentleman with a pale face and light whiskers, whom Mr Tulrumble imports from London to act as his secretary.

SNIGGS, Mr – Predecessor of Mr Tulrumble in the mayoralty of Mudfog.

TULRUMBLE, Mrs – Wife of Mr Nicholas Tulrumble; a vulgar, ignorant woman.

TULRUMBLE, Mr Nicholas – A coal-dealer, who begins life in a wooden tenement of four feet square, with a capital of two-and-ninepence, and a stock-in-trade of three bushels and a half of coals. Being industrious and saving, he gradually gets rich, marries, builds Mudfog Hall (on something which he endeavours to delude himself into thinking a hill), retires from business altogether, grows vain and haughty, sets up for a public character and a great gentleman, and finally becomes Mayor of Mudfog. Having, when in London, been present at the Lord Mayor's show, Mr Tulrumble determines to have one of his own in Mudfog, which shall equal if not surpass it. He make arrangements, therefore, for a grand procession and dinner but the day of his inauguration is dim and dismal, the crowd is unreasonable and derisive, the show is a failure, the dinner is flat, and Nicholas is deeply disappointed. Getting statistical and philosophical, he exerts himself to prevent the granting of a new license to an old and popular inn, called The Jolly Boatmen, and commences a general crusade against beer-jugs and fiddles, forgetting the time when he was glad to drink out of the one and to dance to the other. He soon finds, however, that the people have come to hate him, and that his old friends shun him; he begins to grow tired of his new dignity and his lonely magnificence; and at last he dismisses his secretary, goes down to his old haunt, The Lighterman's Arms, tells his quondam companions that he is very sorry for having made a fool of himself, and hopes they will give him up his old chair in the chimney-corner again, which they do with great joy.

TULRUMBLE, Nicholas Junior – Their son. When his father becomes rich, he takes to smoking cigars, and calling the footman a 'feller'.

TWIGGER, Edward – *called* 'Bottle-Nosed Ned'. A merry-tempered, pleasant-faced, good-for-nothing sort of vagabond, with an invincible dislike of manual labour, and an unconquerable attachment to strong beer and spirits. He is engaged to take part in the procession in honour of the election of Mr Tulrumble as Mayor of Mudfog, and is to make his appearance in a complete suit of ancient brass armour of gigantic dimensions. Unfortunately, however, he gets drunk, makes a most extraordinary exhibition of himself, as well as a laughing-stock of the mayor, and has to be conducted home, where his wife, unable to get the armour off, tumbles him into bed, helmet, gauntlets, breastplate, and all.

TWIGGER, Mrs – His wife.

THE PANTOMIME OF LIFE

(Published in *Bentley's Miscellany*, March, 1837)

DO'EM – A confederate of Captain Fitz-Whisker Fiercy, acting as his livery-servant.

FIERCY, The Honourable Captain Fitz-Whisker – A swindler, who struts about with that compound air of conscious superiority and general blood-thirstiness which is characteristic of most military men, and which always excites the admiration and terror of mere plebeians. He dupes all the tradesmen in his neighbourhood by giving them orders for all sorts of articles which he afterwards disposes of to other dealers by means of his confederate, Do'em.

THE LAMPLIGHTER'S STORY

MR JOHN MACRONE, the publisher of the *Sketches by Boz*, died in 1841, leaving his wife and children in straitened circumstances. For their benefit, Dickens undertook to procure and supervise the publication of a series of voluntary literary contributions. These were issued in three volumes, by Henry Colburn, as: 'The Pic-Nic Papers. By various hands. Edited by Charles Dickens'. The work was illustrated by George Cruikshank and Phiz. It served the purpose for which it was intended, and brought Mrs Macrone the sum of three hundred pounds. Dickens wrote the Preface, and furnished the opening tale, called ' The Lamplighter's Story', which is a narrative version of a farce that he wrote in 1838 or 1839 for the manager of the Covent Garden Theatre.

BARKER, Miss Fanny – Niece to an old astrologer, who takes Tom Grig to be pointed out by the stars as her destined husband. He describes her as having 'a graceful carriage, an exquisite shape, a sweet voice, a countenance beaming with animation and expression, and the eye of a startled fawn'. She has also, he says, five thousand pounds in cash; and this attraction, added to the others, inclines Tom to marry her; but, when he finds that her uncle has borrowed and spent the whole sum in an unsuccessful search for the philosopher's-stone, he alters his mind, and declares that the scheme is 'no go', at which the uncle is enraged, and the niece is delighted, she being in love with another young man.

EMMA – Daughter of a crazy astrologer who has spent fifteen years in conducting fruitless experiments, having for their object the discovery of the philosopher's-stone. Her father designs marrying her to his partner, 'the gifted Mooney'; but he utterly refuses to take her, alleging that his 'contemplation of womankind' has led him to resolve that he 'will not adventure on the troubled sea of matrimony'.

GALILEO ISAAC NEWTON FLAMSTEAD – The christian-names of the son of the crazy astrologer who takes Tom Grig to be 'the favourite of the planets'. He is a tall, thin, dismal-faced young gentleman, in his twenty-first year; though his father, absorbed in chimerical projects, considers him 'a mere child', and hasn't provided him with a new suit of clothes since he was fourteen.

GRIG, Tom – A lamplighter who, on going his rounds one day, is accosted by one of the strangest and most mysterious-looking old gentlemen ever seen. This person proves to be a very learned astrologer, who is on the point of discovering the philosopher's-stone, which will turn everything into gold. He imagines that he has found in Tom a noble stranger, whose birth is shrouded in uncertainty, and who is destined by the stars to be the husband of his young and lovely niece. He therefore takes him into his house forthwith, and introduces him to the lady. She is greatly disturbed, and, suggests that the stars must have made a mistake; but is silenced by her uncle. After this, Tom accompanies the old gentleman to the observatory, where Mr Mooney – another scientific gentleman – casts his nativity, and horrifies him by predicting his death at exactly thirty-five minutes, twenty-seven seconds, and five-sixths of a second, past nine o'clock, am, on that day two months. Tom makes up his mind that, while alive, he had better be rich than poor, and so assents to the proposed marriage. The preliminaries are nearly concluded, when suddenly the crucible containing the ingredients of the miraculous stone explodes with a tremendous crash, and the labours of fifteen years are destroyed in an instant. Moreover, a mistake is discovered in the old gentleman's computation; and it turns out that Tom is to live to a green old age – eighty-seven, at least upon this, not caring for a portionless bride who doesn't love him, he utterly refuses to marry the lovely niece, whereupon her uncle, in a rage, wets his forefinger in some of the liquor from the crucible that was spilt on the floor, and draws a small triangle upon the forehead of the young lamplighter, who instantly finds himself in the *watch-house*, with the room swimming before his eyes.

MOONEY, Mr – *called* 'The Gifted'. A learned philosopher, with the dirtiest face we can possibly know of in this imperfect state of existence. He is so very absent-minded, that he always has to be brought to by means of an electric shock from a strongly-charged battery.

41

A Charles Dickens Chronology

1809 13 June: John Dickens (clerk in the Royal Navy Pay Office, Portsmouth Dockyard) marries Elizabeth Barrow at St Mary-le-Strand, London.

1810 28 October: Frances (Fanny) Dickens born (died 1848)

1812 7 February: Charles John Huffam (Huffham) Dickens (CD) born at Portsmouth.
March: CD baptised in Portsea Parish Church.
24 June: Family moves to Portsea.

1813 March: Alfred Dickens born (died in September)
December: Family moves to Southsea.

1814 June 24: John Dickens transferred to London, probably Somerset House.
Dickens family moves to Norfolk Street, St Pancras, London.

1815 Catherine Hogarth later Mrs CD born.

1816 Letitia Mary Dickens born (died 1893).

1817 John Dickens reappointed to Chatham.

1819 August: Harriet Ellen Dickens born (died 1822).

1820 July: Frederick William Dickens born (died 1868).

1821 Family moves to St Mary's Place, Chatham.
CD attends William Giles's school; writes a tragedy, *Misnar, the Sultan of India*.

1822 Alfred Lamert Dickens born (died 1860).
John Dickens transferred to London. Family moves to Camden Town.
CD left in Chatham with William Giles (schoolmaster).

1823 April: Fanny Dickens becomes boarder at Royal Academy of Music.

December: Mrs Dickens opens a school for young ladies, but without pupils.
CD living at home.

1824 February: John Dickens arrested for debt and imprisoned at King's Bench, later Marshalsea.
Mrs Dickens and younger children join him there.
CD lodging in Camden Town; employed at Warren's Blacking Warehouse through the agency of his cousin James Lamert.
May: John Dickens released.
June: CD removed from Warren's; sent to Wellington House Academy, Hampstead Road.

1825 Dickens family moves to Somers Town.
John Dickens retires with small Navy Pay Office pension.

1826 CD at Wellington House Academy.
John Dickens city correspondent for the *British Press*; it fails.

1827 Augustus Dickens born (dies 1866).
Dickens family evicted for non-payment of rates.
CD removed from Wellington House Academy, and Fanny from Royal Academy of Music.
CD becomes clerk at Ellis & Blackmore, solicitors.

1828 John Dickens working as a reporter for the *Morning Herald*.
CD employed by Charles Molloy, solicitor.

1829 CD learns shorthand; becomes a freelance reporter at Doctor's Commons, sharing Thomas Charlton's box to report legal proceedings.

1830 February: CD admitted reader at British Museum.
May: CD meets banker's daughter Maria Beadnell; falls in love.

1831 CD meets John Forster.
CD working for his uncle John Henry Barrow, reporting for the *Mirror of Parliament*.

1832 CD courting Maria Beadnell.
CD reporting for evening paper, the *True Sun*.
March: CD seeks auditions at Covent Garden Theatre but is ill on the day.

1833   CD produces private theatricals at his home in Bentinck
Street; ends affair with Maria Beadnell. CD's first story 'A
Dinner at Poplar Walk' (later titled 'Mr Minns and his
Cousin') published in *The Monthly Magazine*.

1834   January–August 1835: Eight more stories published in
Monthly Magazine, and another in *Bell's Weekly Magazine*.
CD becomes a reporter on the *Morning Chronicle*. *Street
Sketches* 1–5 published in the *Morning Chronicle*.
September–December: CD meets Catherine Hogarth. George
Hogarth, Catherine's father, commissions *Sketches of London*
for his new paper, the *Evening Chronicle*.
November: John Dickens arrested and detained for debt;
family home broken up.
On release John Dickens goes to lodgings in North End,
Hampstead.
December: Dickens family moves to 21 George Street,
Adelphi.
CD moves to 13 Furnival's Inn, Holborn.

1835   January–August: *Sketches of London* 1–20 published in *Evening
Chronicle*.
May: CD engaged to Catherine Hogarth; takes lodgings at
Queen's Elm, Brompton.
September–January 1836: *Scenes and Characters* 1–12
published in *Bell's Life in London*, two more stories in *The
Monthly Magazine* and twenty *Sketches of London* in *The
Evening Chronicle*.

1836   8 February: *Boz*, first series, published.
10 February: Chapman and Hall suggests first idea of *Picwick*
to CD.
17 February: CD and brother Fred move to chambers at 15
Furnival's Inn.
31 March: First of 20 monthly parts of *Picwick* published.
Two contributions to *The Library of Fiction*, and one to *Carlton
Chronicle*.
Two more *Scenes and Characters* in *Bell's Life*.
2 April: CD marries Catherine Hogarth at St Luke's Church,
Chelsea; honeymoon at Chalk, near Gravesend; return to live
at Furnival's Inn, with Fred Dickens and Catherine's sister
Mary.

20 April: Robert Seymour, illustrator of *Picwick*, commits suicide; succeeded by Hablot K Browne: 'Phiz'.

June: *Sunday under Three Heads* published.

6 August: *Hospital Patient* published in the *Carlton Chronicle*.

29 September: CD and Catherine staying at Petersham.

Strange Gentleman adapted from *Great Winglebury Duel*: begins 60-night run at St James's Theatre.

4 November: CD agrees to edit *Bentley's Miscellany;* he leaves the *Morning Chronicle*.

6 December: *Village Coquettes* produced at St James's Theatre.

17 December: *Boz*. second series, published.

22 December: *Village Coquettes* published.

25 December: Forster introduces CD to Harrison Ainsworth. *Strange Gentleman* published.

1837 1 January: First number of *Bentley's Miscellany* appears; contains the first *Mudfog* piece.

6 January: CD's first child, Charles Culliford Boz (Charley) Dickens born.

21 January: CD elected member of Garrick Club.

31 January: First of 24 instalments of *Oliver Twist* published in *Bentley's Miscellany*.

3 March: *Is She His Wife?* produced at St James's Theatre.

3 May: CD's first public speaking engagement at the Literary Fund Anniversary Dinner.

7 May: Mary Hogarth dies suddenly after a visit to the theatre.

CD, Catherine and Charley retire to Hampstead.

Writing *Pickwick* and *Oliver Twist* suspended for a month.

16 June: Forster introduces CD to William Charles Macready.

July: CD holidays in France and Belgium with Catherine and HKB.

31 August–September: CD and family at Broadstairs.

September: 'Boz' revealed as CD.

30 October: Last parts of *Pickwick* appear.

7 November: CD and Catherine at the Old Ship Hotel, Brighton.

17 November: *Pickwick* appears in one volume.

18 November: Dinner marks publication of *Pickwick*.

1838 30 January–6 February: CD and HKB examine Yorkshire schools.

10 February: *Sketches of Young Gentlemen* published.

26 February: *Memoirs of Grimaldi* published.

6 March: CD's second child, Mary (Mamie) born.

29 March: CD takes Catherine to the Star and Garter Hotel, Richmond, to convalesce and to celebrate their second wedding anniversary.

31 March: First of 20 monthly instalments of *Nicholas Nickleby*.

21 June: CD elected member of the Athenaeum Club.

September: CD and family in the Isle of Wight, staying at the Needles and Ventnor.

29 October–8 November: CD tours the Midlands and North Wales with HKB.

November 5: Forster joins them at Liverpool.

9 November: *Oliver Twist* published in 3 vols. *Lamplighter*, a play, written but not acted.

1839 January: CD begins writing *Barnaby Rudge*.

12–17 January: CD visits Manchester with Harrison Ainsworth and Forster.

31 January: CD relinquishes editorship of *Bentley's Miscellany*.

4–11 March: CD visits Exeter to find a home for his parents; stays at the New London Inn, and settles on Mile-End Cottage, Alphington.

13 March: CD elected to Literary Fund Committee.

March: Last part of *Oliver Twist* appears.

31 April–31 August: CD and family at Elm Cottage, Petersham.

June: First complete edition of *Boz* published. *The Loving Ballad of Lord Bateman* published.

September–October: CD and family at Broadstairs.

1 October: CD completes *Nicholas Nickleby*.

23 October: Serialisation of *Nicholas Nickleby* completed, and published in one volume.

6 December: CD's third child, Kate Macready Dickens born. CD enrols as a student of Middle Temple, but does not 'eat dinners' until many years later.

December: CD and family move to 1 Devonshire Terrace, Regent's Park.

1840   10 February: *Sketches of Young Couples* published.
CD writing *Master Humphrey's Clock*.
29 February–4 March: CD at Bath with Forster, visiting Walter Savage Landor.
March: CD writing *Barnaby Rudge* and *The Old Curiosity Shop*.
3 April: CD, Catherine, and Forster visit Birmingham, Stratford-upon-Avon, and Lichfield.
4 April: First part of *Master Humphrey's Clock* appears.
25 April: The first of 40 instalments of *The Old Curiosity Shop* appears in the fourth number of *Master Humphrey's Clock*.
June: CD and family at Broadstairs.
29–30 June: CD, Forster, and Maclise visit Rochester and Cobham.
27 July–4 August: CD visits his parents in Devon.
30 August–October: CD at Lawn House, Broadstairs, with family.
15 October: First volume *Master Humphrey's Clock* published.

1841   January: CD completes *The Old Curiosity Shop*.
6 February: End of serialisation of *The Old Curiosity Shop*.
8 February: CD's fourth child, Walter Landor Dickens, born.
13 February: *Bar* begins publication in 42 weekly instalments in *Master Humphrey's Clock*.
24 February–3 March: CD and Catherine at the Old Ship Hotel, Brighton.
?12–15 April: Second volume *Master Humphrey's Clock* published.
29 March: CD declines invitation to become Liberal parliamentary candidate for Reading.
19 June: CD and Catherine set off for Scotland.
22 June–4 July: Staying at the Royal Hotel Edinburgh. CD writing *Master Humphrey's Clock*.
25 June: Dinner in CD's honour at Waterloo Rooms, Edinburgh.
29 June: CD granted Freedom of City of Edinburgh.
4–16 July: CD and Catherine tour Scotland, with the sculptor Angus Fletcher.
18 July: CD and Catherine return to London.
1 August–2 October: CD and family at Lawn House, Broadstairs.

9 August: The *Pic-Nic Papers* published, containing *Lamplighter's Story*.

2–5 October: CD and Forster visit Rochester, Cobham and Gravesend.

8 October: CD undergoes an operation for fistula; convalescent during the following weeks.

24 October: Death of George Thomson Hogarth, CD's brother-in-law.

6–20 November: CD, still unwell, goes to Windsor to rest at the White Hart Hotel. *Barnaby Rudge* finished.

27 November: End of *Barnaby Rudge* serialisation.

4 December: End of *Master Humphrey's Clock* serialisation.

15 December: *Master Humphrey's Clock*, vol III, single-volume editions of *The Old Curiosity Shop* and *Barnaby Rudge*.

1842   4 January: CD and Catherine sail on their first visit to Boston, America.

CD meets Longfellow; speaks on international copyright in Boston.

February: CD and Catherine in Worcester, Springfield, Hartford, New Haven and New York.

CD meets Washington Irving.

CD investigates conditions in gaols.

CD speaks on international copyright at Hartford.

March: CD and Catherine in Philadelphia, Washington, Richmond, Baltimore, York, and Harrisburgh. CD investigates gaols in Philadelphia; criticises slavery in Richmond.

April: CD and Catherine in Pittsburgh, Cincinnati, Louisville, St. Louis, Sandusky, and Buffalo.

CD inspects solitary confinement prison in Pittsburgh.

May: CD and Catherine at Niagara, Toronto, Kingston, and Montreal, where CD performs in private theatricals with guards officers.

1 July: CD and Catherine arrive back in England, stay briefly at Broadstairs; then return to London; Georgina Hogarth joins the household.

August: CD and family at Broadstairs.

18 October: CD writing *American Notes*.

October–November: CD, Forster, and Maclise make a 'bachelor' excursion to Cornwall.

31 December: First of 20 instalments of *Martin Chuzzlewit*.

1843   January: First part of *Martin Chuzzlewit* appears.

June: CD rents Cobley's Farm, Finchley, for a month's concentrated *Martin Chuzzlewit* work.

August: CD and family at Albion Street, Broadstairs.

4–6 October: CD presides at opening of Athenaeum Club, Manchester.

October–November: CD writing *A Christmas Carol*.

19 December: *A Christmas Carol* published.

1844   January: CD successfully takes proceedings in Chancery against pirates of his works.

15 January: CD's fifth child, Francis Jeffrey (Frank) Dickens born.

26 February: CD takes the chair at the Mechanics' Institute, Liverpool.

28 February: CD takes the chair at the Polytechnic Institution, Birmingham.

May: CD lets 1 Devonshire Terrace pending a visit to Italy; family move to 9 Osnaburgh Terrace.

June: CD leaves Chapman & Hall for Bradbury & Evans; completes *Martin Chuzzlewit*.

July: *Martin Chuzzlewit* published as a book.

CD family leaves for Italy, arriving at Genoa 16 July.

10 October–3 November: CD writing *A Christmas Carol*.

6 November: CD starts alone for England.

3 December: In London, CD reads *A Christmas Carol* to a group of friends at Forster's house.

December: *A Christmas Carol* published as Chapman & Hall's Christmas Book for 1844.

13 December: CD leaves Paris for Genoa.

6 December: *A Christmas Carol* published.

1845   20 January: CD and Catherine leave Genoa for Rome via Carrara, Pisa and Siena, arriving 30 January.

February–April: CD and Catherine visit Naples; joined by Georgina Hogarth. From Naples, they return to Rome, then visit Florence before returning to Genoa (9 April).

June: CD, Catherine, and Georgina Hogarth leave Genoa for England via Switzerland; joined in Brussels by Maclise, Jerrold, and Forster, and arrive back in London at the end of June.

CD conceives idea for *The Cricket on the Hearth*.

July: CD engages Fanny Kelly's theatre, Dean Street, Soho, for amateur productions.

August: CD family at Broadstairs for three weeks.

21 September: Jonson's *Every Man in his Humour* produced at Fanny Kelly's theatre; CD plays Bobadil.

October: CD writing *The Cricket on the Hearth*.

28 October: CD's sixth child, Alfred D'Orsay Tennyson Dickens, born.

Performance of *The Elder Brother* (Beaumont and Fletcher) at Fanny Kelly's theatre.

December: *The Cricket on the Hearth* published. CD begins writing *Pictures from Italy*.

1846 21 January: First issue of *Daily News* appears; editor CD. *Pictures from Italy* begins publication in it.

9 February: CD resigns editorship of *Daily News*.

2 March: Serialisation of *Pictures from Italy* ends; published as a book.

31 March: CD and family to Switzerland, settle at the Villa Rosemont, Lausanne. CD becomes interested in Swiss prison reform and Haldimand's work for the blind.

CD writing *Life of our Lord* (not published until 1934).

18 May: *Pictures from Italy* published.

27 June: CD begins *Dombey and Son*.

30 September: CD interrupts *Dombey and Son* to write *The Battle of Life*, which begins serialization in 20 monthly numbers.

October: CD completes *The Battle of Life*. First monthly part of *Dombey and Son* appears.

20 November: CD family arrive in Paris for a three month stay *en route* for England. They stay at the Hotel Brighton; then rent 48 Rue de Courcelles, home of the Marquis de Castellane.

19 December: *The Battle of Life* published.

15–23 December: CD in London; attends rehearsals of a version of *The Battle of Life* dramatised by Albert Smith; returns to Paris.

1847 January–February: CD and family in Paris. CD writing *Dombey and Son*.

February: Charley, at King's College School has scarlet fever; CD and family return to London prematurely, staying at the Victoria Hotel, Euston Square because their own house is still let.

18 April: CD's seventh child, Sydney Smith Haldimand Dickens born.

May: CD and Catherine, Georgina Hogarth, and Charley holiday at Brighton.

June–September: CD and family at the Albion Hotel, Broadstairs. CD writing *Dombey and Son*. Begins *The Haunted Man*; not resumed until winter 1848.

July: CD appears at Manchester and Liverpool in *Every Man in his Humour* with a cast of friends and relatives, for benefit of Leigh Hunt and John Poole. The play proper followed on alternate nights by farces: *A Good Night's Rest*, *Turning the Tables* and *Comfortable Lodgings*, or *Paris in 1750*.

CD writes an account of the Tour, 'A New Piljians Projiss', in the character of Mrs Gamp, to be sold to augment the benefit fund. This never appeared because of the failure of the artists to provide illustrations.

September: CD and family return to Devonshire Terrace.

1 December: CD chairs a meeting of Leeds Mechanics' Society.

28 December: CD in Scotland, opening the Glasgow Athenaeum; visits Edinburgh, where Catherine is taken ill, and they stay over the New Year period.

1848   March: Last part of *Dombey and Son* finished.

April: CD and his company give eight performances in London in aid of the purchase and preservation of Shakespeare's birthplace, Stratford-upon-Avon. In *The Merry Wives of Windsor*, CD plays Justice Shallow; they also perform a farce: *Love, Law and Physick*.

Last part of *Dombey and Son* appears; published in book form.

April–July: CD touring with the plays, visiting Manchester, Liverpool, Birmingham, Edinburgh and Glasgow.

Summer: CD and family holiday at Broadstairs.

August: Fanny Burnett, CD's sister, dies.

November: CD at the Bedford Hotel, Brighton; writing *The Haunted Man*.

19 December: *The Haunted Man* published.

31 December: CD, Forster, Leech and Lemon visit Norwich and Yarmouth.

1849   15 January: CD's eighth child, Henry Fielding Dickens born.
February–June: CD and family at Brighton. CD writing *David Copperfield*.

May: First number of *David Copperfield* appears.

30 April: First of 20 instalments of *David Copperfield*.

July: CD and family at Fort House, Broadstairs.

July–October: CD, family, and friends at Bonchurch, Isle of Wight.

1 October: CD's enthusiasm for IoW wanes suddenly; the family returns to Broadstairs.

7 October: In a letter to Forster, CD outlines the details of the proposed journal *Household Words*, an oft-recurring idea which he has worked out at Bonchurch and Broadstairs.

November: CD and Catherine make first visit to Rockingham Castle, Northamptonshire.

1850   30 March: First number of *Household Words* appears; CD editor.

April: CD, Catherine and Georgina Hogarth spend a week at Knebworth to discuss with Bulwer-Lytton his scheme for creating a Guild of Literature and Art to assist needy writers and artists.

June: Dinner at Star and Garter, Richmond, in honour of *David Copperfield*.

CD visits France with Maclise to see plays and pictures.

July: CD and family at Fort House, Broadstairs.

16 August: CD's ninth child, Dora Annie Dickens born in London.

Dickens joins his Catherine for the event; re-joins Georgina and his children at Broadstairs.

October: CD back at Devonshire Terrace. *David Copperfield* finished.

November: Rehearsals at Knebworth for *Every Man in his Humour*, to be given in aid of the Guild of Literature and Art. Three private performances of *Every Man* given in the hall at Knebworth, followed by the farces *Animal Magnetism* and *Turning the Tables*, CD acting and directing.

CD writing *A Child's History of England*.

Serialisation of *David Copperfield* completed; it appears in book form.

1851　January: Performances of *Animal Magnetism* and *Used Up* at Rockingham Castle.

Serialization of *A Child's History of England* begins in *Household Words*.

February: CD visits Paris with Leech and the Hon Spencer Lyttleton.

March: Catherine Dickens suffers a nervous collapse and goes to Malvern to recover.

CD visits her, but is recalled to London to his ailing father.

31 March: John Dickens dies in London.

14 April: CD takes the chair at the General Theatrical Fund meeting. Forster withholds the news until afterwards that CD's daughter Dora Annie has died at Devonshire Terrace.

16 May: CD directs and plays in Bulwer-Lytton's *Not so bad as we Seem* at Devonshire House, Piccadilly, home of the Duke of Devonshire, in aid of Guild of Literature.

27 May: A second presentation at Devonshire House, at which CD plays in his own farce, *Nightingale's Diary*.

The play is published privately.

May–June: CD decides to move his family to a larger house on the expiration of the Devonshire Terrace lease. He decides on Tavistock House, Bloomsbury, and supervises improvements.

May (late): CD and family at Fort House, Broadstairs, for the last time; CD driven out by the incessant noise of German bands and other street musicians.

CD family and Georgina Hogarth move into Tavistock House.

November: Catherine Dickens's only publication, a cookery book *What Shall We Have for Dinner?* appears under the pseudonym Lady Maria Clutterbuck.

CD begins writing *Bleak House*.

1852　March: *Bleak House* begins serialization in 20 monthly numbers.

13 March: CD's tenth child, Edward Bulwer Lytton Dickens born.

July–October: CD's children staying at Camden Crescent, Dover, while he, accompanied by Catherine and Georgina Hogarth, tours in performances of Bulwer-Lytton's *Not so Bad as we Seem* at Derby, Sheffield, Nottingham, Sunderland, Newcastle, Manchester and Liverpool.

Deaths of his friends, Count D'Orsay, in August, and Mrs Macready, in September.

October: CD, Catherine and Georgina Hogarth in Boulogne, experimenting with it as a holiday place, after which they return to London for the rest of the year.

CD working on *Bleak House*; also on *To be Read at Dusk* for *The Keepsake* at about this time.

December: First bound volume of *A Child's History of England* appears.

Christmas Books appears.

1853   January: CD receives ovation and presentations at Birmingham for his services to the Mechanics' institute. At Twelfth Night banquet CD makes offer to Midland Institute. Charley Dickens leaves Eton and goes to study at Leipzig.

CD writing *Bleak House*, and *A Child's History of England*, and editing *Household Words*.

13 June: CD returns to Boulogne to escape nervous breakdown. Catherine and Georgina Hogarth accompany him and the family follow three weeks later.

August: CD completes *Bleak House*.

September: CD completes *A Child's History of England*. Last monthly part of *Bleak House* appears, and it is published in volume form.

October–December: CD sends family home and goes on a trip to Italy with Wilkie Collins and Augustus Egg. Revisits Haldimand's institution. Revisits Genoa, Naples, Rome, Florence, Venice.

Mid-December: CD returns to London.

10 December: *A Child's History of England* ends in *Household Words*. Second bound volume appears.

27 December: CD gives his first public reading, *Christmas Carol*, at Birmingham Town Hall, followed on December 29 by *Cricket*, and *Christmas Carol* again on December 30. Henceforth, reading from his works in London and the provinces occupies much of his time and energy.

1854   6 January: Twelfth Night celebrations at Tavistock House with *Tom Thumb* performed by the family.

January: CD in Preston. CD collecting material for *Hard Times*, which he begins.

1 April: First instalment of *Hard Times* in *Household Words*.

June–October: CD at Boulogne at the Villa Camp de Droite.

CD writing *Hard Times*.

12 August: Last instalment of *Hard Times* appears. It appears this month in volume form.

October: CD returns to Tavistock House.

December: Third and last bound volume of *A Child's History of England* appears.

1855   6 January: Twelfth Night celebrations at Tavistock House: performance of *Fortunio and His Seven   Gifted Servants*.

February: CD spends fortnight in Paris with Wilkie Collins.

May: CD meets again Maria Winter, *née* Beadnell, and suffers disappointment in her.

June: Amateur theatricals at Tavistock House: *The Lighthouse*, *Nightingale's Diary*, and *Animal Magnetism*.

CD begins writing *Little Dorrit*, first called *Nobody's Fault*.

July: CD at 3 Albion Villas, Folkestone.

CD and family winter in Paris. CD writing *Little Dorrit*.

CD sits for Ary Scheffer for his portrait and meets the *élite* of Paris, including George Sand.

1 December: *Little Dorrit* begins serialization in 20 monthly numbers.

1856   14 March: CD pays the purchase money for Gad's Hill Place. Returns to Paris until May.

CD at Boulogne with family.

June–August: CD returns to London.

September: CD writing *Little Dorrit*.

November: Collins's melodrama *The Frozen Deep*.

1857   6, 8, 12, 14 January: *The Frozen Deep* acted at Tavistock House, followed by farces *Animal Magnetism* and *Uncle John*.

February: CD gets possession of Gad's Hill Place.

June: Last instalment of *Little Dorrit* appears, and it appears in volume form.

8 June: Douglas Jerrold, journalist and friend of CD, dies.

4 July: *The Frozen Deep* given as benefit performance for widow of Douglas Jerrold at Gallery of Illustration in Regent Street.

20 July: Walter CD leaves for India.

July: Marital discord between CD and Catherine grows.

August: CD meets Ellen Ternan and she goes with his troupe to Manchester to play in the benefit performances of the *Frozen Deep* on August 21 and 22.

September: CD tours through the North of England with Wilkie Collins.

CD and Collins acquire material for *Two Apprentices*.

3–31 October: *The Lazy Tour of Two Idle Apprentices*, by CD and Wilkie Collins appears in *Household Words*.

1858   February: CD throws himself into work for Hospital for Sick Children.

15 April: CD gives reading in aid of Hospital.

29 April: First of the many public readings for CD's own benefit given at St Martin's Hall, London.

Reprinted Pieces collected in 8th volume of Library Edition of CD's works (Chapman & Hall).

May: CD and Catherine separate.

12 June: CD makes unwise public statement in *Household Words* and quarrels with publishers Bradbury & Evans.

2 August–13 November: First provincial Reading Tour, 44 stops, 87 readings, beginning at Clifton, ending at Brighton, taking in Ireland and Scotland.

1859   28 January: CD chooses title of *All the Year Round* for a new weekly journal.

February: Takes office at 11 Wellington Street, Strand.

March: CD begins writing *A Tale of Two Cities*.

30 April: First number of *All the Year Round* appears, containing opening instalment of *Two Cities*. As owner-editor, CD contributed to it throughout the remainder of his life, and willed his share in it to his son Charley. Chapman & Hall agree to publish the remainder of his books.

28 May: Last number of *Household Words* appears.

Summer: CD at Gad's Hill with daughters, younger sons, and Georgina Hogarth as housekeeper. Moves to Broadstairs for a week at the end of the summer. Finishes *A Tale of Two Cities*.

20 August: First part of *Hunted Down* (in three parts) published in *New York Ledger*.

10–27 October: Second provincial Reading Tour.

26 November: Last instalment of *A Tale of Two Cities* appears.

December: *A Tale of Two Cities* appears in volume form.

1860   28 January: *The Uncommercial Traveller* begins in *All the Year Round*.

17 July: Katey Dickens marries Charles Allston Collins.

27 July: Alfred Lamert Dickens dies in Manchester.

July: CD gives up Tavistock House.

September: CD settles at Gad's Hill as his permanent residence.

October: CD begins writing *Great Expectations*.

November: CD and Wilkie Collins visit Devon and Cornwall.

1 December: First instalment of *Great Expectations* appears in *All the Year Round*.

December: First collection of *Uncommercial Traveller* pieces in book form appears.

1861   March: CD takes 3 Hanover Terrace, Regent's Park, as London base.

CD writing *Great Expectations*. Sydney Dickens appointed to HMS *Orlando*.

March–April: Second series of readings begins at St James's Hill, ending April 18.

June: CD at Gad's Hill; finishes writing *Great Expectations*.

3 August: Last instalment of *Great Expectations* appears, and the work is published in 2 volumes.

28 October: A long series of provincial readings begins at Norwich, taking in Berwick upon Tweed, Lancaster, Bury St Edmunds, Cheltenham, Carlisle, Hastings, Plymouth, Birmingham, Canterbury, Torquay, Preston, Ipswich, Manchester, Brighton, Colchester, Dover, and Newcastle.

October: CD's tour manager, Arthur Smith, dies. Henry Austin, CD's brother-in-law, dies.

October–January 1862: Second provincial Reading Tour.

November: CD Junior, marries Bessie Evans, daughter of CD's one-time publisher.

1862   January: Provincial readings end at Chester.

February: CD takes 16 Hyde Park Gate for three months.

March: Georgina Hogarth seriously ill.

March–June: Series of London readings at St James's Hall, ending in mid-June.

October–December: CD takes Georgina Hogarth and Mamie CD to Paris.

December: CD home for Christmas.

1863   January: CD returns to Paris with Georgina Hogarth and Mamie.

CD gives four readings at the British Embassy, Paris, for British Charitable Fund.

February: CD and his companions return to London.

June: CD gives 13 readings at the Hanover Square Rooms.

12 September: Death of CD's mother. CD begins writing *Mutual Friend*.

November: CD at Gad's Hill.

24 December: Death of Thackeray.

31 December: Death of Walter, CD's fourth child, in India.

1864   January: Frank Dickens starts for India.

February: CD moves London base to 57 Gloucester Place. CD writing *Our Mutual Friend*.

1 May: First of 20 episodes of *Our Mutual Friend* published.

June: CD leaves London and returns to Gad's Hill for the remainder of year.

29 October: Death of John Leech.

December: Swiss chalet arrives at Gad's Hill, the gift of Fechter.

1865   February: CD attacked by pain and lameness in left foot, probably early symptom of thrombosis.

March: CD takes furnished house at 16 Somers Place, Hyde Park, until June.

June: CD takes short holiday in Paris, possibly accompanied by Ellen Ternan and her mother.

CD writing *Our Mutual Friend*.

9 June: CD and Ellen Ternan in serious railway accident it Staplehurst, Kent.

CD uninjured but permanently affected by shock.

November: Last part of *Our Mutual Friend* appears, and the work is published in volume form.

December: Second collection of *Uncommercial Traveller* pieces appears in book form.

1866   March: CD takes furnished house, 6 Southwick Place, Hyde Park. Suffers from heart trouble and general ill-health. CD accepts offer from Chappells of Bond Street to undertake 30 readings.

April: CD shocked by news of death of Jane Welsh Carlyle. Reading tour begins at Liverpool.

June: Tour ends. CD complains to various correspondents of exhaustion, and pain in left eye, hand, and foot. Returns to Gad's Hill for remainder of year.

6 October: Augustus Dickens dies impoverished in Chicago.

December: 'Mugby Junction' published in *All the Year Round*.

1867 January: CD begins new series of 50 provincial readings at Liverpool, taking in Scotland and Ireland.

15 January: CD complains of exhaustion and faintness, and of nervousness produced by rail travel.

May: Death of CD's close friend Clarkson Stanfield.

14 May: Tour ends. After it, CD tells Forster of American offers, and that he is tempted to undertake an American tour.

August: CD suffers severely from pain and swelling in foot, and is unable to walk.

Forster tries to dissuade him from undertaking the American trip. Dolby sails for America to reconnoitre; he reports favourably on American conditions.

30 September: CD telegraphs acceptance to J T Fields in Boston.

October–November: CD writes his last Christmas piece (with Wilkie Collins), *No Thoroughfare*, for *All the Year Round*. This and other Christmas pieces from *Household Words* and *All the Year Round* are now familiar as *Christmas Stories*.

9 November: CD sails for America; arrives in Boston 19 November.

2 December: CD writes home of severe weather and trials of travelling, but enjoys warm hospitality in New England. CD gives first reading in Boston; is now making a clear profit of £1300 a week.

9 December: Gives first reading in New York.

26 December: First production of *No Thoroughfare*.

27 December: In New York, CD calls in doctor to treat persistent cold and catarrh.

1868 January–February: CD still unwell. Comments on improvements in American condition since his first visit. Reads in New York, Brooklyn, Philadelphia, Baltimore, Washington, (where he meets President Andrew Johnson).

February: 'Silverman' published in *Household Words*.

January–March: *George Silverman's Explanation* published in *The Atlantic Monthly*.

January–May: *Holiday Romance* simultaneously begins publication in *Our Young Folks* (USA) and *All the Year Round*.

March: CD revisits Niagara. Complains of being 'nearly used up'. Reads in Rochester, Syracuse, Buffalo, Springfield, Utica, Portland, New Bedford, &c. Returns to Boston.

April: Public dinner given for CD at Deimonico's. Farewell readings in Boston and New York.

22 April: CD leaves New York and sets sail for England.

1 May: CD arrives in England. Appears in better health.

Summer: Throughout summer CD entertains American and other friends at Gad's Hill.

September: CD's youngest son, Edward Bulwer Lytton D, sails for Australia.

5 October: CD starts Farewell Reading Tour for Chappells.

20 October: CD's only surviving brother Fred dies.

November: Reading tour interrupted for anticipated general election. CD works up his 'Murder of Nancy' reading and first presents it privately at St James's Hall, London, on November 14.

1869   January: Readings resume; first public hearing of the *Murder of Nancy* is on January 5.

5 January: First public reading of *Sikes and Nancy*.

22 April: At Preston, CD is ordered by Dr Beard and Sir Thomas Watson to discontinue readings, as paralysis threatens. The audience's money is returned and Dr Beard escorts CD back to London. He is still unwell, but promises Chappells a series of London farewell readings.

CD conceives first ideas of *The Mystery of Edwin Drood*.

July: CD begins writing *The Mystery of Edwin Drood*

October: CD at Gad's Hill.

1870   January: CD visits Ellen Ternan regularly at Windsor Lodge, Peckham.

Suffers much pain in left hand and failure in left eye.

11 January: CD begins Twelve Farewell Readings at St James's Hall.

9 March: CD received by Queen Victoria at Buckingham Palace.

15 March: CD gives final reading at St James's Hall.

1 April: First number of *The Mystery of Edwin Drood* appears, only six of the intended twelve completed when CD died.

30 April: CD attends Royal Academy Dinner; returns thanks for 'Literature'.

May: CD Has to refuse invitation to attend Queen's ball because of illness.

29 May: CD writes last letter to Forster.

7 June: CD drives from Gad's Hill to Cobham with Georgina Hogarth and walks in Cobham Park; expresses to her his desire to be buried at Rochester.

8 June: CD taken ill after a day of writing EdD; it is left unfinished.

9 June: CD dies of cerebral haemorrhage.

14 June: CD Buried in Poets' Corner, Westminster Abbey.

12 August: First bound publication of *The Mystery of Edwin Drood*.

September: Sixth and last part of *The Mystery of Edwin Drood* appears.

42

Some Members of Charles Dickens's Circle

Agassis, Jean Louis Rodolph (1807–73) Swiss–American naturalist, geologist and teacher.

Ainsworth, William Harrison (1805–82) Lawyer, publisher and author.

Andersen, Hans Christian (1805–75) Danish singer, dancer, schoolmaster and folklorist.

Austin, Henry (d 1861) Architect and artist. Married Dickens's sister Letitia (1816–93) in 1837.

Barham, Richard Harris (1788–1845) Author and divine.

Barrow, Charles (1750–1826) Father of Elizabeth Barrow and father-in-law of John Dickens.

—— **Edward** (1798–1869) Son of Charles Barrow, younger brother of John Henry Barrow, and uncle of Charles Dickens.

—— **Elizabeth** *See* **Dickens, Mrs John.**

—— **John Henry** (1796–1858) Brother of Elizabeth Barrow. Author and barrister.

—— **Thomas Culliford** (?1793–1857) CD's Uncle. Civil servant.

Beadnell, Maria (1810–86) CD's first love.

Beard, Dr Francis Carr (1814–93) CD's doctor.

—— **Thomas** (1807–91) Journalist.

Bentley, Richard (1794–1871) Publisher.

Blackmore, Edward – Solicitor; CD's first employer.

Blessington, Marguerite, Countess of (1789–1849) London hostess.

Boyle, Mary (1810–90) Amateur actress.

Bradbury & Evans – CD's publisher after Chapman & Hall.

Brown, Anne, later Anne Cornelius – D family maid.

Brown, Hablot Knight *alias* Phiz (1815–82) Watercolour painter and book illustrator.

Burdett-Coutts, Angela Georgina (1814–1806) Heiress and philanthropist.

Burnett, Henry (1811–93) CD's brother-in-law (wife of Frances). Singer and music teacher.

Carlyle, Mrs Jane Baillie Welsh (1801–66) Scottish poetess. Wife of Thomas Carlyle.

—— **Thomas** (1795–1881) Scottish essayist and historian.

Cattermole, George (1800–68) Painter.

Chapman, Edward (1804–80) With William Hall, CD's first publisher.

—— **Frederic** (1823–95) Cousin of Edward Chapman. Publisher.

Clarke, Mrs Charles Cowden (Mary Victoria née Novello) (1809–98) Author and amateur actress

Colburn, Henry (d 1855) Publisher and magazine proprietor.

Collins, Charles Allston (1828–73) Artist.

—— **Mrs Charles Allston** née Kate Macready Dickens; CD's second daughter.

—— **William Wilkie** (1824–88) Barrister and author.

Cruikshank, George (1792–1878) Artist and caricaturist.

Dickens, Alfred D'Orsay Tennyson (1845–1912) CD's fourth son.

—— **Alfred Lamert** (1822–60) CD's younger brother. Civil engineer and sanitary inspector.

—— **Augustus** (1827–66) CD's youngest brother.

—— **Charles Culliford Boz** (1837–96) CD's eldest son. Bank clerk, tea merchant, paper manufacturer and editor.

—— **Charles John Huffam** *alias* Boz (1812–1870)

—— **Mrs Charles John Huffam** née Catherine Hogarth (1815–79) CD's wife.

—— **Dora Annie** (1850–1) CD's youngest daughter.

—— **Edward Bulwer Lytton** alias Plorn (1852–1902) CD's tenth and last child.

—— **Frances Elizabeth** (Fanny) (1810–48) Musician and teacher. CD's elder sister.

—— **Francis Jeffrey** (Frank) (1844–86) CD's third son.

—— **Frederick William** (1820–68) CD's younger brother.

—— **Henry Fielding** *alias* Harry (1849–1933) CD's sixth son. Barrister.

—— **John** (1785–1851) CD's father.

—— **Mrs John** née Elizabeth Barrow (1789–1863) CD's mother.

—— **Kate Macready** (1839–1929) CD's second daughter. Artist.

—— **Mary** *alias* Mamie (1838–96) CD's eldest daughter. Authoress.

—— **Sydney Smith Haldimand** *alias* Ocean Spectre > Hoshen Peck > The Admiral (1847–72) CD's fifth son. Sailor.

—— **Walter Landor** *alias* **Young Skull** (1841–63) CD's second son. Army officer.

Dolby, George – CD's reading manager 1866 – 1870.

D'Orsay, Alfred Guillaume Gabriel, Count (1801–52) Artist.

Doyle, Richard (1824–83) Artist and caricaturist. Uncle of Sir Arthur Conan Doyle.

Egg, Augustus Leopold (1816–63) Painter.

Emerson, Ralph Waldo (1803–82) American poet and essayist.

Fechter, Charles (1822–79) Swiss actor–manager.

Field, Inspector Charles – Detective.

Fields, James T (d 1880) American publisher and editor.

—— **Mrs James T** (Annie) Wife of the above.

Fildes, Sir Luke, RA (1844–1927) Painter.

Fitzgerald, Percy – A CD admirer and founder of The Boz Club.

Forster, John *alias* Fuz (1812–76) Historian and biographer.

Gaskell, Mrs Elizabeth Cleghorn (1810–65) Novelist of Knutsford.

Giles, The Revd William, FRGS (1798–1856) Baptist minister; CD's first schoolmaster.

Grip – one of CD's two pet ravens.

Haldimand, William (1784–1862) Banker, MP and philanthropist.

Hall, William *See* **Chapman, Edward**.

Harte, Francis Brett (1836–1902) American author.

Hogarth, George (1783–1870) Father of *inter alia* Catherine (CD's wife), Mary, and Georgina Hogarth Lawyer, musician and journalist.

—— **Mrs George** (Georgina) (1793–1863) Wife of George Hogarth; CD's mother-in-law.

—— **Georgina** (1827–1917) CD's second sister-in-law and editor.

—— **Mary Scott** (1819–37) CD's first sister-in-law.

Hood, Thomas (1799–1845) Poet, humorist and editor.

Huffam, Christopher – CD's godfather. RN blockmaker and rigger.

Hunt, James Henry Leigh (1784–1859) Essayist and poet.

Irving, Washington (1783–1859) American lawyer and writer.

Jerrold, Douglas William (1803–57) Author and humorist.

Jones, William (1777–1836) Headmaster.

Kent, William Charles – Editor.

Kolle, Henry William (1808–81) Bank clerk and manufacturer.

Lamert, James – Step-cousin of CD.

Landon, Letitia Elizabeth *alias* LEL (1802–38) Poetess and novelist

Landor, Walter Savage (1775–1864) Poet and author. Godfather to CD's son Walter.

Landseer, Sir Edwin Henry (1802–73) Animal painter.

Layard, Sir Austen Henry (1817–94) Archaeologist and politician.

Leech, John (1817–64) Humorous artist.

Lemon, Mark (1809–70) Writer and editor.

Lewes, George Henry (1817–78) Author.

Linda – A Gad's Hill St Bernard.

Linton, Mrs Eliza Lynn (1822–98) Authoress.

Longfellow, Henry Wadsworth (1807–82) American poet.

Lowell, James Russell (1810–91) American author and diplomatist.

Lytton, Edward George Earle Bulwer-Lytton, first Baron (1803–73) Writer and social reformer.

Maclise, Daniel (1806–70) Irish-born artist.

Macready, William Charles (1793–1873) Actor.

Macrone, John (1809–37) Publisher.

Millais, Sir John Everett (1829–96) Pre-Raphaelite: PRA; PRB.

Milner-Gibson, Thomas (1806–84) MP.

Milnes, Richard Monckton, first Baron Houghton (1809–85) Politician and litterateur.

Mitton, Thomas (1812–78) A friend of CD's boyhood. Solicitor.

Mrs Bouncer (1859–74) Mamie D's white Pomeranian dog.

Ouvry, Frederic (1814–81) CD's friend and solicitor.

Perugini, Carlo (*c* 1839–1918) Artist.

—— **Mrs Carlo** *See* **Dickens, Kate Macready**.

'Phiz' *See* **Browne, Hablot Knight**.

Proctor, Bryan Waller (1787–1874) Solicitor, poet, playwright and biographer.

Rogers, Samuel (1763–1855) Banker, poet, wit and entertainer.

Sala, George Augustus Henry (1828–96) Artist and journalist.

Seymour, Robert (1800–36) Artist and illustrator.

Shaw, William (?1783–1850) Schoolmaster.

Smith, Arthur (1825–61) CD's first tour manager.

—— **Sydney** (1771–1845) Author, divine and wit.

—— **Dr Thomas Southwood** (1788–1861) Minister, doctor and writer.

Stanfield, Clarkson (1793–1867) Marine and landscape painter.

Stone, Frank (1800–50) Painter.

Stowe, Mrs Harriet Elizabeth Beecher (1811–96) American writer and philanthropist.

Stroughill, George – A playmate of CD's childhood.

—— **Lucy** – George's sister and CD's childhood sweetheart.

Sultan – CD's St Bernard-bloodhound cross.

Talfourd, Sir Thomas Noon (1795–1854) Judge and author.

Tennyson, Alfred, first Baron Tennyson (1809–92) Poet.

Ternan, Ellen Lawless (1839–1914) Actress and CD's mistress.

Thackeray, William Makepeace (1811–63) Novelist.

Timber – CD's Devonshire Terrace spaniel.

Turk – CD's Gad's Hill mastiff.

Victoria, Queen (1819–1901)

Wamen, Jonathan – Blacking-factory owner and CD's first employer.

Watson, The Hon Richard (d 1852) Castle owner and amateur actor.

Weller, Christiana – Pianist.

—— **Mary** – CD's nurse.

Williamina – CD's cat at Gad's Hill.

Wills, William Henry (1810–80) Editor.

Yates, Edmund (1831–94) Novelist and journalist.

43

Index of Artists concerned with Dickens's Work

The following list brings together the names of the many artists who were concerned with the illustration of the works over the years. The chief works with which they are associated are indicated by the TLAs; this is not to say that they were necessarily the illustrators of fully-fledged published versions. More detail will be found in the introductions to the works.

Aldin, Cecil; 1870–1835; illustrator and children's author
  Pic

Barnard, Fred; 1846–1896; illustrator and realist painter
  Cop

Brock, Charles Edmund; 1870–1938; illustrator
  COH

Browne, Hablot Knight *alias* Phiz; 1815–82; painter and illustrator
  Bar, Blk, Boz, Chz, Cop, Dom, Lit, MHC, Nic, OCS, Pic, SYC, TTC

Buss, Robert William; 1804–75; illustrator
  Pic

Cattermole, George; 1800–68; painter and illustrator
  Bar, MHC, OCS

Collins, Charles Alston; 1828–73; illustrator
  EdD

Cruikshank, George: 1792–1878; artist and caricaturist
  Boz, OTw

Doyle, Richard; 1824–83 Humorous artist
  BOL, Chi, Chr

Eytinge, Solomon; 1833–1905; American genre painter

Fildes, *Sir* Luke; 1843–1927; painter
  EdD

French, Harry
  Har

Furniss, Harry; 1854–1925 Irish caricaturist
  Blk, Dom, OMF

Green, Charles
  Chi, OCS,

Houghton, Arthur Boyd; 1836–75; book illustrator and painter
  Har, OMF

Landseer, *Sir* Edwin Henry;
  1802–73; animal painter
  COH
Leech, John: 1847–64;
  humorous artist
  Blk, Chi, Chr, THM
Leslie, Charles Robert;
  1794–1859; painter
  Pic
Maclise, Daniel; 1806?–70;
  historical and literary painter,
  portraitist, and book
  illustrator.
  BOL, Chi, Chr, COH, Nic,
  OCS,
Mahoney, J
  OTw
Michael, A C
  Chr
Palmer, Samuel; 1805–81;
  painter
Pears, Charles
  Bar, GEx, OTw,
Pinwell, G J; 1842–75; painter
  Unc
Reynolds, Frank; 1876–1953;
  illustrator
  Cop, OCS, Pic

Seymour, Robert; 1798?–1836;
  popular illustrator, esp
  humorous sporting subjects
  Boz, Pic
Stanfield, Clarkson; 1793–1867;
  marine and landscape painter
  BOL, Chi, Chr, THM
Stone, Frank; 1800–59; painter
  Chz, THM
Stone, Marcus; 1840–1911;
  painter and illustrator
  Lit, OMF
Tenniel, *Sir* John; 1820–1914;
  artist and cartoonist
  THM
Thomson, Hugh; 1860–1920;
  illustrator
  Chi, Pic
Topham, Francis William;
  1808–77; painter
Walker, Frederick; 1840–75;
  painter and book illustrator
  Har, Rep
Webster, Thomas; 1800–86;
  painter
  Nic
Williams, Samuel; 1788–1853;
  wood-engraver
  MHC, OCS

44

A Classified List of Characters &c

The following section arranges those significant Dickens characters that are classifiable in their classes.

The General Index will reveal in which of the works a given character is to be found.

Actors – Master Crummles; Master Percy Crummles; Vincent Crummles; Mr Folair; Jem Hutley; Alfred Jingle; John; Jem Larkins; Thomas Lenville; Mr Larkins; Thomas Lenville; Mr Loggins; Nicholas Nickleby; Mr Pip; P Salcy Family; Smike; Mr Snevellicci; Mr Snittle Timberry; Mr Wopsle

Actresses – Miss Belvawney; Miss Bravassa; The Compact Enchantress; Ninetta Crummles; Miss Gazingi; Mrs Grudden; Miss Ledrook; Mrs Lenville; Henrietta Petowker; Miss Snevelicci

Actuary – Mr Meltham

Adventurers – Mr Jingle; Alfred Lammle

Aeronauts – Mr Green; Mr Green Jr

Alderman – Mr Cute

Amanuensis – Caddy Jellyby

Americans – Mr Bevan; Julius Washington Merryweather Bib; Jefferson Brick; Mrs Jefferson Brick; Oscar Buffum; Cyrus Choke; Hannibal Chollop; Miss Codger; Colonel Diver; Doctor Ginery Dunkle; General Fladdock; Colonel Groper; Mrs Hominy; Mr Izzard; Mr Jodd; Captain Kedgick; La Fayette Kettle; Mr Norris and family; Major Pawkins; Mrs Pawkins; Professor Piper; Elijah Pogram; Zephaniah Scadder; Putnam Smif; Miss Toppit

Apprentices – Noah Claypole; Mark Gilbert; Hugh Graham; Simon Tappertit; Oliver Twist; Dick Wilkins

Architects – Martin Chuzzlewit; Seth Pecksniff; Tom Pinch; John Westlock

Articulator of bones, &c – Mr Venus

Astrologer – Mr Mooney

Auctioneer – Thomas Sapsea

Authors, &c – Theodosius Butler; Miss Codger; David Copperfield ; Mr Curdle; Mrs Hominy; Mrs Leo Hunter; Miss Toppit; Professor Mullit

Babies – Frederick Charles William Kitterbell; Sally Tetterby; Alexander MacStinger

Bachelors – George Chuzzlewit; Nicodemus Dumps; The Single Gentleman; John Jarndyce; Michael; Newman Noggs; Mr Saunders; Felix Tapkins; Tackleton; Mr Topper; Watkins Tottle

Bailiff – Solomon Jacobs

Ballad-seller, &c – Mr Wegg

Bankers – Josiah Bounderby; Mr Meagles; Mr Merdle; Tellson and Co

Barbers – Crofts; Jinkinson; Mr Slithers; Poll Sweedlepipe

Barmaids – Becky; Miss Martin

Beadles – Mr Bumble; Mr Bung; Mooney; Simmons; Sownds; Sowster

Begging-letter writer – Mr Southcote

Bird-fancier – Poll Sweedlepipe

Blind persons – Bertha Plummer; Mr Sampson Dibble; Stagg

Boarding-house keepers – Mrs Pawkins; Mrs Tibbs; Mrs Todgers

Boobies – Bentley Drummle; Edmund Sparkler

Boots – Bailey Jr; Cobbs; Tom Sparks; Sam Weller

Bore – Mr Barlow

Brokers – Mr Brogley; Clarriker; Fixem; Wilkins Flasher; Fascination Fledgeby; Mr Gattleton; Frank Simmery; Grandfather Smallweed; Tom Tix

Burglars – *See Housebreakers*

Butlers – David; Giles; Nicholas

Carpenters – Thomas Joy; Samuel Wilkins

Carriers – Mr Barkis; John Peerybingle

Chambermaid – Mrs Pratchett

Chandler – Tom Cobb

Chapel – Little Bethel

Charity-boys – Noah Claypole; Robin Toodle

Charwomen – Mrs Bangham; Mrs Blockson

Cheap Jacks – Doctor Marigold; Willum Marigold

Chemists – Thomas Groffin; Mr Redlaw

Circus performers, &c – E W B Childers; Emma Gordon; Signor Jupe; Master Kidderminster; Josephine Sleary; Mr Sleary; Miss Woolford

Clergymen, &c – Mr Chadband; Horace Crewler; Septimus Crisparkle; Alfred Feeder; Brother Gimblet; Verity Hawkyard; Melchisedech Howler; Mr Long Ears; Frank Milvey; George Silverman; Mr Sliverstone; Mr Stiggins; Charles Timson

Clerks, &c – Mr Adams; Clarence Barnacle; Mr Bazzard; Bitzer; Young Blight; Alexander Briggs; James Carker; John Carker; Frank Cheeryble; Mr Chuckster; Chuffey; Mr Clark; Bob Cratchit; Mr Dobble; Walter Gay; Tom Gradgrind; William Guppy; Uriah Heep; Mr Jones; Mr Jackson; Mr Jinks; Tim Linkinwater; Jarvis Lorry; Mr Lowten; Mr Mallard; Wilkins Micawber; Augustus Minns; Mr Morfin; Nicholas Nickleby; Newman Noggs; Nathaniel Pipkin; Thomas Potter; Bartholomew Smallweed; Putnam Smif; Mr Smith; Robert Smithers; Horatio Sparkins; John Spatter; Dick Swiveller; Mr Tiffey; Tom; Alfred Tomkins; Mr Tupple; John Wemmick; Mr Wicks; Reginald Wilfer; Mr Wisbottle *See also Parish Clerks*

Clients – Mr Watty; Michael Warden; Amelia; Mike

Coachmen, &c – William Barker; George; Joe; Martin; Sam; William Simmons; Tipp; Tom; Tony Weller; William

Coal-dealer – Nicholas Tulrumble

Collectors – Mr Buffle; Mr Lillyvick; Mr Pancks; Mr Rugg

Constables – Black; Darby; Green; Daniel Grummer; Rogers; White; Williams

Convicts – Alice Brown; Compeyson; John Edmunds; Kags; Abel Magwitch

Corn-chandlers – Octavius Budden; Wilkins Micawber; Uncle Pumblechook

Corporations, &c – Anglo-Bengalee Disinterested Loan and Life Insurance Company; Circumlocution Office; Eden Land Corporation; Human Interest Brothers; Inestimable Life Assurance Company; United Grand Junction Lirriper and Jackman Great Norfolk Parlour Line; United Metropolitan Improved Hot Muffin and Crumpet Baking and Punctual Delivery Company *See Societies*

Costumer – Solomon Lucas

Cricketers – Mr Dumkins; Luffey; Mr Podder; Mr Staple; Mr Struggles

Cripples – Phœbe; Tiny Tim; Fanny Cleaver; Mr Wegg

Dancing-masters – Mr Baps; Signor Billsmethi; Prince Turveydrop

Deaf-mute – Sophy

Detectives – Mr Inspector Bucket; Sergeant Dornton; Sergeant Fendall; Inspector Field; Sergeant Mith; Mr Nadgett; Rogers; Inspector Stalker; Sergeant Straw; Mr Tatt; Inspector Wield; Witchem

Distiller – Mr Langdale

Dogs – Boxer; Bull's-eye; Diogenes; Jip; Merrylegs; Poodles

Dressmakers – Fanny Cleaver (dolls' dressmaker); Miss Knag; Madame Mantalini; Amelia Martin; Kate Nickleby; Miss Simmond

Drivers – *See Coachmen, &c*

Drunkards – Mrs Blackpool; Mr Dolls; John; Krook; Warden

Drysalters – Brother Gimblet; Verity Hawkyard

Dustman – Nicodemus Boffin

Dwarfs – Quilp; Miss Mowcher

Editors, &c – Jefferson Brick; Colonel Diver; Mr Pott; Mr Slurk

Emigrants – Susannah Cleverly; William Cleverly; Dorothy Dibble; Sampson Dibble; Jessie Jobson; Wiltshire; Anastasia Weedle

Engine-driver – Mr Toodle

Engineers – Daniel Doyce; Edwin Drood

Fairies – Grandmarina; Tape

Farmers – Old Benson; John Browdie; Godfrey Nickleby; Martin Stokes

Fishermen – Ham Peggotty; Daniel Peggotty

Footmen – Mercury; Muzzle; John Smauker; Thomas Towlinson; Tuckle; Whiffers

Forgers – Mr Fikey; Mr Merdle

Frenchmen and Frenchwomen – Bebelle; Blandois (or Rigaud); Madame Bouclet; The Compact Enchantress; Charles Darnay (or

Evrémonde); Lucia Darnay; Ernest Defarge; Thérèse Defarge; Monsieur the Face-maker; Théophile Gabelle; Gaspard; Mademoiselle Hortense; Jacques (One, Two, Three, Four, Five); Lagnier (*or* Rigaud); M Loyal Devasseur; Alexander Manette; Lucie Manette; Monsieur Mutuel; St Evrémonde; P Salcy Family; Corporal Théophile; The Vengeance; Monsieur the Ventriloquist

Gamblers – Joe Jowl; Isaac List; Miss Betsey Trotwood's Husband; Little Nell's Grandfather

Gamekeeper – Martin

Gardeners – Mr Cheggs; Hunt; Wilkins

Gentlemen – Mr Tite Barnacle; Sir Joseph Bowley; Mr Brownlow; Mr John Chester; Sir Thomas Clubber; Hon Mr Crushton; Sir Leicester Dedlock; Hon Sparkins Flare; Mr Alexander Grazinglands; Mr Grimwig; Geoffrey Haredale; Sir Mulberry Hawk; Master Humphrey; Sir William Joltered; Hon Mr Long Ears; Nicholas Nickleby; Squire Norton; Samuel Pickwick; Mr John Podsnap; Sir Matthew Pupker; Jack Redburn; Sir Barnet Skettles; Hon Wilmot Snipe; Sir Hookham Snivey; Hon Mr Snob; Hon Bob Stables; Mr Melvin Twemlow; Mr Wardle

Germans – Baron and Baroness von Koëldwethout ; Straudenheim; Baron and Baroness von Swillenhausen

Giants – Gog; Magog; Pickleson

Governesses – Mrs General; Miss Lane; Ruth Pinch

Greengrocers – Harris; Tommy; Richard Upwitch

Grocers – Jacob Barton; Mr Blocker; Joseph Tuggs

Groom – Thomas

Guards – George; Joe

Haberdashers – Mr Omer; Mr Phibbs

Hangman – Ned Dennis

Hop-grower – Mr Chestle

Horse-jockey – Captain Maroon

Hostlers – Hugh; Mark Tapley

Housebreakers – Toby Crackit; Bill Sikes

Housekeepers – Mrs Bedwin; Miss Benton; Molly; Mrs Pipchin; Miss Pross; Mrs Rouncewell; Peg Sliderskew; Mrs Sparsit; Esther Summerson; Mrs Tickit; Agnes Wickfield

Hypocrites – Charity Pecksniff; Mercy Pecksniff; Seth Pecksniff; Julius Slinkton

Impostor – Blackey

Invalids – Bill Barley; Mrs Clennam; Mrs Crewler; Mr Gobler; Mrs Gradgrind; Mrs Skimpole; Mr Tresham

Inventors – Mr Crinkles; Don Diego; Daniel Doyce; John; Professor Queerspeck; Mr Tickle

Irishmen – Frederick O'Bleary

Ironmaster – Mr Rouncewell

Italians – Giovanni Carlavero; John Baptist Calvalletto

Jailer – Mr Akerman

Jews – Barney; Fagin; Aaron Mesheck; Mr Riah

Judge – Mr Justice Stareleigh

Jugglers – African Knife-Swallower; Sweet William

Jurymen – Thomas Groffin; Richard Upwitch

Labourers – Bayton; Will Fern; Joe Wiltshire

Ladies – Princess Alicia; Lady Bowley; Lady Clubber; Lady Dedlock; Mrs Gowan; Baroness von Koëldwethout; Mrs Merdle; Lady Fareway; Lady Seadgers; Lady Skettles; Hon Mrs Skewton; Lady Snuphanuph; Lady Tippins; Baroness von Swillenhausen

Lamplighter – Tom Grig

Landladies – Mrs Bardell; Mrs Billickin; Madame Bouclet; Mrs Craddock; Mrs Crupp; Mrs Lirriper; Mrs Lupin; Mrs MacStinger; Mrs Noakes; Miss Abbey Potterson; Mary Ann Raddle; Mrs Tibbs; Mrs Todgers; Mrs Whimple; Mrs Williamson; Miss Wozenham

Landlords – Bark; The Black Lion; James George Bogsby; Christopher Casby; James Groves; W Gribble; Captain Kedgick; Mr J Mellows; Mr Licensed Victualler; John Willet

Laundresses – Mrs Dilber; Mrs Parkins; Mrs Stubbs; Mrs Sweeney

Law stationers – Mrs Harris; Mr Snagsby

Law student – Percy Noakes

Law writers – Captain Hawdon; Tony Jobling

Lawyers – Sally Brass; Sampson Brass; Samuel Briggs; Sergeant Buzfuz; Sydney Carton; Clarkson; Thomas Craggs; Mr Dodson;

Mr Fips; Mr Fogg; Hiram Grewgious; Uriah Heep; Mr Jaggers; Mr Jerkins; Conversation Kenge; Mortimer Lightwood; Percy Noakes; Joseph Overton; Owen Overton; Solomon Pell; Mr Perker; Mr Phunky; Mr Rugg; Mr Skimpin; Jonathan Snitchey; Sergeant Snubbin; Francis Spenlow; Henry Spiker; Mr Stryver; Mr Tangle; Thomas Traddles; Mr Tulkinghorn; Mr Vholes; Mr Wickfield; Eugene Wrayburn

Literary productions – Considerations on the Policy of removing the Duty on Beeswax; Last Moments of the Learned Pig; Ode to an Expiring Frog; Speculations on the Sources of the Hampstead Ponds, with some observations on the Theory of Tittlebats; the Thorn of Anxiety

Locksmith – Gabriel Varden

Lodging-house keepers – Bully Bark; Mrs Billickin; Mr Bulph; Mrs Lirriper; Miss Wozeham

Lords – *See Noblemen*

Lunatics – Mr Dick (Richard Babley); The Gentleman in Small-clothes; Miss Flite

Magistrates – Alderman Cute; Mr Fang; Mr Nupkins

Manufacturer – Josiah Bounderby

Matrons of Workhouses – Mrs Corney; Mrs Mann

Mayors – George Nupkins; Joseph (or Owen) Overton; Mr Sniggs; Mr Tulrumble

Medical students – Ben Allen; Alfred Heathfield; Jack Hopkins; Bob Sawyer

Member of Congress – Elijah Pogram

Members of Parliament – William Bufrey; Cornelius Brook Dingwall; Mr Gregsbury; Sir Matthew Pupker; Sir Barnet Skettles; Honest Tom; Hamilton Veneering *See also Noblemen*

Merchants – Barbox Brothers (Mr Jackson) ; Cheeryble Brothers; Clarriker; Arthur Clennam; Mr Dombey; Mr Fezziwig; Mr Thomas Gradgrind; Mr Murdstone; Mr Miles Owen; Herbert Pocket; Mr Quinion; Scrooge

Messengers – Jerry Cruncher; Jenkinson; Mr Perch

Military men – Captain Adams; Matthew Bagnet; Major Bagstock; Captain Bailey; Major Banks; Captain Boldwig; Colonel Bulder; General Cyrus Choke; Major Hannibal Chollop; Colonel

Chowser; Captain Doubledick; Captain Dowler; General Fladdock; Tom Green; Colonel Groper; Captain Hawdon; Captain Helves; Captain Hopkins; Major Jemmy Jackman; Captain Kedgick; the Recruiting Sergeant; George Rouncewell; Lieutenant Slaughter; Wilmot Snipe; Lieutenant Tappleton; Captain Taunton; Corporal Théophile; Joe Willet

Milliners – Miss Knag; Madame Mantalini; Amelia Martin

Misers, &c – Uncle Chill; Christopher Canby; Anthony Chuzzlewit; Jonas Chuzzlewit; Arthur Gride; Ralph Nickleby; Scrooge; Bartholomew Smallweed; Grandfather Smallweed

Murderers – Jonas Chuzzlewit; Gaspard; Bradley Hudstone; Mademoiselle Hortense; Captain Murderer; Rigaud; Mr Rudge; Bill Sikes; Julius Slinkton; William Warden

Musical performers – Antonio; Matthew Bagnet; Banjo Bones; Mrs Banjo Bones; Mr Brown; Mr Cape; Frederick Dorrit; Mr Evans; Mr Harleigh; John Jasper; Miss Jenkins; Signor Lobskini; Miss A Melvilleson; Master Wilkins Micawber; Lætitia Parsons; Little Swills; Mr Tippin; Mrs Tippin; Miss Tippin; Mr and Mrs B Wedgington

Nautical-instrument maker – Solomon Gills

Newsmen, &c – Adolphus Tetterby; 'Dolphus Tetterby

Newspapers – Eatanswill Gazette; Eatanswill Independent; New York Rowdy Journal

Noblemen, &c – Lord Decimus Tite Barnacle; Prince Bear; Lord Boodle; Prince Bull; Prince Certainpersonio; Cousin Feenix; Baron von Koëldwethout; Monseigneur; Lord Mutanhed; Lord Peter; Marquis St Evrémonde; Count Smorltork; Lord Snigsworth; Lord Lancaster Stiltstalking; Baron von Swillenhausen; Lord Frederick Verisopht; King Watkins the First

Notaries – Abel Garland; Mr Witherden

Nurses – Mrs Bangham; Mrs Blockitt; Dawes; Sally Flanders; Flopson; Sairey Gamp; Mercy; Millers; Betsey Prig; Mrs Prodgit; Mrs Polly Toodle; Mrs Wickham

Old Maids – Miss Barbary; Volumnia Dedlock; Miss Havisham; Miss Lillerton; Miss Jane Murdstone; Miss Anastasia Rugg; Judy Smallweed; Miss Clarissa Spenlow; Miss Lavinia Spenlow; Miss Lucretia Tox; Rachael Wardle; Miss Witherfield

Orators – Mr Edkins; Mr Magg; Mr Slackbridge

Orphans – Johnny; Lillian

Pages – Alphonse; Withers

Painters – Henry Gowan; Miss La Creevy

Parish Clerks – Solomon Daisy; Nathaniel Pipkin; Mr Wopsle

Paupers – Anny; Little Dick; Mrs Fibbetson; Martha; John Edward Nandy; Oakum Read; Chief Refractory; Refractory Number Two; Old Sally; Mrs Thingummy; Oliver Twist

Pawnbrokers – David Crimple; Mr Henry; Pleasant Riderhood

Pensioners – Mr Battens; Mrs Quinch; Mrs Saggers

Pew-opener – Mrs Miff

Philanthropists – Bigwig Family; Luke Honeythunder; Mrs Jellyby; Mr and Mrs Pardiggle; Mr Quale; Miss Wisk

Philosophers – Doctor Jeddler; Mr Mooney

Physicians – Baytham Badger; Mr Chillip; Ginery Dunkle; Doctor Grummidge; Doctor Haggage; John Jobling; Doctor Kutankumagen; Doctor Lumbey; Alexander Manette; Mr Pilkins; Parker Peps; Doctor Soemup; Joe Specks; Doctor Toorell; Doctor Wosky *See also Surgeons*

Pirate – Lieutenant-Colonel Robin Redforth

Pickpockets – *See Thieves*

Pilot – Mr Bulph

Places (various) – Ball's Pond; Borrioboola-Ghba; Chinks's Basin; Chumbledon Square; Cloisterham; Dingley Dell; Dullborough; Eatanswill; Eden; Great Winglebury; Grogzwig; Haven of Philanthropy; Mill Pond Bank; Chinks's Basin; Mugby Junction; Muggleton; Namelesston; New Thermopylæ; Oldcastle; Old Hell Shaft; Old Mint; Pavilionstone; Plashwater Weir Mill; Pocket-Breaches; Pod's End; Poplar Walk; Port Middlebay; Princess's Place; Rat's Castle; Staggs's Garden; Stiffun's Acre; Tom-all-alone's; Tucket's Terrace; Verbosity; Wilderness Walk

Plasterer – Thomas Plornish

Poets – Mr Slum; Augustus Snodgrass; Mrs Leo Hunter

Policemen – Sergeant Dornton; Inspector Field; Mr Inspector; Sergeant Mith; Parker; Peacoat; Quickear; Sharpeye; Inspector Stalker; Trampfoot ; Williams; Sergeant Witchem

Political parties – Eatanswill Buffs; Eatanswill Blues

Politicians – Lord Boodle; Horatio Fizkin; Major Pawkins; Mr Rogers; Samuel Slumkey

Pony – Whisker

Porters, &c – Bullamy; 'Lamps'; Tugby; Toby Veck

Postmasters – Tom Cobb; Monsieur Gabelle

Postmistress – Mrs Tomlinson

Pot-boy – Bob Gliddery

Prisoners – Mr Ayresleigh; John Baptist Cavalletto; the Chancery Prisoner; William Dorrit; Charles Evrémonde; Doctor Raggage; George Heyling; Captain Hopkins; Horace Kinch; Mr Martin; Wilkins Micawber; Mr Mivins; Neddy; Mr Price; Rigaud; Mr Simpson; Smangle; Mr Walker; Mr Willis

Public-houses – Black Boy and Stomachache; Black Lion; Boar; Blue Dragon; Boot-jack and Countenance; Bush; Crozier; Dolphin's Head; Golden Cross; Good Republican Brutus of Antiquity; Great White Horse; Holly Tree; Jolly Bargemen; Jolly Boatmen; Jolly Sandboys; Jolly Tapley; Lighterman's Arms; Marquis of Granby; Maypole; National Hotel; Nutmeg Grater; Original Pig; Peacock; Pegasus' Arms; Pig and Tinderbox; St James's Arms; Saracen's Head; Setting Moon; Six Jolly Fellowship-Porters; Slamjam Coffee-House; Sol's Arms; The Temeraire; Three Cripples; Three Jolly Bargemen; Travellers' Twopenny; Valiant Soldier; White Conduit House; White Horse Cellar; Winglebury Arms

Pugilist – The Game Chicken

Pupils – Adams; Belling; Bitherstone; Bitzer; Black; Bobbo; Bolder; Briggs; Rosa Bud; Cobbey; David Copperfield; Cripples; George Demple; Miss Edwards; Richard Evans; Adelina Fareway; Miss Ferdinand; Miss Frost; Miss Giggles; Bully Globson; Graymarsh; Harry; Charley Hexam; Miss Jennings; Johnson; Helena Landless; Jemmy Jackman Lirriper; Mary Anne; Mawls; Maxby; Mobbs; John Owen; Miss Pankey; Miss Reynolds; Miss Rickitts;

Miss Shepherd; Barnet Skettles Jr; Smike; Miss Smithers; Sophia; Joe Specks; Steerforth; Bob Tartar; Tomkins; Toots; Tozer; Traddles; Granville Wharton; White

Ranger – Phil Parkes

Raven – Grip

Receivers of Stolen Goods – Bully Bark; Fagin; Joe; Mr Lively

Reporter – David Copperfield

Residences, &c – Abel Cottage; Amelia Cottage; Blunderstone Rookery; Boffin's Bower; Chesney Wold; The Den; The Elms; Fizkin Lodge; The Growlery; Gumtion House; Harmony Jail; Hoghton Towers; Manor Farm; Mudfog Hall; Norwood; Oak Lodge; Rose Villa; Rustic Lodge; Satis House; Stone Lodge; The Warren; Wooden Midshipman

Resurrectionist – Jerry Cruncher

Rioters – Ned Dennis; Hugh; Barnaby Rudge; Simon Tappertit

Robe-maker – Mr Jennings

Saddlers – Old Lobbs; Tipkisson

Schools – Dotheboys Hall; Minerva House; Nuns' House; Salem House; Westgate House

Sciences – Ditchwateristics; Umbugology

Seamen, &c – Old Bill Barley; Captain Boldheart; William Boozey; Mr Bulph; Captain Bunsby; Captain Cuttle; Dando; Dark Jack; Mercantile Jack; Job Potterson; Captain Purdgy; Lieutenant Tartar

Secretaries – Ferdinand Barnacle; Mr Fish ; Mr Gashford ; John; Harmon; Mr Jennings; Layfayette; Kettle; Jonas Mudge; Mr Wobbler

Servants – *Male* Benjamin Britain; Brittles; Deputy; John Derrick; Do'em; Jeremiah Flintwitch; Old Glubb; John Grueby; James; Joe (the Fat Boy); John; Littimer; The Native; Kit Nubbles; Peak; Pepper; Phil; Pruffle; Tom Scott; Sloppy; Smike; Phil Squod; William Swidger; Mark Tapley; Tinkler; Robin Toodle; Job Trotter; Tungay; Samuel Weller – *Female* Jane Adams; Agnes; Anne; Barbara; Becky; Berinthia; Betsey; Biddy; Charlotte; Clickett; Mary Daws; Emma; Affery Flintwhich; Flowers; Goodwin; Guster; Hannah; Mademoiselle Hortense; Jane; Janet; Winifred Madgers; The Marchioness; Martha; Mary; Mary Anne; Caroline Maxey; 'Melia; Miss Miggs; Clemency Newcome; Susan Nipper; Mary Anne Paragon; Clara Peggoty; Mary Anne Perkinsop; Phœbe; Priscilla; Mrs Rachael; Sally Rairyganoo; Robinson; Rosa; Tilly Slowboy; Betsey Snap; Sophia; Willing Sophy; Tamaroo; Tattycoram

Sextons – Bill; Old David; Gabriel Grub

Sharpers – See Swindlers

Sheriff's Officers – Blathers; Dubbley; Duff; Mr Namby; Mr Neckett; Mr Scaley; Mr Smouch; Tom

Shipwright – Chips

Shoe-binder – Jemima Evans

Shops – Wooden Midshipman; Old Curiosity Shop

Shop-keepers – Giovanni Carlavero; Mrs Chickenstalker; Mrs Chivery; Augustus Cooper; Ernest Defarge; Little Nell's Grandfather; Mrs Plornish; Pleasant Riderhood; Straudenheim; Mrs Tugby

Showmen, &c – Tom Codlin; Mr Grinder; Mr Harris; Mrs Jarley; Jerry; Mim; Vuffin

Shrews – Mrs Bumble; Mrs Joe Gargery; Mrs MacStinger; Mrs Marigold; Miss Miggs; Mrs Raddle; Bargh; Mrs Snagsby; Mrs Sowerberry; Fanny Squeers; Mrs Squeers; Mrs Varden

Smiths – Richard; Joe Gargery; Dolge Orlick; John

Societies – All-Muggleton Cricket Club; Finches of the Grove; Convened Chief Composite Committee of Central and District Philanthropists; Glorious Apollos; Infant Bonds of Joy; Ladies' Bible and Prayer-Book Distribution Society; Master Humphrey's Clock; Mr Weller's Watch; Pickwick Club; 'Prentice Knights; Social Linen Box Committee; Superannuated Widows; United Aggregate Tribunal; United Bulldogs; United Grand Junction Ebenezer Temperance Association; Watertoast Association of United Sympathisers

Spaniard – Antonio

Spendthrift – Edward Porrit

Spies – Roger Cly; Solomon Pross

Sportsman – Nathaniel Winkle

Statisticians – Mr Filer; Mr Kwakley; Mr X Ledbrain: Mr Slug

Stenographer – David Copperfield

Steward – Mr Rudge; Job Potterson

Stoker – Mr Toodle

Stonemason – Durdles

Straw-bonnet maker – Jemima Evans

Street-sweeper – Jo

Student – Edmund Denham

Sugar-baker – Gabriel Parsons

Suitors in Chancery – Richard Carstone; Ada Clare; Miss Flite; Mr Gridley; John Jarndyce

Surgeons – Mr Knight Bell; Mr Dawson; Mr Lewsome; Mr Losberne; Doctor Payne; Doctor Slammer; Allan Woodcourt *See also Physicians*

Swindlers, &c – Blackey; Mr Bonney; Do'em; Fitz-Whisker Fiercy; Alfred Jingle; Mr Jinkins; Alfred Lammle; Mr Merdle; Rigaud; Zephaniah Seadder; Montague Tigg; Job Trotter; Captain Walter Waters; Mr Wolf

Tailors – Mr Omer; Mr Trabb; Alexander Trott

Taxidermist – Mr Venus

Teachers, &c – Cornelia Blimber; Doctor Blimber; Mr Blinkins; Old Cheeseman; Mr Creakle; Mr Cripples; Amelia and Maria Crumpton; Mr Dadson; Miss Donny; Miss Drowvey; Mr Feeder; Miss Grimmer; Miss Gwynn; Bradley Headstone; Betty Higden; Latin-Grammar Master; Mrs Lemon; Mr M'Choakumchild; Mr Marton; Charles Mell; Miss Monflathers; the Misses Nettingall; Nicholas Nickleby; Emma Peecher; Professor Piper; Mr Sharp; Wackford Squeers; Doctor Strong; Miss Tomkins; Miss Twinkleton; the Misses Wackles *See also Governesses*

Temperance Reformers – Anthony Humm; Jonas Mudge; Brother Tadger

Thieves – Charley Bates; Bet; Tom Chitling; Noah Claypole; John Dawkins (the Artful Dodger); Doctor Dundey; Aaron Mesheck; Nancy; Mr Shepherdson; Bill Sikes; Tally-ho Thompson; Earl of Warwick

Taodies – Mr Boots; Mr Brewer; Mr and Mrs Camilla; Mrs Coiler; Mr Flamwell; Georgiana; Mr Pluck; Sarah Pocket; Mr Pocket

Tobacconist – Miss Chivery

Toymaker – Caleb Plummer

Toy-merchant – Tackleton

Tramps – John Anderson; Mrs Anderson

Turner – Mr Kenwigs

Turnkeys, &c – Mr Akerman; Bob; John Chivery; Young John Chivery; Solomon Pross; Tom Roker

Umbrella-maker – Alexander Trott

Undertakers – Mr Joram; Mr Mould; Mr Omor; Mr Sowerberry; Tacker; Mr Trabb

Usurers – Anthony Chuzzlewit; Arthur Gride; Ralph Nickleby; Grandfather Smallweed

Vagabonds, &c – John Anderson; Mr Click; Bob Miles; Edward Twiggs; Winking Charley

Valets – See Servants

Verger – Mr Tops

Vessels – The Beauty; the Cautious Clara; the Family; the Royal Skewer; the Scorpion; the Screw; the Son and Heir

Vestrymen – Mr Chib; Captain Banger; Mr Dogginson; Mr Magg; Mr Tiddypot; Mr Wigsby

Waiters – Ben; Christopher; Ezekiel; Jack; John; Miss Piff; William Potkins; Mrs Sniff; Thomas; Miss Whiff; William

Watermen – Dando; Jesse Hexam; Mr Lobley; Roger Riderhood; Tommy

Weaver – Stephen Blackpool

Wharfinger – Mr Winkle Sr

Wheelwright – Mr Hubble

Widowers – Mr John Dounce; John Podgers; Tony Weller

Widows – Barbara's Mother; Mrs Bardell; Mrs Bedwin; Mrs Billickin; Mrs Bloss ; Mrs Brandley; Mrs Briggs; Mrs Budger; Mrs Clennam; Mrs Coiler; Mrs Copperfield; Mrs Corney; Mrs Crisparkle; Lady Fareway; Mrs Fielding; Flora Finching; Sally Flanders; Mrs General; Mrs Gowan; Edith Granger; Mrs Gummidge; Mrs Guppy; Mrs Heep; Mrs Jiniwin; Mrs Markleham; Mrs Maplesone; Mrs Mitts; Mrs Nickleby; Mrs Nubbles; Mrs Pegler; Mrs Skewton; Mrs Sparsit; Mrs Starling; Mrs Steerforth; Mrs Taunton; Lady Tippins; Mrs Tisber; Mrs Wardle; Mrs Woodcourt

45

Three Letter Abbreviations used for Dickens's Works in the Index

Bar	Barnaby Rudge		Mud	The Mudfog Association
BBB	Barbox Brothers		Mug	Boy at Mugby
Blk	Bleak House		Nic	Nicholas Nickleby
BOL	The Battle of Life		NUS	New Uncommercial Samples
Boy	Boy at Mugby		OCS	The Old Curiosity Shop
Boz	Sketches by Boz		OMF	Our Mutual Friend
Chi	The Chimes		OTw	Oliver Twist
Chr	A Christmas Carol		Pic	Pickwick Papers
Chz	Martin Chuzzlewit		Rep	Reprinted Pieces
COH	The Cricket on the Hearth		Rom	Holiday Romance
Cop	David Copperfield		Sil	George Silverman
Dom	Dombey and Son		SPT	The Seven Poor Travellers
DrM	Doctor Marigold		SUP	Some Uncollected Pieces
EdD	Edwin Drood		SYC	Sketches of Young Couples
GEx	Great Expectations		TGS	Two Ghost Stories
Har	Hard Times		THM	The Haunted Man
Hol	The Holly Tree		TTC	A Tale of Two Cities
Hun	Hunted Down		Unc	Uncommercial Traveller
Leg	Mrs Lirriper's Legacy			
Lit	Little Dorrit			
Lod	Mrs Lirriper's Lodgings			
Lug	Somebody's Luggage			
MHC	Master Humphrey's Clock			

Oliver asking for more – George Cruikshank

Index of Characters, Places &c

BAPS, Mr and Mrs, **Dom**

BARBARA and her mother, **OCS**

BARBARY, Miss, **Blk**

BARBOX BROTHERS, **BBB**

BARDELL, Mrs Martha, Master Tommy, **Pic**

BARK, Bully, **Rep**

BARKER, Miss Fanny, **SUP**

BARKER, Mr William, **Boz**

BARKIS, Mr and Miss, **Cop**

Barkis, Mrs, **Cop**

BARLEY, Old Bill and Clara, **GEx**

BARLOW, Mr, **NUS**

BARNACLE, Lord Decimus Tite, Mr Tite, Clarence and Ferdinand, **Lit**

BARNEY, **OTw**

BARSAD, John, **TTC**

BARTON, Mr Jacob, **Boz**

BATES, Charley, **OTw**

BATTENS, Mr, **Unc**

BAYTON, **OTw**

BAZZARD, Mr, **EdD**

BEADLE, Harriet, **Lit**

BEADLE, The, **Boz**

BEAR, Prince, **Rep**

BEATRICE, **BBB**

Beauty, The, **Rom**

BEBELLE, **Lug**

BECKWITH, Mr Alfred, **Hun**

BECKY, **OTw**

BEDWIN, Mrs, **OTw**

Beeswax, Considerations on the Policy of Removing the Duty on, **Boz**

BEGGING-LETTER WRITER, The, **Rep**

Begs, Mrs Ridger, **Cop**

BELINDA, **MHC**

Bell Yard, **Blk**

BELL, Mr Knight, **Mud**

BELLA, **Boz**

BELLE, **Chr**

BELLING, Master, **Nic**

BELVAWNEY, Miss, **Nic**

BEN, **SPT**

BENSON, Old, Young and Lucy, **SUP**

BENTON, Miss, **MHC**

BERINTHIA, **Dom**

BERRY, **Dom**

BET or BETSY, **OTw**

BETSEY, **Pic**

BEVAN, Mr, **Chz**

BEVERLEY, Mr, **Boz**

BIB, Julius Washington Merryweather, **Chz**

BIDDY, **GEx**

BIGBY, Mrs, **Rep**

BIGWIG FAMILY, The, **Rep**

BILER, **Dom**

BILL, **OTw**

BILL, Uncle, **Boz**

BILLICKIN, Mrs, **EdD**

BILLSMETHI, Signor , Master and Miss, **Boz**

BIRTHS. MRS MEEK, OF A SON, **Rep**

BITHERSTON, Master, **Dom**

BITZER, **Har**

BLACK, **Rep**

Black Boy and Stomachache, The, **Mud**

BLACK LION, The, **Bar**

BLACK, Mrs, **Rom**

BLACKEY, **Rep**

BLACKPOOL, Stephen and Mrs, **Har**

BLADUD, Prince, **Pic**

BLANDOIS, **Lit**

BLANK, Mr, **Mud**

BLATHERS and DUFF, **OTw**

Brobity, Miss, **EdD**

BROGLEY, Mr, **Dom**

BROGSON, Mr, **Boz**

BROKER'S MAN, The, **Boz**

BROOKER, **Nic**

Brooks of Sheffield, **Cop**

BROWDIE, John and Mrs, **Nic**

BROWN, **Rom**

BROWN, Miss Emily, **Boz**; **SUP**

BROWN, Mr, **Boz**; **Mud**

BROWN, Mrs and Alice, **Dom**

BROWNLOW, Mr, **OTw**

BROWNS, The three Miss, **Boz**

Buchan's Domestic Medicine, **Lit**

BUCKET, Mr Inspector and Mrs, **Blk**

BUD, Miss Rosa, **EdD**

BUDDEN, Mr Octavius, Mrs Amelia and Master Alexander Augustus, **Boz**

BUDGER, Mrs, **Pic**

Buffam, Oscar, **Chz**

BUFFER, Dr, **Mud**

BUFFEY, The Right Hon. William, MP, **Blk**

BUFFLE, Mr, Mrs and Miss Robina, **Leg**

Buffs, The, **Pic**

BUFFUM, Mr Oscar, **Chz**

BULDER, Colonel, Mrs Colonel, Miss, **Pic**

BULL, Prince, **Rep**

Bull, The, **Pic**

BULL'S-EYE, **OTw**

BULLAMY, **Chz**

BULLFINCH, **NUS**

BULPH, Mr, **Nic**

BUMBLE, Mr and Mrs, **OTw**

BUMPLE, Michael, **Boz**

BUNG, Mr, **Boz**

BUNSBY, Captain Jack, **Dom**

Burgess and Co, **Dom**

Bush, The, **Pic**

BUTCHER, William, **Rep**

BUTLER, Mr Theodosius, **Boz**

BUZFUZ, Serjeant, **Pic**

C

CALTON, Mr, **Boz**

CALVETTO, John Baptist, **Lit**

CAMILLA, Mr John or Raymond and Mrs, **GEx**

CAPE, Mr, **Boz**

CAPTAIN, The, **Boz**

CARKER, Harriet, James and Mr John, **Dom**

CARLAVERO, Giovanni, **Unc**

CAROLINE, **Chr**

CARSTONE, Richard, **Blk**

CARTER, Mr, **Mud**

CARTON, Sydney, **TTC**

CASBY, Christopher, **Lit**

Catechism, Overhaul your, **Dom**

Cautious Clara, The, **Dom**

CAVALETTO, John Baptist, **Lit**

CERTAINPERSONIO, Prince, **Rom**

CHADBAND, The Revd Mr and Mrs, **Blk**

CHANCERY PRISONER, The, **Pic**

Charitable Grinder, **Dom**

CHARLES and LOUISA, **SYC**

CHARLEY, **Blk**; **Cop**; **Hol**

CHARLOTTE, **OTw**

CHARLOTTE and EDWARD, **SYC**

CHARLOTTE, Miss, **SYC**

Cheap Jack, **DrM**

CHEERYBLE BROTHERS, **Nic**

CHEESEMAN, Old, **Rep**

COPPERNOSE, Mr, **Mud**

CORNEY, Mrs, **OTw**

Corpse Common, **SUP**

COUNTESS, The, **Rep**

CRACHIT, Bob and Mrs, Belinda, Martha, Peter and Tim, **Chr**

CRACKIT, Toby, **OTw**

CRADDOCK, Mrs, **Pic**

CRAGGS, Mr and Mrs Thomas, **BOL**

CREAKLE, Mr, Mrs and Miss, **Cop**

CREWLER, Revd Horace, Mrs, Miss Caroline, Miss Louisa, Miss Lucy, Miss Margaret, Miss Sarah and Miss Sophy, **Cop**

CRICKET ON THE HEARTH, The, **COH**

CRIMPLE, David, **Chz**

CRINKLES, Mr, **Mud**

CRIPPLES, Mr and Master, **Lit**

CRISPARKLE, The Revd Septimus and Mrs, **EdD**

CROFTS, **SYC**

CROOKEY, **Pic**

CROWL, Mr, **Nic**

Crozier, The, **EdD**

CRUMMLES, Mr Vincent, Mrs, Master, Master Percy and Miss Ninetta, **Nic**

CRUMPTON, Miss Amelia and Miss Maria, **Boz**

CRUNCHER, Jerry, Mrs and Young Jerry, **TTC**

CRUPP, Mrs, **Cop**

CRUSHTON, The Hon. Mr, **Pic**

CURDLE, Mr and Mrs, **Nic**

CUTE, Alderman, **Chi**

CUTLER Mr and Mrs, **Nic**

CUTTLE, Captain Edward, **Dom**

D

DADSON, Mr and Mrs, **Boz**

DAISY, Solomon, **Bar**

DANCING ACADEMY, The, **Boz**

DANDO, **Boz**

DANTON, Mr, **Boz**

DARBY, **Blk**

DARNAY, Charles and Mrs Lucie, **TTC**

DARTLE, Rosa, **Cop**

DATCHERY, Dick, **EdD**

DAVID, **Nic**

DAVID COPPERFIELD, **Cop**

DAVID, Old, **OCS**

DAWES, **Lit**

DAWKINS, John, **OTw**

DAWS, Mary, **Dom**

DAWSON, Mr, **Boz**

DEAF GENTLEMAN, The, **MHC**

DEDLOCK, Sir Leicester, Lady Honoria and Volumnia, **Blk**

DEFARGE, Monsieur Ernest and Madame Thérèse, **TTC**

DEMPLE, George, **Cop**

Den, The, **Pic**

DENHAM, Edmund, **THM**

DENNIS, Ned, **Bar**

Deportment, Model of, **Blk**

DEPUTY, **EdD**

DERRICK, John, **TGS**

DETECTIVE POLICE, The, **Rep**

DEVASSEUR, M Loyal, **Rep**

DIBBLE, Mr Sampson and Mrs Dorothy, **Unc**

DICK, Little, **OTw**

EDWIN, **Hol**

Effort, Making an, **Dom**

ELECTION FOR BEADLE, **Boz**

ELLIS, Mr, **Boz**

Elms, The, **Lit**

EM'LY, Little, **Cop**

EMILY, **Boz**

EMMA, **Pic; SUP**

EMMELINE, **Hol**

ENDELL, Martha, **Cop**

ESTELLA, **GEx**

EVANS, Mr, **Boz**

EVANS, Mrs, Miss Jemima and Miss Tilly, **Boz**

EVANS, Richard, **OCS**

EVENSON, Mr John, **Boz**

EVRÉMONDE, Charles, **TTC**

EZEKIEL, **Boy**

F

F's AUNT, Mr, **Lit**

F's Aunt, Mr. *See Mr F's Aunt,* **Lit**

FACE-MAKER, Monsieur The, **Unc**

FAGIN, **OTw**

Family, The, **Rom**

FAN, **Chr**

FANG, Mr, **OTw**

FANNY, **Rep**

FAREWAY, Lady, Mr and Adelina, **Sil**

Fascination Fleldgeby, **OMF**

Father of the Marshalea, **Lit**

FEE, Dr W R, **Mud**

FEEDER, Mr, B A and Revd Alfred, M A, **Dom**

FEENIX, Cousin, **Dom**

FENDALL, Sergeant, **Rep**

FERDINAND, Miss, **EdD**

FERN, Lilian and Will, **Chi**

FÉROCE, M, **Rep**

FEZZIWIG, Mr, Mrs and the Three Misses, **Chr**

FIBBETSON, Mrs, **Cop**

FIELD, Inspector, **Rep**

FIELDING, Miss Emma, **SYC**

FIELDING, Mrs and May, **COH**

FIERCY, The Hon. Captain Fitz-Whisker, **SUP**

FIKEY, **Rep**

FILER, Mr, **Chi**

Finches of the Grove, **GEx**

FINCHING, Mrs Flora, **Lit**

Fine figure, A, of a woman, **GEx**

FIPS, Mr, **Chz**

FLADDOCK, General, A cor

FIRST OF MAY, The, **Boz**

FISH, Mr, **Chi**

FITZ-MARSHALL, Charles, **Pic**

FIXEM, **Boz**

Fizkin Lodge, **Pic**

FIZKIN, Horatio, Esq, **Pic**

FLADDOCK, General, **Chz**

FLAM, The Hon. Sparkins, **SUP**

FLAMWELL, Mr, **Boz**

FLANDERS, Sally, **Unc**

Flare, Hollow down by the, **OMF**

FLASHER, Wilkins, **Pic**

FLEDGEBY, Mr, **OMF**

FLEETWOOD, Mr, Mrs and Master, **Boz**

FLEMING, Agnes and Rose, **OTw**

FLIGHT, A, 564

FLINTWINCH, Affery, Ephraim and Jeremiah, **Lit**

FLIPFIELD, Mr, Mrs, Miss and Mr Tom, **Unc**

FLITE, Miss, **Blk**

GRAN, Mrs, **Leg**

GRANDFATHER, Little Nell's, **OCS**

GRANDMARINA, Fairy, **Rom**

GRANGER, Mrs Edith, **Dom**

GRAYMARSH, **Nic**

GRAYPER, Mr and Mrs, **Cop**

GRAZINGLANDS, Mr Alexander and Mrs Arabella, **Unc**

GREAT EXPECTATIONS, **GEx**

Great National Smithers Testimonial, **Blk**

Great White Horse, The, **Pic**

Great Winglebury, **Boz**

GREAT WINGLEBURY DUEL, The, **Boz**

GREEN, **Rep**

GREEN, Lucy, **Unc**

GREEN, Miss, **Nic**

GREEN, Mr and Mr Junior, **Boz**

GREEN, Tom, **Bar**

Greens, Wait till the greens is off her mind, **Blk**

GREGSBURY, Mr, **Nic**

GREWGIOUS, Hiram, Esquire, **EdD**

GRIDE, Arthur, **Nic**

GRIDLEY, Mr, **Blk**

GRIG, Tom, **SUP**

GRIME, Professor, **Mud**

GRIMMER, Miss, **Rom**

GRIMWIG, Mr, **OTw**

GRIMWOOD, Eliza, **Rep**

Grind, One demd horrid, **Nic**

GRINDER, Mr, **OCS**

GRIP, **Bar**

GROFFIN, Thomas, **Pic**

GROGZWIG, Baron of, **Nic**

GROPER, Colonel, **Chz**

GROVES, James, **OCS**

Growlery, The, **Blk**

GRUB, Gabriel, **Pic**

GRUB, Mr, **Mud**

GRUBBLE, W, **Blk**

GRUDDEN, Mrs, **Nic**

GRUEBY, John, **Bar**

Gruff and Tackleton, **COH**

GRUMMER, Daniel, **Pic**

GRUMMIDGE, **Mud**

GRUNDY, Mr, **Pic**

GULPIDGE, Mr and Mrs, **Cop**

GUMMIDGE, Mrs, **Cop**

Gumtion House, **Rep**

GUNTER, Mr, **Pic**

GUPPY, Mrs and William, **Blk**

GUSHER, Mr **Blk**

GUSTER, **Blk**

GWYNN, Miss, **Pic**

H

HAGGAGE, Dr, **Lit**

Halsewell, The, **Rep**

HAMLET'S AUNT, **Cop**

Hampstead Ponds, Speculations on the Source of the, **Pic**

Handel, **GEx**

HANDFORD, Julius, **OMF**

HANNAH, **Nic**

HARD TIMES, **Cop**

HARDY, Mr, **Boz**

HAREDALE, Mr Geoffrey and Miss Emma, **Bar**

HARKER, Mr, **TGS**

HARLEIGH, Mr, **Boz**

HARMON, John and Mrs, **OMF**

Harmonic Meetings, **Blk**

Harmony Jail, **OMF**

HARRIS, **Pic**

HARRIS, Mr, **Boz; OCS**

HARRY, **OCS**

JARLEY, Mrs, **OCS**
JARNDYCE, John, **Blk**
JASPER, John, **EdD**
JAYE, **Boz**
JEDDLER, Dr Anthony, Grace and Marion, **BOL**
JELLYBY, Mr, Mrs, Caroline and Peepy, **Blk**
JEM, **Boz**
JEMIMA, **Dom**
JEMMY, Dismal, **Pic**
JENKINS, Miss, **Boz**
JENKINSON, **Lit**
JENNINGS, Miss, **EdD**
JENNINGS, Mr, **Boz**
JENNINGS, Mr, **SUP**
JENNY, **Blk**
JERRY, **OCS**
JINGLE, Alfred, **Pic**
JINIWIN, Mrs, **OCS**
JINKINS, **Boz**
JINKINS, Mr, **Chz**
JINKINS, Mr, **Pic**
JINKINSON, **MHC**
JINKS, Mr, **Pic**
JIP, **Cop**
JO, **Blk**
JOBBA, Mr, **Mud**
JOBLING, Dr John, **Chz**
JOBLING, Tony, **Blk**
JOBSON, Jesse, Number Two, **Unc**
JODD, Mr, **Chz**
JOE, **Chr; Dom; EdD; TTC**
JOE, The Fat **Boy**, **Pic**
JOEY, Captain, **OMF**
JOHN, **Boz; Dom; NUS; Pic; Rep; SUP**
JOHN, Mr, **SYC**
JOHNNY, **OMF**
JOHNSON, **Dom**
JOHNSON, John, **SUP**

JOHNSON, Mr, **Nic**
Jolly, **Chz**
Jolly Bargemen, The, **GEx**
Jolly Boatmen, The, **SUP**
Jolly Sandboys, The, **OCS**
Jolly Tapley, The, **Chz**
JOLTERED, Sir William, **Mud**
JONATHAN, **OMF**
JONES, George, **OMF**
JONES, Mr, **Boz**
JORAM, Mr and Mrs **Cop**
JORKINS, Mr, **Cop**
JOWL, Joe, **OCS**
JOY, Thomas, **Rep**
JUPE, Signor and Cecilia, **Har**

K

KAGS, **OTw**
KATE, **Dom; Pic**
KEDGICK, Captain, **Chz**
KENGE, Mr, **Blk**
KENWIGS, Mr, Mrs and Morleena, **Nic**
KETCH, Professor John, **Mud**
KETTLE, La fayette, **Chz**
KIBBLE, Jacob, **OMF**
KIDDERMINSTER, Master, **Har**
KINCH, Horace, **Unc**
KINDHEART, Mr, **Unc**
KING, Horace, **Unc**
KITTERBELL, Mr Charles, Mrs Jemima and Master Frederick Charles William, **Boz**
KLEM, Mr, Mrs and Miss, **Unc**
KNAG, Mr Mortimer and Miss, **Nic**
KOLËDWETHOUT, Baron and Baroness Von, **Nic**
KROOK, Mr, **Blk**

LONGFORD, Edmund, **THM**
LONG-LOST, The, **Unc**
LORRY, Mr Jarvis, **TTC**
LOSBERNE, Mr, **OTw**
LOUISA, **SYC**
LOVETOWN, Mr Alfred and Mrs, **SUP**
LOWTEN, Mr, **Pic**
LOYAL DEVASSEUR, M, **Rep**
LUCAS, Solomon, **Pic**
LUFFEY, Mr, **Pic**
LUMBEY, Mr, **Nic**
LUPIN, Mrs, **Chz**
LYING AWAKE, **Rep**

M

M'CHOAKUMCHILD, Mr, **Har**
MACKIN, Mrs, **Boz**
MACKLIN, Mrs, **Boz**
MACMANUS, Mr, **Rep**
MacSTINGER, Alexander, Mrs, Charles and Juliana, **Dom**
MADDOX, John, **SUP**
MADGERS, Winifred, **Leg**
MAGG, Mr, **Rep**
MAGGY, **Lit**
MAGNUS, Peter, **Pic**
MAGOG, **MHC**
MAGWITCH, Abel, **GEx**
MAKING A NIGHT OF IT, **Boz**
MALDERTON, Mr Frederick and Mr Thomas, **Boz**
MALDERTON, Mr, Mrs, Miss Marianne and Miss Teresa, **Boz**
MALDON, Jack, **Cop**
MALLARD, Mr, **Pic**
MALLET, Mr, **Mud**
MAN FROM SHROPSHIRE, The, **Blk**

MANETTE, Dr Alexander and Lucie, **TTC**
MANN, Mrs, **OTw**
MANNERS, Miss Julia, **Boz**
Manor Farm, **Pic**
MANSEL, Miss, **Rep**
MANTALINI, Mr Alfred and Madame, **Nic**
MAPLESONE, Mrs, Miss Julia and Miss Matilda, **Boz**
MARCHIONESS, The, **OCS**
MARGARET, Aunt, **Boz**
Margin, Leaving a, **GEx**
MARIGOLD, Dr, Mrs, Little Sophy and Willum, **DrM**
MARKHAM, **Cop**
MARKLEHAM, Mrs, **Cop**
MARKS, Will **MHC**
MARLEY, The Ghost of Jacob, **Chr**
MAROON, Captain, **Lit**
Marquis of Granby, **Pic**
MARSHALL, Mary, **SPT**
MARSHALSEA, Father of The, **Lit**
MARTHA, **Boz; Dom; OTw**
MARTHA, Aunt, **BOL**
MARTIN, **Pic**
MARTIN CHUZZLEWIT, **Chz**
MARTIN, Jack, **Pic**
MARTIN, Miss, **Lug**
MARTIN, Miss Amelia, **Boz**
MARTIN, Mr, **Pic**
MARTON, Mr, **OCS**
MARWOOD, Alice, **Dom**
MARY, **Boz; Pic**
MARY ANNE, **Gex; OMF**
MASTER HUMPHREY, **MHC**
MASTER HUMPHREY'S CLOCK, **MHC**
MATINTER, The two Misses, **Pic**

Muddle, It's a' a, **Har**

MUDDLEBRAINS, Mr, **Mud**

MUDFOG ASSOCIATION, The, **Mud**

Mudfog Hall, **SUP**

MUDGE, Mr Jonas **Pic**

MUFF, Professor, **Mud**

Mugby Junction, **Boy**

Muggleton, **PIC**

MULL, Professor, **Mud**

MULLINS, Jack, **OMF**

MULLIT, Professor, **Chz**

MURDERER, Captain, **Unc**

MURDSTONE, Mr Edward and Miss Jane, **Cop**

MUTHANED, Lord, **Pic**

MUTUEL, Monsieur, **Lug**

MUZZLE, Mr, **Pic**

MYSTERY OF EDWIN DROOD, **EdD**

N

NADGETT, Mr, **Chz**

NAMBY, Mr, **Pic**

Namelesston, **NUS**

NANCY, **OTw**

NANDY, John Edward, **Lit**

National Hotel, **Chz**

NATIVE, The, **Dom**

Nature and Heart, **Dom**

NECKETT, Mr, Charlotte, Emma and Tom, **Blk**

NEDDY, **Pic**

NEESHAWTS, Dr, **Mud**

NELL, Little, **OCS**

NEMO, **Blk**

NETTINGALL, The Misses, **Cop**

New Thermopylæ, **Chz**

NEW UNCOMMERCIAL SAMPLES, **NUS**

NEW YEAR, The, **Boz**

New York Rowdy Journal, The, **Chz**

NEWCOME, Clemency, **BOL**

NICHOLAS NICKLEBY, **Nic**

NICHOLAS, **Boz**

NICKLEBY, Mrs, Mr Godfrey, Nicholas the elder and younger, Ralph and Kate, **Nic**

Nimrod Club, **Pic**

NINER, Miss Margaret, **Hun**

NIPPER, Susan, **Dom**

NOAKES, Mr, **Mud**

NOAKES, Mr Percy, **Boz**

NOAKES, Mrs, **SUP**

NOBODY, **Rep**

NOBODY'S STORY, **Rep**

NOCKEMORF, **Pic**

NODDY, Mr, **Pic**

NOGGS, Newman, **Nic**

NOGO, Professor, **Mud**

NORAH, **Hol**

NORRIS, Mr, Mrs and the two Misses, **Chz**

NORTON, Squire, **SUP**

Norwood, **Dom**

Note of, When found, make a, **Dom**

NUBBLES, Mrs, Christopher or Kit and Jacob, **OCS**

Nuns' House, **EdD**

NUPKINS, George, Mrs and Miss Henrietta, **Pic**

Nutmeg-Grater Inn, **BOL**

O

O'BLEARY, Mr Frederick, **Boz**

Oak Lodge, **Boz**

OAKUM-HEAD, **Unc**

Ode to an Expiring Frog, **Pic**

OLD CURIOSITY SHOP, The, **OCS**

PEGGY, **Rom**

PEGLER, Mrs, **Har**

PEPLOW, Mrs and Master, **Boz**

PEPPER, **GEx**

PEPS, Dr Parker, **Dom**

PERCH, Mr and Mrs, **Dom**

PERKER, Mr, **Pic**

PERKINS, Mrs, **Blk**

PERKINSOP, Mary Anne, **Lod**

PERRYBINGLE, John and
Mrs Mary, **COH**

Peruvian Mines, **Dom**

PESSELL, Mr, **Mud**

PET, **Lit**

PETER, Lord, **Boz**; **SUP**

PETOWKER, Miss Henrietta,
Nic

PHENOMENON, The Infant,
Nic

PHIB, **Nic**

PHIBBS, Mr, **Rep**

PHIL, **Rep**

PHIZ, **Pic**

PHŒBE, **BBB**

PHOEBE, or PHIB, **Nic**

PHUNKY, Mr, **Pic**

PICKLES, **Rom**

PICKLESON, **DrM**

PICKWICK PAPERS, The,
Pic

PICKWICK, Samuel, **Pic**

PICWICK, Mr Samuel, **MHC**

PIDGER, Mr, **Cop**

PIERCE, Captain and Miss
Mary, **Rep**

PIFF, Miss, **Boy**

Pig and Tinder-box, The, **Mud**

PIGEON, Thomas, **Rep**

PILKINS, Mr, **Dom**

PINCH, Tom and Ruth, **Chz**

PIP, **GEx**

PIP, Mr, **Chz**

PIPCHIN, Mrs, **Dom**

PIPER, Mrs, **Blk**

PIPER, Professor, **Chz**

PIPKIN, Mr, **Mud**

PIPKIN, Nathaniel, **Pic**

PIRRIP, Philip, **GEx**

PITT, Jane, **Rep**

Plashwater Weir Mill, **OMF**

PLORNISH, Mr and Mrs, **Lit**

PLUCK, Mr, **Nic**

PLUMMER, Caleb, Bertha
and Edward, **COH**

POCKET, Mr Matthew, Mrs
Belinda, Alick, Fanny,
Herbert, Jane, Joe and Sarah,
GEx

Pod's End, **Har**

PODDER, Mr, **Pic**

PODDLES, **OMF**

PODGERS, John, **MHC**

PODSNAP, Mr John, Mrs and
Miss Georgiana, **OMF**

Podsnappery, **OMF**

POGRAM, The Hon. Elijah,
Chz

POLLY, **BBB**

POODLES, **NUS**

POOR MAN'S TALE OF A
PATENT, **Rep**

POOR RELATION'S
STORY, **Rep**

Poplar Walk, **Boz**

Port Middlebay, **Cop**

Portable Property, **GEx**

PORTER, Mrs Joseph and
Miss Emily, **Boz**

POTKINS, William, **GEx**

POTT, Mr and Mrs, **Pic**

POTTER, Mr Thomas, **Boz**

POTTERSON, Miss Abbey
and Job, **OMF**

PRATCHETT, Mrs, **Lug**

RUGG, Mr and Miss Anastasia, Lit

RUMMUN, Professor, **Mud**

Rustic Lodge, **SUP**

S

SAGGERS, Mrs, **Unc**

SALCY, P, Family, **Unc**

Salem House, **Cop**

SALLY, **Boz**

SALLY, Old, **OTw**

Salwanners, The, **Bar**

SAM, **Pic**

SAMPSON, George, **OMF**

SAMPSON, Mr, **Hun**

SANDERS, Mrs Susannah, **Pic**

SAPSEA, Mr Thomas, **EdD**

Saracen's Head, The, **Pic**

SARAH, **Boz**

Satis House, **GEx**

SAUNDERS, Mr, **SYC**

SAWYER, Bob, **Pic**

SCADDER, Zephaniah, **Chz**

SCADGERS, Lady, **Har**

SCALEY, Mr, **Nic**

SCHOOLBOY'S STORY, The, **Rep**

SCHUTZ, Mr, **Rep**

Scorpion, The, **Rom**

SCOTT, Tom, **OCS**

Screw, The, **Chz**

SCROO, Mr, **Mud**

SCROOGE, Ebenezer, **Chr**

SENTIMENT, **Boz**

SERAPHINA, **Lod**

Setting Moon, The, **Rep**

SEVEN DIALS, **Boz**

SEVEN POOR TRAVELLERS, The, **SPT**

SEXTON, The Old, **OCS**

SHARP, Mr, **Cop**

SHARPEYE, **Unc**

SHEPHERD, Miss, **Cop**

SHEPHERD, The, **Pic**

SHEPHERDSON, Mr, **Rep**

SHORT, **OCS**

Shoulder to the wheel, Putting the, **Blk**

SHROPSHIRE, The Man from, **Blk**

SIKES, Bill, **OTw**

SILVERMAN, George, **Sil**

SILVERSTONE, Mr and Mrs, **SYC**

SIMMERY, Frank, Esq, **Pic**

SIMMONDS, Miss, **Nic**

SIMMONS, **Boz**

SIMMONS, Mrs Henrietta, **OCS**

SIMMONS, William, **Chz**

SIMPSON, Mr, **Boz**; **Pic**

SINGLE GENTLEMAN, The, **OCS**

Six Jolly Fellowship-Porters, The, **OMF**

SKETCHES BY BOZ, **Boz**

SKETCHES OF YOUNG COUPLES, **SYC**

SKETTLES, Sir Barnet, Lady and Barnet, **Dom**

SKEWTON, The Hon. Mr, **Dom**

SKIFFINS, Miss, **GEx**

SKIMPIN, Mr, **Pic**

SKIMPOLE, Harold, Mrs, Arethusa, Kitty and Laura, **Blk**

SLACKBRIDGE, **Har**

Slamjam Coffee House, **Lug**

SLAMMER, Dr, **Pic**

SLAUGHTER, Lieutenant, **Boz**

SLEARY, Mr and Josephine, **Har**

SLIDERSKEW, Peg, **Nic**

SPENLOW, Mr Francis, Miss
  Clarissa, Miss La Vinia, Miss
  Dora and Miss Dora, **Cop**
SPHYNX, Sophronia, **OCS**
SPIDER, The, **GEx**
SPIKER, Mr and Mrs Henry,
  Cop
SPOTTLETOE, Mr and Mrs,
  Chz
SPRODGKIN, Mrs, **OMF**
SPRUGGINS, Mr Thomas
  and Mrs, **Boz**
SQUEERS, Wackford, Mrs,
  Miss Fanny and Wackford
  junior, **Nic**
SQUIRES, Olympia, **Unc**
SQUOD, Phil, **Blk**
ST EVRÉMONDE, Marquis,
  Marquise, Charles and Lucie,
  TTC
St James's Arms, The, **SUP**
St JULIAN, Mr Horitio, **Boz**
STABLES, The Hon. Bob, **Blk**
STAGG, **Bar**
Stagg's Gardens, **Dom**
STALKER, Mr Inspector, **Rep**
STAPLE, Mr, **Pic**
STARELEIGH, Mr Justice, **Pic**
STARLING, Mrs, **SYC**
STARTOP, Mr, **GEx**
STEAM EXCURSION, The,
  Boz
STEERFORTH, Mrs and
  James, **Cop**
Stiffun's Acre, **Rep**
STIGGINS, The Revd Mr,
  Pic
STILTSTALKING, Lord
  Lancaster, **Lit**
STOKES, Mr Martin, **SUP**
STRANGE GENTLEMAN,
  The, **SUP**

STRANGE GENTLEMAN,
  The, **SUP**
STRAUDENHEIM, **Unc**
STRAW, Sergeant, **Rep**
STREETS, THE NIGHT,
  Boz
STRONG, Dr and Mrs Annie,
  Cop
STRUGGLES, Mr, **Pic**
STRYVER, Mr, **TTC**
STUBBS, Mrs, **Boz**
STYLES, Mr, **Mud**
SUMMERSON, Esther, **Blk**
Superannuated Widows, **Blk**
Suturb, **Chz**
SWEEDLEPIPE, Paul, called
  'Poll', **Chz**
SWEENEY, Mrs, **Unc**
SWEET WILLIAM, **OCS**
SWIDGER, George, Milly,
  Philip and William, **THM**
SWILLENHAUSEN, Baron
  and Baroness Von, **Nic**
SWILLS, Little, **Blk**
SWIVELLER, Dick, **OCS**
SWOSHLE, Mrs Henry
  George Alfred, *née* Tapkins,
  OMF
SWOSSER, Captain, **Blk**
SYLVIA, **Sil**

T

TACKER, **Chz**
TACKLETON, **COH**
TADGER, Brother, **Pic**
Take care of him: he bites, **Cop**
TALE OF TWO CITIES,
  TTC
TAMAROO, **Chz**
TANGLE, Mr, **Blk**
TAPE, **Rep**
TAPKINS, Mr Felix, **SUP**

Tough, sir—tough, and de-vilish sly!, **Dom**

TOUGHEY, **Blk**

TOWLINSON, Thomas, **Dom**

TOX, Miss Lucretia, **Dom** ·

TOZER, **Dom**

TRABB, Mr, **GEx**

TRADDLES, Thomas, **Cop**

TRAMPFOOT, **Unc**

Travellers' Twopenny, The, **EdD**

TRENT, Frederick and Little Nell, **OCS**

TRESHAM, **BBB**

Tricks, I know their, **OMF**

TRIMMERS, Mr, **Nic**

TRINKLE, Mr, **Rep**

TROTT, Mr Alexander, **Boz**

TROTT, Mr Walker, **SUP**

TROTTER, Job, **Pic**

TROTTERS, **OCS**

TROTTY, **Chi**

TROTWOOD, Mr and Miss Betsey, **Cop**

TRUCK, Mr, **Mud**

TRUNDLE, Mr, **Pic**

Tucket's Terrace, **Rep**

TUCKLE, **Pic**

TUGBY, **Chi**

TUGGS, Mr Joseph, Mrs, Miss Charlotte and Mr Simon, **Boz**

TUGGSES AT RAMGATE, The, **Boz**

TULKINGHORN, Mr, **Blk**

TULRUMBLE, Mr Nicholas, Mrs and Nicholas Junior, **SUP**

TUNGAY, **Cop**

TUPMAN, Tracy, **Pic**

TUPPLE, Mr, **Boz**

Turn up, Waiting for something to, **Cop**

TURVEYDROP, Mr and Prince, **Blk**

TWEMLOW, Mr Melvin, **OMF**

TWIGGER, Edward and Mrs, **SUP**

TWINKLETON, Miss, **EdD**

TWIST, Oliver, **OTw**

TWO GHOST STORIES, **TGS**

Tyrolean Flower-act, The, **Har**

U

Umble, I'm very, **Cop**

Umbugology, **Mud**

UNCLE TOM, **Boz**

UNCOMMERCIAL TRAVELLER, **Unc**

United Aggregate Tribunal, **Har**

United Bull-Dogs, **Bar**

United Grand Junction Ebenezer Temperance Association, **Pic**

United Grand Junction Lirriper and Jackman Great Norfolk Parlour Line, **Leg**

United Metropolitan Improved Hot Muffin and Crumpet Baking and Punctual Delivery Company, **Nic**

UPWITCH, Richard, **Pic**

V

Vale of Tauton, The, **Blk**

Valiant Soldier, The, **OCS**

VARDEN, Mrs Martha, Dolly and Gabriel, **Bar**

VAUXHALL GARDENS BY DAY, **Boz**

VECK, Margaret and Toby, **Chi**

VELASCO, Rinaldo di, **DrM**